I0545487

Extraordinary Praise for Jim Geraghty and
The CIA's Dangerous Clique Series:

"Geraghty has hit another homerun! *Hunting Four Horsemen* is an absolutely electrifying thriller. Fantastic plot, pacing, and characters. Bravo!"

—**Brad Thor, #1** *New York Times*-**bestselling author of** *Near Dark*

"A thoroughly researched thriller [*Between Two Scorpions*] with a threat vector I wish I'd come up with—and a bite of humor rarely seen in the genre."

—**Brad Taylor, author of** *Daughter of War* **and the** *New York Times*-**bestselling Pike Logan series, retired U.S. Army Special Forces Lieutenant Colonel**

"Powerful, real, and relevant, Jim Geraghty's *Between Two Scorpions* is a well-written and dynamite page turner and a welcome addition to the thriller genre."

—**Mark Greaney, #1** *New York Times* **Bestselling Author of** *Mission Critical*

"Jim Geraghty is one of the most insightful and cutting writers in the country.

—**Ben Shapiro, author,** *The Right Side of History* **and founder of The Daily Wire**

GATHERING FIVE STORMS

GATHERING FIVE STORMS

A DANGEROUS CLIQUE NOVEL

JIM GERAGHTY

DISCUS BOOKS

ALEXANDRIA, VIRGINIA

ISBN: 978-1-7337346-4-6 (paperback)

To
A+C+A

Still My Everything

TABLE OF CONTENTS

CHAPTER ONE

B y every measure, the operation was a success, but it marked the first time Katrina Leonidivna had ever vomited on her target.

The target's name was Douglas Hitti, and considering the rogues' gallery that Katrina had taken down over the course of all of her years with the Central Intelligence Agency, Hitti was a comparably minor-league threat to the United States and the world. Paraphrasing a former president, Katrina's husband Alec had labeled Hitti a "kindler and gentler" financier of global bioterrorism.

***

Hitti had steadily climbed the greasy pole of Washington to run a lobbying shop and was a registered foreign agent for several foreign countries. A little more than two years ago, while in a schmooze-and-booze-filled trip to Berlin, at a cocktail party thrown by one of his clients, someone—Hitti couldn't even remember who—introduced him to an up-and-coming member

1

of the German Bundestag legislature—Shakira Erikat. Hitti was used to meeting bland, fat, boring politicians on these trips, but Shakira was a striking and charming young woman. He was a little smitten, and she seemed to pick up on it, and she invited him to the private after-party.

It was there, in the private back room of marvelously reviewed restaurant, Hitti met Shakira's "special friends"—all wealthy, all interested in international affairs, and as the night wore on, he realized, all passionate critics of Israel—although they reflexively insisted their views were merely "anti-Zionist." As the night wore on further, Hitti observed that their definition of *Zionist* had expanded to include just about every Jewish person involved in any government anywhere—and that Shakira's crowd believed these Jewish politicians and donors and bankers had been working together in a sinister secret conspiracy to manipulate policies and world events for decades, perhaps centuries. At one point, Hitti contemplated asking, if the world's Jews had been secretly controlling world events behind the scenes, why do things keep going so badly for Jews? Between the targeted terror attacks, anti-Israel boycotts, flourishing anti-Semitism on college campuses, and so on, if Jews ran the world, they were doing a terrible job of it. But Hitti held his tongue and nodded, acknowledging the powerful counterargument that Shakira Erikat was extraordinarily hot and seemed to be into him.

One thing led to another—more specifically, a white-hot enjoyable one-night stand—and Hitti eagerly signed up with Shakira's new crowd, who had nicknamed themselves the Shedim, after a demon in Jewish mythology. Hitti sometimes thought it all seemed like wealthy drunks cosplaying cloak-and-dagger—but the networking was spectacular, and he never knew when Shakira might be in Washington and invite him up to her hotel room.

About two years later, Shakira called out of the blue and said she needed all of the Shedim members to transfer large amounts of cash to certain accounts, to support a spectacular mission to undermine Jewish influence in world affairs. Hitti initially hesitated. Her instructions were specific and bizarre—withdraw some amount between $9,000 and $9,999 in cash, keep a small random amount of a few hundred dollars or so, and deposit the remaining cash into a different account that she provided—and repeat the process each day, with the specific account that would receive the money changing each day.

Hitti figured Shakira was running a money-laundering effort designed to avoid the attention of the authorities. When Hitti pressed her on why he should agree to pay roughly $65,000 a week, she pointed out that her friends in the Shedim network had easily referred close to $10 million in work to his consulting firm each of the past two years, and she figured a major portion of that ended up in Hitti's pockets. Asking for weekly payments amounting to $3.3 million per year to finance "a biological research project" to solve "the Jewish question," was, in her mind, a bargain.

In his gut, Hitti knew Shakira Erikat was breaking the law. Her words "biological research project" struck him as the sort of evasive, vague euphemism he had recommended his clients use plenty of times. A few years back, he had advised an institution with close ties to Bashar al-Assad's regime to refer to the uses of chlorine, sarin, and sulphur mustard gas on civilian targets as "unfortunate toxic events." Whatever Shakira was willing to say the project was, it was probably much worse—and Hitti decided he didn't want to know any more details. He agreed to transfer the money, but said he wanted to discuss this further, in person. And not on any phone line or e-mail. She agreed, and he looked forward to her returning to Washington—knowing there was no telling how their evening meetings would end.

But a few days later, Douglas Hitti saw the news coverage reporting that the Federal Bureau of Investigation had arrested Shakira Erikat, an arrest that allegedly coincidentally occurred in the same time and place that the bureau was running a biological weapons response training exercise at Fox Plaza in Los Angeles.

Hitti sensed with dread that his agreement to move some money from one account to another had been part of Shakira's aborted attempt at developing a biological weapon. He contemplated running, but realized he knew plenty of lawyers, and had a decent chance of pleading down to a lesser charge—if he was ever charged at all. Almost six weeks had passed, and the FBI still hadn't kicked down the door of his office or home.

***

Katrina felt an unfamiliar wave of nausea pass over her. She swallowed hard.

She had been in this situation dozens of times before. Sometimes she was wearing a headscarf and veil and sitting on a carpet in some tent or corner of Afghanistan or Pakistan; more often she was wearing a smart business suit and concealed weapon in a European capital. The world had thousands of go-betweens, middlemen, fixers, and facilitators who worked with terror groups, extremists, mercenaries and three times as many wannabes and five times as many con men. The late Rafiq Tannous, blown to kingdom come by a bomb in a Berlin café by the terrorist group Atarsa, was typical of the sort. Greedy, convinced they were charming when they were not, convinced they were careful when they were not, and unburdened by a conscience.

Most often Katrina Leonidivna's cover identity was that of Katrina Alimova, the representative of a small oil and natural gas oligarch from Uzbekistan who was looking for an illicit way to get his money out of the country, buy weapons, support some jihadist cause, or do something else illegal. The agency had quietly recruited a real-life small-time Uzbek businessman, Zayniddin Tashmuhamedov, to play the part and confirm any inquiries into Katrina's background. Katrina had all the right paperwork, financial records, passport, and she spoke Uzbeki like it was her native language—in part because it was, even through she immigrated to the United States in her first year of life and was raised in Queens.

She rarely needed to wear a wire. At first, hidden long-distance parabolic microphones did the trick. Then the National Security Agency perfected the ability to remotely turn on, and tap into, the microphones of the cellular phones of the people around them, using dozens of unknowing civilians as unwitting spies. Even if the fixers kept their phones turned off during their meetings—the smarter ones did—Dominica "Dee" Alves and her former colleagues at the NSA would usually pinpoint their cell phones shortly after the meeting and remotely copy and download the phone's entire contents at the first opportunity.

Besides, recording a conversation was most useful for collecting evidence, and the Central Intelligence Agency rarely worried about proving a case in a court of law. The CIA team nicknamed the Dangerous Clique simply kept hunting for the next big rising star on the international terrorism scene and arranged for an early retirement, usually in the form of "random violence" that didn't seem all that random or an accident that didn't look too much like an accident. They wanted their targets' colleagues to strongly suspect, but never quite know for certain, that the suddenly departed had been sent to Hades by the CIA.

But this was the first time Katrina had pursued a target while pregnant.

And while Douglas Hitti was seen as a relatively small fish, he was seen as one of the best possible leads to bigger fish—and he stood out as one of the rare American members of the Shedim network, a rabidly anti-Semitic secret group of Europeans who had been willing to finance a project to develop an ethnic bio-weapon, a virus that would only afflict those with particular genes.

The FBI, represented by special agent Elaine Kopek, wanted Hitti arrested, and to make an example of him. The U.S. Department of Justice, represented by prosecutor Geraldine Murphy-Fitzal, wanted the same—with a smooth conviction, and no grounds for mistrial or lengthy appeals. Hitti knew plenty of good lawyers, and the financial resources to afford them. The CIA, represented by Katrina's immediate supervisor, Raquel Holtz, cared much less about sending Hitti to jail; she wanted his contacts and what he knew about other Shedim members— particularly if anyone else was still dreaming up plots involving bioweapons.

Dee's friends at the National Security Agency had success-fully vacuumed up a mountain of Hitti's communications and financial transactions going back decades, but they still wanted Hitti to help them separate the wheat from the chaff and they hadn't yet been able to hack his iPhone. The Department of the Treasury, represented by senior enforcement agent Minnie Black, wanted to seize Hitti's money and assets, which were considerable.

And Katrina's other teammates, her husband, Alec, and her friend Ward, had argued that by choosing to finance bioterror-ism, Hitti deserved, at minimum, to be brought into govern-ment custody through a rough-and-tumble process that clearly communicated the wrath he had invited upon himself. Alec and Ward weren't on the scene at the moment, but they had made their opinions clear before departing on their mission to Europe.

"Rich bastards always think they can buy their way out of trouble," Ward had said with a Sam Elliott–esque smile. "Some of my happiest moments are the ones where I see that look in their eyes, when they realize they can't buy their way out of an oncoming punch."

"We're professionals," Katrina responded evenly. A careful observer would notice her statement was not a promise to not hit him.

"Yeah, and this guy tried to help lunatics unleash a second worldwide plague, right on the heels of Covid," Alec emphasized. "It's better for the world if everybody understands that if they try to do that, the arsenal of democracy will happily put them in a full body cast."

***

Two FBI surveillance vans were parked outside the high-end restaurant specializing in New Orleans–style cuisine. In the closer one, Elaine, Minnie Black, and two FBI agents who looked like they could be starting middle linebackers all sat, too close, and listened to Katrina's conversation with Hitti.

"Come on, come on, that's gotta be more than enough for an indictment!" Black muttered.

"We've got enough for an indictment, now we want enough so that he knows we've got a slam-dunk conviction, so he gives up his buddies," Elaine noted.

"Katrina's good, but this guy's going to get spooked and run," Black warned. "I want this bastard to be watching when we take all of this stuff away."

"Stuff?"

"Hitti's got a real nice boat he keeps in Alexandria," Black said with an eager smile. "He just finished a bunch of upgrades, spent a fortune." She held up her hand, at about forehead height.

"Here's sex," Black declared. She lowered her hand about a half an inch. "Here's how I'm going to feel, seizing the boat of this guy, right in front of his eyes. It's almost as good."

Elaine shook her head, wondering where the Treasury Department had recruited Black. "Trust Katrina. She's handled guys way tougher than this in all kinds of far-flung armpits of the world. Think of this waiting as…" Elaine paused and thought of Black's comparison, "… foreplay."

Black laughed. "I have a righteous impatience for comeuppance."

***

Katrina's gradual courtship of Hitti had run sufficiently smoothly, but the moment she finally brought up the word *Shedim*, she saw that Hitti realized she was probably a government investigator.

"Would you excuse me?" Hitti slipped from the booth without waiting. Katrina glared, and she could see it in his eyes—. Hitti knew he was caught and was going to try to make a run for it. She scooted out from the booth and was barely two paces behind the fleeing lobbyist.

Hitti ran and knocked over a waiter with a large serving platter of four entrees, attempting to cut through the kitchen. Katrina leaped over the waiter and the overturned plates of sea scallop amandine, duck jambalaya, and raw oysters on ice. Katrina's sense of smell had seemed to be on steroids in the past month, and thus any scent that others smelled hit her like a wave, the kind of overwhelming olfactory tsunami found at land-fills, morgues, and Lush cosmetic stores at the mall. Smashing through the doors to the kitchen, Hitti scrambled past cooks and made it to the kitchen's back door, and Katrina quietly fumed that the FBI did not, as promised, have every exit covered.

Bursting through the kitchen's back door leading to the dumpsters, Hitti tried to escape down a back alley.

For many years, Katrina's body had been her second-most important tool, next to her mind. Throughout adolescence and early adulthood, she had trained in martial arts and when she thought, her body responded. By the time she joined the agency, her thoughts and actions were one—instinct and reflex. But now, with some other little person under construction deep within her, her body seemed to have come up with a mind of its own, or perhaps it had simply gone on strike, refusing to work as she had trained it. Suddenly, every increasingly frequent trip to the bathroom felt like Niagara Falls. Exhaustion caught up with her much quicker than usual, and if her sense of smell grew any stronger, police would ask her to track down missing persons like a bloodhound. And much to her husband's delight, Katrina felt like her breasts were inflating to a size that would make a *Playboy* centerfold jealous.

None of this was ideal for a footrace against a fleeing lobbyist-turned-terrorism-financier, but even when her body was going haywire, and when she felt like a tired, part-bloodhound, breast-inflated Victoria's Secret model who desperately needed to pee, she retained the capacity to dig down deep and tap into her reserve 55-gallon-drums of sheer willpower.

Maybe the FBI and Treasury teams have the end of the alley covered, Katrina thought. *But I can't let them know I need them, that I can't catch up with this slick lobbyist creep—*

One foot in front of the other, right arm extended out in front of her as far as she could reach ... toward the end of the alley, Katrina caught up to Hitti, reached up and out and grabbed him by the back of his collar—his legs lost their balance and he tumbled to the ground, and Katrina nearly tripped over him and fell, too. But steadying herself, she reached down as he was trying to get back to his feet and threw Hitti up against a brick wall that had recently been defaced with purple graffiti spelling out STORMCLOUDS ARE GATHERING.

"You're not going anywhere!" she bellowed.

"I swear, I didn't know what she was going to do with the money!" Hitti screamed, holding his hands up.

"Oh, really?" Katrina spat. "You just handed her all that money, no questions asked? What did you think was going to happen?"

Hitti just looked away, but Katrina reached up, grabbed him by the chin, and forced him to make eye contact.

"Shortly before he died an extremely painful death, your buddy Vincent Van Der Groot told my team that you guys called yourself Shedim, *demons* in Jewish mythology, to taunt the Jews you would be targeting," she seethed. Katrina's connection to her Bukhari Jewish heritage waxed and waned as the chapters of her life passed, but the fact that she had the genes that the Shedim bioweapon targeted had rekindled her interest in her ancestors' faith. Or maybe it was impending motherhood. In the matrilineal perspective of Judaism, her child would be Jewish—and also, with half her genes, possibly vulnerable to the virus the Shedim envisioned.

"But I don't think you called yourself Shedim for that," Katrina hissed. "The term means malevolent, violent, destructive. I think you picked that name because deep down, all of you *knew* what you were planning was evil, and you *liked* it that way. You're not misunderstood. You're not mixed-up ideologües, hiding behind the safe label 'anti-Zionist.' You *knew* it was genocide … and you *wanted* it!"

By now, Elaine Kopek, Minnie Black, and two other FBI agents had emerged from the two surveillance vans. Someone in the bureau with a sense of humor had chosen the fake company names Foundation Building Inc. and Discount Operating Joists. The jokester hadn't thought through what would happen if the target under surveillance realized what other institutions shared those acronyms.

Kopek and Black blocked off the end of the alley.

"Nowhere to run, Hitti!" Black declared, holding her 17M Glock level with two hands, her feet square.

Katrina released Hitti from her tight grip. Hitti, sweating and shaking, seemed to be on the verge of a breakdown from fear, guilt, and shame.

"I'm gonna be sick," Katrina said, her voice suddenly getting much quieter.

"Yeah, this guy makes me sick, too," Elaine said, removing handcuffs. "Read him his—"

Then Elaine realized Katrina's queasy expression. The CIA senior case officer croaked, "No, I mean, I'm gonna be si—"

And then Katrina retched and deposited what was left of her breakfast all over Hitti's shirt, pants, and shoes. Everyone recoiled let out short yelps of shock. Katrina looked up, mortified.

"Don't worry about it," Elaine declared. "He had it coming."

Black burst out laughing as Hitti reacted to the regurgitation with disgusted groans. "That's almost as good as seizing his boat," she observed.

Elaine turned to Hitti, as the other two agents, cringing, turned the shocked, now-filthy lobbyist up against the wall and applied handcuffs. "Douglas Hitti, you have a right to an attorney. You're also really going to need a dry cleaner."

***

Two hours later, Katrina returned from the bathroom to the small conference room in the nearby FBI headquarters building where Raquel, Dee, Elaine, and Geraldine awaited. Black had departed to enjoy her long-awaited boat seizure.

"Let's get the debriefing over with," Katrina moaned, collapsing into a chair.

The quartet of women all answered with variations of, "we can wait!"

Katrina put her face in her hands, groaned loudly, and then recomposed herself. "Oh, God. I can handle terrorists. I can handle lunatics cooking up bioweapons. But suddenly one whiff of cilantro has me reenacting scenes from *The Exorcist!*" She threw her head back and looked to the ceiling. "And in front of all you guys! This is so embarrassing!"

Geraldine was the first to laugh. "Katrina, with both of my girls, my body went haywire just about every day. I had to excuse myself from a tense negotiation of a plea deal for an informant six times in one hour because I had to pee so much. There's nothing wrong with you—this happens to almost everyone."

Elaine put her hand on Katrina's shoulder. "And if I had a dime for every rookie agent who barfed upon seeing their first dead body, I would have ..." She paused. "Like, two dollars."

Raquel nodded. "Special Agent Black said she's putting in her report to Treasury that you caught Hitti in a footrace, overcoming great physical adversity. You did fine. Don't beat yourself up over this."

"I can keep doing this," Katrina grimaced. "Just force my way through it. It's the way I've done everything else."

Raquel nodded. "Katrina, we talked about this. I'm not going to yank you. I'm also not going to make you do anything you don't feel comfortable doing. We're just going to take this day by day. We don't usually have case officers in the field while they're pregnant. The agency has guidelines on this but no strict rules—and even if it did, I would ignore them in favor of what you felt was right for you."

Dee gave Raquel a look, and Raquel glared back, as if to say, *You bring it up!*

Dee cleared her throat. "That said, Katrina, you do know it's okay to slow down a little during the pregnancy, right?" She tread carefully, fearing Katrina would interpret this as nudging her toward the sidelines.

Much to Dee's pleasant surprise, Katrina did not leap out of her chair and bite her head off. Instead, she just let out a long sigh.

"I don't want to slow down, I just want the world to stop speeding up," she muttered.

Raquel sensed her cue. "No one in this room, or this building, would think badly of you if you took a different role for a few months—or however long you needed."

"I never thought I'd be in this position," Katrina said softly. "From puberty, doctors told me it was unlikely I could have children. Not impossible, just … maybe a one-in-ten chance in ideal circumstances. I'd be the last of the Leonidivnas, the only child of two only children. And the way I live my life was all the wrong circumstances—the travel, the hours, the wear and tear. Year by year, Alec and I figured it was just not a possibility for us. We talked about adoption. We talked about whether we wanted to have kids while doing work like this. We talked about someday stepping back into jobs with less travel, less danger, more predictability … stable desk jobs where you can go home at night and be a mom."

"And a dad," Elaine added.

"And now … this," she gestured to her midsection. "It's like the world is telling me that I can have this thing I always wanted, but I can't keep the other things in my life that make me who I am."

"You're going to be a great mother!" all four women said simultaneously—and then they all swore they hadn't rehearsed it.

Katrina nodded. "I'm really looking forward to it. But I still want to be me."

Geraldine shook her head. "Katrina, I'm never going to tell you what to do, but can I tell you what I had to learn the hard way?"

"Sure, just … we should grab some food soon, because now all of a sudden I'm ravenously hungry."

"Well, you're on an empty stomach," Elaine dryly observed.

Geraldine chuckled a bit, more at the memories of herself early in her first pregnancy than Katrina's sudden hunger. "My thinking was just like yours before we had our first child, and I'll tell you it straight, now: You cannot be the same person you were before you become a parent. You're going to change. But you don't necessarily turn into the spit-up-on-your-shirt, always-wearing-sweatpants, bloated, exhausted, stressed-out caricature of new moms that our society loves to terrify women with. You grow into a different version of yourself—in some ways, a better one. Yeah, you're pulled in a million different directions. Yeah, it feels like there's never enough time, never enough sleep, you're always keeping a million plates spinning and trying to keep them crashing to the floor."

Geraldine seemed to be growing more agitated, the more she remembered. "The girls are in school now, and yet I still find cheese sticks in my purse, and half-finished juice boxes are everywhere, and—"

"Geraldine, where are you going with this?" Katrina asked.

Geraldine steered back from her tangent of stress. "It takes time, and you're going have bumps in the road, but at some point, after your child is born, you're going to feel like a woman in full," Geraldine assured her. "You won't have work–life balance. It will always feel imbalanced. But you'll step back and be amazed at what you've done, and you'll look at your child—or who knows, someday, maybe children—and you'll wonder how you ever could have felt complete without your little one."

Katrina took a moment to contemplate her friend's words, which were meant to be reassuring but had the opposite effect. Change was inevitable, and just as she had grown seemingly comfortable with who she was, what she did, and how she did it—she was being sucked into some sort of chrysalis that would inevitably forever change her—with no guarantee that she would like who she was on the other side.

"Let's get some pastries."

CHAPTER TWO

UPTOWN MÜNCHEN SKYSCRAPER
MUNICH, GERMANY
1 A.M., JUNE 15, 2021

Hermann Schmalenbach felt like his heart had somehow jumped up to his throat as his body was hurled off the rooftop. He plummeted, face-first, and from his view, the pavement seemed to be rushing toward him, gathering speed, heading to an impact that would destroy his body…

…and then he felt an intense sharp pain around his ankle, a jolt that reverberated through his body, and he slammed against the glass wall of the skyscraper. Schmalenbach's plunge suddenly and inexplicably halted, ten stories before violent impact with the alley pavement below. Trembling from shock and fear, he felt himself being painfully pulled up the side of the skyscraper by his ankle, floor by floor, and then four hands grabbed him and hauled over the parapet, back onto the roof.

"If we have to throw you off the roof again, Schmalenbach, next time we're gonna do it without the wire around your ankle," his gruff, red-bearded interlocutor warned, grabbing him by the lapels and roughly shoving him in a sitting position up against the parapet.

Schmalenbach struggled to catch his breath. "Please! No! Who are you? You can't do this to me!" All Schmalenbach could remember was being the last one in to leave his office, managing trade agreements between Singapore and Germany, and stepping onto an elevator, where two men were waiting. Something about the two men had seemed off—they hadn't looked German—and they must have jabbed him with a taser or something. He passed out, and awoke to feel himself being thrown over the side of the skyscraper's roof.

The bearded man's taller partner sighed in exasperation. "Here we go again. Another guy who expected the cops to show up at his door, reading him his rights," he said, rolling his eyes. "Do we look like cops to you? Are we wearing badges?"

Schmalenbach's eyes widened. "CIA?"

The bearded man grinned. "Ya frightened yet?" Then he widened his menacing smile to show his teeth.

"We're not interested in *arresting* you for your role in financing the Shedim network's attempt to purchase biological weapons," Alec announced. "For all intents and purposes, right now, just think of us as Batman. We have no jurisdiction. We just find you and make you squeal."

"What do you want?" Schmalenbach asked, trembling.

"Schmalten—Schmalben—I'm just going to call you Schmoobie," Alec said with an odd, casually irritated tone, as if he was dealing with an unwanted phone sales pitch. "Schoombie, I've got a problem. See, I'm about to become a dad."

Schmalenbach stared back in confusion. "Congratulations?"

***

"Thank you! It's terrific," Alec said, his face lighting up with genuine joy for a moment, before shifting back to what was supposed to be his game face. He did a lousy job of hiding how much he was enjoying interrogating the terrified German.

"But before the fruit of my loins arrives, Schmoobie, I've got a job to do. I have to *fix the world*," Alec said, squinting, attempting to make clear to the German that he was not exaggerating.

"My child cannot grow up in a messed-up world like this: Terrorist groups like Atarsa, pandemics like Covid. I mean, somebody tried to blow up Nashville because he feared a conspiracy of lizard people. Lizard people, Schmoobie! I swear, the world is spinning off its axis. And then you Shedim bastards tried to wipe out millions of people with a genetically engineered virus. You just danced a jig on my last nerve, pal. I've had it. No more Mr. Nice Unaccountable Constitutionally Dubious Secret Government Assassin."

Schmalenbach sweated and stammered. "My colleagues said the man who offered to make the virus was lying to us, and that he never made the virus—"

"Yeah, but you didn't know that he was running a con when you agreed to pay the guy millions," Ward said, wagging his finger. "Just because you didn't *get* a real virus doesn't mean you didn't want to *use* a real virus, which makes you every bit as dangerous. Being gullible doesn't really get you off the hook." He removed the wire that had been secured around Schmalenbach's ankle. "Or maybe it does, in the bad way."

Schmalenbach started to insist he knew nothing, but Alec cut him off. "Now, Schmoobie, I can fix the world by having you turn yourself in to Interpol and telling them all about your Shedim friends, so that you guys get shut down like a receiver stuck on Revis Island. Or I can fix the world by *just throwing you off the roof again, this time without a safety line.* Six of one, half a dozen of the other. *Fark etmez*, as the Turks say. But one way or another, tonight I'm crossing you off my to-do list."

"I'm not a terrorist!" Schmalenbach insisted. "I just—"

This time it was Alec who suddenly snapped, grabbing Schmalenbach by the throat and shoving his head hard against the stone parapet.

"No, you just *paid* for it!" Alec snarled, with a swift and unexpected raging ferocity so intense that even Ward was taken aback. Ward wondered just how much his old friend had put his emotional instability behind him.

"Every time my friends and I witness one more innocent life torn apart by some terrorist, we know there's somebody who made money on the deal," Alec hissed. "Somebody who sold the bomb parts or the fake passports or some other necessary building block of massacres! You've lived well, Schmoobie! Enjoyed the high life paid for with blood money! Your happy days are over now! When we grabbed you this evening, it was part of this message we keep trying to send, but no one seems to want to hear!"

Alec leaned in and whispered in Schmalenbach's ear. "The doors of this dangerous world swing both ways. None of you are safe from us."

Ward put a hand on Alec's shoulder, and it was as if Mr. Hyde turned back into Dr. Jekyll. Alec stepped back, shook his head as if ridding it of cobwebs, and took a deep breath.

Ward handed Schmalenbach a phone. "Call and confess, with lots of details, including bank account numbers."

Schmalenbach glared. "This is a coerced confession."

Ward nodded. "Uh, yeah, that's the point. I'm glad we understand each other. Now what's it going to be, Schmoobie? Prison?" He gestured over the edge. "Or pavement?"

***

A few minutes later, a black SUV peeled away from the Uptown München skyscraper. In a few moments, Munich police would ascend the stairs to the rooftop and find Hermann Schmalenbach, tied up and thoroughly bruised, the burner cell phone at his feet. At that point, he would become the problem of Germany's public prosecutor general. Winning a conviction of Schmalenbach might be challenging, as he would no doubt justifiably argue that his confession was coerced by mysterious strangers claiming to work for the CIA, and with it, all of his bank records should be inadmissible. But even if a German judge dismissed the case, an audio recording of Hermann Schmalenbach's confession would be anonymously sent to every major publication in Europe, ensuring the destruction of his reputation.

"I'd rather see him rotting in a cell," Ward grumbled as he sped through the streets.

"Think of it as using cancel culture to our advantage," Alec replied. "No one's ever gonna work with Schmoobie after they know he's been financing bioweapons research. And there are a lot of people who would be perfectly happy to kill the guy once they hear about his dirty deeds. The local Mossad will probably whack him during their morning coffee break. It's the circle of life, Simba."

Ward glanced at his longtime partner in the field.

"You keeping it cool, buddy?" Ward asked. "For a moment back there, I thought Gleefully Murderous Alec had returned, and I don't like seeing you like that." Then, after realizing the two men had come perilously close to genuine and vulnerable human affection, Ward added, "It really throws me off, because I'm supposed to be the bad cop."

Alec looked out the window.

"Were you like this before your first child was born?" Alec asked. "Feeling like … the world's a mess, everything's falling apart, and you're about to bring a defenseless little child into it?"

Ward chuckled.

"Alec, when my first daughter was born, Iraq was turning into a bloodbath, North Korea set off a nuke, Israel and Hezbollah were bombing the crap out of each other, it felt like there was a school shooting every other day … same crap, different year," he shook his head. "The world's always a mess. There's never a time when it's 'safe' to bring a child into the world. You love your wife, you make a baby, and you figure it out and life goes on, no matter how messed up the world is."

Alec offered his own bitter laugh. "Today, that looks like the good old days," he snarked. "No pandemic, no riots over presidential election results, no looking over your shoulder wondering who's selling you out to China. We've been doing this for a long time, and I'm not sure the world is in better shape than when we started. *Change* is not a synonym for *improvement*."

Ward snorted. "The world may not be better than when we started, but *your world* is better than when we started. And it's going to get even better when your little one arrives, trust me. Children turn your lives upside down, and then one day you find yourself realizing you don't know how you ever lived without them."

Alec nodded. "Good talk, buddy. You should write a book on parenting."

Ward laughed and flexed his bicep. "Nah, I'd rather write a book about heavy lifting."

CHAPTER THREE

That should just about do it, Harvey thought, wiping sweat from his brow. It was strapped into place, secure for the journey, or at least as secure as he could make it. He wished he could test what he had built, but that was obviously impossible. He was certain he had followed the instructions carefully, step by step.

Harvey knew many people would see what he was about to do as drastic. Everyone used to laugh at him, when he used to tell stories about his dog talking to him. They had sent him to a doctor, and when he described hearing voices—it took a while for him to figure out it wasn't just his dog doing the talking— they put him in a state-run facility that was supposed to be for "treatment" but that turned out to be just a different kind of pain, doled out by indifferent guards and doctors who didn't seem to want to be there any more than Harvey did.

Harvey Lawrence Godula knew people in town thought he was a nut. Over the years, lots of doctors had given him lots of different kinds of medicine, and none of them seemed to do any good. He used to have friends, but the voices made it harder and harder for him to maintain those connections. He noticed how his friends and acquaintances looked at him differently.

They didn't return the phone calls, always made excuses when he invited them over, didn't invite him to the big neighborhood barbeque. That therapist had told him to make connections with people, to feel like he was a part of something, but no matter how many times he tried, it never seemed to work.

He could hear them in the hum of the ceiling fan, or the air conditioner, or the heating vent—like someone talking on the other side of a door, or some radio that was left on in another room. It was rarely easy to hear what they were saying … but they never seemed to go away. *Audio pareidolia* was what one doctor called it, insisting that there were no voices or music, and that Harvey's mind was just interpreting random sounds and noise as a person's voice, looking for a pattern in the regular hums, buzzes, and clicks.

That answer didn't really satisfy Harvey. He sensed it was something more, and possibly something sinister. He wondered if it was ghosts, or angels, or demons, or spirits of some kind. But eventually Harvey determined it wasn't voices, it was *signals*. Someone was broadcasting, or perhaps directly targeting him with these signals. Harvey spent a lot of time on the Internet and knew the government had all kinds of secret projects that had hurt innocent people, from MK-Ultra to aboveground nuclear testing during the Cold War that spread fallout upon civilians. For a decade, a leading endocrinologist irradiated the testicles of prisoners in Oregon and Washington. The U.S. Army paid to have blister agents tested on prisoners at Holmesburg Prison in Pennsylvania. Much more recently, Raytheon had tested a "pain ray" energy weapon on prisoners at the Pitchess Detention Center, with the enthusiastic support of the Los Angeles County Sheriff's Department.

Harvey had figured it out. The voices all around his house were part of a secret government experiment, on him, and God knew how many other innocent people. Everyone Harvey told this to reacted by telling him he was nuts—clearly, the government had gotten to the doctors and authorities and pressured them to paint Harvey as crazy. Lawyers wouldn't listen to him. Everyone kept telling him that the answer was more hospitalization, more therapy, more medication. His friends, the sheriff, the mayor—all of them told him that if he kept disrupting public meetings by showing up and railing about the government's sinister plot, he would end up in an institution again.

About a month after one of Harvey's town council meeting tantrums had gone viralw on social media, with lots of mockery, a strange, beautiful little answer showed up at his door, out of the blue. Simple instructions, on clean, typewritten notes. A pile of cash. Instructions on how and where to buy ammonium nitrate without arousing suspicion, mixed in with other farm goods and materials. A map of a quarry, and where the company kept the blasting caps. Detailed instructions and a blueprint.

And soon, Harvey's bomb would be used where the letter had confirmed the signals were coming from.

The Central Intelligence Agency's headquarters building in Langley, Virginia.

CHAPTER FOUR

LIBERTY CAMPUS
TYSONS CORNER, VIRGINIA
JUNE 15, 2021

After the effort against Hell-Summoner and the Shedim network, the CIA's Dangerous Clique had moved offices, *again*, and Katrina found herself with her own small windowless office instead of the cubicle in the old space. Raquel still enjoyed the largest office—needed for her hoarder-worthy collection of paper files, because she didn't trust computers, the Internet, or electronic data systems. Dee had her own workspace in one corner, with four or five computer monitors and a humming series of computers that had spurred a lot of Tron jokes from Alec.

The Dangerous Clique didn't get many visitors to its office suite in the Liberty Crossing Intelligence Campus in Tysons Corner. The group's reluctance to work closely with others was right there in the nickname, Raquel observed. Katrina was surprised when she heard a knock on the door to her office.

Patrick Horne.

Horne and Katrina had entered the agency the same year, trained together at the Farm and had worked together early on—before their paths veered apart suddenly and dramatically. Polished, professional, and ambitious, Horne had climbed the Langley ladder until he was right-hand man to his mentor, the late CIA Director William Peck. Horne had been assigned the task of determining who had poisoned the former director during the Atarsa terrorist attacks two years earlier.

After two fruitless years—during which Peck passed away, succumbing to an infection of Covid-19—the current director, Barbara Stern, closed the investigation. Peck's poisoning, while indisputably tied to the Atarsa attacks, remained a stubborn mystery with far too many unanswered questions, joining the ranks of the 2003 Ricin letters, the 2008 Times Square bombing, the 2017 Las Vegas mass shooting, and the Metcalf sniper attack.

Katrina figured the inability to generate even a single solid lead would leave Horne with something of a damaged reputation within the agency. Yet somehow Horne had landed on his feet with the Office of the Executive Secretariat, coordinating all the correspondence for the director of national intelligence.

"Hey, I heard the Hitti takedown got a little messy yesterday! How are you feeling?"

"Better, thanks for asking," Katrina said, measuring Patrick's approach carefully. Patrick's choice of words could reflect genuine concern... or he could be subtly mocking her about her digestive eruption.

Katrina had long ago stopped trying to figure out what made Patrick tick. He acted like a genuine friend when he wanted to—but he seemed to turn off his charm, warmth, and affection at will. His working relationship with Raquel ran hot and cold from year to year, building to mutual respect and then backsliding into a bitter professional rivalry. He was usually brusque and dismissive of Dee unless he needed something. And Patrick could rarely hide his contempt for Alec. Yet Patrick hadn't interacted with the team at all during the months they were hunting down Hell-Summoner.

"Alec back yet?"

"Comes back this afternoon. Apparently, Hermann Schmalenbach shared a lot of information with Interpol," Katrina said. She assured herself she was simply expressing genuine spousal pride, and not trying to needle Patrick.

"Terrific," Patrick said, smiling with his mouth but not his eyes. "But you tell him to be careful out there. Particularly if he's going to be a dad." Then his expression softened a bit, and Katrina could sense something resembling genuine concern trying to claw its way out of him. "He's a lucky man, and even if I think he is an idiot, I'd hate to see his luck run out."

Katrina could have been gracious, but she sensed Patrick had intended to needle her with the "messy" comment, so she picked at one of Patrick's professional scabs. "Hey, I've been meaning to ask—when Stern shut down your Peck poisoning task force, did you guys have any leads you never got to follow up on?" Katrina knew the answer was *no*, and she wanted to see how Patrick would handle her query.

Patrick shook his head in frustration and pursed his lips. "The best lead we had was an intern at the television studio who was on a student visa from Saudi Arabia. But if it was him, he covered his tracks too well. No clear ties to Atarsa. Nothing suspicious on his phone. He went back to Saudi a bit before the pandemic."

"Convenient," she observed.

CHAPTER FIVE

SOMEWHERE IN THE SEEMINGLY ENDLESS
SPRAWL OF THE NORTHERN VIRGINIA SUB-
URBS
JUNE 16, 2021

Katrina loved her gynecologist, Dr. Amber Beryl. In a world where everything seemed to be unraveling toward chaos, Dr. Beryl was an hour-long vacation, serving as a de facto psychotherapist, holistic healer with tea recommendations, wise big sister, and career and marriage coach all rolled into one, as well as making sure Katrina's parts down under remained healthy. She had a vague sense of what Katrina did for a living—it involved a lot of foreign travel, stress, and unexpected injuries—and she was as thrilled as anyone when Katrina called, saying the pregnancy test had come back positive. And she was equally thrilled when she herself confirmed, shortly thereafter, that Katrina's initial peeing on a stick hadn't generated a false positive.

But it was time, as Dr. Beryl put it, for the "baton to be passed" to an obstetrician and had recommended Dr. Isaiah Mikołajczak. Dr. Beryl figured that Mikołajczak, a mid-life immigrant from the border region of Poland and Lithuania, might find something in common with the Uzbeki-born Katrina.

"Call me Doctor Miko!" the doctor insisted, upon meeting Katrina and Alec and ushering them into an examination room. "Doctor Beryl is vunderful, isn't she?"

Katrina was a keen student of human behavior, and she had suspected that Dr. Beryl was more nervous about her pregnancy than she let on. As everyone felt the need to remind her, any pregnancy past forty was considered high risk. The medical community had invented the perfectly insulting label, "geriatric pregnancy." By the calculation tables of the reproductive research world, Katrina's odds of becoming pregnant had been about one in twenty. Seemingly everyone—her parents, Alec's parents, Dr. Beryl—felt the need to prepare her for the possibility of stillbirth or miscarriage. Mid-conversation, Katrina and Alec suddenly realized both sets of parents were speaking from painful experience that had deliberately never been brought up in their lifetimes.

Yet, more than 100,000 American women gave birth after forty each year, and Katrina was in phenomenal shape for her age—not just in appearance but in blood pressure, blood sugar, resting heart rate, cholesterol, and almost every other measurement. Still, today's ultrasound felt like a big step— only a few more weeks, and it would feel safe to tell other people.

"I've been terrible with that," Katrina confessed on the drive over with Alec. "They say don't tell anyone for the first three months, but how am I supposed to hide this? How am I not supposed to share the best news we've gotten since ..." She realized she couldn't remember. "I mean, thanks to the restaurant chase, I think I've contained the news of my pregnancy to the CIA, FBI, NSA, Department of Justice, Department of the Treasury ... and I guess Douglas Hitti has a strong suspicion of why I barfed all over him."

Alec shook his head in mock disapproval. "Very bad, sweetheart! I thought you kept secrets for a living. I've just told Ward, my brothers, Elaine's husband, Joe ... oh, and I guess Hermann Schmalenbach."

Katrina stared back and threw up her hands in mock outrage. "Seriously? At least I kept this secret contained to just one continent!"

But in Dr. Miko's examination room, the doctor kept going on and on about the risks of her pregnancy, with his thick Eastern European accent. "Particularly vor a voman of your advanced years!"

Alec suppressed a scowl and realized Dr. Miko reminded him of Frank Gorshin when he played the Riddler on the 1960s *Batman* television show. No doubt Dr. Miko thought he was doing the couple a favor—nudging them to emotionally prepare for the worst-case scenario. Alec was wondering just what the heck he was supposed to do with the possibility of fate, or destiny, or God, or someone giving him a child, and then cruelly snatching it away before he could see his child's face. Be happy, but not too happy? Be prepared for the life-altering change of parenthood, but be prepared to lose it all at a moment's notice? All of the advice for parents grappling with a high-risk pregnancy seemed painfully generic: *Listen to your partner. Eat a healthy diet. Do not eat raw meat.* As if at any given moment, they would be relaxing in their home when Katrina would suddenly be attacked by steak tartare. No, Alec had concluded, the only way to get through this was to ignore what he couldn't control—which was almost everything—and focus on what he could control, which was look for opportunities to find some bad guy and beat the snot out of him. On paper, Hermann Schmalenbach might have just revealed all his secrets if he had been threatened with prosecution. But Alec had decided throwing Schmalenbach off a building was a healthy way to deal with pregnancy-related stress.

But Dr. Miko's sudden reaction to the ultrasound was unreadable.

"What? What is it?" Alec demanded, a million nightmare scenarios running through his head, even though he had sworn he wouldn't think about something going wrong. "Does our child have two heads or something?"

Katrina squeezed Alec's hand, bracing herself for the worst.

"In a manner of speaking, yes!" Dr. Miko chuckled. "Congratulations, Meester and Meesus Lee-oh-need-iv-na. You're having tvins!"

"Tvins?" Alec repeated, not quite understanding.

"*Twins!*" Katrina gasped.

CHAPTER SIX

D
r. Miko had told Alec and Katrina a lot more things about the pregnancy, but after the revelation of the twins, every time the obstetrician spoke, the only thing Alec heard was the trombone sound used for the voices of adults in the Charlie Brown *Peanuts* cartoons. Had Alec's mind and ears continued their longtime working relationship, he would have heard that the bottom line was that there was no reason for concern, yet. Dr. Miko emphasized that Katrina should avoid stress. This recommendation just caused Katrina to start laughing hysterically, to the obstetrician's confusion.

Once they were in the car, Katrina said she was supposed to go to a late afternoon meeting at CIA headquarters in Langley. Alec asked if, considering the day's amazing news, she wanted to take the rest of the day off. She declined, and he asked again. She declined again, and Alec asked why it was so damn important to go to this meeting.

"Because I said I would be at this meeting, and until I am physically incapable of doing my job, I am going to do my job and keep my word!" Katrina burst with terrible fury.

"You are having twins!" Alec screamed, and then he laughed at himself, and then felt his eyes fill with tears, and then he started laughing at the fact that he was crying, and he looked over and Katrina was doing the same thing.

"Okay, *now* I'm scared!" she laughed. "Oh, God, two babies in me? Two? Twins?"

"Tvins!" Alec corrected her, mimicking Dr. Miko's accent. "Zat is ee-fen vurse!"

"Now we have to agree on two names!" Katrina marveled.

Alec stared ahead, dazed, overjoyed, and terrified, all at once. "How are we going to do this? I figured we could handle this because we could double team him—or her! But now...them? We're going to have to cover man-to-man! God help us if you had triplets, we would have to cover them zone!"

***

The forty minutes or so from the obstetrician's office to the Central Intelligence Agency south entrance gate on Dolley Madison Boulevard was the happiest Katrina and Alec had ever been while fighting traffic.

The idiot who belatedly realized he was in the wrong lane and had to get back in, the moron who sat through the first ten seconds of a green light looking down at his phone, the maniac who accelerated on the last millisecond of a yellow light at the intersection—Alec greeted their vehicular imbecility with uncharacteristic patience, good cheer, and forgiveness, because for once, everything seemed right with the world. He and Katrina were going to have two children. An instant family! Two heartbeats on that monitor!

"*Tvins!*" he kept shouting at random intervals, triggering a new round of giggling in Katrina. He kept having to wipe tears as he drove. Everything that had seemed so wrong in the world had been washed away by a tide of surprise and joy. The God he had doubted so often was giving him this overwhelming gift, one he didn't feel he deserved.

Katrina was contemplating who they should tell, and in what order, and how on earth she was going to make it to three months before telling everyone who didn't already know. But as they waited in the line of traffic to enter the south entrance, her blissful vision of impending double parenthood was interrupted by an odd question from Alec.

"How many years have you been coming to this building?" Alec asked.

"Twenty-two years next spring," Katrina answered. "Why?"

"Have you ever seen a tractor-trailer use this entrance?" Alec asked, suspiciously.

Katrina's eyes widened. "Not at this hour, and not one like that," she said, seeing the large tractor-trailer that was about to pull up to the guard shack.

"There's always a chance he's just some idiot who made a wrong turn," Katrina said, dipping her head and checking to see if the Glock in the glove compartment was loaded.

"Or he's al-Qaeda or ISIS or Atarsa!" Alec said, suddenly veering out of the line of cars and making a U-turn.

"Alec!" Katrina shouted. "Don't—"

And then she heard the gunshots.

Alec swerved to the side of the road, hit the brake, reached down to unbuckle his safety belt, and threw his body on top of Katrina.

"Ow! What the hell do you think you're doing?"

"Protecting my family!" Alec barked at her. "Keep your head down! And your belly down! And—just keep everything down!"

They heard more gunshots, and the sounds of guards shouting.

Katrina fumed underneath her husband's body. For how many years had she run toward a threat instead of hiding from it? And now, with two babies inside her, her husband just assumed she was the one who needed protection? "Alec, right now, your weight on top of me is a greater threat to me than anybody outside with a gun."

Alec poked his head up above the seats and looked behind their car at the guard shack. A small army of uniformed CIA federal protective service personnel were converging upon the tractor-trailer truck. The officers seemed to be shouting a lot, half waving some units closer, half waving others to stay back or move farther away.

Alec got off Katrina. She poked her head up and watched.

Finally, one of the guards, gun drawn, approached Alec's side of the vehicle, and motioned to roll down the window. Alec did so, his mind momentarily pausing to realize that the *roll down the window* gesture had long outlasted manual window controls in cars.

"Are you two all right?" the guard shouted.

Alec and Katrina answered affirmatively.

"We're doing great, she's having twins!" Alec shouted.

The guard stared back in confusion.

"Uh, great," he shouted back with a wave. "Please stay in your car for now, sir, we're dealing with an emergency situation—"

Katrina leaned over and asked the guard what had happened.

But before the guard could answer, the three officers who had opened the back of the tractor-trailer were shouting one terrifying word, over and over again.

BOMB! BOMB! BOMB!

CHAPTER SEVEN

JUNE 16, 2021
REMARKS BY THE PRESIDENT ON THE WAY TO
MARINE FORCE ONE

THE PRESIDENT: It's been a tough day. This after-noon—excuse me, morning, as you all know, a terrorist attacked—attempted an attack—that we've been talking about, and worried about, that the intelligence commu-nity has assessed—has undertaken—tried to undertake an attack. The terrorist attempted, tried, to detonate a truck bomb at the entrance to CIA headquarters. The George Bush—the effect would have been terrible. Had the bomb gone off, the casualties would have been enormous.

Only the quick action of the guards at the little—the entrance checkpoint—stopped today from being a dark day. A really dark day. They took action, and the bomber was killed before the bomb could be exploded, the bomb could be detonated.

I've been engaged all day, in constant contact with CIA Director Stern, Barb Stern, great woman—the FBI, the military commanders here in Washington and the Pentagon as well as overseas. And my commanders here in Washington and in the field have been on this with great detail, and you will have a chance to hear more from them at some point.

The situation on the ground is still evolving, and I'm constantly being updated. These American law enforcement officers who gave their lives—I mean, risked their lives—it's an overused word but it's totally appropriate here—are heroes, heroes who have been engaged in a dangerous, selfless mission to save the lives of others. They are a part of simply what I call the backbone of America. They are the spine of America. The heart. The spleen. the best the country has to offer.

To those who carried out this attack, as well as anyone who wishes America harm, know this: We will not forgive. We will not forget. We will hunt you down and make you pay. I will defend our interests and our people with every measure at my command.

Q: Mr. President, is there any sense of who the bomber was, was he part of a terror organization or acting alone, or—

THE PRESIDENT: We don't know anything about that yet. I haven't been told anything about that.

Q: Mr. President, is there any sense whether there is potential for more attacks? Should Americans be concerned—

THE PRESIDENT: We don't know anything about that, either. What I can tell you, I will tell you, and I really mean it here, I'm not being facetious—is that the risk today is the same as yesterday. It's like my dad used to tell me—and I'll never forget this—he was driving in his car, and he told me—he was a wise man, my dad—he told me you couldn't walk out the door in the morning without taking a risk. Risk is part of life. You just have to live with it. You just live with it. You live with it until you die. And that's what we're going to do. Live with it, I mean. Not die with it. I mean, yes, eventually we all die. But—

WHITE HOUSE PRESS SECRETARY: The president really needs to be going! Thank you, everyone!

THE PRESIDENT: Yes, thank you! Thank you, everyone!

***

Twenty minutes later, the Secretary of Homeland Security gave his on-camera statement, clarifying any confusion from the president's off-the-cuff remarks on the way to Marine Force One. Shortly after noon, a tractor-trailer truck containing explosives had been stopped at the main employee entrance to the George Bush Center for Intelligence, more commonly known as CIA headquarters, in Langley, Virginia. The perpetrator did not successfully detonate the bomb; after having a brief, confusing, and hostile exchange with the guards, he was shot and killed by Federal Protective Service personnel. So far, there was no indication that the perpetrator was part of a group, or that more attacks were expected—but all the usual targets—federal buildings, airports, train and subway stations—would have an increased police presence as a precaution.

CHAPTER EIGHT

LIBERTY CROSSING INTELLIGENCE CAMPUS
JUNE 17, 2021

The next day, productivity within the halls of CIA headquarters declined considerably—less out of fear than by the fact that everyone wanted to figure out who was behind the attack. The evening before, the FBI Washington Field Office announced the name of the perpetrator as Harvey Lawrence Godula. The overwhelming majority of CIA personnel suspected he was a patsy who had been armed and enabled by someone else. (The turf fights between the agency and the FBI over who had responsibility for the investigation had been brief but spectacular. The FBI Director won the argument when they pointed out that they, along with Fairfax County police, had jurisdiction over the 1993 shooting of CIA employees by Mir Aimal Kansi, a Pakistani immigrant. Kansi had killed two CIA employees and wounded three more before escaping, and it took four years to catch him, even after he was named to the FBI's Most Wanted list.)

The Dangerous Clique had collectively lost interest in that update on the Shedim network that was supposed to run in one of next week's presidential daily briefings, overtaken by the news that Katrina and Alec were having twins, and the mystery of who was behind the attempted bombing.

"Harvey Lawrence Godula, age fifty-five," Raquel read off from the latest internal update. "Lived in a remote cabin outside of Roanoke. The neighbors keep saying, 'He was the quiet type, kept to himself mostly.'"

"Please don't say he believed in lizard people," Alec muttered.

"You're close," Raquel said, exhaling and revealing long-simmering exasperation. "The guy wrote letters to the CIA a lot of years back, demanding to know why we made his dogs talk to him."

"That's insane!" Dee exclaimed. "Any secret program that could make dogs talk would be entirely under the jurisdiction of the NSA."

"Bargain-basement Son-of-Sam knockoff," Ward growled. "The bigger question to me is how a lone nut gets his hands on a truck full of ammonium nitrate?"

"Every government agency in the country is trying to figure that out," Raquel continued, reading off the update. "The FBI searched his house and determined that two months ago the guy opened his front door and finds on his doorstep a giant pile of cash, detailed instructions for legally purchasing ammonium nitrate in a way that wouldn't attract attention or suspicion, detailed instructions on how to assemble the bomb, and a map to Langley's front door. All in neatly typewritten notes."

"That's what Atarsa did, only supersized," Katrina muttered, rubbing her temples. "Find someone troubled, teach them how to cause large-scale chaos, and then disappear, leaving no fingerprints."

Dee winced. "You don't think Atarsa is back, do you?"

"Copycats, maybe, but not the original crew," Alec said quickly. "Almost all of them are dead, the rest in prison."

Katrina noticed a pensive look on Raquel's face.

"What is it?" Katrina asked.

Raquel exhaled slowly. "There's another angle here that I think I need to share with you guys. And I hate to say it, but this could be really bad news."

Alec did a double take. "I'm sorry, was the attempted bombing the *good* news?"

"I'm starting to think the truck bomb was intended for us, specifically," Raquel declared gravely. "This morning the mail cart brought something that didn't make sense until I just read the FBI report about neatly typewritten notes. I need to show you something."

She disappeared into her office and returned a minute later with two plastic bags and a pair of rubber gloves. She snapped one of the rubber gloves onto her hand.

"My prostate's fine," Alec insisted.

Raquel ignored his joke and opened one of the plastic bags. She removed a blank white envelope postmarked from McLean, just down the road from CIA headquarters. The letter had no return address; the mailing address was simply:

THE DANGEROUS CLIQUE
CENTRAL INTELLIGENCE AGENCY
WASHINGTON, D.C. 20505

Raquel noted the mailing address and zip code was the publicly known one, used by the CIA's public affairs office and encouraged for anonymous informants. She them removed a single trifolded 8.5-by-11-inch piece of paper, with one typewritten phrase in the middle.

THE DANGEROUS CLIQUE WILL PAY
FOR ITS CRIMES FROM 2003

"This was sent to CIA headquarters, not Liberty Campus. It took a few days for it to get forwarded. Meaning whoever sent it thought we worked at Langley, not here. I think it's possible that whoever set up Harvey Lawrence Godula with his truck bomb wasn't targeting the CIA in general. They may have been specifically trying to kill us and using him to do it."

For a long moment, Raquel's team stared back in stunned silence. Ward looked over the note.

"Shit," he declared.

Raquel said she hadn't had a chance to have the letter forensically tested, to match it against the letters described by the bureau.

"The moment I tell anyone outside this room about this letter, everything changes. The FBI takes over the investigation and will want to review all our case files, going back to 2003. They'll want a protective detail on all of us, maybe our family members. Our whole lives get turned upside down, and we're living one step short of being in the witness protection program, not that a personal protective security detail is going to do much if somebody parks truck bombs in front of our homes."

Katrina shook her head. "I do not want to spend the rest of this pregnancy living as a prisoner in my own home, giving birth under armed guard!" she fumed. "And it wouldn't be the right response, anyway! Whoever's targeting us doesn't know that much about us! They targeted the wrong building. If they knew where we lived, they would have started there. They don't know where we are at any given moment."

"Yet," Alec added.

Katrina looked at the paper. "We don't necessarily have to tell our bosses about this letter, do we?"

Raquel sat back in her chair. "Very, very few people outside the U.S. intelligence community know the term *Dangerous Clique*. Hell, not many people outside this room use it. It's particularly strange that they would know our nickname but not where we work."

Ward cleared his throat with a rumble. "How about that mole we've been hearing rumors about for the past decade or so?"

Raquel exhaled slowly, thinking it over. "If it is, it means something changed recently. One of the few advantages we've had these past few years is that, as far as we could tell, the mole—or *moles*—either didn't know we exist or what we do or didn't care or see any value in leaking anything about us."

Alec nodded grimly. "For years, our colleagues outside this room have constantly labeled us 'an idiotic waste of resources.' And now it finally pays off!"

"But this?" Raquel gestured to the letter. "The last two words are the biggest clue. 'From 2003.' Whoever it is, they probably don't realize that the thing with the kids was the only significant mission we did that calendar year. Merlin thought one bull stampede through the china shop per year was sufficient."

"Assuming they're not misremembering the year, or trying to throw us off the trail," Katrina noted.

Alec started chuckling. He got up, paced around the room, continued to giggle, and then stood behind his chair, digging his hands into the chair back.

"Buddy, you doing all right?" Ward asked, cocking an eyebrow in concern.

"Sweetheart?" Katrina asked cautiously.

"I'm fine!" Alec giggled. "I'm totally fine!"

He suddenly lifted up his chair and banged it against the floor a few times, in a sudden explosion of rage.

"Alec!" Katrina exclaimed.

"One day!" Alec fumed. "One friggin' day between you and I getting maybe the best news of our entire lives—Twins! *Twins!*—and learning someone's trying to kill us!" Alec's eyes were wide, and the veins in his neck and forehead were throbbing. "What, a whole week was too much to ask? A weekend? It's just … what did we do to deserve this? Katrina, haven't you and I done enough good things in our lives to deserve just a little stretch of peace and quiet?"

"Of course you guys have done enough good things!" Dee exclaimed before anyone else could speak. "But that's not the way life works."

"Hey, hey, Alec, this is nothing new for us!" Ward said, getting up and putting a hand on Alec's shoulder. "Everybody's always trying to kill us, man. Atarsa, Hell-Summoner, everybody before—this is just another day at the office. Same stuff, different day."

Alec shook his head. "No, my friend, it's not quite the same."

He slowly walked over to Katrina's chair.

"Because whoever's out to get us, they may not even realize it, but ..." Alec put his hands on his wife's shoulders.

"They're trying to kill our children, too."

CHAPTER NINE

T he team concluded that they would urge their relatives to "visit Aunt Edna," the code phrase that meant leaving town for at least a week and varying their routines to ensure they're not being monitored or followed. In the aftermath of the attempted truck bomb attack, all intelligence community personnel were being urged to take additional precautions.

The agency helpfully sent around a memo to all employees entitled "Ten Things You Can Do to Help Your Personal Security." The instructions included varying the routes of their commute—the memo ignored that all commutes ended in the same location—and helpfully suggested they "maintain situational awareness of your surroundings at all times." Katrina murmured that she wished the same advice could be communicated to all drivers on the Beltway.

The memo concluded with the plea, "if you see something, say something," followed by a paragraph from the agency's lawyers declaring that racial or ethnic profiling in threat assessment would not be tolerated in any shape or form.

Alec crumpled up the memo. "They should just print up a brochure: *So You've Learned Someone's Trying to Kill You.*"

Katrina stared at a map of the world in frustration and wondered just what the Dangerous Clique would need to achieve to earn office space with a window. All the windows at Liberty Campus were double-paned and specially treated to guard against laser beams that an enemy spy could aim at the window, detect the vibrations and theoretically, at least, hear what was being said inside.

The threat against her and her team shouldn't feel all that different.

Dee would search through the NSA's intercepts to see if anything pointed to an attack against the team—although no one expected to find something, as that would be the sort of information that would get red-flagged immediately.

And they agreed to consult the one person at the FBI they trusted, the now supervisory special agent Elaine Kopek who had been dragged, kicking and screaming, into a management position in the aftermath of her successful work against Hell-Summoner and the Shedim network. The Hitti surveillance was supposed to be her last field work for a while. But about two weeks after her promotion, Kopek started trying to figure out what infraction would be perfectly calibrated to keep her employed by the bureau but to get her demoted back into field work, so she would never have to attend a budget planning meeting again.

Upon hearing the news later that afternoon, Elaine was concerned, but not quite alarmed.

"The world has a finite number of people," she began. "Only a certain number of people know you exist. An even smaller number know what you—I guess technically *we*—did in 2003. I'm pretty sure even I only know half the story. An even smaller number would be pissed about it, and an even smaller number would have the motive, means, and opportunity to target you."

"Well, that's sort of the catch," Ward sighed, rubbing the bridge of his nose. "Everybody we crossed paths with back then is dead."

The team all looked at one another awkwardly.

Elaine looked around the table incredulously.

"Everyone? Really? Every last co-conspirator and hired gun and money-launderer and mook? You know, at the bureau, we don't have these issues," she sighed.

"The Branch Davidians could not be reached for comment," Alec chirped.

Elaine frowned. "That wasn't us, that was ATF! Do all federal agents look alike to you?"

After a moment of studying the note, Elaine turned her attention back to her teammates.

"I only ran across you lovable lunatics at the tail end of all that. Just who else did you piss off in 2003?"

Ward let out a little chuckle. "This is gonna take a while."

2002

CHAPTER TEN

CIA HEADQUARTERS
HAROLD HARE'S OFFICE, SEVENTH FLOOR
SEPTEMBER 1, 2002

"**H**appy anniversary," acting deputy director Harold Hare said, pouring two tumblers of Scotch. His office was small but cozy. The drink cart was right out of a 1960s advertising agency, and the crystal decanter and glasses looked far too nice to be sitting on a side table in a federal government office. Hare would only say his drinkware had been stolen from a palace of a not-too-friendly country.

"This past year has been…more than I ever could have imagined," Raquel said, shaking her head. "I just hope I've done enough with the opportunity I was given."

A little more than a year ago, CIA Director George Tenet had asked Hare to head up a comprehensive review of the agency and determine what it was doing well, what could be improved, and what glaring problems needed to be addressed. Hare wasn't sure if the assignment was as important as Tenet made it sound, or whether it was just another study group whose recommendations would end up in a file cabinet somewhere. Raquel Holtz, a bright mind who had transferred to the analytic corps after some operations work in the Balkans, had been persuaded to be Hare's executive assistant—a role some young women in Raquel's position would find slightly demeaning, but she had been assured it would be a good way to make connections.

Ten days into the job, the morning had barely begun when someone yelled that a plane had flown into the World Trade Center. They were watching when, seventeen minutes later, a second plane hit the second tower and everyone's thoughts of an accident were dispelled. Tenet's security detail had pulled him out of a breakfast at a downtown Washington hotel and was rushing back to headquarters. Hare turned to Raquel and shoved a legal notepad into her hands. "Everything we're supposed to do just changed. We're not proposing changes, we're making changes. Wherever I go today, you come with me. No matter who's there, you come in, clearance be damned. You're going to write down every instruction, every idea, and anything that could be important because by the end of the day I won't remember it all."

The rest of the day, week, month, and year had been a whirlwind. Hare was right—sweeping changes came to the CIA, enacted as they went along, and the Hare study turned into a widely read evaluation of those changes and what had been learned along the way, sometimes the hard way.

"You can skip the modesty, Raquel," Hare said. "You got thrown into the fire and rose to the occasion. Good people were wearing out from stress and exhaustion and burnout and pressure left and right. And don't think I didn't notice that exhausting as it all was, you loved it. Stress drives you. You're a managerial adrenaline junkie. You'll get bored without it. You've handled everything right by my side, and I know I am not the easiest man to work for. All the big names on the seventh floor know who you are now—Tenet, McLaughlin, Cofer Black. Some people are going to hate you for being associated with me, but I like to think you end up with more friends than enemies."

Raquel beamed. "I wouldn't have it any other way." She had been waiting for an opportunity like this, having spent the past decade in the quietly frustrating "really impressive but not quite the best" category at almost every level—Thomas Jefferson High School for Science and Technology in Virginia, the College of William & Mary, and graduate school at Tufts. Raquel had been high academic honors but just short of salutatorian, "best teammate" but not team captain in field hockey, top quarter of her agency entry class—an endless series of ranking among those who were inevitably described by ceremony speakers as "exemplary, but too many to mention." The most powerful chip in the world wouldn't be found in the laboratories of Dell or Intel, but on Raquel's shoulder.

"They're going to want you to manage a team," Hare said. "I've told them you've got leadership capabilities. Don't get too excited. You'll be running a team monitoring some quiet corner of the world, not hunting for bin Laden."

"I wouldn't want that job," she said with a chuckle. "I worry more about the terror mastermind that we don't know about yet. If we had just raided one camp at the right time … everything would be different. I want to find the guy who wants to be the next bin Laden and cut short his career before he's even got a real terrorist group."

"You've been listening to my complaints and taking careful notes," Hare chuckled.

"Just as you instructed," she shot back. "We're a big agency. Layers of management and bureaucracy—mostly good people, but we're like an aircraft carrier, we don't turn on a dime. Changing anything takes a long time. The enemy works in cells of just a couple of guys. I don't want to send a big, slow-moving institution against a small, nimble, always-changing, always-adapting enemy. We're always going to lose that fight eventually."

"What would you do? If you had all the authority and power and budget you needed?" Hare asked, a twinkle in his eye. "Because we're in that rare moment where I might just have enough clout to make something happen."

CHAPTER ELEVEN

JANUARY 2003

What Harold Hare had promised and what he had delivered turned out to be no closer than distant cousins. The promised office space in Langley never materialized, nor did the alternative at the Intelligence Community Campus in Brookmont, Maryland. For a while, it looked like the new team wouldn't have any office space at all. But finally, a small suite of offices at the Liberty Crossing Intelligence Campus was opening up, after a CIA group focusing on Russia was ordered to reduce its staff and budget. Putting so many resources into watching Russia made little sense now that Vladimir Putin was a trusted ally in the war on terror.

The new office's official title was Counterterrorism Liaison and Intelligence Quality Utilization Executive. Harold Hare liked it because it sounded important, but no one would be able to figure out what exactly it meant their job was.

Raquel's first hire was Katrina Leonidivna, whom she had encountered at the Farm before working for Hare, a burgeoning friendship interrupted by Katrina's rapid deployment to Uzbekistan and then Afghanistan. But Katrina still had a few more weeks to complete for her temporary duty with the Global Jihad Unit. Katrina had strongly encouraged Raquel to hire her husband, Alec Flanagan, who was apparently too exuberant for his colleagues tracking terrorism financing in the Office of Transnational Issues.

Alec proved to be twice as exuberant once he was alongside Raquel.

"I've studied how everybody organizes their small counter-terrorism teams, paying a lot of attention to the lesser-known, under-the-radar ones," Alec began. "Taiwan's Thunder Squad, Austria's EKO Cobra, Iceland's Viking Squad."

"Why do they all sound like defunct football franchises?"

"I've drawn up an all-star team of nine possible recruits, both from within the agency and other branches of the intelligence and military. Call us … the *Tenacious Ten*!"

Raquel scanned the list.

"I've got the budget for half this."

Alec just mimicked his gesture from a moment earlier: "Call us … the *Fiery Five*!"

"The rest we'll have to borrow intermittently from their current employers. Let's start with finding a hacker."

CHAPTER TWELVE

NATIONAL SECURITY AGENCY
9800 SAVAGE RD.
FORT GEORGE G. MEADE, MARYLAND
THE CLOSING DAYS OF JANUARY 2003

"**W**e're putting together a team at Langley and we're looking to borrow someone with serious cyber and hacking skills, possibly long-term," Raquel began. "We need someone smart, creative, adaptable—the kind of person who can handle any problem thrown their way without flinching."

The man behind the desk stared back blankly and her and Alec, with the fluorescent lights above him reflecting in the lenses of his glasses. Jonathan Smythe had been staff director for the National Security Agency's Threat Operations Center for a bit more than two years.

Ever since the movie *The Matrix* hit theaters a few years earlier, Smythe's colleagues had given him the deeply unwanted nickname Agent Smith, in part because of his surname and in part because his receding hairline and stark features made him resemble Hugo Weaving a bit. Because he hated the jokes and hated that anyone could see him as a soulless computer program walking around in a gray suit,

Smythe did his best to maximize the inflection in his voice and never sound too robotic.

"And *why* did you *specify* in your *message* that you were *interested* in an NSA employee who had just *completed* all necessary *training*?" Smythe asked in a singsongy voice that dispelled any suspicions that he was a robot and confirmed all suspicions that he was a weirdo.

Raquel shifted in her chair. "Well, we need somebody who knows all the tricks, but who hasn't been around so long, they've picked up recognizable habits or gotten set in their ways."

"We need someone bright but morally flexible," Alec explained, making his requirements sound more normal than they were.

Smythe nodded.

***

"These are our FRESHEST recruits," Smythe said, as they stood in the doorway of a large classroom, watching a crop of mostly twentysomethings—generally government bureaucrat drones, one or two who looked like former military, and one or two nose-ring-wearing rebels—sit through a mandatory training course on FISA warrants.

"Like anybody's ever going to care about that stuff," Alec scoffed at the training video.

"Twenty-four desks, twenty-three recruits," Raquel counted. "Who's missing?"

"We *had* an early *washout*," Smythe said, betraying a little irritation. "Someone *chose* to start hacking into *our* systems on the *first* day."

Raquel cringed, but Alec's eyes lit up. "Really?" he asked excitedly. "Now I've got to meet this person."

***

The "washout" had just been terminated with prejudice and completed several hours of having her superiors threaten criminal charges. Alec and Raquel found her walking to her car in the Fort Meade parking lot.

"I wasn't there long enough to have a desk to clean out," she spat.

Alec summed up the personnel file he'd been given a few minutes earlier. "Dominica 'Dee' Alves, born in Little Havana, Miami, Florida. Raised by a single father, you were running the books for your father's restaurant by the time you were twelve, skipped a grade in high school, won a full scholarship to the University of Miami, transferred to Carnegie Mellon. Off-the-charts grades in computer sciences."

"Why did you apply to NSA and not CIA?" Raquel asked.

"Because the CIA is a bunch of snobs who never gave my grandfather the credit he deserved," Dee shot back. "He was a doctor who came over in 1959 and informed the local CIA station about what he was hearing from patients about Castro's goons running around the city. They didn't even reimburse him for parking fees."

Alec leaned over and whispered in Raquel's ear: "We had a station in Miami?"

"Yup, for most of the sixties, at one point the second-largest in the world next to Langley," Raquel whispered back.

Dee kept fuming while they whispered. "Smug, arrogant WASPs! The Old Boy's Club, picking from the Ivy Leagues, with their good breeding and Skull and Bones and 'jolly good show, old chap. Let's have some tea!'"

Alec furrowed his brow. "Are you under the impression that everyone at the CIA is British?"

Raquel elbowed him, and he continued. "Because we're not! In fact, we're going to be really different from anything you're picturing. See, our team's going to operate from a different philosophy. On our seal, it's going to say, 'quae iuris est, si tu non adepto deprensus.'"

Dee was intrigued. "I'm Latina, but I don't speak Latin."

Alec responded with utter glee. "It means, 'everything is legal if you don't get caught.'"

CHAPTER THIRTEEN

EARLY FEBRUARY 2003

E dward "Ward" Dale Rutledge waited in the room, deep within
in the bland office building with suspiciously serious security
in a nondescript office park northern Virginia. Shortly after
returning from Afghanistan, he had completed his application
to become one of the Central Intelligence Agency's paramilitary
operations officers, the tough-as-nails assignment with the somewhat less-than-intimidating acronym P-MOO.

Some government contractors had been hired to design the
space to be soothing and relaxing, and to draw visitors' attention
away from the one-way mirror. The result looked like a police
interview room redecorated by Marriott.

Finally, a tall but distinctly unintimidating man around his
age in a suit entered through the door, nodded, and sat across
from him at the table.

The man nodded, smiled, and checked the paper in the file
in front of him. "Are you the one who went after al-Qaeda in
Afghanistan, and they said was..." he read carefully from the
paper in the file. "Quote, 'irrationally exuberant in the use of
explosives,' unquote?"

Edward nodded. "When you say 'they,' I assume you mean
my commanding officers. Because the al-Qaeda guys I bombed
didn't say much of anything."

The man picked up a pen, and made a check mark somewhere on the paper in front of him. "Good answer. Why do you want to join the CIA?"

Ward studied the man across the table. He was clearly a civilian, comfortable in a suit, perhaps a little overcaffeinated.

"I could give you a long song and dance about my values, but ... since I was nineteen, and was in Oklahoma City when the bomb went off, I have wanted to introduce my foot to the ass of anybody and everybody who wanted to harm innocent people. The Army helped me do that in Kosovo and Afghanistan. But a lot of the mission felt like mop-up. It was the Jawbreaker guys with CIA who got to be the tip of the spear. I don't want to spend my prime fighting years patrolling villages and sorting out disputes between tribal chiefs. I want to find the next bin Laden and put his head on a pike and leave it on the White House lawn as a message to all the other wannabes. And then ... when the world is safe for my kids to grow up in ... then I'll sit back and take some cushy desk job."

Ward stared at the man across the desk and couldn't get a read on whether his interviewer was horrified or thrilled. He winced. "Was the head-on-a-pike thing too much?"

"Nope, just right," the man grinned wildly. "You're hired. Welcome to the CIA, or at least an experimental team under the deputy director. I'm Alec Flanagan."

"You're gonna be on this team? You're less old and crotchety than I pictured."

The man did a double take.

CHAPTER FOURTEEN

CIA HEADQUARTERS
FEBRUARY 7, 2003

The final recruit was Patrick Horne, a case officer who had just completed a tour in Warsaw, Poland, who had been one of Alec's best friends when he first joined the agency. But he had sensed friction with Patrick ever since he had proposed to Katrina. Raquel had noticed that Patrick had seemed uninterested until she had mentioned Katrina was joining the team, when he suddenly asked where he needed to sign to make it official.

There were other team members who had been bumped down to the "when we have the budget" list.

Thomas Wells was another CIA applicant currently with U.S. Air Force intelligence, who boasted he could fly anything. He was yet another American man whose career path was heavily influenced by watching Tom Cruise fly, ride a motorcycle, and win over Kelly McGillis in *Top Gun*. Alejandro Serrano de la Verde, who was currently one of the "crash and bang" driving instructors down on the Farm, helping future case officers perfect their skills in crashing through roadblocks, evade pursuing vehicles, and disabling moving vehicles. Raquel thoroughly studied his record and concluded that behind the wheel, he offered a combination of Mario Andretti, Evel Knievel, and David Letterman on a late-night commute home in Connecticut.

Because it hadn't been initially clear that the Global Jihad Unit would let Raquel's new team have Katrina, Raquel had contemplated recruiting one of her classmates from the Farm, a strikingly beautiful case officer of Japanese ancestry named Sanai Sato, currently working in Hong Kong. Alec had characterized Sanai as "90 percent of my fiancée's skills, and 160 percent of her attitude." But GJU had signed off on Katrina's departure, and it was now just a matter of arranging transport out of Afghanistan.

With an empty chair for Katrina, the group met in a small conference room on the seventh floor of CIA headquarters, adjacent to deputy director Harold Hare's office. Even with walls and doors that were supposed to be soundproof, the seventh floor of CIA headquarters felt like Grand Central Station, with groups coming and going. Between the ongoing war against al-Qaeda and the increasing expectations of an invasion of Iraq, the agency had arguably never been busier.

"I think John McLaughlin is trying to squeeze me off the seventh floor, so let's keep this meeting short," Harold Hare began. He looked at Raquel, Alec, Dee, Ward, Patrick, and the empty chair for Katrina, and felt distinctly underwhelmed. For a man code-named Merlin, this trick felt like he was pretending to remove the tip of this thumb.

"Well, seeing you all here together for the first time, I can say all of you have a distinctive record of..." Merlin looked down at his briefing packet. "... existence."

Raquel nodded, having experienced plenty of meetings and briefings where she had to put the best spin on bad news. "Merlin, when you gave me this assignment, I set out to assemble the best of the best. What you see before you is the very best of who was left over after almost everyone else was assigned to handling Iraq."

Ward furrowed his brow and looked around the table, trying to tell if he was being hazed.

Merlin waved his hand. "I'd like all of you to select a suitable test run. Nothing fancy. Just find some low-level troublemaker who hates America and has big ambitions and put him out of commission. Doesn't need to be fatal. Compromised and disgraced is fine."

"Well, where's the fun in that?" Ward asked, not entirely joking.

Raquel's replacement as Merlin's aide knocked, entered, and whispered something in his ear. Irritated, the deputy director checked his watch. "Dammit, Tenet moved the meeting up. Look, you're all smart, just find something and send me a memo." Merlin rose and quickly departed, grumbling something about how McLaughlin kept stealing his magic tricks.

The team—already code-named CLIQUE—sat around the table, exchanging looks, wondering if Merlin was forgetting about them already.

Raquel sighed. "Anyone have any ideas?"

"I'm glad you asked!" Alec leaped out of his chair and went over to the room's screen, eager to showcase what he had wanted to pitch to Hare.

A moment later, Alec brought up the correct file, and the screen illuminated a map of the China–India border.

"I'm going to first tell you a little bit about a country called Tibet," Alec began, chipper and cheery. "Tibet is an Asian country almost completely surrounded by mountain ranges. It is an extremely spiritual country, practicing a form of Buddhism. For many centuries the leader of Tibet has been known as the Dalai Lama. In 1950, Communist China invaded Tibet, and seized control of the entire country. In 1959, the Dalai Lama was forced to flee to India, and has lived in exile ever since. Upon the death of each Dalai Lama, his spirit is believed to pass into the body of a newborn infant. An exacting series of tests are performed to discover this boy's identity, who is then rigorously trained to fulfill his great responsibilities. The Dalai Lama is confirmed by a second spiritual leader, called the Panchen Lama. The Dalai Lama and the Panchen Lama recognize each other's reincarnations."

Dee raised her hand. "Are you Buddhist?"

"No, I'm a bad Catholic with excellent taste in old television shows," Alec shot back. He brought up in next image on the PowerPoint presentation. "This is the last known photo of Gedhun Choekyi Nyima, who would today be about fourteen years old. Back in 1995, the Dalai Lama announced he was the eleventh Panchen Lama in the Gelugpa school of Tibetan Buddhism. He was six years old at the time."

"He's just a kid!" Ward exclaimed.

"Yes, most six-year-olds are," Alec responded dryly. "Unfortunately, shortly after the announcement, the Chinese government kidnapped the Pachen Lama, because they wanted to install their own substitute who would be loyal to Beijing. They tried, but most Buddhists rejected the Chinese-appointed one. The true Panchen Lama, Gedhun Choekyi Nyima, has never been seen in public since his abduction."

Patrick finally stopped looking at the empty chair where Katrina was supposed to be. "You want the five of us to bust this kid out of some Chinese prison camp?"

"Well, we can't, because somebody else already did that," Alec said. "Several months ago, on the information-trading website called the Grand Bazaar, someone offered a lot of money for the location and security protocols around the Panchen Lama—and within a week, somebody paid."

Alec removed a handful of photocopied briefing packets out of a folder and slid one across the table to each of his new teammates. Dee started nodding as she glanced through the briefing report on the Grand Bazaar.

"Then, about a week later, the agency's China desk reported that the Panchen Lama was indeed taken from where he was living under the constant surveillance of the Chinese government. Everybody thought this was Tibetan Buddhists rescuing him. But the kid hasn't reappeared, and the Dalai Lama and Tibetan Buddhists insist they don't have him. All evidence the CIA can access suggests the Tibetans are launching a genuine effort to find him—and the Chinese are looking for him, too. From what we can tell, some third party kidnapped the kid from his kidnappers."

Ward looked back to the picture of the Pachen Lama, almost shaken by the six-year-old boy's full and innocent eyes. "This all sounds like a big deal. How have we not heard about any of this?

"Well, we're about to bomb Saddam Hussein back to the Stone Age, and that's using up a lot of oxygen in the room," Raquel remarked.

"I want to find Gedhun Choekyi Nyima and liberate him from whoever kidnapped him the second time, before the people who kidnapped him the first time find him."

"Oh, is that all?" Patrick scoffed. "One does not simply walk into a clash with Chinese state security. But let's assume we succeed in finding this kid. Then what do we do?"

"Return him to Tibet and the Dalai Lama," Alec answered firmly. "Or at the very least, let this boy choose his own fate."

Raquel let out a long, deep breath. "This is not a small test run," she declared.

"Raquel, no one else in the American government, or any of our allies, is even looking for him," Alec pleaded. "We've got stations and listening posts all around the world, and the NSA can pick up radio stations in your fillings. At minimum, a little time and effort should reveal who kidnapped him from China. How do we know if we can find him unless we try?"

Raquel looked at the file before her, and a Tibet Buddhist artist's sketch of what he might look like today. "He would be fourteen or so today?" Alec nodded. She looked hard at her new teammate. "Alec, your intense interest in finding a missing teenager wouldn't have anything to do with your past experience with missing persons cases?"

Alec bristled, a little offended that Raquel would even subtly bring up the topic of Sarina Locke, the girl from his teenage years who had disappeared from a small, wealthy town in Connecticut. The official explanation from the cops was that Sarina had run away, but Alec remained convinced she had been kidnapped, even though he never found any significant evidence of a crime.

Alec composed himself. "We can't fix Saddam Hussein by ourselves. We can't fix al-Qaeda. But this? This we can fix."

Dee raised her hand again. "Before we reach any final decisions... would you mind if I took some time to see what I can find on the Internet and signals intercepts about this kid's disappearance? Maybe I can find something that the China desk missed."

Raquel thought for a moment, then finally nodded. "Fine, but you seem awfully certain that the NSA will be eager to work on tasking requests from someone they just fired."

Dee stared back, puzzled. "Oh! I guess I could give them tasking requests, but I figured it would just be easier to use the CIA's network access to hack what we need out of NSA."

CHAPTER FIFTEEN

CIA HEADQUARTERS
FEBRUARY 10, 2003

Three days later, the members of the team had reassembled in the conference room, with the same empty chair because Katrina's departure had been delayed. This time Dee had arranged the PowerPoint presentation.

"By the end of 2001, everybody in the world realized we were in a new world, particularly for spying. Last year somebody—we don't know who—came up with the idea of creating an eBay for secrets. The Grand Bazaar," Dee declared.

Alec nodded. "I had a feeling you were already familiar with it."

"Oh, I've browsed it," she said, beamingly. "I just didn't have the savings to buy the classified portions of the defense budget of Belarus. Or, you know, any particular need to read it."

The conference room door opened, and Harold Hare and his new aide entered and took their seats at the far end of the table. "Please, continue," he gestured.

"The Grand Bazaar site gets ten percent of every transaction, and the NSA calculates whoever's running it must have made tens of millions by now."

Hare interrupted. "We've had some of our secrets sold on it, but we've also used front companies to buy information that would be difficult for us to obtain otherwise."

Alec cleared his throat. "So, if I want to know who bought a piece of information on that site a couple months ago—"

"Good luck," Dee laughed. "That's going to be like looking for a needle in a haystack."

Alec furrowed his brow. "Actually, finding a needle in a haystack is really easy if you have a powerful enough electromagnet."

Ward chuckled. "No, you burn down the haystack."

"Or, because we're not pyromaniacs, we put the whole haystack in water, because the straw floats, and the needle sinks," Patrick interjected.

Raquel marveled at the team before her. "Do all of you spend time thinking about how to find needles in haystacks?"

Dee shook her head. "This particular haystack is a Dark Web."

Alec rolled his eyes. "Yes, yes, I know. It's spooky and there are spiders and cobwebs and the metaphor is heavy-handed—"

Dee shook her head again and remembered she was not dealing with fellow techies. "No, I mean that's literally what people say a network like this should be called, a *dark web*. It doesn't show up on Google or Alta Vista or other search sites. Any website that requires a password to access is technically part of this 'deep web.' A dark web would be another step on top of this—the only way to visit is to know the URL, and you often need a special browser to access the site."

Alec stared back, trying to understand. "Go on."

"When your computer goes to connect to one of these deep web sites, they go through onion relays—basically proxy servers," Dee explained. "They call them onion relays because they have a lot of layers, and each one only decrypts a little bit. Thus, when you connect to the Grand Bazaar, it doesn't know who you are. And those onion relays change, every ten minutes or so. Even if you tried to trace back the route, it would change before you could finish."

Alec smiled and snapped his fingers. "Unless you had the fastest decryption software in the world!"

She shook her head. "No, probably not even with that." Alec stared back, crestfallen.

"The Grand Bazaar is even trickier because it doesn't keep regular hours. The site goes down for hours at a time, almost every day—seemingly random, although I think there might be a pattern. When users get through, everybody tries to cut their deals as fast as they can, because they don't know how long the site will remain up."

Hare stared at Dee's complicated diagram of how onion relays worked. "What pattern?"

"I think whoever's running it is operating in a time zone close to ours—the site is almost always down from two a.m. local to six a.m. local," Dee began. "But like I said, trying to find the Grand Bazaar through traceroute commands is a fool's errand—you're never going to be able to track it back through all the onion relays fast enough. I'd say you do the opposite—you sort out everything else that can't be the Grand Bazaar, like separating the needle from the straw."

She gestured over at a map of the world on one wall. "The Grand Bazaar could be set up anywhere—all you need is a place for servers and a connection to the web. But if you're setting up a place to buy information stolen from every government in the world, from the U.S. to Russia to China to Israel to everybody else, you're making enemies everywhere and so you need *amazing* secrecy."

Dee went over to a whiteboard and quickly sketched boxy skyscrapers with little dots for windows. "Every person who builds your system, every person who operates it, they're a security risk. And if you're in some office tower, who knows who walks in from the janitorial staff or something, right? Building security guards or safety inspectors or some other person could come in and see something they shouldn't. Or the building catches on fire and firemen come in. Then there's the lifestyle question. You're making a ton of money and all you're doing is hosting servers? Sooner or later, somebody would start asking questions. Like, the first thing I started doing when I heard about this was searching for known hackers who had bought new yachts."

Alec shook his head. "Idiot criminals, putting all that planning into stealing the fortune and no thought into hiding it once they've got it. Doesn't anybody study money laundering anymore?"

"I think whoever set up the Grand Bazaar is working someplace remote. Someplace nice. Where you can enjoy the good life relatively cheap, so no one thinks it's weird that you're throwing around money. Your Swiss bank or Caymans or wherever account keeps getting bigger, but you're living large on just a few thousand a month. Eventually, in a year or two, you've made a couple hundred million and retire to the Riviera or something."

She sketched a desert island with a palm tree, and then drew a radar dish sticking up out of the palm tree.

"If you're running a major dark web intelligence auction site from one of the nicest corners of a third world country, close to our time zone, and because of concerns about reliability of Internet cables and phone lines, you would probably want to do it with your connection through a satellite."

"You can connect to the Internet through satellite?" Alec asked.

"Sure," Dee shrugged. "It will probably be common someday. But for now, it's a little glitchy—"

"—which might explain when the site goes down," Hare noted.

"Somewhere out there, between 60 degrees and 105 degrees west latitude, in an isolated corner of a country with a low cost of living, you're going to see a satellite dish sticking out in the middle of nowhere—but like, a *nice* middle of nowhere. And I'll bet the Grand Bazaar is in the server right underneath it."

***

It took Deputy Director Harold Hare a lot of favors to call in, but within two days, the National Security Agency could confirm that a large portion of web traffic activity that matched the web traffic activity connected to the Grand Bazaar site on this newfangled "Dark Web" was indeed being transferred through a satellite, and that all of the traffic went down to one satellite dish, sticking out in a patch of jungle just outside Tulum, Mexico. When the Grand Bazaar website was operating, a lot of data was going back and forth from that satellite dish. When the Grand Bazaar website stopped operating, data stopped flowing to and from that dish. NSA analysts concluded there was an eighty percent chance that site was the Bazaar.

"That area has a giant network of caves, a lot of them underwater," Dee said. "Miles and miles, dozens of entry points. Dos Ojos—Two Eyes. Tulum, Mexico. Under continual exploration since its 1987 discovery, the Dos Ojos underwater cave system extends for an estimated fifty-one miles, filled with crystalline, balmy freshwater accessible via twenty-eight known sinkholes—locally called *cenotes*." She pronounced it say-*noh*-tays.

"So, you find some dry corner of the cave network no one else has found, put in all your servers on portable generators, one dish sticking up through the jungle to catch the signal from the satellites … and you operate your site in the middle of nowhere … but you still get to enjoy the good life on the beach."

"Sounds like surf's up," Ward chuckled.

CHAPTER SIXTEEN

CIA HEADQUARTERS
LANGLEY, VIRGINIA
FEBRUARY 12, 2003

H arold Hare said he had about ten minutes to spare for a briefing, and so Dee and Alec ran through what they had learned with the approximate verbal speed of "Motormouth" John Moschitta, famous for 1980s commercials for Fed Ex and MicroMachines, who had set the records in the Guinness Book for articulating 586 words per minute.

The CIA deputy director known as Merlin nodded and tried to follow along, as facts about the kidnapping of Gedhun Choekyi Nyima and the likely location of the Grand Bazaar came at him like a wind tunnel. His eyes widened occasionally, and he nodded.

"On a scale of one to ten, my interest in the location of this Dali Lama junior is about a two," Hare began, crushing Alec's hopes with the casualness of stepping on an ant. "Tibet hasn't been a priority of this agency since Nixon."

He turned to the page that focused on the satellite photos of the cenotes caves, and the lone satellite dish in the jungle, not far from a seemingly abandoned unpaved road.

"But I would indeed love to know who's operating the Grand Bazaar and where and why," Merlin said, rubbing his chin. "Whoever's running that site has gained access to secrets this agency hasn't. Once we know for certain that this is where it's being operated … we have a variety of options to leverage that into actionable intelligence."

He nodded. "Go. Send your team down there, do surveillance, confirm that it's really the Grand Bazaar and not drug smugglers or pirate radio or something like that. But I insist—and I cannot emphasize this enough—keep a low profile. What day is today?"

"February 12," Patrick answered.

Merlin winced. "Global Jihad Unit was supposed to have traded Katrina to us by now, but she's not going to be back in time. I'll remind Kabul Station she's overdue to get home. Until then, you're in luck. There's a legend on the ops side who I know is available and looking for his next assignment. Michael Thomas Davies, but everyone calls him Big Mike. Let him run things in the field, and everything will turn out fine."

***

LIBERTY CROSSING INTELLIGENCE CAMPUS FEBRUARY 15, 2003

"Big Mike" lived up to his name—a six-foot-eight mountain of a man of Dominican heritage, jet black skin, barrel-chested and muscles upon muscles. His biceps were the size of Alec's thighs.

Upon his arrival in the small bullpen of cubicles, Big Mike ignored Alec's outstretched hand and demanded everyone's attention.

"Shut your mouth and open your ears, accountant!" Big Mike bellowed so loudly that Dee thought the cubicle walls were going to shake.

"I have fought and killed on six continents, and it would have been seven except there wasn't a single dumb bastard willing to piss me off in Antarctica. I ultramarathon in Death Valley to unwind. I snapped my first neck in Grenada, and I've been on a warpath ever since. I've spent more of my life in enemy territory than I've spent sleeping. I take day trips to North Korea, vacation in the Balkans, and took a sabbatical in Hell. I think the bunch of you are the saddest excuses for CIA I've ever seen. Damn 9/11 and damn Iraq. Scraping the bottom of the barrel. Y'all look like interns. Old George Tenet must be desperate, got me babysitting a bunch of kids like this. You listen up, because I don't repeat myself: every moment you're around me, you do exactly what I tell you to do, exactly the way I tell you to do it. You don't breathe without my permission, you get me? I don't care if this is a routine investigation of a potential hacker or whatever the hell the mission briefing says. You act like everyone outside of this room is planning to kill you."

Patrick, Ward, and Dee nodded.

"Travel office arranged flights to Cancun International Airport tomorrow. Our usual contacts will ensure our firearms clear customs. Be early."

He glared at Alec, who was doing a poor job of hiding his shock.

"And you might not like me very much right now, but you rest assured, accountants and hackers and—" he paused at Ward.

"Seventy-Fifth Ranger Regiment Special Operations with two tours, including Task Force Sword and a raid on Mullah Omar's compound," Ward growled back. "If you really want to get into that kind of a measuring contest."

Big Mike nodded and smiled. "Okay, this guy I like."

He turned to Alec and Dee. "All of you accountants and hackers should know that no matter how much you may think I'm a dick, no matter how much you think my expectations are unrealistic and my attitude is nasty and mean for as long as I'm breathing, I'm gonna make sure you come back alive."

CHAPTER SEVENTEEN

BAGRAM AIR BASE
AFGHANISTAN
FEBRUARY 16, 2003

K atrina's transport out of Afghanistan and back to the Western hemisphere would be on a U.S. Air Force C-130, but the timing was undetermined until it arrived. She had been told shortly before midnight, and then closer to three in the morning, and now the Air Force crews were hoping it would arrive before dawn.

"It reminds me of the airlines back home," she shrugged.

More than seven thousand U.S. and allied service members lived and worked at Bagram, a fenced-off camp of the Special Operations forces and home of the allied forces' Bagram detention center, a compound surrounded by an eight-foot wall and razor wire just across from the PX.

Earlier in the evening, Katrina enjoyed her "farewell party," which featured a half dozen British SAS who had somehow obtained two bottles of Johnnie Walker and accelerated their consumption as the evening went on.

In May, Katrina had been on assignment with a small CIA team, having started as a glorified translator and increasingly winning her senior teammates' confidence as she noticed details about the body language of the tribesmen they encountered. Some days the CIA team's contacts, negotiations, and questioning of local tribes went well; many days it proceeded with great tension, and a few times it got violent.

Katrina's team was in Patkika province, which borders Pakistan, when the coded radio traffic burst alive with frantic messages. Near the town of Khost, an Australian SAS team was under fire from the Taliban, al-Qaeda, or possibly both, and reported that they were considerably outnumbered. Katrina's team calculated that just getting to the site of the Australians would require traversing in some of the most difficult mountainous terrain possible.

But Katrina insisted, observing that the four of them with their small arms could at least help the Australians escape. The CIA team suited up and mobilized in the direction of the Australians. The good news is that U.S. AC-130 and helicopter gunships eventually arrived and barraged the Taliban fighters. The bad news was that the Taliban fighters fled in the direction directly toward Katrina's team, and she and her team found themselves in an intense firefight with the remaining Taliban fighters. Katrina's team faced its own dire odds, until they were effectively rescued by a British Special Air Service team that had been operating on the Pakistani side of the border, a detail that was redacted and erased from all official records. The dozen or so Taliban fled across the border, but because it wasn't marked, the battle just continued into North Waziristan. By the end of the day, the CIA team and the British SAS had fought well past the border line, with, the final report estimated, ten enemy KIA. The action wasn't technically illegal, as the coalition's rules of engagement allowed them to cross and fire into Afghanistan as a matter of "hot pursuit." But any acknowledgment of U.S. or coalition presence on Pakistani territory threatened to further destabilize Pakistani General Pervez Musharraf's shaky hold on his country, much less word that the CIA had crossed over and killed Muslims.

Now a half dozen of the more-than-slightly-inebriated British SAS men had fought alongside her that day had decided it would be hilarious to serenade her with a parody of Queen's "Killer Queen," crooning off-key, *"She's a killer queen, gunpower and kerosene, dynamite with an M-16, guaranteed to blow your mind anytime! She's like the Baroness, puts the sex in Semtex, if you're on her list, you'll dieeee!"*

Katrina laughed and acted like she loved it. Inside, she was mortified. She had naively believed that the high-stakes work at the Central Intelligence Agency would get her male colleagues to put aside their attraction and not feel compelled to remark that she had been blessed, or cursed, with exotic Eurasian looks and a figure to rival Monica Bellucci's. It was a tactical advantage, no doubt; the men around her, friend or foe, seemed regularly surprised that she could fire a gun and hit the target. But most mornings she woke up just wanting to be a regular and respected part of the team—and he hated the notion that she was someone else's prize to win.

But the Brits weren't done. The two ringleaders of the Katrina Leonidivna Fan Club looked like opposites; one was lean and tall, the other stocky, large-headed, and barrel-chested. Katrina had nicknamed them Jeeves and Wooster in her mind. Jeeves and Wooster brought a heavy long case over and unlocked it.

Katrina gasped.

"A crack shot woman like yourself shouldn't be using anything less than the finest British firearms available!" Wooster boasted. "Accuracy International's L96A1 sniper rifle—when you absolutely, positively need someone dead at a range of six hundred meters or more!"

"I'm going to have a hell of a time getting this through customs," she joked. She thanked them, tried to decline the gift, and inquired twice to make sure they had cleared the gift with their superiors.

"Plenty of 7.62 NATO cartridges, too," Jeeves added.

Katrina told others she was handling the stress of her time in Afghanistan with relative ease, despite everything she had seen. And it wasn't completely a lie; she had kept anxiety and fear at bay with a relentless focus upon her work, the next mission, the next objective, the next piece of the intelligence puzzle, the next interview with a tribal leader in the next village.

But in the past two weeks, her rotation had wound down and her operations tempo slowed considerably. What was starting to worry her were the increasingly frequent nightmares, and how they strangely didn't seem to have any discernable connection to her Afghanistan experiences. She often dreamt she was in a forest, looking for Alec. In the dream, she knew that he had been abducted. Sometimes she heard the growls of bears, or insect-like chittering. In Katrina's dreams, she wasn't menaced by Taliban or al-Qaeda fighters, but sometimes mustached strongmen out of a nineteenth-century circus or black-hatted thugs who looked like they stepped off of a pulp novel cover. Once a bald, peak-eyebrowed Ming the Merciless–esque wizard had been throwing books upon a burning pyre, commanding the blaze to walk with him, and another time Salma Hayek had commanded an army of slithering snakes to chase Katrina. (She attributed that one to some troops at Bagram watching *From Dusk Till Dawn* the previous night.) When Katrina awoke from the nightmares, she was sweating—and she distinctly felt that the nightmare was not about what she had experienced in the past but was some sort of deep, recessed corner of her mind warning about a danger to come.

"Back to quiet life?" Jeeves asked.

"Or are you headed to Iraq next?" Wooster probed.

"Neither," Katrina answered. "My fiance's about to head out on some surveillance operation in Mexico, and I'm assigned to join him upon arrival."

Katrina sighed. "They said the whole thing's supposed to be a cakewalk."

CHAPTER EIGHTEEN

SOMEWHERE IN THE JUNGLES OUTSIDE TU-
LUM, MEXICO
FEBRUARY 18, 2003

T he gun pressed against Alec's temple was another clear indi-
cator that the first mission had gone terribly wrong, exceptionally quickly.

The first was the truck that seemed to come out of nowhere,
t-boning the CIA team's leading Land Rover, right on the driver's
side door, knocking their vehicle tumbling off the road into a
ditch. Big Mike had sworn and raged that the density of the jungle meant that intersections were almost impossible to see until
you arrived at them—and for a split second, Ward in the shotgun
seat and Alec in the back seat had wondered if the truck hitting
them had been a genuine accident.

The truck timed the impact to hit the driver's side dead center, and the momentum from the impact sent the Land Rover
rolling over into a ditch, finally stopping upside down. Alec
couldn't tell if he had blacked out. His head was pounding. His
seat belt had saved him.

Big Mike wasn't moving. His massive arms hung down like
slabs of meat in a butcher shop, while his body strained against
the seat belt. The rest of his team would not know until much later
that besides the obvious contusions and head injuries sustained
from the accident, the impact and intense blunt chest trauma

from the crash triggered Takotsubo cardiomyopathy, causing the left ventricle of Big Mike's heart to change shape and get larger.

Alec reached up to Big Mike's neck and felt for a pulse. Nothing.

Alec heard in his head Big Mike's pledge in the office: *"For as long as I'm breathing, I'm gonna back sure you come back alive."*

The autopsy would conclude that Big Mike's peak condition for his age would have allowed him to survive either the accident injuries or his left ventricle's inability to contract properly, but not both simultaneously. Hanging upside down in his seat, Big Mike suffered the equivalent of a heart attack and died within a minute of the crash.

The men gathering around the crashed vehicle in the jungle clearing wore military fatigues and black masks. Ward wondered if they were genuine Zapatista rebels, or simply dressed that way. They were north and east of the Zapatista territories in Mexico, but as that conflict had calmed somewhat, grizzled veterans of jungle warfare—both Zapatista and PRI militias—had looked for work elsewhere. Whoever was operating out of the Tulum caves had apparently plenty of eyes in the jungle and ambushed their vehicle perfectly.

The masked men rushed in, made their superior numbers and clear kill shots obvious, and dragged Ward and Alec from the vehicles, pulling the Americans' guns from their holsters. When they realized Big Mike had no pulse, they left him in his seat, hanging upside down.

Ward swore quietly.

"How good's your Spanish?" he muttered to Alec.

Alec was still trying to get his head to stop spinning, or the world to stop spinning.

"Mal," Alec said, squinting and wondering why everyone was shouting so loudly.

"Think they plan to kill us?" Ward said under his breath.

Alec groaned and bent over, holding his head and trying to remember if he was supposed to put his head between his legs if he had a concussion. "They probably want ransom."

One of the men pressed his gun against Alec's temple and yelled something threatening in Spanish.

"Can you tell what he's saying?" Ward asked.

Alec winced, nodding, as the masked assailant gestured toward their truck.

"I think he wants us to attend a presentation about the enormous deal he can give us on a beachfront timeshare."

Ward chuckled, somewhat surprised and reassured that Alec was still keeping it together enough to crack a joke. "Whatever you do, don't sign the contract."

Vaguely understanding the orders of their assailants, Alec climbed into the back of the truck that had rammed their Land Rover off the road. "Oh, wait, I misheard him. He's threatening to make us buy a farm."

***

Only two factors mitigated the sudden, nearly overwhelming disaster surrounding Alec and Ward. The first was that about a mile behind them from the site ambush, Patrick Horne and Dominica "Dee" Alves were following in a second Land Rover, and Katrina was supposed to be flying into Cancun later that day. Alec and Ward hadn't seen or heard anything indicating that the other half of the team had encountered their assailants—no screams, no gunshots, no shouting.

The other piece of good news was that as far as they could tell, the transponders in their vehicles and hidden in their gear were still operating. The moment Patrick and Dee saw the crashed Land Rover, they would relay the call for help. Raquel could help

Mexican authorities track them down fairly quickly, and with any luck, that rescue effort would begin shortly.

Then again, they had just demonstrated that the only luck they had was bad—and Big Mike had just paid the ultimate price.

The masked rebels bound their hands behind them, put them in a truck, and drove them less than five minutes down the road. Then the truck turned, slipped through a thick pseudo-fence of bushes, and into a small camp by a cave entrance that was so thoroughly covered with vines, an observer could miss it, or think it was some curtain. Ward and Alec realized they had nearly driven up to the front door of the Grand Bazaar operator's headquarters complex.

Ward counted two armed masked men in the truck cab, and five more in the back of the canvas truck with them. As they emerged from the truck, Ward counted two more masked men by the cave entrance, and two guys who weren't wearing masks, one fat and one skinny, a Mexican Laurel and Hardy. If this was indeed where a major illicit intelligence-trading website was being run, they might be the tech guys. An eleven-man operation, he calculated, making it nearly impossible to fight their way out of here. Maybe they could sneak out at night if they saw an opportunity.

Then Ward realized it was an eleven-man and one-woman operation. A middle-aged Mexican woman with still-striking features emerged from the cave and strode up to the still-bound Alec and Ward and evaluated them carefully.

"What are American military men doing in my part of the jungle?"

CHAPTER NINETEEN

U pon seeing Big Mike's body, Dee had a tough time keeping her emotions under control. Patrick wasn't doing that much better—and he couldn't hide it.

"He's dead, Raquel!" he shouted into his satellite phone. "Big Mike is dead! Alec and that Grizzly Adams Army Ranger have disappeared! The Land Rover's wrecked, broken parts all over the road, and it looks like whoever did this took all the gear, too. There are tire tracks from what looks like a, a big giant truck! This is it! Abort! Surveillance and observation are not gonna happen!"

Back at Liberty Campus, Raquel was listening, and watching them from above on a grainy, satellite image that was updated every thirty minutes. Apparently, all of the good spy satellites had been retasked to watch Iraq. Raquel fumed to the technician that the overhead surveillance images had all the sharpness and clarity of Monet watercolors. The confused technician asked if he was the one who painted the dancing can-can girls in France.

"Take a deep breath, Patrick," Raquel instructed, with surprising calm. "Can you see where the tracks lead off to? We can make the calls to get Mexican police and even domestic military units moving, but we need to figure out where they are. The transponders went down the road a bit, and then stopped sending a signal—my guess, somebody unfriendly found 'em and smashed them. Once we have a location, we can launch a rescue. But I need you to go see if—"

"What, go see if I can find who took Alec and the Ranger? With what, Raquel? This peashooter?"

Raquel didn't bother to argue that the Heckler & Koch Mark 23 in his belt holster was hardly a "peashooter."

"Go rescue Alec with Little Miss Sunshine the hacker to watch my back?" Patrick exclaimed incredulously. Dee looked up, a little offended that her new teammate deemed her useless. "Big Mike was the one who was supposed to be running this operation, Raquel! He was the guy who was supposed to keep the rest of us alive! Now we're stuck out here like sitting ducks, we don't know the territory, and we're just supposed to hope that whoever killed Big Mike doesn't come back here and do the same to us? That's your plan?"

Raquel tried arguing with her increasingly panicked officer in the field. Patrick Horne was no slouch. He had completed ops training on the Farm and earned a sterling evaluation during his first assignment working in Poland, playing cat and mouse with the Russian Foreign Security Bureau agents in Warsaw. But Horne's comfort zone was mingling at embassy parties and the slow seduction process of convincing foreign government officials to commit treason by compromising their government's secret information. Running around in the jungle, knowing that someone had just killed the gargantuan special forces veteran who was supposed to be running the mission was miles outside of his comfort zone.

"Katrina's on her way, Patrick," Raquel said. "She's landed in Cancun. Just sit tight—"

A steady stream of profanities crackled down the line.

"I'm not sitting tight, Raquel! There are cops in Tulum. I'm going back to get them. A lot of them. And someone has to get a team out here to recover Big Mike's body."

"Ward and Alec need your help!" Raquel implored.

"Alec friggin' Flanagan has bitten off more than he could chew, just like I warned him," Patrick fumed into the phone.

"I told him I'll help his team, not play Rambo rescuing his ass because he was stupid. And Raquel, if you're smart, you won't let Katrina risk her neck to do the same."

Before Raquel could object, Patrick hung up the phone.

"Wait, you're leaving?" Dee exclaimed. "We can't just leave this—" she gestured to the crash.

Patrick got back behind the wheel of the Land Rover. "Get in, it's not safe here."

Dee stared at Patrick, worrying that he had snapped. "Do we have Katrina's number? Could we call her, tell her to—"

Patrick turned the key and started the engine. "I'm going back to Tulum and getting every cop I can find. Either get in or don't, but I'm driving away in ten seconds." He stared at her, waiting for her to get in.

Dee's incredulity turned to anger. "Some teammate you turned out to be! You're not even willing to try looking for them! And you didn't even ask me what I thought we should do!"

Patrick glared. "You're a hacker. If I have trouble rebooting my computer, I'll ask you what to do."

Dee exploded in a series of curses and insults in Spanish.

"You talk too much," he said, shaking his head, and shifting the Land Rover into drive. He did a K-turn and hit the gas, headed back to Tulum as fast as he could.

And Dee stood by the side of the road alone, realizing her situation had just gotten much worse.

***

Dee started walking back down through the jungle road for about five minutes, until she started wondering if walking by the side of the road made her an easier target for whoever killed Big Mike. Then she tried walking parallel to the road, through the jungle, but within a few minutes, the problems of this approach were undeniable: her feet kept sinking into mud, she tripped over a tree root, she was being eaten alive by mosquitos, and she thought she saw a snake.

She stood, sweating, frustrated, and confused, trying to determine the safer option, when she heard a voice behind her.

"Don't move." It was a woman's voice—firm, but not menacing.

Dee reacted instinctively, ignoring the instruction. A woman with a long gun strapped to her back stepped out from behind a tree.

"Who are you?"

"I'm Katrina Leonidivna. Where the hell is my fiancé?"

CHAPTER TWENTY

D ee explained what she knew.

"And to think, I worried the bunch of you would run into trouble without me," Katrina deadpanned.

Katrina said that her cell phone had stopped working a short time ago; it didn't appear to be the battery, as far as she could tell, making her wonder if the locals had activated some sort of jamming equipment. She had left her rental car a quarter mile back, around the bend. Before her phone had gone out, Raquel had said that while she didn't know exactly where Alec and Ward had been taken, it couldn't have been far.

"Take me to the crash site," Katrina instructed, and Dee didn't argue.

"Raquel and Alec talk about you like you're some sort of, I don't know, Wonder Woman or—"

"Yeah, I'm pretty good," Katrina nodded. "Let's just hope that you and I putting our heads together can figure out some way to get Alec and this Ranger out of whatever mess they're in."

Dee realized she was smiling. At least this Katrina woman seemed to think she could be useful.

After a few minutes, they found the crash site, and nothing had been disturbed. The tracks of the truck tire were still clear.

"I'm going to see if I can get a look above the tree line to where the truck headed," Katrina declared. "Stay here."

"Oh. Were you afraid I was going to join you up there?" Dee asked, as Katrina, rifle slung over her shoulder, put her arms around the tree truck and just started shimmying up the tree like it was a jungle gym.

Dee took deep breaths as she waited. If nothing else, now she had Katrina, and she felt like that made her much safer already.

A moment later, she shimmied back down the tree. "The truck isn't that far away—it's like a little camp over by some rock outcroppings and maybe a cave. If I can get a concealed spot with a good vantage point, I can take out a bunch of them with the sniper rifle," she thought out loud. "But the moment they're under attack, I assume they'll do something with the servers you're supposed to hack."

Dee nodded. "I would bet anything they've got some sort of remote auto-erase program to protect their clients' data. Maybe even some sort of bomb or incendiary to physically ruin the hard drives."

Katrina scratched an itch on her chin.

"I guess that means you'll just have to hack their systems *before* I attack."

***

Alec's head had finally stopped pounding from the crash. But the woman in front of him—who called herself Consuela—was now irate that he and Ward hadn't honestly answered why they were here. Ward had given her implausible claims of getting lost looking for the beach.

"Liar! Do not waste my time with this! I have a lie detector. Do you want to see it?" Consuela hissed.

Ward's persona switched from the hapless tourist to the more authentic impatient tough guy veteran who began the previous year in a war zone in Afghanistan. "Sure. Why not?"

She walked over to a table that her men had been keeping their distance from and picked up what seemed like a normal piece of Tupperware.

"Careful, Ward," Alec murmured. "She's gonna make us attend a potluck."

Consuela approached, peeled open the lid to the Tupperware dish, and held it under Alec and Ward. Inside were dozens of tiny brown spiders, ranging in size from a quarter inch to three-quarters of an inch long—the biggest ones were the size of a quarter. Alec recoiled, without knowing what they were.

"The jungle is full of these, brown recluse spiders. One of the few spiders with six eyes, instead of eight—perhaps the extra two are left here, in Dos Ojos caves. They are highly venomous, and their wounds turn into lesions and gangrene. The venom attacks the whole body system—rashes, fever, vomiting. There is no anti-venom. Do you realize what happens if I order my men to shove your hand into this bowl?"

Alec stared in dread. "Something like Paul Atreides' Pain Box?" She frowned, not understanding the reference.

Ward scoffed. "Lady, I'm from Oklahoma. Up there, we've got spiders big enough to commit carjackings."

Consuela fumed, sealed the Tupperware container, and put it back on the table.

"Very well, my Oklahoma strongman," she hissed. "Then how about *this* as a lie detector?"

She turned and from the small of her back drew a Smith & Wesson .357 Magnum revolver, surprisingly compact, with stainless steel that gleamed so brightly Ward momentarily thought it was silver, with a pearl handle. It was a distinctive, stylish signature weapon for a woman who was used to commanding the room.

Ward nodded. "That looks pretty effective."

With a smile, Consuela boasted that she had informants and eyes watching every port and road in the state of Quintana Roo, particularly Cancun International Airport. Two U.S. military men arriving from Washington sent up red flags throughout her organization. With the world on the brink of war, the tourist traffic in Cancun and Tulum had slowed to a crawl; even in civilian clothes, Big Mike and Ward had looked like American military. By the time their Land Rover was approaching, Consuela and her men knew they were looking for her, and she demanded to know why.

Alec shook the cobwebs loose and straightened himself up.

"This *is* the operating site of the infamous intelligence-trading site the Grand Bazaar, right?" he asked. "We would like to do business."

Consuela glared at him warily. Ward looked irked that Alec was abandoning their meager cover.

Alec pointed to the satellite dish, just barely rising above the trees, above the rocky outcropping that housed the cave entrance. "We have a really good hacker, who followed the ..."

He suddenly realized he didn't really know what the NSA had followed back to this spot. "... yellow brick road until we came to Oz. We're here to make you an offer."

Consuela raised an eyebrow. "I'm listening."

Alec had no time for introductions, and he found himself genuinely curious about the woman before him.

***

If he had time to chat, he would have learned that she went only by the name Consuela, because she had been born into Mexican drug cartel royalty. She had always dreamed of building her own empire, separate from her father's. She saw how quickly drugs could destroy a person, and she detested how the cartel culture largely saw women as disposable playthings. She realized that information could be, in the right circumstances, even more valuable than drugs or guns, and set up her own business as an information broker—first for cartels, then for governments in the region. One or two near-death experiences with hot-tempered clients convinced her to cater to a more refined clientele of governments overseas.

After 9/11, Consuela realized every government on the planet was changing its policies, postures, and arsenals in the name of counterterrorism—and every state would pay well for secrets of rival countries. She considered herself one of the world's most successful women entrepreneurs, rising entirely in secret—and she would soon have accumulated sufficient fortune to enter any industry she wanted and found a new business empire, this one entirely legit. She wasn't sure yet if fashion, real estate, or a winery was more to her liking. Of course, along the way, she had killed more than a few men who threatened to spill her secrets.

"What kind of offer?" she demanded.

***

"I'm Alec Flanagan, and on behalf of the Central Intelligence Agency, we would like to buy the Grand Bazaar."

This took Ward by surprise, as this had not been part of the plan. "Excuse me?" She studied Ward in particular. "I thought you were here to raid me."

Alec laughed, almost convincingly. "Raid you? Ma'am, look at us! You ambushed us like we were a bunch of amateurs on our first mission! Do you really think that the CIA would just grab a bunch of insufficiently trained misfits and throw them together, send them off into the jungle and say 'Hey, good luck raiding that compound with lots of armed guards! Try not to get shot, rookies?'" He laughed, and Ward laughed, too, perhaps a little too hard. As the saying went, it was funny because it was true.

Finally, Consuela cracked a smile. "No, I guess not."

Alec tried to hide his big exhale of relief. "We're not here to spy on you. We're here to make you a very lucrative offer. We're the United States federal government, we don't believe in trying to save money. You've managed to create a massive intelligence-gathering operation, and rather than try to steal all your secrets, we figure it would be easier to simply purchase your whole operation outright."

Her face grew stern. "You are not going to take over something I built from the ground—"

"Whoa, whoa, whoa!" Alec interrupted. "We don't want to *take over*. We don't want to *run* it. The last thing we need is another underfunded pension program. We just want to be silent partners with an all-access pass. You keep doing what you're doing, we give you a blank check, and we use the Grand Bazaar to … keep tabs on an increasingly dangerous world."

Consuela studied Alec. "Why should I believe you?"

Alec straightened his posture, offended. "I'm Alec Flanagan. My specialty is money laundering."

"Prove it," Consuela ordered.

He stared back, bluffing, as if she was being ridiculous. "Well, that's going to be tough, because it's not like CIA case officers walk around carrying ID." Ward smiled inwardly. Alec wasn't a case officer; he was a forensic accountant.

"You must have some way to prove this," Consuela insisted.

Alec shook his head. "What, like Harrison Ford in *Clear and Present Danger*, where he just presents his business card to the doorman at the cartel kingpin's mansion? Ma'am, look at me. Look at him. This is not a Tom Clancy novel."

Ward glared with indignation. "Speak for yourself! *I* could fit in very well in Clancy."

Irritated, Consuela raised her gleaming, pearl-handled revolver and pointed it at Ward's head again. "Prove it now, or my men will use your friend as fish bait."

Ward gave Alec a hard look that said, *Sure, I can try to grab her gun, and I might even succeed, but then her men will open fire on us and we will get shot to pieces, and then we're not just dead, we're dead on our first mission as a team and I am not dying humiliated, man.*

Alec's eyes widened, and he took a deep breath. "Okay. Do you ever do business with anyone in the Irish Republican Army?"

She regarded Alec suspiciously.

"I'll take that stony silence as a yes. Call your contact up and ask him if Joseph Flanagan in Connecticut ever did him or his organization any favors."

Consuela took out her satellite phone.

***

A thousand feet to the south of where Consuela was standing—and slightly below—Katrina and Dee had followed an opening in the Dos Ojos cave complex to an important juncture.

"I figured with the dish sticking out of the jungle there, the Grand Bazaar's servers had to be nearby," Katrina declared. "You check that passage, I'll check this one."

Katrina was mildly impressed with Dominica "Dee" Alves so far. Most NSA tech specialists would be wilting in the heat, terrified from the capture of the rest of the team, going into flight-or-fight mode from the danger, and/or whining from suddenly being thrust far from their area of expertise. Dee had accepted a handgun, flashlight, and three minutes of instruction on how to move quietly through jungle and caves.

After a few moments, Katrina heard an excited whisper: "Katrina! Katrina, I found it!" Katrina rolled her eyes and fumed that they hadn't brought a secure communications system. Katrina followed the sound of Dee's voice and found her much less excited.

"I found it, but it's bad. Sure, I can get to the mainframe and server and the generators. It's just down this declining, curved passage over here. I got about a quarter of the way when I saw it. But between us and where I need to get is a pit, tripwires, a land mine … everything except a giant boulder ready to come down and roll right over us."

"Huh?" Katrina shone her flashlight around, looking for the boulder.

"Never mind," Dee said, concluding Katrina didn't watch many movies. "The point is, they've booby-trapped this way to keep folks like us out. We're going to have to find another way."

"I've just spent a year in Afghanistan, and the Taliban like to hide in caves," Katrina said, getting out night vision goggles and wire cutters. "Same kind of tripwires, triggers, and traps."

Dee's eyes bulged. "You seriously want to defuse all that and then have us just walk in and start stealing their data?"

Katrina nodded. "Just another day at the office, right?"

***

Consuela ended the call on her satellite phone with laughter and warm farewells. It had taken fifteen agonizingly tense minutes.

"My contact said that Joseph Flanagan was indeed a big help to his old friends … a long time ago."

"Refresh my memory, Alec, who's Joseph Flanagan again?" Ward asked. He figured it was some idiot cousin of Alec's who spent the eighties building car bombs,

"Dad is almost at retirement age, but he's a banker, and much like Congressman Peter King, he was always telling people to diversify by putting some of their money in that *other* kind of an IRA," Alec explained, returning his focus to Consuela.

"Back when Dad was running money to Noraid, he taught me a lot about how to move money around without people noticing,"

Alec began. "For example, if you've got a particular big-ticket item you would like to buy, like a top-of-the-line private jet or something, it might be easier for us to just give you unlimited access to the jet ourselves and register it to some innocuous front company. That way, you don't even have to pay taxes or maintenance and fuel costs yourself. In fact, maybe it makes sense to just have the front company hire you as a 'consultant'"—Alec paused to make air quotes—"and provide you with a legitimate form of taxable income, so you can spend as much as you like without arousing suspicion from tax authorities."

Consuela raised her eyebrows, as if this American might have some useful suggestions after all. "Now I believe you."

Ward looked over at Alec.

***

Dee had explained the technical details of what she was doing to get access to the Grand Bazaar's secrets and had been pleasantly surprised when Katrina hadn't told her it was boring or incomprehensible jargon.

"How long will it take?" Katrina asked.

"To get all of it? Hours," Dee declared. "I went first for the data on the transactions related to the kid from Tibet. I've got those days almost done, so determining who bought the information about the kid should be relatively easy. But there's just a treasure trove in here—"

"I am going to take a position to cover the guys," Katrina said. "I want to launch this rescue as soon as possible. Dee, if I see any indication these guys are going to kill my fiancé, I'm going to start shooting, which means you will need to get the hell out of here immediately. I cannot make any promises about how much time you've got, so prioritize what you want to steal."

Dee nodded.

Working on this team was a lot more exciting than she expected.

***

Consuela, Ward, and Alec were now seated at a picnic table not far from the cave entrance. Her men had seemed to relax. Those who had rifles were cradling them gently, and those with pistols had holstered them.

"Go back to what you were saying about the private jet," Consuela ordered.

"Well, it's like that saying, you don't want to own a yacht; you want a friend who owns a yacht who invites you out on it all the time," Alec said, rubbing his wrists where he had previously been bound. "That way, they handle all the upkeep and maintenance, and you get all the enjoyment. All the benefits, none of the costs. And this way, even if everything goes wrong, and the government comes after you, they're seizing the assets of the dummy corporation, not your personal assets and, legally, they can't tie anything to you."

Ward nodded as Alec started discussing elaborate methods of hiding income from government authorities and laundering illicit income. The forensic accountant was keeping his cool, talking about what he knew best, calming and intriguing Consuela by giving her information everyone always wanted to know—how to get rich, or in her case, even richer. Ward noted there was something salesman-like about Alec, almost entertaining, disarming this dangerous woman with humor.

Ward wondered if the whole encounter might end with pleasantries and a promise of a business lunch when the meeting was suddenly interrupted by a loud alarm emanating from inside the cave.

A moment later, the fat and skinny Mexican Laurel and Hardy ran out, shouting to Consuela.

Once again, their panicked expressions and the tone of their yelling voices offered a lot of context clues to Alec and Ward's limited Spanish skills. "Someone tripped the automatic defenses!" "The Grand Bazaar is erasing itself!"

Consuela rose from her seat and drew her revolver, pointing it directly at Alec.

***

Somewhere inside the cave network, Dee was swearing a lot.

***

Conseula's white outfit suddenly exploded in red.

"Sniper!" one of her men shouted, but it was too late. The shooter in the jungle switched from her focus on precision to fully automatic, spraying waves of rounds toward the men. Alec, Ward, and all of Conseula's men ducked and scrambled.

Ward leaped on top of the nearest guard, and rolled to have the massive guy on top of him—whether *El Gordo* realized it or not, Ward was using his body as a human shield, hoping Consuela's goons would hesitate to fire for fear of hitting one of their own men.

Alec ran for cover and realized the man in front of him was waving a gun in his direction and shouting angrily in Spanish. The only thing within reach, upon the nearby table … was the Tupperware container.

Alec raised his hands … then grabbed the container, lifted the lid, and tossed the bowl full of spiders at the man—who immediately panicked, and started brushing the arachnids off of his clothes, waving his gun around wildly.

Alec thought he had a free path to the relative cover of the jungle, but then one of Consuela's bigger goons tackled him to the ground. His meaty fist came down on Alec's face, smashing the American's nose. he roared with anger. "Your people killed Consuela!" he snarled in English.

Alec wiggled under him, nose gushing crimson like a geyser, and contemplated his options.

"Did she pay you in advance?" Alec screamed desperately.

The man recoiled in confusion. "*Que?* What? No, we are paid at the end of the week, cash—"

"So why are you punching me, instead of looking for Friday's payroll?"

Alec could almost see the light bulb going off above his assailant's head.

"*Donde esta el dinero?*" Alec asked. "Usted can grab-o el mucho dinero muy pronto!"

The thug sprang to his feet and started running toward the cave complex. Alec grinned, surprised he hadn't been killed yet.

Ward had finally wrestled a gun out of one of the gang member's hands ... and he raised it, looking around—and realized that as quickly as the sniper attack began, it had ended. The bodies of Consuela and five of her men lay strewn around the camp, all hit in their center mass. The rest of Consuela's men had run for it, except for the one who tore off into the cave complex, determined to find where Consuela kept her cash.

"What the hell just happened?" Ward shouted, wide-eyed, nostrils flaring, adrenaline pumping.

Alec, trying to wipe the blood from his nose and mouth, let out a little chuckle.

A lone woman emerged from the jungle, her rifle now at eye level, carefully scanning for any movement as she approached the camp.

"Ward Rutledge, meet the most beautiful woman in the world," he said, his face lighting up, despite the little tributaries of blood that insistently dribbled down out of his nose. "Katrina Leonidivna, soon to be Katrina Flanagan."

Katrina resisted the urge to rush over to her fiancé, scanning the perimeter where the jungle met the camp's edge for a few more minutes.

"Alec, I told you to be careful until I got back," she said, concluding that the threat had receded. She lowered her gun and gave her fiancé a withering look. "You call *this* being careful?"

CHAPTER TWENTY-ONE

FEBRUARY 20, 2003
CIA HEADQUARTERS
HAROLD HARE'S OFFICE

"**B**ig Mike was a legend," Harold Hare sighed. "Oh, he could be a pain in the ass, an ego a mile wide, but he always answered the call. The man's been shot at more times than our range on the Farm, and he dies from a car accident and heart attack." Hare shook his head.

Before him, in his office, were Katrina, Alec, Dee, Ward, Raquel, and Patrick.

"I think it would be good for you guys to make it to Arlington for his burial," the man code-named Merlin declared. "Beyond that awful consequence, I'm fairly certain I specifically said I didn't want the Grand Bazaar destroyed."

"Yes, Merlin, we survived being held at gunpoint and getting caught a fierce firefight, thanks for asking," Alec interrupted.

Dee figured that was her cue. "Unfortunately, sir, once the intrusion alarm was tripped, the files started erasing themselves and the hard drives started burning, with, from what I could see after it started, some sort of jury-rigged system using roadside flares. I did get the data we were looking for, along with data on some other transactions that might prove useful."

"But with the proprietor dead and the computer systems down, the Grand Bazaar is out of business forever," Merlin grumbled. "Which precludes the option of this agency ever using it as a resource in the future."

Raquel nodded. "Yes, but now we don't need to worry about the Grand Bazaar selling any of our secrets any longer."

***

LIBERTY CROSSING INTELLIGENCE CAMPUS
FEBRUARY 23, 2003

It took a little while for Dee and the NSA to decrypt the files, and then match the account transactions and the identities of who owned which account. Each time Dee went back to Fort Meade for help, they became slightly less resentful of her.

"Here's the account that purchased the security protocols for the Pachen Lama," Dee began. "Here's the username. Here's the bank account. The bank account is under the name Busina Ahmahdov, which is a known alias of the mercenary Magdalena Kurbikka Vagabova, a.k.a.—"

Katrina's face fell as she read the name.

"*Magda.*" In just one word, Katrina packed in contempt, anger, resentment, annoyance, and, Alec wondered, perhaps just a tiny dollop of fear.

"Friend of yours?" he asked.

Katrina let out a long, seething sigh. "Late last year, in Afghanistan, we kept hearing stories about some foreign woman helping the Taliban." Katrina spat the name. "Magda."

"The Taliban wanted help from a woman?" Alec asked skeptically. "You and your buddies must have put the fear of God into them."

"Fear of us, really," Ward chuckled with a bit of pride.

"After a couple of months of daisy cutter bombs and AC-130s, the Taliban were desperate for help from anyone," Katrina said with a satisfied smile. Ward nodded in agreement.

"We think they used a bunch what was left of their opium money to hire her," Katrina continued. "Either she was Chechen, or she was recommended by the Chechens, the intelligence was a little fuzzy on that. I'm pretty sure she's Chechen, and I wonder if she's either one of the Black Widows or trained by them." The Black Widows were widows of Chechen rebels killed in the separatist war with Russia, who dressed all in black, almost never showed their faces, and who told their hostages that they loved death more than others loved life.

Katrina stared at a blank wall, starting to get lost in her memories of a few months ago.

"The closer we got to the Pakistani border, the more we heard about this woman. Locals said she was trying to get the Pakistanis to attack coalition forces. We started hearing a woman's voice on the radio, urging the locals to fight us. She used this Chechen proverb: 'A brother without a brother is like a falcon without a wing.' Then, right before the end of the year, some Pakistani border guard crossed over into Afghanistan—right near a patrol at the border post near Shkin, where I was assigned as a translator, making sure the local allied tribes are playing nice. Our guys order him to return to his side—he does, but then he takes cover, and starts firing at our guys, shooting one of our guys in the head—thank God somehow he didn't kill him, he got evac'ed to Germany. But all hell breaks loose. They're firing at us, we're firing at them—this is the exact scenario every unit near the border wanted to avoid. Finally, somebody on our side called in an air strike on the building. Takes out the sleeper, but that also blew up our working relationship with the Pakistanis. Things still aren't fixed. Magda wanted to prevent Pakistan from cooperating with us—and she did it."

Raquel brought up a file from the agency's secure servers. "According to the file, Magda's believed to have worked for the Chechen militias, Macedonia's National Liberation Army, the Kadar Zone, the Mahidi militia in Indonesia. The whore isn't choosy."

"Most whores aren't," Ward observed.

Katrina stared at the undated surveillance photo on the screen.

"This world isn't big enough for her to hide."

2021

CHAPTER TWENTY-TWO

LIBERTY CROSSING INTELLIGENCE CAMPUS
JUNE 18, 2021

"Big Mike! Jeez, there's a name I haven't heard in a long time," Alec marveled. "Rest in peace, Mike. You were a jerk to me, but everybody else loved you."

"Consuela Zambada Cardenas, daughter of a prominent early drug cartel head, proprietor of the Grand Bazaar intelligence-trading site, confirmed dead, 2003," Elaine read aloud, studying the transferred files from the Mexican government. "No known close associates, no known offspring. No indication her dad's cartel ever blamed the CIA or our particular team for her death. Her surviving lieutenants signed on with various other cartels and militias. About two thirds have been either shot or otherwise killed in the intervening almost two decades." She shook her head. "Whoever is after you guys, it's not because of this."

Alec stared ahead, frustrated and stumped. "Great. Now I don't know who's trying to kill us, or whether that should have been, 'whomever is after you guys.'"

Dee looked quite smug at the far end of the table.

"What are you grinning about?" Katrina asked.

"I remembered all that when you asked me to pull all the files for Elaine," Dee announced. "It got me thinking whatever happened to the old Grand Bazaar cave complex. I made a call. Mexico City Station checked with state police and found rumors that someone's been using the old cave network in Tulum."

"You could drive right past that place and never know it," Ward recalled. "Who's hiding in there, drug cartels?"

Dee shook her head. "You're not gonna believe this. Local rumor mill says honest-to-God pirates of the Caribbean."

The team exhaled various scoffs of disbelief or surprise, but Katrina studied the satellite image of the location. "I think I'd like to see who chose to set up shop in Consuela's old hideout."

"You want to go down to Mexico and rattle the cages of some pirates?" Alec smirked. "Or you just want to see…"

He paused, dramatically putting his sunglasses on with a flair that David Caruso would envy, and turned to his wife.

"… who they *Arrr*."

Raquel, Dee, Elaine, and Ward groaned.

Katrina stared at her husband and shook her head. "How did I know that the first aspect of fatherhood you would embrace would be dad jokes?"

***

THE COAST NEAR TULUM, MEXICO
JUNE 21, 2021

The new "tenants" used a cave entrance much closer to shore, not far from where an inlet made a natural harbor, sheltered from the waves. In the inlet were a trio of luxury yachts.

A quartet of rough men watched Alec and Katrina as they approached from the nearest road. As they raised their rifles, Katrina pointed to the sky, and the guards could suddenly hear the whine of the drone.

"Ese es un dron de fuego del infierno," Katrina calmly declared.

The men nodded in understanding and lowered their rifles but did not put them down. Katrina switched to English. "We just want to ask your boss some questions."

"Ustedes go bang-bang a nosotros, el drone-o make-o ustedes go muy grande ka-boom-o," Alec warned with elaborate hand gestures, demonstrating a fluency in the Spanish language equaled only by former New York City mayor Mike Bloomberg.

The largest guard shook his head in disapproval. "Please speak English. My people have suffered enough."

Two men watched them warily, still cradling their rifles, while the other two men, the apparent bosses, intensely debated whether to take the visitors to their superior. Glancing upward nervously at the drone, they nodded. They went to check Alec and Katrina for weapons, but Alec put up a hand and gestured *stop.*

"We've got a drone with Hellfire missiles. The two of us bringing two more guns in there isn't really going to change anything."

A few moments later, they were brought to the harbor, walking the passerelle of the largest yacht. The large deck by the bow hosted what felt like a royal court. A pair of lounge chairs closest to the bow served as a pair of thrones. About a dozen scantily clad babes, male friends, and hangers-on made up the entourage of the royal couple. Another dozen men, some openly armed, some a little more subtle, stood guard.

"It's like the set of every *Miami Vice* episode," Alec marveled.

The hangers-on parted like the Red Sea, and Alec and Katrina got a good look at who had taken over the Tulum cave complex.

Katrina realized she hadn't seen that face since he disappeared on the Island of the Dolls in Mexico City two years earlier: Juan Comillo, the ruthless mercenary operating under the *nom de guerre* Jaguar and his partner in crime, Esmerelda.

"*Jaguar!*" she exclaimed.

Alec's eyes bulged. *"You!"*

Jaguar's posture changed, and he leaped out of the chair, reacting with similar angry shock. *"Ustedes dos bastardos entrometidos de la Agencia Central de Inteligencia!"* he fumed. *"Perdí un condominio fabuloso porque apareciste!"*

"He said—" Katrina began.

"I got the gist of *bastardos*, thank you," Alec interrupted. "You tried to kill me! And apparently ever since you gave us the slip, you've been playing Juanny Depp in yet another *Pirates* sequel!"

He got a good look at Esmerelda. "What's new, pussycat?" She still looked amazing in a black bikini, but her eyes suggested she was calculating how close her nearest gun was, and whether she could kill both of them.

"Give me one good reason I shouldn't have my men kill you," Jaguar seethed.

"Do you want to get droned? Because that's how you get droned," Katrina warned, pointing to the sky.

Jaguar nodded. "Very well, that is one good reason."

Katrina walked over and pulled up a chair, acting like she owned the yacht herself. "Don't act like you're the victim here, Jaguar. You were working with Gholam Gul and the whole Atarsa crew."

Esmerelda scoffed. "Really? We're going to get a lecture about unsavory associates from the Central Intelligence Agency?"

Katrina leaned forward. "What are you doing here? How did you find this harbor and cave complex?"

Jaguar stared at Katrina in confusion, then he and Esmerelda looked at each other, and they both laughed.

"Are they high?" Alec asked.

Jaguar and Esmerelda muttered some exchange to each other, and then Jaguar gestured for them to come closer.

"Have your husband have a seat," he said with uncharacteristic friendliness. "Suddenly everything makes a lot of sense."

"To you, maybe," Katrina said, as Alec approached and sat down.

"Can I get you anything?"

Before Alec could say anything, Katrina responded, "Answers."

"When the pandemic hit, Esmerelda and I closed up shop with our independent contracting work in Mexico City—"

"You mean murder-for-hire and street gang management," Katrina answered.

"—and we turned to new opportunities in the field of maritime transport and acquisitions."

"You mean piracy."

Jaguar explained that even before the pandemic, the Gulf of Mexico and Caribbean were thinly policed. By carefully monitoring the habits and patterns of police forces, coast guard units, and harbor patrols, he and Esmerelda systematically determined gaps in security and what to steal—cash, passports, jewels, equipment, what was most easily fenced. It was during this period they had infamously stolen one of the three yachts and been photographed, ending up on the cover of *Time* magazine. Despite the seeming fame of that particular heist, Jaguar and Esmerelda had simply laid low in a beach community for a few months.

After a while, their problem became storing what they stole; they accumulated laptops, cell phones, top-of-the-line scuba tanks and dive gear, lots of liquor, Cuban cigars, jewelry of all kinds—creating a backlog as he carefully looked for ways to fence what he stole.

And then, Jaguar explained, this pair reached out to him, asking if he had ever run across a particular CIA team.

"Someone is looking for you, and they have deep pockets," Jaguar said with chuckle. "Two women. Surprisingly young, maybe college age. They asked about you—or at least some sort of CIA unit called Camarilla Peligrosa."

"Oooh, that sounds way better than *Dangerous Clique*," Alec observed.

"I said I had … crossed paths with you about a year back, but that I expected to be compensated for sharing my expertise. They mentioned these caves and the natural harbor as a good site to relocate our business."

Katrina and Alec glanced at each other. Whoever was targeting them had extensively researched their history.

"Jaguar, what did you tell them about us?" Katrina demanded.

"That despite my copious and extensive secrecy measures, you found Francis Neuse on Snake Island and knocked on my door and went through my place," Jaguar said, unable to hide his resentment about the disappointing results of that endeavor. "That Esmerelda went after you with a tough bunch of her hermanas, and you killed six of them, put two more in the hospital for weeks."

Across the table, Esmerelda fumed, staring at Katrina with a glare of pure hate. "I think about that night quite often."

Katrina met the glare. "I wish that could have been avoided," she said softly. She tilted her head. "But your team was trying to kill us, your boyfriend here was working with a terrorist death cult to devise panic-inducing psychotropic drugs, and as I recall, you killed the doorman in cold blood, so no, I'm not exactly torn up by the guilt."

Esmerelda seethed. "How do you sleep at night?"

"Mostly on top of me," Alec shot back. "Now tell us more about this pair looking for us."

Jaguar put his hand on Esmerelda's, and that gesture seemed to calm her for a moment.

"None of us used real names," Jaguar began. "They contacted me using the code name Gemini. At first, I thought they were with some foreign intelligence service that wanted to track you down to capture you and interrogate you—Russians, maybe. But if I had to guess, judging from their accents, I would say they were Americans."

Katrina and Alec exchanged the briefest unnerved look.

"What did they look like? White? Black?" Alec asked. When the Mexican criminal couple furrowed their brows, he rolled his eyes, sighed, and added, "Not that their race matters! I hate anyone who is trying to kill me equally, no matter their race, creed, or color. Oh, and gender identity and sexual orientation, too."

Jaguar and Esmerelda looked at each other. "Mixed race, maybe? Hard to place. Skin like coffee with cream in it. Tanned."

"Well, that narrows it down to somewhere between Tilda Swinton and Idris Elba. How much cream do you put in your coffee?"

Katrina backtracked to an earlier point. "Wait, you said 'young, maybe college age.' Did they look like they were alive in 2003?"

Jaguar seemed perplexed by the question. "Eighteen years ago? If they were, they would have been very young. Toddlers, maybe. Or maybe just infants, hard to say."

Katrina and Alec exchanged another concerned look, as this was not what they were expecting at all. The possibility of Americans trying to kill them felt like a betrayal. The notion of someone using particularly young Americans to help study them felt exceptionally insidious.

"Great, we're being hunted down by the Mata Haris of Generation Z," Alec sighed. "Maybe we'll get lucky and they'll be too distracted because they're always posting on Instagram."

"The kids aren't on Instagram anymore, honey, they've all moved on to TikTok," Katrina gently corrected. "They might as well just upload their most sensitive data to Chinese State Security directly." She turned to Jaguar. "I don't suppose these young women told you where they were going?"

Jaguar chuckled.

"As a matter of fact, they said they had an upcoming meeting in Budapest."

2003

CHAPTER TWENTY-THREE

LIBERTY CROSSING INTELLIGENCE CAMPUS
FEBRUARY 28, 2003

A long stretch of days, filled with research from every conceivable source, had uncovered nothing about why the Chechen mercenary Magda would want to kidnap a teenage Tibetan prophet.

Raquel began the next meeting with the bad news. "We've got no leads on Magda, but—"

"Wait, how can that possibly be?" Alec fumed. "A Chechen woman somewhere in Afghanistan or Pakistan, working for the Taliban? That's got to stick out like Tony Bennett at a Gwar concert!"

"We've got no leads on Magda, but we've got a lead on one of her regular associates," Raquel announced. "One of the middlemen she uses regularly, Vasco Gianni, is on the guest list for the Japanese embassy's big Foundation Day party in Budapest on March fifth."

"Wait, Foundation Day was February 11," Katrina noted. She had spent a particularly memorable semester abroad in Japan.

"Apparently, security worries forced them to push it back a bit, and they're making it an Emperor's birthday and we're almost at Vernal Equinox Day celebration, too."

"Who's Gianni?" Katrina asked.

It took a moment for Dee to bring up the file, softly singing to herself, "Who's Gianni, she said, and smiled in her special way…"

Katrina stared back in confusion, not recognizing Dee's song. "Vasco Gianni is some shady gray market fixer out of Naples. Back in the nineties, he started branching out into connecting buyers and sellers of private security services—that is, mercenaries. End of the Cold War put a lot of soldiers out on the street, and the Serbians were hiring anybody who was experienced. Everybody forgets, Greek volunteers participated in the Srebrenica massacre."

"The damn Serbs," Raquel muttered quietly, thinking of one particular Serbian source named Stanko and his twisted dark soul. She recomposed herself. "Either MI6 and Interpol don't have a photo on Vasco Gianni, or they weren't willing to look hard enough when we asked. But Interpol said they had heard that late last year one of Vasco's deals went terribly bad and somebody in either the Italian or Albanian mafia put his head through a plate glass window, cutting his face to ribbons."

"Got it," Alec nodded. "We're looking for a guy who looks like he got plastic surgery with a can opener."

EMBASSY OF JAPAN
BUDAPEST, HUNGARY
MARCH 5, 2003

The rings on each of Katrina's hands were "cat rings"—silver, with two points sticking out like stylized cat ears—which, once turned out on her knuckles, would ensure her punches would inflict a little extra pain to any assailant. The pen in her purse hid a thin three-inch blade, and her hair sticks were a pair of sharp ceramic pointed weapons.

While preparing in an agency safe house, Ward was unimpressed. "You know none of that's useful when shooting starts, right?"

"Unlike any of the guns you're carrying, all of this gets through the metal detector at the door," Katrina shot back. "That's why Alec and I are going inside, and you're a block down in an SUV."

In foreign capitals, almost every embassy threw a big party on their country's national day. Sometimes the embassies rented out a luxury hotel ballroom for their big celebration days, but often they preferred to host them on the embassy grounds, in large conference rooms or open courtyards.

For spies, these parties were the bread and butter of their work, and an excellent opportunity to meet foreign officials who could someday be persuaded or blackmailed into betraying state secrets. The guest lists were rarely strictly enforced, and having a black diplomatic passport was usually enough to be welcomed inside. The open bar often helped loosen tongues, and honey-traps were not that rare. Diplomats who found the parties boring could always amuse themselves with a game of "spot the spook." Clues were the embassy officials who were vague about their duties, but always had a lot of questions about what everyone else's were. Any embassy rooms with sensitive materials were locked up, but if you wanted to break into a sensitive part of an embassy, the national day party was probably your best opportunity of the year.

The CIA's station in Budapest wasn't thrilled to hear that some new team was coming into town and needed to be at the party—but they were assured that the operations of Harold Hare's team wouldn't interfere with any ongoing agency operations.

A string quartet played soft music, and Alec and Katrina danced, looking over each other's shoulders as they scanned the crowd.

"Diplomats," Alec murmured with disapproval. "World's on the brink of war, we're hunting down kidnappers, and the striped-suit set still finds time to throw a fancy party. This feels a little frivolous and detached, doesn't it? We're on orange alert—or maybe it's up to burnt sienna, I have to check the Department of Homeland Security paint swatches."

"This is how the official cover crowd makes connections," Katrina corrected him. "For a man whose career requires the legitimate channels of foreign relations, you don't appreciate diplomats."

"Will Rogers said, 'Diplomacy is the art of saying "nice doggie," until you can find a rock.'"

Katrina slowly pulled them away from the dance floor. "Near the door, you see that pair? Tall woman facing away from us—the guy next to her is a slab of beef and he thinks his makeup is concealing those scars on his face, but it doesn't."

Alec chuckled. "Heeeere's Gianni!" Katrina didn't recognize his impersonation of Ed McMahon.

Katrina approached Vasco and declared, with a warm smile, that she hadn't seen him since the Romanian embassy party late last year.

Vasco smiled back, trying and failing to hide his admiration for Katrina's curves, snugly packed inside her silk Asian floral-print dress. He said he wasn't at the Romanian party and that she must be thinking of someone else. Within a few minutes they were laughing and getting to know each other with small talk, and Vasco stood quite close, occasionally running his hand on her back, slipping lower to the small of her back, feeling through her silk dress.

The tall woman, who had drifted away from Vasco, noticed Alec was watching them with suspicion and leaned in close.

"Don't worry, Vasco is an incurable flirt, but he's not going to steal her away," she chuckled in English. "He may try, but he probably won't."

Alec turned and realized the woman, in her heels, was as tall as he was. She had blond hair, striking Eastern European features, a smile that projected confidence but predatory eyes, and Alec couldn't quite place her accent. Russian? Romanian?

"I'm not worried," Alec declared. "I never let the toilet paper run out, I can kill spiders and open tight jars and I'm phenomenal in bed. Compared to that, what's he got?"

The woman laughed and introduced herself as Ana Abdura, a trade analyst for a multinational firm, hoping the likelihood of war in the Middle East wouldn't disrupt the export deals she had in the works.

"You're American?" Abdura asked.

"I am what I am, love it or hate it," Alec said, taking a swig of his drink and bracing himself for a lecture on unilateralism, imperialism, colonialism, materialism, or some other malady of the world that ended in *ism*. But Abdura just chuckled and seemed to be sizing him up. At his shrug she laughed, and placed her hand on his chest, running it down toward his waist. Alec couldn't tell if she was being forward or subtly checking for a weapon.

Vasco and Katrina started slowly floating back toward their partners in the corner of the party, and the pair introduced themselves. Alec noticed Katrina was studying Abdura closely. He doubted it was jealousy.

"This must be an uncomfortable time for you as an American," Vasco said. "The streets of the whole world are filled with people demanding you turn away from war."

"Yeah, well, the nice thing about being an American is that our leaders don't answer to the streets of the whole world, they answer to us," Alec shot back with a polite screw-you smile. "And despite all those protests, I don't think anybody's going to miss having Baghdad run by the Middle East's version of the Manson Family. What's the Coalition of the Willing up to now? Forty-six? Forty-seven countries?"

"Yes, I heard the other day that Micronesia is helping the war effort by sending a crate of coconuts," Abdura dryly mocked. "Surely you recognize that many countries' governments are publicly supportive but privately just waiting for your armies to fall flat on their faces in Iraq."

Alec noticed that Katrina was still scrutinizing Abdura closely but ignored it and pursued the truly undiplomatic course of saying what he really thought. "Oh, really? Because the last government that made that bet was last seen running away from Kandahar," Alec declared with a smug chuckle. "Did you know that since the Americans arrived, the Taliban's wives no longer walk ten paces behind their husbands, and instead now the Taliban make their wives walk ten paces ahead of them?"

Abdura looked at him skeptically. "I hadn't heard that. Are you claiming the U.S. coalition has already imported Western gender equality, and that's why the Talban wives now walk ahead of their husbands?"

"No, it's because of the land mines."

Katrina noticed that Abdura didn't laugh. Instead, her tone stiffened a bit. "It would be foolish to underestimate the anger of a unified Muslim world. Despite their differences, all the factions oppose an invading outsider. In one of my recent travels, I encountered many Muslim men who said they could put aside their internal differences against an outsider. It's like an old Chechen proverb, *A brother without a brother—*"

"*—is like a falcon without a wing*," Katrina said, finishing Abdura's sentence.

"I'm glad we've finally met in person, *Magda*," Katrina declared in recognition.

Abdura—Magda—stared back in defiance, knowing she had been caught. "I have no idea what you're talking about," she said so evenly and unconvincingly that it was almost a pro forma denial.

"Niiiiiice doggie," Alec muttered.

Everyone reacted at the same time. Katrina reached out to grab Magda, and she wrenched her arm away and struck Katrina, right in her chest. Katrina lost her grip and stumbled back, doubling over and wincing as pain radiated out from her breast. Alec tried to throw his glass at her, but Gianni's fist seemed to teleport directly between his eyes.

It was a small miracle that Alec didn't topple instantly; he just wobbled on suddenly rubbery legs, seeing stars and extending his arms to hold his balance like he had just completed forty consecutive rides on the tilt-a-whirl at the carnival. His foe simply crouched and brought a leg around, whacking Alec behind the knees. Alec's legs buckled and he tumbled to the floor.

From the floor, Alec moaned, "Sweep the leg, Gianni!"

The rest of the party stopped and turned their heads in concern at the commotion. Gianni and Magda headed for the door.

Recovering, Katrina raised from her doubled-over squat and kicked off her high-heeled shoes. She tore after them in her bare feet. "Alec, I'm going after Magda, you focus on Gianni!" She yelled into the radio built into her bracelet. "Support, where are you?"

Alec scrambled to his feet and tried to shake away the blur and the pain and throbbing in the middle of his face and the seeming Niagara Falls of blood that was coming from his nose, fuming that he had been on two field operations so far and gotten punched in the nose twice.

Focus on Gianni? He could barely focus his vision. He shook his head, and spotted a waiter with a circular silver tray of drinks. Gianni had nearly made it to the doorway.

"Time to Captain America these two," Alec declared, yanking the tray away from the waiter, sending the drinks crashing to the floor. Alec wound up, hurled the serving tray like a Frisbee ...

…and watched the silver disc fly across the room, completely missing where Magda and Gianni were a second earlier and clanging off the head of some ambassador.

Alec winced. "I hope he wasn't from the coalition of the willing."

***

Katrina had prepped herself to chase the pair to the ends of the earth—but her hunt ended abruptly when she tripped on the cold stone just outside the embassy entrance, landing hard and face-planting on the driveway. The Japanese embassy security guards rushed to help her, but they only got in her way. She angrily barked in Japanese that she was fine, but the guards pointed out that her lips were bleeding, and Katrina realized her kneecap was killing her, new explosions of pain bursting like fireworks from her thigh to her shin.

Rain had started to fall, and she realized there was no way she was going to sprint over the puddles. She spoke into her wrist.

"Ward, it's up to you now!"

"Got bad news, Katrina," she heard in her earpiece.

Ward reported that he had chased Magda and Gianni to the end of the street—where they had hopped on the back of Ducati motorbikes and evaded him.

An hour later—after the U.S. ambassador had to personally get Alec out of trouble for throwing the silver serving platter—an agency doctor checked them out at the safe house. He diagnosed Katrina with a chipped tooth, scrapes and bruises, and he suspected a hairline fracture in her kneecap.

"You must have genes for pain tolerance that is off the charts," the doctor marveled.

"It's not the genes—my dad complains about every toothache," Katrina answered flatly. "It's just willpower."

2021

CHAPTER TWENTY-FOUR

LIBERTY CROSSING INTELLIGENCE CAMPUS
JUNE 24, 2021

D ee's message to the rest of the team was frantic.
"NSA just flagged this!" she practically shouted as the rest of the team entered the office. Katrina could tell Dee had been coping with the stress of the potential threat to their lives by dramatically increasing her caffeine intake.

"Four e-mail accounts connected to terror groups we thought had gone dormant just used translations or variants of the term *Dangerous Clique*. What's more, they're all talking to each other." She clicked to bring transcripts and visualizations of the data to her giant monitors.

Alec turned to Ward. "This is the kind of bad news I've come to associate with Mondays."

"It's Thursday," Ward observed.

"Yes, but now it *feels* like a Monday!"

"Which groups? Who's using them?" Katrina asked, settling into her chair.

"Get this: First, the Conspiracy of Fire Nuclei."

"That Greek anarchist arsonist terrorist group?" Katrina exclaimed with genuine surprise. It took a lot to shock Katrina but hearing that long-forgotten name crossed the threshold. "I thought they went out of business years ago!"

"As far as anybody knew, they did! Everybody connected to them is either dead or in prison," Raquel said, equally befuddled. "We're absolutely certain this account is connected to that group?"

"Yes, although technically, someone new could be using an old account," Dee nodded, before moving on to her next batch of visualizations. "The second group is another blast from the past: the Afrikaner Resistance Movement."

"Ah, more commonly known as the Dyslexic Nazi Party," Alec chirped, pointing to the image of the group's three-pointed swastika. "Apartheid's been dead for a generation, but these guys still carry a torch. You would think they were marching in Charlottesville or something. We haven't run across any of them since ... what, late Bush, early Obama?" Katrina nodded.

Dee continued. "Third group, out of Bangladesh, the ISIS Bengals."

"Even tougher than the ones in Cincinnati," Ward observed, studying the screen.

"And, finally, completing the weirdest quartet of obscure terrorist groups we've fought in our increasingly odd careers, Ansaru," Dee declared with a flourish. "The al-Qaeda-affiliated Nigerian Islamists who Boko Haram thought were too extreme."

Katrina, Alec, Ward, and Raquel stared at the monitors, displaying facts about the four groups, all dangerous and willing to kill innocent people, but wildly divergent, even opposed, in their ideologies and philosophies. The more the team looked at the messages and updated dossiers, the more their faces contorted into expressions of confusion.

Ward scratched his beard. "I think I can summarize my initial analysis as ... *huh*?"

"This makes no sense!" Raquel declared. "What the hell brings together Greek Anarchists, South African white supremacists,

Bangladeshi ISIS, and Nigerian al-Qaeda? By every measure, these guys should be at each other's throats."

"Well, they probably all hate us for killing a bunch of their guys over the past eighteen years," Ward declared.

"I think it's kind of inspiring to see white supremacists and African Islamists finally putting aside their hatred and divisions and working together to try to kill us," Alec quipped. "You see, we're a uniter, not a divider."

"Could any—or all—of these groups be behind the truck bomb?" Dee thought out loud.

"Or the 2003 reference is meant to throw us off the trail," Katrina mumbled, before feeling a bit of analytical inspiration. "Or, the two women who Jaguar mentioned have been traveling around the world, meeting with all of the groups we've ever fought. They've been researching our history, assembling our enemies list…"

"Spider-Man and the Sinister Six!" exclaimed Alec.

After a moment, Alec realized no one around him understood the reference. "In the Spider-Man comics, all of his enemies realized they could never beat him alone, so they finally decided to team up. Doctor Octopus, Electro, the Vulture—every time, they almost beat Spider-Man, and he usually has to rely on their internal infighting to escape."

Raquel stared at Alec. "You're contending that whoever's trying to kill us isn't inspired by Sun Tzu or von Clausewitz or Sayyid Qutb, but by Stan Lee?"

"Somebody—maybe one of these groups, maybe somebody else—is assembling our Sinister Six," Alec speculated. "They're looking around the world for our old enemies, recruiting them, and teaming up."

"According to the e-mails, they're all meeting in Budapest in a couple of days," Dee declared. "Someplace called the Budapest Labyrinth."

CHAPTER TWENTY-FIVE

KÜLÖNLEGES KIVÉTELEK
LEHEL STREET
BUDAPEST, HUNGARY
JUNE 29, 2021

Sergei Markov had just had a terrible day, and only the brothel could relieve his stress.

He was not a man used to disappointment. A hard-edged Russian in his late fifties, and the leader and primary proprietor of the Iron Wolves mercenary team, Markov had run and executed dozens upon dozens of assassinations, from Spetsnaz GRU—roughly the Russian equivalent of Delta Force—to CHVK Vagner, a private paramilitary term owned by oligarch Yevgeny Prigozhin, to his current small "boutique" private elimination team. Sergei proved that he and his team, time and again, were the most reliable option for ensuring a foe of the Russian government ended up dead, often in brutal, bloody, and mysterious ways.

But a few months ago, the Iron Wolves came home empty-handed from a job in Salzburg, Austria. Some bioterrorist-for-hire had reached out to Russian intelligence services through discreet and secure channels, offering the ability to engineer a virus targeting particular genes. This mad virologist, calling himself Hell-Summoner, implied that Russia's long-term headaches with Chechens, Georgians, or even a significant portion of Ukrainians could be quickly alleviated through the malevolent application of biological tinkering. The Russian government wasn't intrigued enough to pay Hell-Summoner's massive fee. But Vladimir Putin's regime *was* intrigued enough to hire the Iron Wolves to meet with the bioterrorist-for-hire and kidnap him and beat answers out of him. That particular mission fell apart when some clumsy group of Americans, also on the hunt for Hell-Summoner, spooked his representative and sent him scurrying. The Iron Wolves added this American team—allegedly nicknamed Opasnaya Klika or Dangerous Faction—to their enemies list and returned to their other work.

Markov thought his luck had changed when an old Serbian contact, Stanislav "Stanko" Radic, passed along word that he had arranged a meeting with America's Dangerous Faction in a chapel in Nis, Serbia. Markov and his team arranged what was supposed to be a perfect trap to ambush the Americans as soon as they drove up to the chapel...except the Dangerous Faction arrived armed to the teeth and in full body armor, landing in a heavily armored helicopter like the ones used in the U.S. raid on Osama bin Laden's compound. The ensuing shootout killed Stanko and his companion, but none of the Americans.

After Serbia, Markov *really* hated this American team, and notified the Iron Wolves' contacts that he was willing to pay money and give away one of his $2,500 bottles of Stoli Elite to the source who could help him hunt down the Dangerous Faction. Much to Markov's pleasant surprise, another figure who was hunting for the team was eager to share more information about them—including a list of their past foes.

With that information, it was very easy to set another seemingly perfect trap, this time in Budapest. They had found long-dormant e-mail accounts connected to four of the terrorist groups the Dangerous Faction had fought over the years. Using light encryption, they sent messages indicating representatives of the four groups would meet in the subterranean tunnels of the Budapest Labyrinth. Russian assets in Washington, D.C., had confirmed that several Americans, some of whom were connected to the CIA, had hastily arranged trips to Budapest.

The FSB had loaned the Iron Wolves some officers to play the roles of the terrorist group representatives. The Labyrinth staff had been bribed to ensure certain locked doors were unlocked, and certain doors meant to be unlocked would be locked.

Having staked out all the key access points, the Iron Wolves prepared to cut the electrical power and lights, and using night vision goggles, turn the labyrinth into a horror movie, methodically hunting down and murdering every last member of the Dangerous Faction. Markov felt the location was fitting, because during the years Hungary was part of the Soviet empire, the labyrinth had been used as a torture chamber.

And then, damning it all…the Dangerous Faction never showed up. They seemed to disappear once they departed the Budapest airport. The Iron Wolves and the FSB operatives reran the operation the next day, and then the day after that. But no Americans ever entered the labyrinth those days.

Somehow, the CIA team must have figured out it was a trap.

And with considerable effort and expense turning out for naught, and he and his teammates disappointed and irritated, Markov chose to go ahead with his celebration plan anyway.

The name of the brothel—Különleges Kivételek—translated to *Special Exceptions*.

Hungary had legalized and regulated prostitution since 1999. But the onetime hotel manager Moric Vajda envisioned something bigger and better—a true luxury experience that the country's wealthiest men—and women—would shell out top dollar to experience all manner of sexual partners, with absolute discretion. Vajda's establishment truly took off with the second election of Viktor Orbán as prime minister in 2010, and his Fidesz party with its slogan of "God, nation, family."

Orbán began his career in politics in the late 1980s as an anti-communist activist with little time for religion. But as he grew older, he grew more religious, and wrapped himself in Christianity as he pursued increasingly controversial policies that certain other Western countries deemed xenophobic and increasingly autocratic. As Orban publicly embraced the church, the men of his party did so, too—making the traditional adulterous habits of powerful politicians and businessmen a bit more dangerous to their reputations. Hungary's most politically powerful movers and shakers now had a pious, moral, and righteous image to maintain—which made the ever-present temptations of the flesh even more alluring.

Special Exceptions expanded to fill a vacuum. To outsiders, it was just another luxury bar and private club for the rich and well connected, with the familiar overstuffed leather chairs and couches, dim lighting, cigars, and cognac. Moric Vajda had himself put out several articles and rumors that described the club as stuffy, stiff, and formal, a lackluster gathering place for flaccid old men slowly pickling their livers.

But the entertainment was usually string quartets, vocalists, or other small musical groups, with the twist of often performing with little or no attire. Up the grand staircase, a series of twelve small private rooms, connected with secret doors and passageways, provided private quarters for the club's premier services. The rooms were soundproof and equipped with all manner of furniture, equipment, and toys for intense erotic activities. The staff included the usual bartenders and waitresses, as well as a surprisingly wide range of professionals.

Moric Vajda obsessively emphasized to every employee that the foremost priority of the institution was discretion. Vajda guaranteed his patrons that their extracurricular dalliances would never be revealed—and the considerable private security ensured that. By the standards of a career military man, Sergei Markov, the club's security represented better-than-average rent-a-cops. But to the typical excessively imbibing patron, jealous spouse, or nosy journalist, the club's bouncers were an imposing and impenetrable barrier.

As far as Hungarians knew, parliament, cabinet members, captains of industry, and cultural elites were good Christians, honoring their marital vows, traditional values, and family—with special exceptions.

The FSB quickly realized the useful blackmail potential of this institution, and years ago had sent Sergei Markov and the Iron Wolves to ensure the long-term cooperation with Moric Vajda. Vajda had no interest in getting into a fight with Russian mercenaries but realized that if any of the FSB blackmail schemes were ever exposed, his club's reputation would be instantly ruined. Vajda made Markov a counteroffer: if the FSB never blackmailed his clients using his prostitutes, he would become a source for Russian intelligence, and give Markov and his team permanent memberships to the club.

Sergei Markov had planned on a celebratory visit to Special Exceptions, but the Americans' refusal to step into the trap blew up those plans. Instead, the visit to the full-service brothel represented a chance to blow off steam from an infuriatingly disappointing mission. The FSB team had returned to their regular duties, but that night Markov, his right-hand man, the bald giant Dimitri Guryanov, and his striking redheaded infiltrator, Zoya Zakrevskaya, would work out their frustrations on the staff of Special Exceptions.

Moric Vajda had decided that the presence of three Russian mercenaries would be better obscured by a busy night than a quiet one. So all of the rooms were booked, and plenty of other patrons waited, drank, flirted, and fooled around downstairs, enjoying the music and waiting for the upstairs rooms to be ready.

Inside one of those upstairs rooms, Sergei Markov sat in an overstuffed easy chair next to a bed with pink silk satin sheets. This was not his favorite private room in Special Exceptions. This particular boudoir was decorated with a million shades of pink from rose to salmon to bubblegum to hot pink, as if someone had created a room from a life-sized Barbie Dream House and then decorated it with slaughtered flamingos, cotton candy, and slices of ham.

Markov had told Vajda he had none of his usual preferred girls in mind, and to surprise him with tonight's selection. Considering the room, he expected to get a blond bimbo, a life-size Barbie doll to match the room.

He was pleasantly surprised when the girl entered, and she was nothing like what he expected. Her skin was olive or tan, and Markov initially couldn't quite tell if she were Latina, Asian, or from somewhere in the Middle East. Instead of the usual lacy lingerie favored by most of the women in the club, this woman of the night was wearing a full head-to-toe bodysuit that seemed to combine leather and metal, almost armor-like, making her look like some sort of dominant-minded warrior goddess. She had a spectacular figure, although she was perhaps a bit heavier than the typical cover girl/supermodel. Her boots were up to her knee but flat-footed, and she wore black leather gloves. Her entire face except her eyes were obscured by a white and gold feminine Venetian Volto mask. Over her shoulder, she carried a black leather satchel that had a few objects sticking out, indicating her agenda for the evening—a riding crop and a small flogger.

Markov was thrilled, and his heart started pounding. She must be new, and her style was completely different from Vajda's other women. This woman didn't say a word but seemed to be smiling with her eyes as she locked the door behind her. She approached confidently, fearlessly, almost like a predator. Markov was used to getting what he wanted from women, and showing him the back of his hand—or more—if they were difficult. This one would be a challenge, a worthy opponent. She would try to break him, and he was eager to show he was unbreakable. By the end of the night, he would break her.

Markov sat back, feeling a surge of sexual anticipation and excitement, and took off his shirt. "I've been looking for a woman like you for a long time," he said in accented English. He unzipped his fly and started taking off his pants.

"*Da, ya uveren, chto u tebya yest,*" the seductress responded playfully.

Chalk it up to insufficient blood flow to the brain; in ordinary circumstances, Markov would have realized that a woman who wasn't supposed to know who he was, answering a question that he asked in English with an answer of "Yes, I am sure you have" in Russian was a sign that something was terribly wrong.

As the seductress reached into her bag of tricks, Markov's brain had just stopped being overruled by another organ … when she whipped out a Glock with a long silencer attached to the barrel.

***

"*Privet*, Sergei Markov," Katrina Leonidivda said, removing her mask to reveal a satisfied smile.

Markov's jaw dropped and his eyes widened. For a split second he contemplated trying to jump atop her and grab the gun, but he realized he had literally been caught with his pants down.

"I regret to inform you that you will be getting a completely different form of action this evening," Katrina declared, a little giddy at how easy that had been. Markov's reputation was that of a man as hard as stone, but apparently even he let his guard down in the right circumstances.

He went to pull up his pants, and Katrina told him to leave them where they were.

"We're going to have a little pillow talk," Katrina teased. "I'm going to ask the questions, and you're going to tell me your dirty secrets. But not the fun ones."

"My colleagues are in the adjacent rooms," Markov said coolly. "You know Dimitri Guryanov? With one hand, he can squeeze a man's skull like a grape."

"Yes, I'm sure he can," Katrina purred condescendingly.

"*Dimitri!*" Markov yelled, with a frantic warning in Russian, then stopped when Katrina aimed her Glock at his head.

The secret door to the right opened. Markov smiled at Katrina, waiting for his gargantuan right-hand man to barrel through the doorway and tackle her.

Instead, Ward entered.

"Dimitri's taking a nap, Marko. First, your giant guy isn't all that tough after a jab of muscle relaxant," Ward said, capping a syringe and tossing it into a neon pink trash bin. "Second, the, uh … hostess he was with didn't seem all that disappointed when I pulled his massive body off of her. A man that big, a woman that small? You've got to think about her needs, comrade. I've got two words of advice you really have to pass along to the big boy: Reverse. Cowgirl."

Katrina had to bite her lip to not laugh—partially at Ward's irreverence to Markov, and at Markov's obvious sense of horror that he and his team had just been completely trapped after failing to trap the Americans.

"There's still Zoya," Markov declared, more of a plea than a boast.

"Ah, yes, your redheaded infiltrator," Katrina scoffed. Everyone in the room turned their eyes to the other wall, where a bookcase full of books that had been selected for having pink dust jackets stood awkwardly in the center of the wall. Pink paint had started to scrape off the brass hinge of the secret door, now not so much of a secret.

"Zoya?" Markov called out.

"Zoya?"

There was an awkward moment of silence. Katrina tapped her earwig.

"Alec?"

"I've got her." Alec's muffled voice was audible from behind one of the walls, and a moment later, the floor-to-ceiling bookcase shifted, and the room's other secret door opened.

Alec entered, tugging along a redhead wearing a black silk robe. She had been blindfolded with a leather strap and gagged with a pair of silk scarves, and her arms were handcuffed behind her. Zoya Zakrevskaya was thoroughly captured and overpowered by Alec, and Katrina and Ward realized that somehow Alec had done it in the adjacent room without any sound or perceivable sign of struggle. Over the years, Alec had intermittently pleasantly surprised his teammates, but nabbing Zoya in complete silence was way beyond his usual abilities.

"Look, I'm not saying I'm the greatest covert operative of all time," Alec shrugged in unconvincing modesty. "But I do think this makes me a first-ballot hall of famer."

Katrina tilted her head and looked at Alec and his captive suspiciously, while Ward furrowed his brow, as skepticism washed over him like a wave.

"Wait, how did you..." Ward started to ask, squinting. "There's not a mark on either one of you."

Alec looked offended. "What, you don't think I could—"

"No!" Katrina and Ward answered simultaneously.

Alec exhaled in frustration with their disbelief. "Okay, *fine!* When I entered the room, she was already blindfolded and handcuffed, and there was nothing left for me to do but grab her! Are you happy now?" Alec fumed. "Apparently this is how Moscow's top femme fatale lady-killer relaxes when she's off the clock, and she was waiting for the Hungarian version of Christian Grey. I got there first, through the secret door, and locked Fabio Von Goulash out. I'm not even sure if she realizes this isn't part of her scheduled scenario. For all I know, she might have previously arranged a 'captured by the Americans' fantasy."

Katrina looked her over, thinking of a frantic chase and nearly drowning in water tunnels underneath the streets of Salzburg, Austria. She stared at the blindfolded, gagged woman, and calculated what bad consequence she deserved for working with the Iron Wolves.

"You're trying to kill us," Katrina declared.

Markov smirked. "The powers of observation of the CIA are a wonder to behold."

Irritated, Katrina took the riding crop with her other hand and whacked Markov across the face. It was definitely not playful.

"Next time I use the Glock," she warned, as Markov wiped his painfully stinging face and found blood on his hands. "Who told you about our old enemies?"

Markov spat blood and a series of curses in Russian. Alec shoved Zoya onto the bed and took a step closer to Markov.

"Look, Boris Badinov, my wife's got a gun, a whole bag full of instruments for inflicting pain, she's wearing Kevlar in her corset, and she's full of pregnancy hormones. Trust me, this is not the night to be difficult."

But Markov just glared.

Alec was about to serve up another round of insults, but Ward raised his hand.

"Look, Marko, your big guy Dimitri's out cold in the next room, and it's real easy for me to put a gun against his head and remove one Russian mercenary from this world," Ward declared.

"You guys have the résumés of demons and make the Khorasan Group look like the Little Sisters of the Poor. You want Dimitri to live? Talk fast."

Markov exhaled, surveying the room and considering his options.

"I wish I could tell you, but I suspect the person who told us was simply a cutout," Markov shrugged. "We met with two young women, American. They might as well be cheerleaders. Someone wants you dead and was willing to help us kill you. But the people who told us about your old foes, these two girls— they're middlemen."

Katrina studied his face for any signs that the Russian was making up his answer. "What makes you so certain?"

"Professional instincts," Markov answered evenly. "I'm not sure they were old enough to drink in your country."

Katrina nodded. "How did they find you?"

Markov met her glare. "After Serbia, every Russian intelligence asset knew we were looking for an American team, the Dangerous Faction."

"Dangerous *Clique*, damn it, not Dangerous Faction!" Alec corrected. "Jesus Christ! All I ever wanted to do is strike fear in the hearts of evildoers, but we're stuck with this ludicrous branding issue! That's it, Katrina, when we get back to Langley, I'm hiring a publicist!'

Markov ignored him. "The two women walked into our consulate in New York and said they had information about you, and were willing to share it, for no cost."

Katrina stared at Markov. As far as she could tell, this was the truth.

"Did these two young women say why they wanted to see us dead?" Katrina demanded.

Markov shrugged. "I never thought to ask."

Katrina nodded—not caring why someone wanted someone else murdered seemed quite Russian of him. She gestured to her husband.

"Alec, go lock Zoya in a closet or something."

"Fine, but I'm only doing this because you're wearing that outfit."

After Alec left, Katrina nodded at Ward, who nodded back. Ward disappeared back into his secret doorway. It was just Katrina and the Russian mercenary again, and Markov smiled.

"Now that I have been cooperative ... I don't suppose you will give me what I came into this room for?" He leered at her.

Ordinarily, Katrina would have expressed her repugnance quickly and painfully, perhaps hitting him with the gun. But she studied him up and down and quietly came to a conclusion.

"You're trying to kill me, Sergei," she declared evenly. "You're not the first, and I doubt you'll be the last. And in my line of work, you're almost a routine professional hazard."

She raised her silenced Glock until it was level with Sergei's head.

"But as my husband just mentioned, Sergei, I'm pregnant ... and that means you're trying to kill my children, too. And that's the sort of problem that requires a permanent solution."

Markov's eyes widened, as he realized Katrina intended to kill him.

"*Bozhe moi!*" Markov exclaimed. "This is not how you work! Atarsa, the Summoner of Hell, the Shedim leaders—you sent them to prison!"

"Yes, but that was before I became a mother," Katrina affirmed, with a calmness that terrified the Russian mercenary. "My tolerance for risk is dramatically lower now."

Before Markov could speak, he heard a muffled gunshot through the secret doorway from the other room, leading to

Dimitri's chamber. Markov noticed Katrina didn't flinch, meaning she was expecting to hear the gunshot. She entered this room, knowing that once Dimitri was no longer needed as leverage against Markov, Ward would execute him. Markov realized Katrina had always intended to kill him.

Markov suddenly felt cold sweat everywhere, most notably at the thought of the indignity of dying with his pants around his ankles. "If you kill me, the FSB will come after you—"

"No, they won't," Katrina asserted. "Right now, my husband is whispering in Zoya Zakrevskaya's ear that she should tell the FSB you and Dimitri were killed by a Chechen hit squad. If she repeats that tale, she lives happily ever after in the Red Room." She thought for a moment. "Either Christian Grey's or Black Widow's, her choice. But if she mentions us, it just starts up the cycle of vengeance again, with all of our friends targeting her."

Katrina paused, getting a little satisfaction in Markov knowing, in his final moments, that no one would ever avenge his death.

"Katrina, you must let me be killed somewhere else," Markov pleaded. "This is not a warrior's death. This is embarrassing. I will be remembered as a fool—"

"That's not my problem," Katrina declared.

"You don't want to do this," Markov begged.

"It's not the way that I want it, Sergei. It's just the way that I need it."

She pulled the trigger, making a mess of red on the pink wall behind the Russian mercenary. The soul of Sergei Markov went to Hades.

2003

CHAPTER TWENTY-SIX

MARCH 13, 2003

This time Katrina had uncovered the useful information, nudging the agency's Tokyo station to get the Japanese Public Security Intelligence Agency to figure out how Magda and Gianni had gotten on the guest list for the embassy party and why they were rubbing elbows with the diplomats in Budapest. The Japanese embassy was mortified that two individuals with such unsavory reputations had managed to get into their party, and diligently began inquiring who the two had spoken to there and what they had discussed.

"Magda was at the party because she and Gianni were trying to contact a man named Abu al-Saqat, nicknamed AAS, who's reportedly hiding in Jordan somewhere, and they believed someone at the party might know how to contact him."

"Who's Abu al-Saqat?" Ward asked.

"It's a fake name, translates to *Father of the Fallen*," Katrina declared.

A day later, when they gathered in the seventh floor's undersized conference room, Merlin had a useful lead.

"I called up an old friend in Jordanian intelligence," Merlin began. He elucidated that Jordan's General Intelligence Directorate did not know where Abu al-Saqat was, but they were fairly certain he was still in their country, and they had just arrested a known associate. Merlin had negotiated that they could fly to Amman and witness the questioning.

"What's he being charged with?" Alec asked. Merlin only laughed.

Merlin explained that King Abdullah II had quietly assented to the coming invasion—he realized he had no ability to stop it, and his father's decision to back Saddam Hussein against the Americans in the early 1990s blew up in his face. Nonetheless, the king was preparing to reap the whirlwind, with Merlin darkly joking that the country was "caught between Iraq and a hard place."

Jordanian cooperation with U.S. military had to be minimized and kept secret; the people of Jordan overwhelmingly opposed an American invasion of Iraq. The invasion promised to create a colossal mess and ongoing crisis right next door, and Jordan already had absorbed hundreds of thousands of Iraqi exiles from the last time the Iraqis fought the Americans. Jordanian intelligence knew that Iraqi spies and secret police were operating in Jordan's cities. The United Nations and various international aid groups were already preparing for a massive wave of refugees to come pouring over the border, setting up massive camps. Jordan was a poor country, with no oil and just one major port, surrounded by problematic neighbors. They had tried to reform their economy, but 9/11 had ruined the tourism industry. The war promised to at least interrupt, if not completely end Iraqi oil exports to Jordan, which Hussein sent to Jordan at deeply discounted prices, as well as disrupting $300 million in Jordanian exports to Iraq.

Jordan was a powder keg, with a war about to start just across the border. And now the team had the opportunity to fly right into the middle of it.

"This is arguably our single most important ally in the War on Terror, a Muslim pro-Western monarchy with actual good human sourcing on the ground in terror groups," Merlin emphasized. "When you're over there, I want you to act like the Queen of England is giving you a personal tour of Buckingham Palace, and she's letting you pet her corgis. You will bend over backward to be respectful and appreciative. Every time they clear their throat, you're going to say you completely agree."

AMMAN, JORDAN
MARCH 15, 2003

"Beware the Ides of March," Alec moaned.

Alec, Katrina, and Ward arrived in a country that reminded Ward of a small town in Oklahoma right as the tornado sirens began wailing. The U.S. government had just named a dozen Iraqi officials whom it accused of war crimes, declaring that they would likely stand trial after the war—which was a de facto admission that war was coming soon. Saddam Hussein had invited chief United Nations weapons inspectors Hans Blix and Mohamed ElBaradei to Baghdad, apparently believing that America would never launch an attack while he was hosting U.N. officials. Thousands of protesters had gathered around the U.S. Embassy in Amman, under the watchful eyes of the kingdom's military and security forces, but most other residents of Amman realized that protests were not going to stop the momentum toward war, right on their doorstep. Shops closed early, heavy metal gates pulled down and locked. Every sound of a distant plane spurred people on the street to look to the sky, wondering if it was a military jet signaling the invasion had begun, or even worse, some sort of preemptive strike from Hussein aiming a Scud missile at Israel and falling terribly short.

Much to the team's surprise, their counterparts in Jordan's General Intelligence Directorate instructed them to meet at a high floor suite at Le Royal Hotel in Amman.

When they entered the hotel suite, the first thing Katrina noticed was the plastic sheeting covering the floor. "Head on a swivel, guys, someone's expecting a mess," she muttered under her breath to her teammates.

"*Lethal Weapon 2*," Alec observed. She looked at him with confusion, but he didn't have time to explain.

When they entered the next room, they saw why their Jordanian hosts had taken that preparation. A middle-aged man sat handcuffed to a chair, with a swollen black eye, puffy lip, and blood trailing from his nose, down his chin, onto his shirt, and down onto the plastic sheeting above the plush carpet.

"What the hell did you do to this guy?" Alec exclaimed. Two massive men wearing sunglasses stood at either side of him, wiping a handkerchief across their knuckles.

Their Jordanian contact, Euyun, gave his American guests a disapproving look. "Motivation," he said, removing his glasses and wiping them.

Alec was horrified. "Well, if you want him to talk, you probably want to leave his mouth and mind intact," he shot back.

"The squeamish guests can wait in the other room if they like," Euyun said, sizing up Ward and Katrina.

"We've seen worse in Afghanistan," Katrina declared. "May we ask him some questions?"

Euyun appeared to be in his late forties, bags under his eyes, and dark hair that was starting to recede. His pants, and his jacket over the back of a chair on the other end of the room, were from a fine suit, and his dress shirt matched. Aside from his tired eyes, he looked like he could fit in in any executive boardroom anywhere in the world.

The Jordanian security official looked at her and turned to Ward, as if he expected him to say something. After a moment of Ward staring back, Euyun's eyebrows raised a fraction, revealing he was surprised that a woman spoke for the American group. After a moment, he nodded.

"As long as we're present," Euyun said softly.

"Alec, get him some water."

Euyun smiled a bit as Alec quickly rushed to get a glass of water, like a servant.

Katrina lifted the cup to the man's lips and let him drink. After a moment she subtly stepped and leaned back, waiting for him to spit it. But he swallowed it.

"I don't know if you feel a need to not cooperate out of a sense of honor," she said in Arabic that was technically proficient but didn't quite nail the accent. "But you've demonstrated that you wouldn't fold or quit easily. You've done your job. Now just answer some other questions and let's end this and get you out of here."

The imprisoned man looked at her warily from his non-swollen eye.

She asked Alec for the photos of Magda.

"Have you ever seen this woman before?" He shook his head, and answered something in Arabic that seemed to amuse the Jordanian security officials.

"He says most of the women he sees are veiled," Katrina translated, smirking a bit. "She's looking for AAS—Abu al-Saqat," Katrina declared. The man tried not to react, but something about the length of his blink—just a split second longer than normal one—suggested the name was significant to him.

"Why do you think she would be looking for him?" Katrina asked. He shrugged. One of the Jordanian security men stepped forward, but Katrina raised an arm. The hulking bruiser looked at Euyun, and his boss gave him a head shake that told him to back off, for at least a moment.

Katrina leaned closer. "I know you don't know, but I asked what you think," she said. "What's so special about AAS?"

The man shook his head. He wouldn't talk. But he did look at Ward, and then Alec.

"Who do you think they are?" Katrina asked in Arabic. "Westerners. They don't look like you or me. They're Americans. I don't know what the General Intelligence Directorate will do with you. If you're in this situation, probably nothing good. But if you answer questions the Americans have, these men in this room look good to their bosses. You've become useful to them. And that probably means something better. This is your big opportunity. This is that little bit of control over your fate that you have. If I were you, I would use it."

The man took a deep breath. He appeared to be considering his options. Katrina rose.

Euyun studied her closely.

"Conduct many interrogations in Afghanistan?" he queried.

Katrina didn't answer. She knew from experience that men who were tortured would talk, but they would often just say whatever their captors wanted to hear. If she wanted the truth, the threat of torture, and the fear of the unknown, was a much more useful tool than pain itself. Besides, some men who were fighting for a cause they believed in saw the endurance of pain as an honorable sacrifice, a noble demonstration of their valor.

Ward approached, and squatted right in front of the prisoner, getting to his eye level.

"Just start telling us things you know about AAS," he said.

The man took another deep inhale, and much to their surprise, answered in English.

"Nobody's sure what Abu al-Saqat's real name is," the prisoner said. "I'm pretty sure he's Egyptian. You hear the accent in his voice sometimes. He told a story about being imprisoned there, so I'd guess he was with the Muslim Brotherhood at some point, or maybe Egyptian Islamic Jihad. He's told stories about fighting the Soviets in Afghanistan toward the tail end of the occupation, but half the men in certain neighborhoods tell stories like that. I know when Afghanistan was done, he hooked up with Hamas. Maybe al-Qaeda, too, before they went big-time— he traveled in the same circles. He doesn't see as well in one eye. He lost the tips of two fingers from trying to build a bomb. He limps, so there was some other wound to his leg."

Ward stared angrily. "Are you telling me this guy's al-Qaeda?"

The prisoner shook his head. "No. If he ever was, he isn't anymore. This part he told me late one night. At some point, despite all his sacrifices, he decided that all of these groups were worthless, that they didn't keep their promises, and he doesn't believe them anymore. He's not interested in a reward in paradise any longer. He wants his reward in the here and now. He's a mercenary. He started by recruiting his old buddies who were similarly disillusioned."

Katrina was intrigued. "So, he looks like a jihadist, and hangs out with jihadists, but he's not a jihadist?"

Euyun raised his hand. "That's enough."

***

Despite the objections from Katrina and the others, Euyun ordered his men to move the prisoner to "the other place" and ushered the Americans into a hotel suite across the hallway.

Euyun then made a series of phone calls. After a frustrating wait, he returned to the hotel room.

"My apologies, I needed clearance to share certain secret information with you," Euyun began. "It turns out my government knows Abu al-Saqat by another name. A code name and reputation. Emir al Eblis—the Devil's Prince."

"Boy, that guy's presumptuous," Alec snarked, rolling his eyes. "There's only one Prince." He was about to add, "and he's from Minnesota," but he remembered Merlin's orders about being respectful to his hosts.

Euyun stared back in confusion for a moment, and then shook his head and continued. "For years, we've heard about someone calling himself the Devil's Prince, assembling jihadist burnouts and putting together teams of experienced terrorist thugs and foot soldiers. He's no jihadist, he's a…" He paused, looking for the right words. "He's a nihilist capitalist. His ethical awakening is that he now wants to kill for money, not faith."

"Great," Ward spat. "He's quit blowing people up in the name of the Almighty, and now he's just blowing people up in the name of the almighty dollar."

"Well, you can't really blame a guy like that for reevaluating his career path," Alec observed. "It's hard to find experienced suicide bombers."

"If someone in our region needs a bunch of ruthless killers, with no ties to a state, they can go to Emir al Eblis' Brotherhood, or Brotherhood of the Devil," Euyun continued. "Emir al Eblis negotiates the best deal he can for those who sign up with him."

"That's even worse," Alec said, shaking his head. "This guy's a terrorist recruiter *and* a union rep."

Katrina turned to Euyen. "Where do we find Emir al Eblis?"

"This is where it gets complicated," Euyun sighed. "We're in the crosshairs of the jihadists even more than you are. In their eyes, we're apostates, and should be killed first. For years, Emir al Eblis has taken men from the ranks of the terror groups and steered them in a different direction, often beyond our borders. As far as my government is concerned, the Brotherhood of Eblis is not an enemy."

Katrina was stunned. "Excuse me?" She gave Euyun a hard, suspicious look. "I guess certain governments in this neighborhood never know when they might need a mercenary group for some off-the-books operations."

Euyun shrugged. "I cannot confirm or deny, because I do not know. I do know that we cannot allow you to harm Emir al Eblis, or Abu al-Saqat, or whatever he's calling himself these days. He is too useful to our security interests. My government is already doing you a great favor regarding our neighbor in Iraq. This is not a time to ask for more."

"How about the fact that Magda is looking for him? Because she's an enemy of the United States," Katrina said fiercely.

"She tried to kill our guys in Afghanistan, nearly started a shooting war between the coalition and Pakistan, and now she's trying to negotiate a contract with Abu Saqat's Terrorist Local Union 241!" Alec's voice grew louder and angrier. "How on earth can it be in the Kingdom's interest to protect these two?"

Euyun winced and thought over the Americans' argument. After a moment, he concluded, "Magda is not an ally of my government, and Abu al-Saqat's protection does not extend to her, even if she's a client of his."

"Real simple, my friend," Ward declared. "If we can find AAS, we can find Magda. And if we find them together, then we'll just be really, really careful when we start shooting."

Euyun smirked. "Careful when you shoot? I may ask the Chinese Embassy in Belgrade for a second opinion." He took a deep breath. "Last we heard, Emir al Eblis was traveling with a group of nomadic Bedouin goat herders whose grazing pattern extends to Ad Deir, the monastery at Petra."

Ward couldn't hide his surprise. "What's an SOB like him doing with a bunch of nice folks like Bedouin goat herders?"

"Oooh, I know this one!" Alec interjected. "The Bedouins have legendary hospitality. Rough life in the desert—their culture doesn't allow them to turn away guests. It can be a matter of life and death. The saying is a guest can stay for three days before a Bedouin host will even ask their name."

Euyun nodded, mildly impressed his American visitors knew much of anything about his country. "And here I thought you were the dumb one! It's not quite that extensive, but yes, Emir al Eblis probably is taking advantage of the Bedouins welcoming outsiders and not asking too many questions."

"Isn't Petra a little conspicuous for a guy trying to avoid attention?" Katrina asked.

Euyun chuckled grimly. "Did you see many other passengers on your flight here? Did you see many tourists in the hotel lobby below us? 9/11 destroyed our local tourism industry along with the towers. Not many Westerners are itching to get on a commercial airliner to visit an Arab country right next door to Iraq." Euyen's expression darkened. "Our trickle of visitors stopped entirely after that USAID worker was assassinated right outside his home here in Amman."

"We were briefed before we arrived," Katrina nodded grimly. "You guys are certain it was al-Qaeda?"

"Some madman calling himself Abu Musab al-Zarqawi," Euyun replied.

CHAPTER TWENTY-SEVEN

PETRA, JORDAN
March 16, 2003

The Treasury at Petra was best known to Westerners as the site in the climax from *Indiana Jones and the Last Crusade*, as the hidden home of the Holy Grail. In reality, Petra was the preeminent tourist attraction of Jordan, nominated as one of the seven wonders of the world, a spectacularly preserved historical and architectural treasure, consisting of whole buildings carved into the rose-colored stone of the valley.

The visitors' center had one extraordinarily bored staffer manning the ticket booth and two soldiers who were napping.

Al-Siq was the narrow pathway between two high rock walls that led to the spectacular site of the Treasury. Those who had only seen the movie would be surprised to see that much more was just offscreen to the right of the Treasury—an entire valley with courtyards and burial chambers carved into the sides of the canyon—the Urn Tomb, the Silk Tomb, the Corinthian Tomb, and the Palace Tomb. A little farther was the Great Temple and the Blue Chapel.

Despite being where desert met the mountains, Petra intermittently got wet in the winter months, and when Katrina, Ward, and Alec arrived, a cloud fog hung low over the tops of the mountains. It felt almost ready to drizzle. The wind picked up, sending clouds of sand and the occasional small whirlwind in the corners—Westerners called them "dust devils," but certain Arabs contended those small whirls of dust were signs of djinn, supernatural creatures.

To make the ascent to the Monastery, visitors had to travel a one-mile winding path along the side of a fairly steep mountain, ascending about 650 feet. The walkway was about three feet wide, with no guardrails, and empty air and a steep fall down the side of a rocky mountain on one side, and a sheer rock wall on the other.

"This pathway does not meet the standards of the Occupational Safety and Hazard Administration," muttered Alec as he made the ascent. He marveled that this was considered a perfectly safe tourist attraction—yet if he stepped just a few feet to his left, he would probably plummet to his death.

"This path is smooth and easy compared to Afghanistan," Katrina observed.

Ward suddenly halted and held up his hand, gesturing for his teammates to stop. He crouched down, and the others mimicked him.

"What is it?" Alec whispered.

"This is a really good spot for an ambush," Ward observed. "Nowhere to go but forward or back, easy pickings from that ridge over there."

"How can you be so sure?" Alec asked.

"Because that's what I would do if I were them," Ward murmured. He drew his gun.

The crack of a rifle shot echoed through the canyon—and a few flakes of stone fell on Ward's head, where the shot hit, several feet too high.

"Take cover!" Ward instinctively shouted, flattening himself.

"Take cover where?" Alec swore. "I'm crammed in here tighter than Chris Farley in a wet suit!"

Katrina thought she had seen a flash from the ridge and fired a shot in the direction. She worried her pistol wouldn't have the range.

"Looks like Magda found AAS!"

A few more shots hit the rocks, above their heads.

"Why are they shooting at us?" Alec said, trying to see any movement on the opposite ridgeline. "How do they know we're not tourists?"

"Because there are no tourists here!" Katrina snapped.

A few more shots embedded into the cliff face, both above and below them; apparently the range of the assailants' weapons wasn't any better than the handguns the American trio had brought.

The gunfire slowed, then stopped.

They heard the engines before they saw them emerging from over the mountaintop—a pair of giant Russian Mi-26 cargo transport helicopters that looked like they were being held together with duct tape. Long, ungainly, and massive, the first helicopters of this model rolled off the production line in 1980, and versions of the chopper had been sold to the militaries of Algeria, Belarus, Cambodia, India, Mexico, and the Jordanian Air Force. But the pair carrying Magda, Emir al Eblis, and his men must have been long since retired from military service, and sold, and resold to a series of owners who skimped on maintenance. These two helicopters had once been the workhorses of some air force's cargo transport fleet, but those glory days were a long time ago. Alec realized Emir al Eblis' men must indeed be burned-out jihadists who were no longer afraid to die, if they voluntarily had boarded rusting death traps like those.

Between the wind and cloudy conditions, and the less-than-reliable condition of the aircraft, the pair of helicopters were not swiftly swooping up, up and away. It was almost like they were both standing on a slow, steady invisible escalator that only gradually took them up and around the cliff's edge where Katrina, Ward, and Alec stood.

One helicopter hung lower than the other, effectively blocking a clear shot at the higher one.

Bursting with frustration, Ward unleashed everything he had toward the rotor mast.

And either one or more of Ward's shots hit pay dirt, or something inside the tired aging Russian avionics just gave up and died. The thick rotor mast spat smoke, and the rotors slowed—the helicopter shuddered; it seemed like pieces were starting to fly off like the first pieces of a struck pinata. The pitch of the rotor's whine grew lower, then higher, as the pilots desperately tried to will it to keep climbing higher into the sky. And after a few shaky moments of wobbling, the Mi-26 seemed to right itself, and chased after its sibling, much higher in the sky.

And then, after getting perhaps a half a mile farther away from Katrina, Ward, and Alec's cliff… the rotors suddenly made a sickly coughing noise, belched black smoke from the mast, and, without warning, just stopped.

And one helicopter dropped like a stone, disappearing with a crash over the mountain's ridge.

"Whoa!" Alec gasped. "Hell of a shot, man!"

"I think that chopper was going down, no matter what I did," Ward said, squinting and shaking his head. "Think one that was Magda's?"

Katrina shook her head. That was the second chopper; as the first one passed, through the window, Katrina was certain she could see a woman's features.

Magda.

CHAPTER TWENTY-EIGHT

"While you were out, I did your job for you," Dee gleefully announced.

She brought up the first key piece of information, a series of documents written in Chinese, with English translations appearing a moment later.

"First, eight former Chinese military guys were found dead in an apartment in Hong Kong," Dee announced. "The authorities first thought it was alcohol poisoning, and then it turned out to be poisoned alcohol. I found these guys because I was conducting a long and extensive review of figures known to be tied to Magda. She and Vasco Gianni paid these Chinese guys collectively a couple hundred grand in two payments. One shortly before Gedhun Choekyi Nyima disappeared from Chinese house arrest, one shortly after."

"Are the Chinese investigating who killed these guys?"

Dee shook her head. "Doesn't sound like it, apparently they've got their hands full, freaking out about some new virus floating around out there. SABS or SADS or something like that."

"It's SARS, but don't worry about it, forget it," Alec muttered.

"Magda hired these guys, paid them, and then, we think, poisoned them to cover her tracks," Raquel surmised.

"Bitch," Katrina spat. Alec was surprised that Magda was getting under his wife's skin.

"But that's not the big news. Magda gets her payments shuffled through a lot of front companies. Accounts in the Caymans, Switzerland, shell corporations, gold shops. She used to use Chinese fei-chien—that's *flying money*—and now she's using hawala more often, and she might be branching into the Black Market Peso Exchange that's big in South America. Anyway, tracing those payments all the way back to the original source is like finding Waldo. But just like that striped-shirt little bugger, I found him. You're not going to believe it."

She typed and brought up a file to the screen.

"The guy's an American."

CIA HEADQUARTERS
LANGLEY, VIRGINIA
MARCH 19, 2003

When Raquel called Merlin and said the team needed to update him immediately, he fumed that there was a little thing called the impending invasion of Iraq that was occupying almost all of his waking hours.

But Merlin agreed to start his day in the cramped conference room off of his office. The CIA's deputy director seemed in a particularly irritated and scowling mood. Raquel hoped it was simply sleep deprivation and stress.

The presentation began with an image of a smiling middle-aged, gray-haired, slight but somehow slightly paunchy man, standing on a balcony overlooking Central Park.

"Linus Strauss," Raquel announced. "Silicon Valley guy who made a fortune in the dot-com boom. He cofounded GlobeScape with Lennon Silver and sold his shares before they tanked with the whole EasyFed debacle. He made something like twenty million. After the dot-coms crashed, Strauss took his fortune and went to Wall Street, and was making an even bigger fortune ... when he was in lower Manhattan on nine-eleven."

Merlin's eyebrows raised. "Oh."

"He survived with only minor injuries, but apparently the experience radicalized him," Katrina continued, having spent the past hour cramming as if she had a final exam on Linus Strauss. Thankfully, the man had a considerable public paper trail online. He even had a blog. "Strauss got divorced and became an outspoken atheist, giving speeches and writing essays and op-eds declaring that all organized religions are threats to humanity."

"He knows it wasn't a bunch of nuns and rabbis who crashed the planes, right?" Alec muttered.

"Linus Strauss has basically put a big chunk of his fortune into hiring Magda and recruiting the Brotherhood of Eblis," Raquel declared, pointing to photocopied bank records. "Magda contacted the Grand Bazaar, bought the information on where the Pachen Lama was being held, then hired a group of Chinese mercenaries to kidnap him. After collecting the Pachen Lama, she rewarded the mercenaries with a bonus of whiskey, wine, and fine liquors, all of which were laced with type A botulism toxin."

Merlin squirmed in his seat. "She killed them with *Botox*?"

Alec nodded. "Yeah, but the good news is, their skin looked great."

Dee brought up a new document on the screen:

From: Visionary912@outlook.com
To: 9039768@hotmail.com
Subject: MOVE UP TIMETABLE

NEWS SAYS WAR WITH IRAQ IS IMMINENT, CAN'T WAIT ANY LONGER
WE'LL DO IT HERE

GRAB FOUR MORE AT RANDOM, BUT MEETING
SPECIFICATIONS
THURSDAY 2100 LOCAL

"That message, sent late last night from Linus Strauss to an account used by Magda, tells us almost everything," Raquel declared. "'Four more at random' says to me four more kidnappings – maybe four more kids. 'Do it here' I suspect is his penthouse apartment at 55 Central Park West at 66th Street. Everything Dee uncovered points to him still being in Manhattan. 'Thursday 2100 local' says whatever he's doing, he's doing at nine tonight. That gives us"—she checked her watch—"just over twelve hours."

"It also tells us his caps lock key is stuck," Alec snarked. "This guy's got no time for punctuation! He's in a hurry! He wanted to do this to protest the war, or maybe in his mind, this will prevent the war. Tonight, his grand plan becomes real."

Merlin's fingers tapped the table nervously. "What is 'it' that he wants to do?"

"Merlin, I have no idea, but whatever it is, it isn't good," Raquel said. "You don't kidnap people, including a kid, because you've got so much purity and goodness in your heart."

Merlin sighed. He seemed unusually irritated.

"And what is it you want me to do?" he asked.

"Get the FBI to raid his place now," Raquel answered. "I'd bet my next paycheck that Gedhun Choekyi Nyima is in that apartment, and probably Magda and the Brotherhood of Eblis, too. If they're not there now, they're gonna be there tonight."

Hare stared back at her for a long, silent moment. Finally, he cleared his throat.

"Before we move to that, I want to take a moment to make sure all of you appreciate the gravity of the colossal mess you've created, in just a few weeks on the job," Merlin grumbled.

Ward tried to suppress a wince. He knew the crashed heli-copter hadn't been part of the plan.

"I wanted a low profile," Merlin fumed. "In a matter of weeks, you've destroyed the Grand Bazaar and killed the proprietors. You got into a fight at an embassy party in Budapest and appar-ently gave the Hungarian foreign minister a concussion with a metal Frisbee."

Alec cringed.

"And now my very good friends in Jordanian intelligence—who have been absolutely vital in our efforts against al-Qaeda and preparations for Iraq—are livid with us because Emir al Eblis, or Abu al-Saqat, a figure they explicitly told you not to touch, was killed in a helicopter crash, right after you went to confront him over Magda! Right after you assured one of their intelligence officials, and he quoted you directly, 'if we find them together, then we'll just be really, really careful when we start shooting.'"

Now Ward couldn't hold in his wince any longer. Alec noticed.

"Merlin, helicopters crash all the time," Alec insisted.

Merlin seethed. "Particularly when they're full of bullet holes, Flanagan!"

Katrina exhaled. "Sir, did they find Abu al-Saqat's body?"

"Parts of it, they think," Merlin spat. "By the time Jordanian authorities got to the crash site, the hyenas had gotten to the corpses. They're trying to do DNA confirmation."

Merlin's fingers tapped the table in a syncopated beat of building irritation.

"Now…I knew, when we set up this team, we would have growing pains," Merlin seethed, pausing to chuckle at the under-statement of *growing pains*. "I knew finding the right people would be challenging in this environment. But in three weeks, you've managed to create a new significant headache for this agency and me on three continents! We no longer have the Grand Bazaar as a resource! You ran through the Japanese embassy party like the bulls running through Pamplona! And a man the Jordanian government asked us to avoid harming is now in the digestive tract of desert hyenas!"

Merlin was livid and rose to his feet.

"I'd have to literally be Merlin the magician to make this mess disappear! And now you want me to call up the FBI and have them raid a New York City multimillionaire with deep pockets and a lot of good lawyers on speed-dial, based upon your hunch that he's planning something sinister involving a kidnapped boy?"

Raquel met Merlin's gaze, rose to her feet, and answered before anyone else on the team could say anything.

"That's precisely it, sir. We've gone out and gotten you the best information we can. It's in your hands now."

Merlin sat back down, drummed the table some more, and fumed in silence for a moment. Then he checked his watch.

"Damn it, I have to go," he muttered. "Raquel…because I trust you, after so much you've done for me, I will pass this information on to my colleagues in the FBI. I am not promising they will do anything. And you, Alec, and the rest of you, will go home. Stay home. We're about to invade Iraq. The whole country's on edge, waiting for another attack. Some nut just drove his tractor into a pond on the National Mall and is threatening to blow himself up. Just stop."

He turned to leave, but Katrina wasn't done yet. "Sir, Magda is in on this and she's already a sworn enemy of the United States, and we think she's headed to New York City or is there already. If that doesn't qualify as counterterrorism—"

Merlin turned, grouchily, and pointed a finger at her. "Katrina, not another word. I've let you guys run wild for far too long. In a matter of hours, this agency may have Saddam Hussein square in its crosshairs and have a chance to end a war with the first shot—or we may end up blowing up a body double. My plate is full. All lines are busy now, please call back later."

Hare left.

CHAPTER TWENTY-NINE

Alec stood up. "I'm going after Strauss anyway."

Raquel shook her head. "No, you're not."

"Let's get some guns, put on some masks, and kick down the door and stop him ourselves!"

"First, we're not cops," Raquel countered. "We do what you're proposing, we're vigilantes. Even if it works, we could go to jail."

Ward raised his hand, as if he was a bright student being ignored. "And that's one of the better scenarios. You're assuming no NYPD rookie sees us wearing masks and carrying guns and doesn't shoot us out of panic. The whole city's on the highest alert, meaning a bunch of tense cops with itchy trigger fingers, just looking for somebody who looks like a terrorist. Second, you heard the old man. We would be violating orders. That's a firing offense."

"And if we don't do something, Strauss and Magda and the Brotherhood probably kill that child, and maybe four more!" Katrina said. "And maybe we could have done something to stop it. You want to live with that for the rest of your life?"

Alec was elated that Katrina hadn't ruled it out. But Ward seemed offended, swearing under his breath, rubbing his mouth, and rising to his feet.

"I can't believe I left my guys, right as they're about to invade Iraq, to be stuck here with you guys," he fumed. "Ugh, what the hell was I thinking?" He rubbed his eyes.

Alec and Katrina exchanged a look.

"Okay, Ward, wait!" Alec begged. "Just hear me out."

He sat back down.

"And before I get started, I'm only going to tell this story once. Katrina and Raquel have heard it."

Katrina raised her eyebrows. She wasn't sure Alec would ever be willing to tell the rest of the team this.

"My junior year of high school, I'm friends with this girl Sarina Locke. Sweet girl. Smart. She had … she had the smile of an angel. We weren't dating, but … I don't know, maybe it would have turned into something. One autumn night, after our crowd gets together to study—yes, we were all nerds—she just disappears. Vanishes, no trace. No note, no signs of struggle at her home. She just doesn't show up to school one day and her parents have no idea where she went. Her dad was a drinker, her mom had a drug problem, and everybody in town—cops, teachers—everybody gets convinced she ran away. But I know she didn't. I *know* it. She wouldn't run, it wasn't in her nature. Behind all that artsy-alternative stuff, she had a will of iron."

Dee's eyes wandered to Katrina and wondered if Alec had a type.

"A week goes by, then a month, then two months … and after a while, it's like the whole town just forgets about her. Life goes on, but it couldn't for me. I … apparently started going a little nuts about this. My grades tanked. I tried doing my own investigation—keep in mind, I'm sixteen years old. I actually found a fingerprint in her room that didn't match her or her parents … Anyway, it's been years and years, and no one ever found any trace of Sarina Locke. As far as the world knows, back in the nineties, she just"—he snapped his fingers—"disappeared, just like that. No body, no clues, no tips, no trench-coated Robert Stack narrating the story of her disappearance. It felt like she was erased from the world, and I was the only one who noticed the change."

Katrina noticed that Ward was riveted by the story—and Dee, too. Raquel had indeed heard the story from Alec before, but there was something more vulnerable in his account at this moment.

"She's the coldest of cold cases now. Sarina's parents are dead, she didn't have any siblings, her grandparents died when she was young. I never heard her discuss cousins, aunts, or uncles… Our friends all moved on. No one is even looking for her anymore."

While telling the story, Alec had stopped making eye contact with them.

"There's nothing I can do about the disappearance of Sarina Locke. There are a lot of problems in this world that I cannot solve. There's nothing I can do about al-Qaeda. There's nothing I can do about Saddam Hussein and his army."

He reached for the photo in the file front of him.

"But this son of a bitch? Linus Strauss and Magda and this gang of jihadist washouts kidnapping a kid, maybe a bunch of children? Right now, I have the ability and the opportunity to come down on them like a ton of bricks. And if, after I do all that, Merlin wants to fire me? Fine. I'll do something else with my life. Dad wanted me to be a banker anyway."

"Alec, none of us want to do nothing. It's just that some of us would rather not get fired," Raquel countered.

"Or fired twice in two months," Dee corrected.

"If we do this and we fail, at least we tried. We didn't just sit here as something terrible was about to happen. And if we do this and succeed… we're legends," Alec said. "And oh, we will have proven that this nutty idea of Merlin's actually can do something good."

Dee cleared her throat. "Or there's another outcome. Magda and the rest could, you know, kill us."

Katrina smiled. "She'll try."

CHAPTER THIRTY

On paper, FBI Special Agent Elaine Kopek should have been entering the prime of her career. She had known, by the time she had finished reading *The Silence of the Lambs* in high school, that she wanted to be a real-life Clarice Starling. Kopek had excelled at UPenn, double-majoring in criminology and international relations. After acceptance to the FBI Academy, she found herself gravitating to spy-catching over profiling gruesome serial killers. She had been one of the few in her class out of Quantico to seek assignment to counterintelligence, which was widely perceived as a less glamorous and consequential division. Within the culture of the bureau, mobsters and gangsters were still public enemy number one, and kicking down doors and making high-profile arrests was seen as the pinnacle of the bureau's mission—not following suspected spies and going through garbage cans, looking for evidence of dead drops.

The 9/11 attacks prompted the bureau to transfer Elaine Kopek to counterterrorism duties, first in the Philadelphia and then the New York field offices, handling the avalanche of tips about potential jihadists. The vast majority of these tips amounted to false alarms and paranoia, and Elaine thought her current boss enjoyed sending her out to talk to lunatics. Elaine had spent much of her recent years training on the firearms range, running track and practicing close-quarters combat ... just so she could spend day after day talking to tin-foil-hat-wearing shut-in single men convinced that their falafel delivery guy was an al-Qaeda sleeper. Even worse, Elaine's polite, gracious, and professional demeanor often amounted to the warmest and most pleasant attention these lonely men had received from a woman in ages, ensuring that she quickly collected a small army of extraordinarily socially awkward admirers that Langley, Frohike, and Byers would have found weird.

When her parents asked her how work was going, she said the counterterrorism part of the job was slow but that she had made great progress as an involuntary therapist to the outer boroughs' paranoid loners.

Elaine knew that she was, relatively speaking, still the "new girl" in the New York office, and that this was something akin to hazing a rookie. If she complained or objected to her waste-of-time assignments and dirty work, she was likely to immediately earn the label of a whiner who couldn't cut it. The FBI had long since accepted women agents, but that didn't mean that their male counterparts and superiors always welcomed them with open arms. The bureau was, in many ways, the ultimate masculine culture, filled with men who saw themselves as the strongest, toughest, and the best of the best, who threw around their weight with swagger. Ironically, the FBI was still grappling with the ramifications of the betrayal of FBI Special Agent Robert Hanssen, who had proven to be the most dangerous double agent in the agency's history. Hanssen felt overlooked and unappreciated and fumed that in a world that needed brilliant analytical minds to track crime and Russian spies, the FBI still prized the men who kicked down doors, with everyone marinating in a machismo that devalued brainpower and celebrated firepower.

Elaine's immediate superior, a dour, tall, Italian American named Raphael Davino, was probably the kind of man who appalled Robert Hanssen—but that wouldn't have bothered Davino, as Hanssen was a traitor. Davino had trained his entire young adult life to be the man who took down the mafia—and then the RICO act steadily eroded La Cosa Nostra's sinister influence power in American life. Since 9/11, Davino spent most of his days chasing down reports of jihadist terrorist groups, listening to wiretaps and chat room discussions of suicide bombers and poisoning water supplies and the glories of martyrdom. Davino missed the rational selfishness of his old mafia targets.

But as afternoon turned into evening, Elaine was certain Davino was messing with her. He had the audacity to claim that Harold Hare, the deputy director of the CIA, had called up the bureau's New York office and said that an agency team believed that a retired Wall Street multimillionaire, Linus Strauss, was working with mercenaries and jihadists to kidnap a group of children, and the children were being kept at 55 Central Park West at 66th Street.

CHAPTER THIRTY-ONE

During the summer of 1984, the building at 55 Central Park West at 66th Street had been badly damaged in a fire, and completely gutted inside and rebuilt with an underground parking garage and freight elevators, while preserving the building's art deco design, which dated back to 1929. Built by the architects Schwartz and Gross, the building stood out a bit from its neighbors because of the flaxen-colored fluted projections in the base that looked a bit like teeth rising up out the ground. For some reason, residents of the building kept encountering other New Yorkers who had heard stories that the building had been designed by an insane doctor involved in the occult, and that he had conducted dark, demonic rituals on the rooftop. Residents insisted that they saw no clear evidence that they resided in a "huge, superconductive antenna that was designed and built expressly for the purpose of pulling in and concentrating spiritual turbulence" but that they had persistent hot water problems and they were pretty sure somebody was stealing their mail.

Even with the mid-'80s upgrades, 55 Central Park West was considered second-tier compared to the nearby Upper West Side residences of the rich and famous. Linus Strauss was a mere multimillionaire, not a billionaire, and Dee and Alec's analysis of his available—meaning hackable—financial records indicated Strauss burning through his fortune quickly—from a net worth well beyond $25 million three years ago at the height of the dot-com boom to a "mere" $5 million or so now, not counting his considerable personal real estate holdings.

Dee had managed to obtain the floor plans on file with the city's Department of Buildings. Ward didn't like what he saw. Linus Strauss' twelve-bedroom, two-level penthouse apartment was a maze. There was one elevator bank that opened on a small lobby that featured the apartment's one main front door, as well as a separate back door leading to one of the building's four stairwells that must have been required by the fire marshal. By Manhattan standards, the rooms were gargantuan. But they were all connected with blind corners, long, tight hallways, one main staircase in the main hall connecting the floors, and two separate circular staircases on opposite sides. The one spot that really intrigued Ward was the massive balcony overlooking Central Park.

If there was some way to drop down from above, and if no one inside was looking up at the right moment, it would offer a perfect entry point for a raid. Unfortunately, 55 Central Park West towered above its neighbors. Ward briefly imagined hang-gliding onto the balcony, or parachuting down, and realized that elaborate plans like that offered far too many ways for something to go terribly wrong.

CHAPTER THIRTY-TWO

U.S. Department of Justice

Federal Bureau of Investigation

Washington, D.C. 20535-0001

APRIL 28, 2003
TO: R. MUELLER, B. GEBHARDT, W. SKINNER, G. COLE, S. BOOTH, A. CROSS, J. WOO
FROM: E. KOPEK

The accompanying material, and transcription and description below, is confidential and approved for your eyes only. The attached video file was recovered by bureau agents in the aftermath of ██████████████████ at 55 Central Park West at 66th Street. While the actions of Linus Strauss are no longer under active investigation, the details of the events leading up to ██████████████████ remain classified and what follows offers key context as to Strauss' motivations, mindset, and ultimate goals.

THE SUBMITTED, UNPUBLISHED OP-ED

In late 2001 and early 2002, experiencing what was likely undiagnosed post-traumatic stress disorder from being in lower

Manhattan during the 9/11 attacks, Linus Strauss developed an obsessive and paranoid belief that all of the world's organized religions provided, as he put it on his personal blog, "an assembly line for violent extremism." Strauss was quick to emphasize that he did not blame Islam specifically for the 9/11 attacks; he insisted that Christianity, Judaism, Hinduism, and Buddhism were all equally likely to lead a believer to terrorism.

By the summer of 2003, Strauss had become an outspoken and controversial critic of organized religion and its impact in the world. He also told his shrinking group of friends and associates that he felt he was not given the respect and attention he deserved. He submitted the attached document, ESSAY 1, to the *New York Times* to run on its op-ed page, strongly suggesting to the editors that it should be the lead piece in the Sunday Review section the weekend before the one-year anniversary of the 9/11 attacks. The editors sent it back with a polite rejection, which, according to Strauss' remaining friends and acquaintances at that time, he saw as a personal insult.

The essay was 10,000 words, much longer than even the longest op-ed pieces the newspaper runs. The theme can be sufficiently summarized by the opening paragraphs.

One year ago, a cloud enveloped me in lower Manhattan, and I inhaled particulate matter that, in all likelihood, included human remains that had been crushed down to fine powder.

That occurred to me—and so many people suffered such great losses that day—because of a dispute that is ultimately, religious. We do not worship as al-Qaeda does, and in their minds, for that we must die. Now there is talk of our Christian religious fundamentalist president launching a modern-day crusade against the world of Islam by invading Iraq, pushed along by the Jewish

Zionist extremist Ariel Sharon in Israel. The forecast for the future is more wars of religion, more bloodshed, more terrorism, more violence, and more suffering. All because these factions insist their imaginary man in the sky commands them to do this.

The only alternative to this accelerating death spiral of religious warfare is a rapid worldwide societal shift away from religion—enforced by law and police powers, if necessary. History shows us the territories of the former Soviet Union were a fractious, bloody hodge-podge of Orthodox Jews, Muslims, and others. Shortly after assuming power, the new Soviet government determined that organized religion was incompatible with the Marxist spirit of scientific materialism, and took bold, decisive action to liberate the Soviet people from the burden of their ancestors' faith traditions. The closure of churches, synagogues, and mosques was not without some controversy, but it put an end to religious divisions, and turned the Soviet Union into a society where Jews and Muslims felt as respected as any other Soviet citizen.

The doctrine of state atheism should not be seen, as some claim, as fundamentally un-American and a violation of the principles of a country founded by those seeking freedom. It should be seen as the natural evolution of the founding principle of the separation of church and state, and an extension of the presidential oath of support and defend the Constitution of the United States against all enemies, foreign and domestic. All doctrines that ask adherents to put their own decision-making process through an approval process of an imaginary wise man in the sky is one that is inherently dangerous. People who can answer "because God says it must be so" to any question can justify anything—injustice, cruelty, oppression, assault upon their neighbors and fellow citizens.

This next step in human evolution, tossing aside the ancient superstitions and bonds of religious belief, will undoubtedly encounter resistance. Perhaps the clearest way to demonstrate to those that there is no God worth killing for is a vivid demonstration that God is not protecting anyone. If we thoroughly dispel the notion of God's love, we can dispel the notion of God's will—and finally step, united, into a better future.

Assessing the strengths and weaknesses of Strauss' argument is beyond the purpose of this memo, but contending the Soviet Union was "a society where Jews and Muslims felt as respected as any other citizen" suggests he had a blinkered and incomplete understanding of history at best. Several pages later, Strauss offers an odd and vaguely ominous conclusion:

Throughout human history, the Voices have attempted to guide us towards a state of peace that is as calm and silent as a grave. The path is clear and the answers are there, if only we will listen.

THE VIDEO

The video begins with Linus Strauss seated at his desk in his home office. From what we can determine from past publicity photographs of Strauss in his office, his desk has been turned away from its usual location with its back to the window, toward the doors to the large grand hall used for entertaining in his penthouse apartment. Strauss' desk has been cleared of its usual computer, papers, photo frames, or other personal markers. A long, square knife is on his desk, and Strauss picks it up.

WOMAN'S VOICE: When you're ready.

[Note: We are awaiting voice analysis to confirm this is the Chechen mercenary Magda.]

STRAUSS: This is a shechita—wait, I want to start again. We'll cut that out. Okay, ready? Three, two, one…

Hello. I'm Linus Strauss. And by the time you see this, you've probably heard about what I did. I wanted to take a few moments to explain what you should learn from what I have done.

This is a shechita—a ritual slaughter knife, used in the preparation of animals in accordance with kosher teachings. This is a very old one, probably from 1910 or so, made in Kaliningrad, Russia. Most of you watching this don't even know where that is, because you're so ignorant, so poorly instructed. This came over from there with some immigrant family, one that was probably devout, faithful, and God-fearing.

I had to sharpen it, after I hired someone to steal this from the Jewish Museum not too far from my home. You see, this is a symbol of the madness of theism, the notion that some old man in the sky is always watching us, and gave our ancestors strict rules, and the old man will be very angry with us if we break those rules. Really, would God care what knife we use to cut meat? He would want us to use the special knife? Please.

It's all nonsense, and I'm going to prove it to you today. You need to see through the illusion. This illusion of God ordering us to march around and obey and kill in his name—Allah, Jesus, Buddha, they're all the same, no real differences.

[Strauss clutches the knife, and rises from his desk, walking a few steps over to the office doors. He opens them and enters the great hall. Five children, ages eight to fourteen, are bound, blindfolded, and gagged on the floor. Video analysis indicates that there are two gunmen, identified as Abbas al-Falsi and Raqif al-Annan, on the sides of the room.]

STRAUSS: These are five children from all five of the so-called great faiths. Christianity, Islam, Judaism, Hinduism, and Buddhism. This one here, Gedhun Choekyi Nyima, is apparently some prophet or something to the Buddhists—and China fears him so much, they kidnapped him and kept him under house arrest. I had originally wanted to find four other children who were important to their faith communities—a relative of the Chief Rabbi of Israel, or the Pope, or a kid from the Mormon Tabernacle choir. But I've been forced to act quickly, so my associates just grabbed these four other kids off the street. There's nothing special about them. They were just in the wrong place at the wrong time.

All of those faiths discuss a noble divine being watching over the innocent children of the world.

And I'm going to take this knife and I'm going to kill all of these innocent children. And as I do this, I will ask all of you watching this: Where is God? Every day we're confronted with the injustices of the world—cancer, car accidents, massacres, shootings, overdoses. And yet people not only still believe; they believe to the point where they are willing to kill in his name.

When you see me kill these children, ask yourself, could God possibly exist? And if he does, why didn't he stop me? You see—

[SOUND OF GUNSHOTS FROM ANOTHER ROOM]

STRAUSS: What the hell was that?

After the sound of the gunshots, Strauss ran over and apparently believed he turned off the camera. He did not, but the camera got knocked over and the image on the screen is just a bookcase. For the next several minutes, sounds of a struggle can be heard, including people yelling, "Abbad is dead," "Strauss, put the knife down," "That's right, I'm going to walk out of here," "Meaning has no meaning! Man has triumphed! The voices were right! The throne is empty, which means I can sit upon it!" and many, many more gunshots.

CHAPTER THIRTY-THREE

MARCH 19, 2003

Ward needed common firearms. If they ended up in a gun-fight, they were going to leave rounds in their targets or whatever was behind and around them, and Ward wanted the ammunition to be as common on New York City's streets as cigarette butts. But because they might need to fight from room to room, Ward wanted at least one shotgun—a nice broad spray in the direction of the target, with less chance of penetrating walls and hitting a hostage in an adjacent room. But because they were attempting to avoid arousing suspicion, Ward need it to be concealable. He selected a Remington Model 870 TAC-14—under twenty-seven inches long, fourteen-inch barrel, six-shot, 12-gauge. But he concluded he didn't want Alec running around with a shotgun. Once they were on the penthouse floor, they had to minimize the risk of injuring hostages, so the team would need precision.

Glocks, Ward concluded. Common, reliable, a good capacity of seventeen rounds, easy to reload, and mild recoil. The overwhelming majority of NYPD officers carried Glocks; if anyone saw them shooting, they might think they were undercover police, Ward surmised. They he wondered how difficult it would be to get counterfeit NYPD badges to wear around their necks on chains. But the more realistic the fake badge, the longer it would take to obtain, so Ward scrubbed the idea as being too time-consuming.

Katrina seemed competent with firearms, although Ward figured her hands would be more comfortable with a smaller, more compact gun. Dee had no interest in carrying a gun, and Ward wasn't going to make her. Ward wanted her away from the line of fire, keeping any of the building's civilians away from the firefight, and ready to get an ambulance there quick and hit the panic button and get the real NYPD on scene. Raquel had tested well on the range and mentioned something about being in the field in the Balkans but had never been under fire. Ward suggested she be the one to watch the garage and block off an escape route.

"Like Argyle!" Alec exclaimed, but no one else on the team understood the reference.

CENTRAL PARK WEST
NEW YORK CITY

Alec and Ward parked Ward's truck two blocks away. They sat for a moment before beginning the operation.

"*Sidet' na chemodanakh,*" Alec blurted out. "It means 'sit on your suitcases.' Old Russian superstition. Before a big journey, you pause for a moment. You take a deep breath and calm yourself. It's supposed to ensure no demons follow you on your journey."

Ward stared at Alec skeptically.

"When I learned Katrina and her family were Uzebeki immigrants, I studied up on everything I could find about old Soviet traditions, hoping to impress her," Alec explained.

Ward shook his head and took a deep breath. He had to blurt it out.

"Look, Alec, we're about to kick down a door, and on the other side are a half dozen or so men who will kill you just as easily as look at you. I've fought these kinds of men before. What's the worst firefight you've ever been in?"

Alec scoffed. "You were with me in Mexico!"

"You threw spiders at a guy. What else?"

"There was Prague."

"You threw a serving platter at a guy's head. What else?"

"Jordan!"

Ward closed his eyes and exhaled again. "I would have been safer invading Iraq."

Alec bristled with defensive irritation, but Ward suddenly turned, reached over, and grabbed Alec by the shoulder and pointed a gloved finger in his face. "Look, Alec, I've got a fiancée who I want to make a whole lot of babies with someday. I'm not dying because of your inexperience. When we go up there, and it hits the fan, you're going to freeze at first. It happens to everybody. Shock, adrenaline, fight-or-flight instinct. Just take the moment and shake yourself out of it. But once the shooting starts, whatever you do, do not hesitate, capeesh? Do not hesitate. Say it with me. I will not hesitate."

"I—I will not hesitate," Alec answered.

"You just hesitated while saying you won't hesitate! You're not reassuring me, man!" Ward fumed with growing frustration.

"I'm not gonna hesitate!" Alec said louder.

Ward nodded and got out of the truck. For a moment, he looked skyward.

"If you're up there, man, we need all the help we can get," Ward muttered.

***

Katrina, Dee, and Raquel entered through the back entrance to the parking garage. They had just bought construction site walkie-talkies.

Alec and Ward entered through the front door. If the building had a doorman, he wasn't working tonight; they waited until someone else entered and grabbed the front door before it closed and locked again. The two men stepped into an alcove off the lobby and geared up.

Ward had removed his black tactical helmet from his backpack and strapped it on. Ward's Army Surplus store bulletproof vest covered about half of what he wanted, and he now carried a small backpack, two holstered Glocks, multiple magazines, and a shotgun, the butt handle of which, strapped over his shoulder, was visible. Ward's belt pouches contained a small flashlight, two pairs of handcuffs, a hidden handcuff key, zip ties, a collapsible baton, a knife, a restraint cutter, and a multi-tool. He was in tactical black from head to toe, with elbow and knee pads, gloves, and there was a ballistic mask with a painted skull hanging from his belt.

Alec had his own holstered Glock and five magazines, as well as his own ill-fitting, too-small-for-effective-protection vest and was carrying a small container labeled LIQUID NITROGEN.

An elderly man saw the two men and did a double take.

Alec realized how out-of-place they must have appeared. "Hi," he greeted with a friendly wave.

The old man stared at Alec and Ward with intense concern.

Alec gestured with his thumb upstairs. "Somebody saw a cockroach on eighteen."

"This is a counterterrorism training exercise, sir," Ward said. "I need you to go into your apartment and ... and, um, keep your head down and stay low."

The man's eyes bulged. "Stay low? If this is just an exercise—"

"He's trying to reassure you, and he's doing a really bad job," Alec interrupted. "This is totally not an exercise, we're federal agents, sort of—well, he's military—and there are some really dangerous people on the top floor of this building."

"Should I call 911?" the frightened man asked.

"No!" Alec and Ward exclaimed simultaneously, then each one looked at the other for an explanation.

Then both men blurted out a jumble of contradictory and particularly unconvincing explanations and excuses: "We're getting our teams in position—" "And they're tapping the phones—" "And the radio signals could set off—" "We need the element of surprise—"

The old man, now utterly terrified, tried to crouch down, and told them, "I'll hide in the laundry room downstairs!" He scuttled away.

"That went great!" Alec exclaimed sarcastically. "I think we came across as the most trustworthy guys this side of Joe Isuzu."

Ward shook his head as the elevator doors opened. He pressed the door for two floors below the penthouse, intending to take the stairs from there.

"Here we go."

***

The elevator doors creaked and slowly closed … and then Alec and Ward realized the building's elevators were ludicrously slow. Even worse, their final tense pre-battle moments had a soundtrack brought to them by the Muzak version of Queen's "Another One Bites the Dust," softening the anthem until it had all the hard edge, aggression, and confrontational spirit of "The Girl from Ipanema."

Alec and Ward stood, staring straight ahead, as the elevator slowly, oh, so slowly, ascended.

Finally, Alec turned to Ward. "You know, at this moment … I just made my peace with the death of Freddie Mercury, because it means he never lived to see his life's work turned into this auditory maple syrup that makes Barry Manilow look edgy."

"What's with all the jokes, man?" Ward asked. "Was CIA your backup career after bombing at stand-up?"

Alec bristled.

"Look, we both have our ways of dealing with our crap! You've got that 'Rangers lead the way' and 'hooah' stuff, and that's great for you. But I don't have that! I crack jokes!" Alec said, all of his resentment bubbling to the surface. "Two years ago, I was supposed to be tracing bank accounts tied to car bombs in Belfast, but instead lower Manhattan got flattened, my fiancée just spent most of a year playing Mata Hari in Jihad-istan, and I think the guy who used to be my best friend now hates me because the love of my life picked me instead of him! In just the last month, some crazy Mexican woman wanted to stick my hand into a bowl full of spiders, I think that Gianni-come-lately broke my nose, the Jordanians think I'm a wimp because I don't think torture works, my geriatric inscrutable boss thinks I'm incompetent, and some poor kidnapped Buddhist prophet kid is gonna die unless you and I go out there and frickin' Jack Bauer our way through a bunch of killers who didn't have the moral fiber to stay in al-Qaeda! It's all a little stressful, you know? But somehow, I'm still alive! So, so far, I think I'm doing okay, and cracking jokes works for me!"

Ward chuckled.

"All right, buddy. Let's make these guys die laughing."

CHAPTER THIRTY-FOUR

Raquel had taken her position in the garage. Dee and Katrina had climbed the stairs and were three and a half floors from the penthouse when someone quickly emerged from the apartment hallway, onto the landing they had just passed. She crouched to a kneel and raised her firearm.

"FBI! Hands where I can see them!"

Katrina exhaled with frustration, slowly turned, raised her hands and saw a woman in an FBI raincoat.

"Of all the possible times, *now* you show up?" Katrina fumed. She looked behind the woman. "Where's your backup?"

"That's—who are you?"

"We work for Langley, and we have reason to believe a dangerous mercenary and at least one kidnapped child are on the top floor of this building," Katrina said quickly, lowering her hands. "Please tell me Harold Hare sent you."

Elaine eyed her warily. "You've got a Glock in that holster. Arms back up, against the wall, I'm going to remove it."

Katrina shook her head in exasperation.

"We don't have time for this. Either you go upstairs and stop those guys, or we do. I'd rather do it with you alongside me."

"You got any ID?"

"Do you think agency officers walk around with badges that say *CIA*? I'm going to put this as clearly as I can, agent—"

"Kopek."

"Agent Kopek, I'm sure you're well trained, but I can disarm and disable you in less than a minute if I need to. Right now, I can use all the backup I can get. I'd really rather have your butt alongside mine when I kick down the door upstairs, but I can just as easily put you out of commission. Make up your mind."

***

Elaine stared for a moment and noticed the blond woman next to the impatient Eurasian still had her arms up. This pair did not seem like anything she had pictured as a CIA team, but if they had a hostile intent, they hid it well.

Elaine sighed and lowered her weapon. "Okay, I'm convinced. My coworkers warned me that the CIA was secretive, arrogant, and demanding, so it looks like you're the real deal." She shook her head. "Tell me about this mercenary."

"Chechen, worked with the Taliban in Afghanistan, ruthless, strong, tall," Katrina recited, turning her attention to the landing above. "Well-trained in hand-to-hand combat, weapons, almost certainly armed, probably more than one firearm. Always has an escape route. Already got away from us in Budapest and Jordan. Amoral enough to kidnap kids, and probably psychotic enough to kill them. Oh, and she's a woman."

"Another milestone for women's equality," Elaine said sardonically. "Go, us."

Dee reached into her bike messenger satchel and removed a surveillance photo of Magda. Then she held up two other photos of Alec and Ward.

"See this guy? See this guy? Don't shoot them!" Dee instructed. "They're on our team."

Elaine took a moment to study the images and commit the faces to memory. "Great. Any chance we can take these guys down without it turning into the OK Corral, or are—"

At that moment, they heard gunshots on the floor above.

"Apparently not," Katrina declared dryly.

***

Ward thought he had a good plan. Strauss' penthouse apartment had a rear door that connected to the other staircase. He had guessed that the door would have two or three locks—definitely a standard doorknob lock and a deadbolt, and, Ward had guessed, a chain or a bar bolt lock. That would keep out most would-be burglars or intruders who got into the building. But Ward figured few burglars came prepared with a container of liquid nitrogen, or a spray pump designed to get the liquid nitrogen into crevices like the tight space between a door and a doorframe. Put enough liquid at negative 320 degrees Fahrenheit around any metal, even steel, it will get brittle and crack like an eggshell after a sudden, strong impact.

The plan was for Ward to spray the lock and, with the locks now ready to snap like twigs, hold his position with Alec watching his back. Katrina was to emerge from the other stairwell to the elevator lobby by the apartment's grand front door. Whether or not she encountered a Brotherhood of Eblis guard, her job was to create a racket and get the attention of Strauss, Magda, and the Eblis Brothers focused on the front door. With them distracted, Ward would pop through the back door, eliminate anyone in the room closest to the back door, and work his way through the rooms, with Alec as backup, looking for the Panchen Lama.

If Katrina got past the guard at the front door, the plan was for her to advance and together they would corner those inside the apartment in a pincer movement. Ward had given everyone more magazines than they could ever conceivably need. If anyone on the CIA team encountered stiff resistance—and Strauss had hired Magda and the Eblis Brothers specifically for their capacity for stiff resistance—they were to find the best cover they could, hunker down, fire a lot of rounds, and attempt to get their opponents to burn through their ammunition.

Raquel and Katrina had concluded that NYPD SWAT, already on the highest alert, could probably handle the Eblis Brothers even better than they could. They just needed to get the NYPD flooding the building, ready to respond to shots fired. As residents of the building called 911 and reported hearing steady bursts of gunfire on the floors above, the city would mobilize the Emergency Service Unit, which had considerable experience with heavily armed adversaries and hostage situations.

Dee would keep anyone on the floor below from heading up toward the line of fire, and her job was to let the rest of the team know the moment NYPD was on scene. Raquel was the backstop, ensuring that if Strauss, Magda, or anyone else got past them, they wouldn't get away in a vehicle.

If the NYPD arrived quickly, and there was no immediate threat to the Panchen Lama, the plan was for the Dangerous Clique to fall back, ditch their weapons down the garbage chute, and blend in with the evacuating residents. The NYPD would get the credit for rescuing the Panchen Lama, and hopefully the question of who Strauss and his mercenaries had been shooting at would forever remain a mystery.

***

The plan would have worked, but apparently somebody within the apartment heard the hissing of the liquid nitrogen being applied through the doorframe. The two Eblis Brothers closest to the back door realized it was likely a precursor to someone trying to get in and fired their guns at the door. Ward had been in a crouching position when he heard the shots, the surprise knocking him off-balance. From a sitting position, Ward kicked the door open; the frozen locks snapped like they were made of balsa. He caught a glimpse of the two bearded men in the room—at least four shots whizzed above his head, piercing the wall above him. He fired his shotgun into the room, and that seemed to force the assailants inside to retreat through the door-way. The door was open, but the element of surprise was gone, and advancing into the apartment was going to be exponentially harder. The operation had fallen apart in a matter of seconds.

He turned back, at Alec, who was crouched down in the stairwell, wide-eyed, pulse racing, breathing heavily, and still holding his Glock, pointed at the floor.

Ward suppressed an urge to scream at his new partner, and simply spoke softly.

"So, should I just print up an invitation to this firefight, or—"

"Dammit!" Alec realized. "I hesitated, didn't I?"

CHAPTER THIRTY-FIVE

Katrina and Elaine learned they had slightly different methods for clearing a doorway, but they figured it out and found themselves at the apartment's front door, in a small lobby with the elevators behind them. Behind the door they could hear shouting in Arabic, and what Katrina was pretty sure was a mix of Russian and Chechen.

"Ring the doorbell," Katrina suggested.

Elaine shook her head and took a position by the right side of the doorframe. "This is the FBI! Open up!"

After a moment, they heard a series of locks being unlocked. Elaine furrowed her brow. Terrorists almost never just opened the door when you gave them an order.

The door's hinges were on the left, and so it swung open to the right—and all Elaine could see was the muzzle flash from a gun, firing indiscriminately into the lobby. If she wasn't pressed against the wall, she might have been in the line of fire. The hand with the gun had just crossed the threshold of the doorway when she heard gunfire from the other side of the door—first the gun fell, then the hand dropped, and the body of Abbad, one of the larger and more rotund members of the Brotherhood, wheezed and bled from the floor.

It took Elaine a moment to realize Katrina had shot Abbad three times, pressing her Glock right up into the tiny sliver of open space—maybe a half an inch—between the door and the doorframe, in between the hinges.

"Nice shots," Elaine said, a bit horrified.

"Big, close target," Katrina shrugged. "Anybody else in the entrance foyer?"

Elaine peeked out. "Looks clear from nine to about eleven or twelve o'clock!"

Katrina peered through the space between the door and the doorway.

***

"What the hell was that?" Strauss repeated as he stormed out of his office, having left five blindfolded, gagged, and tied-up children behind him, and infuriated that Magda's taping of his presentation had stopped. "Magda, I paid you a fortune! I expected you and these men to handle all of this!"

"Be quiet!" Magda ordered. "Take one of the children to use as a hostage! Don't go back into your office, there aren't any other exits from that room. Gianni, what is—"

An exceptionally concerned Gianni burst through the entryway.

"Magda, I don't know how they found us, but they found us!" He swore a lot in Italian. "Somebody in the back, and Abbas said he heard someone yelling 'FBI' at the front!"

Magda calculated. She had posted Abbad at the front door with Abbas. Jasem and Hamid were at the back. Kadir had been posted upstairs. With her and Gianni, she had seven armed, trained mercenaries who could protect Strauss. Strauss clearly wanted to finish his elaborate execution ceremony, but an FBI team could be upon them any minute now.

"Abbad is dead!" Abbas yelled.

Six mercenaries, Magda realized.

Gianni looked at her with palpable desperation. "Let's get the hell out of here, Magda! We can't spend any money if we're dead or in prison! Let's get out before—"

"Like hell you are!" Strauss suddenly roared, with a burst of rage that belied his relatively diminutive stature. He waved the ceremonial cutting blade with theatrical glee. "I paid you for a job, and that job isn't done! You don't get to just walk out of here and try to live well on my deposit! Until my mission is complete, you belong to me!"

Gianni was somewhere between panicked and insulted that Strauss had the nerve to threaten him. Gianni raised his pistol. "How's about you shut the hell up, you rich ass!"

"Magda, your boyfriend is greedy and stupid," Strauss hissed. "He should aim his gun someplace besides my head, because apparently he doesn't realize that *if he kills me, none of you get paid!*"

"Gianni, what are you doing?" Magda screamed. This was just like his negotiations last year with the Albanian mafia that had ended so badly. His emotions ran away with him—paranoia, suspicion, fear.

Gianni's mind was racing and sweat seemed to be ejecting from every pore in his body. "You think I care about your damn fortune, you madman? All of your rambling nonsense about proving the end of God and the opening of the doors and that crap? I just wanted a fat payday! I'm not spending the rest of my life in prison for y—"

Gianni never finished the sentence. From the second-floor staircase, Kadir had heard the argument, and he had quickly calculated that Gianni was threatening to kill the man who was going to transfer the rest of the funds that constituted their payment.

In one fluid motion, Kadir raised his gun and fired four shots in Gianni's direction—two hit their mark, one in Gianni's ribs, another penetrating the top of his skull.

Thinking the shots had come from an FBI assault team member, Magda reacted instinctively, swiftly turning, raising her gun, and pulling her trigger a half dozen times. She realized she had taken down one of her own men, sending Kadir into whatever was beyond this life.

Four mercenaries, she realized.

Strauss looked at her, stunned, and let out an awkward giggle.

"Well, I guess I don't have to worry about your loyalty," Strauss said.

"I can't have done all this for nothing," she murmured to herself in shock. She hadn't loved Gianni, but she respected him. If the mercenary profession had been conducive to friendships, he would have been a friend with benefits.

She clenched her eyes and shook the shock and horror away. Judging from the sound of gunfire in the other rooms, neither the front nor back door offered a safe exit. The balcony was far too high to jump and there was no way Linus Strauss was going to climb down to a window on a floor below.

You just need to get past the assault team, she told herself. Any hallway, any stairwell, any of the elevators, any other floor. She could dump her guns, scream like an American, and pass for a terrified resident of the building.

"Get back into your office and transfer the funds," she ordered Strauss. "Otherwise, I walk now. I'm going to hold them off as long as I can, then try to slip past them. Do your little ceremony. But I can't stay and run the camera."

***

Abbas, whose job was to man the front door, realized that the pair of invaders who had killed Abbad were tough. He fired what he felt was a devastating barrage, and then just waited. But once it started, the return fire from the invaders never seemed to stop. First one Glock, sending seventeen rounds, then another—almost rhythmic, one gun firing while the other reloaded in steady, methodical synchronization. Abbas realized shooting at civilians was much easier.

Realizing he was outgunned, Abbas retreated and hid in a hall closet. He heard two people go past him—women's footsteps, he suspected—and after a few moments of quiet, opened the closet door and made a mad dash toward the front door and the stairwell. Behind him, he heard a woman yelling *"Stop! FBI!"* and, he could hear her hot on his heels. He just kept running, through the front door, to the stairwell, and down the stairs.

***

Magda was pleasantly surprised that the shooting by the front door had finally stopped. She realized she had another maneuver if an FBI team was about to burst into the room. She dashed to the kitchen and dumped her guns and spare cartridges into the garbage can. She took a kitchen knife and cut herself, gently, on the side of her head and slightly across part of her chest, about an inch below where the neck met the shoulder. She winced as she bled. But now, when she encountered an FBI team, she could cry and go hysterical, screaming about how Linus Strauss had come after her with a knife. Despite Magda's size and strength, she could play the delicate Eastern European damsel in distress. She had fake paperwork to back up her cover story as a Georgian aspiring ballerina who had been promised a chance to come to America and be on Broadway, and who had been tricked into a shady mail-order-bride service. In Magda's experience, men loved to play the hero.

But she suddenly sensed she wasn't alone and looked up. A woman had silently entered the kitchen.

Magda recognized her as the woman from the embassy party in Budapest.

"Hello, Magda," she said, unable to hide her satisfaction.

***

Linus Strauss' two-level penthouse apartment on 55 Central Park West featured a spectacular balcony on the eighteenth floor, offering a stunning view of Central Park's sheep meadow and to the east, Tavern on the Green across the street.

The balcony's glass door from the apartment shattered, with Katrina crashing through it, skidding to a stop against the stone wall edge. A second later, the glass door frame swung open, as a livid Magda stormed through, hell-bent on finishing the job.

The takedown didn't go as Katrina envisioned. She had kept her gun level—down to fewer rounds than she had wanted, after the seemingly endless gunfight by the foyer—but Magda had kicked it out of her hand, and it skidded behind the spacious kitchen's massive refrigerator. Katrina tried not to think about how if she had simply shot Magda after saying hello, the Chechen mercenary wouldn't be coming at her with the meat cleaver.

Katrina had to defend herself with a serrated bread knife, a piece of cutlery just barely up to the task. The two women had inflicted a few minor cuts upon each other, and then Katrina tried to lead her out to where she hoped Ward or Alec would be available to put a round or two in Magda and neutralize her. But a steady exchange of gunfire continued from the direction of the back door, indicating Ward and Alec were still pinned down.

Right by the balcony door, Magda had caught up to Katrina and—with muscles drawing on a runaway fountain of adrenaline—thrown her through the glass door.

And now the tall Chechen mercenary was in bloodlust.

"I survived the Russians!" Magda swore in Russian—not knowing, or caring, if Katrina could understand her. "I survived the Americans! And you! You little girl, you sad little kitten, you think you're going to be the one who beats me?"

Magda had Katrina pinned against the balcony's stone wall, and kicked Katrina like she was a soccer ball, over and over again, wherever Katrina's bloody hand wasn't there to try to block it.

Katrina reached out—all that was within her grasp were shards of broken glass.

Katrina took the closest piece of glass and stuck it right into the back of Magda's right ankle—deeply cutting, or perhaps even severing Magda's Achilles' tendon. Magda threw her head back and unleashed a primal scream of pain, clenching her eyes and howling curses of some long-forgotten ancient demon.

Katrina took the opportunity to spring back to her feet— or at least, she tried to spring. "Found your Achilles' heel," she muttered.

But Magda, wheezing, somehow set aside the pain and grabbed Katrina, getting her right arm around Katrina's neck and trying to squeeze her into unconsciousness, using the inside of her elbow like a vise. Katrina still had the broken glass and kept stabbing and slicing downward into Magda's leg. Somehow, the taller Chechen woman, still running on pure adrenaline, seemed to have disconnected all the nerve endings in her body communicating pain. Katrina felt like life itself was being choked out of her, and the shard of glass slid from her grip.

No, she thought. *I've got a wedding to plan. Things to live for.*

Katrina shoved her right hand into the crick of Magda's elbow and pushed, loosening the constriction around her neck, just a bit, but enough. Then, with her left hand, Katrina grabbed Magda's right wrist, getting further control over her opponent's limb and loosening it further. Their bodies slammed against the balcony wall and railing.

"You're going down," Katrina exhaled.

Magda spat on the back of Katrina's neck and hair. "You can't stop me—"

Using her own hip as a fulcrum, Katrina extended Magda's arm and used it like a lever—Magda felt her arm and upper torso suddenly being pulled over the precipice—and suddenly her feet were off the ground, and gravity was yanking her further and further.

"Fine, I won't stop you," Katrina groaned, giving Magda one final yank that pulled her foe's arm out of the socket, and put more of her body weight over the edge. With her right arm, she pushed into Magda's armpit like it was a shot put—the momentum became unstoppable.

Magda's eyes grew wide as she realized this seemingly obvious inferior foe had somehow managed to toss her off the balcony. Katrina watched as Magda plummeted to the street below, slamming into the roof of an SUV parked below, setting off the car alarm.

Katrina exhaled with satisfaction.

"The ground stopped you."

***

Katrina opened the balcony door—a gesture that seemed a little ridiculous, considering how her body had created a person-sized opening in the door glass—and stumbled in. She realized that at some point during the fight, she had lost her walkie-talkie. Where was everyone?

She walked through an archway and saw the dead bodies of Gianni and Kadir. Two less to worry about, she decided, and knelt down, wincing with pain, checking them for weapons and keeping their pistols for herself.

After a moment, a tense Elaine emerged, having run from the direction of the front door. "There you are! Your friend Raquel and I grabbed that guy in the parking garage, she's sitting on him. NYPD should be here any minute."

Elaine looked around. "What happened to Magda?"

"Hit by a car," Katrina said tersely, without any further explanation. "Where are the guys?"

From across the apartment, they heard Ward's voice. *"Strauss, put the knife down!"*

***

Ward was retreating out of Strauss' office. Katrina and Elaine wondered what was making the Army Ranger back up.

A few moments later, when Ward was about eight to nine feet away, Strauss emerged through the doorway, holding a knife to the throat of a boy—the Pachen Lama. Strauss grinned.

"That's right, I'm going to walk right out of here—"

"Kid's a head shorter, Strauss," Ward barked. "Put the knife down, or you're history."

"You won't shoot," Strauss taunted. "You look trained by the war machine, I'm sure you're familiar with cadaveric spasms. Traumatic death, limbs and muscles stiffen. Shoot me, and I might put this knife through the boy's carotid artery, and you would see that gruesome sight every time you closed your eyes until the day you die."

Ward winced. In Afghanistan, he had been clearing a house when some Taliban goon whose name they had never learned tried to ambush them, jumping through a doorway with a Kalishnikov rifle. Ward reacted quickly, and, following training, fired a green-tipped 5.56mm round through the head of his attacker, tearing off enough skin and flesh to reveal the skull. But the round didn't immobilize the attacker instantly and as he fell, he fired the rifle. One of Ward's teammates was shot in the foot, another grazed his arm. He knew *tango shot*, even in the head, did not automatically mean *tango dead* or even *tango neutralized*.

Ward breathed so heavily his nostrils flared. "I'm sending you straight to hell, you evil f—"

"I've already seen hell in that massive cloud overtaking me in lower Manhattan!" Strauss bellowed. "Hell, heaven, people don't realize that if the gates are open, no one's coming through, no one's answering our calls! The day has come! The world is finally ready to open its eyes! Meaning has no meaning! Man has triumphed! The voices were right! The throne is empty, which means I can sit upon it!"

Ward realized that every time he had confronted a jihadist, he had tuned out his screaming in whatever foreign language the bastard used for his final words. Understanding what his target was saying made it all creepier.

The thoroughly bloodied Katrina took a position flanking Ward on his right. Elaine did the same on Ward's left. Upon seeing Katrina, Strauss looked shaken for a moment.

"Where's Magda?" Strauss asked.

"She took the quickest way down to the street," Katrina announced nonchalantly, wiping blood away from her eyes. "Your bodyguard fell hard, Strauss. There's no one left to protect you anymore. NYPD's on its way, the Brotherhood of Eblis are all dead."

Ward internally pumped his fist at that update. Katrina looked around and realized who was missing.

"Ward, tell me Alec is okay."

"He's peachy, he didn't pee on himself too much and I think he winged one of them. He's watching the back door."

Elaine cleared her throat. "Great, now let's deal with the problem in front of us! Strauss, drop the knife, release the child, and get down on your knees!"

"There's nothing left," Katrina concluded.

"Then I've got nothing left to lose, which makes me more dangerous, not less," Strauss warned.

"Linus Strauss, you've got three guns pointed at your head," Elaine declared. "What you do in this moment will determine if you have any life beyond this moment. Now, here's what's going to happen: I'm going to walk over to you and you're going to release that boy from your grip. I'm going to take him away from you, and you're going to let me do it."

"Come close to me, and this knife will cut your throat," Strauss warned.

"I very much would like to see you try," Katrina declared, stepping closer and actually smiling. "You're a fiftysomething ex–Wall Street multimillionaire who's been living comfortably, sedentary, arteries clogged with cholesterol, sky-high blood pressure, whose heart is probably beating two hundred times a minute, probably seconds away from cardiac arrest. I just spent a year doing covert work in Afghanistan, shivving Taliban goons twice my size, men who've spent their whole adult lives beating women. Against you? I like my odds."

About six feet away from Strauss, she raised her free hand and gave a little *come at me* wave.

"I'll kill him, and you can never undo that," Strauss sneered. "You can never undo that—"

Katrina took one defiant step closer. "I'm going to count to three, and on three, you're going to—"

Katrina's sentence was interrupted by a deafening BLAM and then Strauss' head exploded in red. The knife clattered on the ground as his body fell to the floor. He experienced cadaveric spasms, but they had no consequence.

Katrina turned to Ward, but she realized he hadn't fired, and was as surprised by the shot as she was.

Elaine gasped, then scanned the room, trying to see where the shot had come from. "Dammit! Show yourself!"

A door in the back of the grand hall swung fully open, revealing Alec, who had been silently lining up his shot through the doorway crack for the past few minutes. Alec's hand was shaking from adrenaline, his eyes wide, his breathing heavy.

"He never saw me!" Alec gasped, a combination of shock, exhilaration, and trepidation that matched the expressions of shock on the faces of Katrina, Ward, and Elaine. "He never saw me!"

Elaine realized what had happened. "Ward, grab the kid, let's get him out of this room."

Breathing heavily, Alec turned to Ward, a somewhat delirious, confused smile on his face.

"I didn't hesitate!"

CHAPTER THIRTY-SIX

"Elaine Kopek, FBI."

"Alec Flanagan, CIA."

They stood in the doorway, watching the coroner prepare the body bag in the other room.

"You always shoot the guy when your teammate's trying to talk him down?"

Alec looked down at the diminutive but indisputably tough FBI agent.

"It's my first time," Alec said softly. "He didn't see me. I had the shot. I knew I could save the kid." He exhaled, and after a moment, looked at Ward, who was approaching. "And I didn't *hesitate.*"

"Clear and square," Ward nodded. "Now we just hope you didn't just traumatize the kid for life."

The higher-ups of NYPD and quite a few FBI agents—including Raphael Davino—had arrived once Kopek had radioed in what had transpired at 55 Central Park West. Four of the children had already begun the process of being brought back to their parents, with counselors on hand to help the families begin to process the trauma of the kidnapping. But there was still a question of what would be done with Gedhun Choekyi Nyima.

About two hours after Alec's shot, the official investigation of the crime scene at the penthouse at 55 Central Park West had a surprising visitor, and the small groups of forensics teams,

NYPD detectives, New York office FBI personnel all parted like the Red Sea as he entered the apartment.

CIA deputy director Harold Hare.

Hare spoke briefly with Davino and then turned his attention to his team, a clique who had proven to be as spectacularly dangerous as he feared.

"We're telling the Chinese that when you guys got here, the kid was gone," Hare began. "If we're lucky, they'll believe us. I thought about telling them Strauss had killed him, but they would demand to see the body."

"What's going to happen to him?" Katrina asked.

"He's going into New York's child protective services tonight. In the morning, I'm going to reach out to the Dalai Lama's people through back channels. Ideally, Gedhun Choekyi Nyima will be quietly moved to a family that will take care of him and let him live his life away from the spotlight. He can't go back to Tibet. Maybe Bhutan, maybe India. But the Chinese never acknowledged his escape."

"But the kid gets to live a normal life, right?" Alec asked.

Hare looked at the blood on the floor, and was thankful it was Strauss', not a child's.

"For a while, at least," Hare sighed. He knew some would want the child—soon a young man—to reassume the responsibilities of his faith. And the Chinese would still be keeping their eyes open for him.

Hare turned away from the blood and turned to the team and gave them a disapproving look.

"And tomorrow morning—or more likely, the day after—the NYPD will announce that Linus Strauss was killed by an intruder during an attempted burglary."

"What?" Alec exclaimed.

Merlin studied at the team standing before him.

"Oh, I'm proud of what you did here tonight, but that doesn't mean I can sing it from the rooftops," Merlin began, almost chuckling. "While you guys were doing this, we went to war. Again. U.S. and coalition forces launched the attack on Baghdad tonight. The American public is tense enough—the last thing they need to know is that some Silicon Valley millionaire tried to go on a child-murdering spree and managed to smuggle a bunch of jihadists and a Chechen mercenary into the country."

He paused. "And, technically, Linus Strauss was indeed killed by an intruder."

Alec's jaw dropped, and he tried to formulate an objection or question, but his mouth and throat could just make brief *eh-uh-huh* noises. Ward folded his arms and shook his head.

Katrina spoke up. "Wait, sir, you're just going to cover it all up?"

"It beats telling anyone that the team I put together went rogue and without authorization, started shooting up Central Park West," Merlin declared. "We're arranging a very plausible explanation that the NYPD investigation will confirm—that someone broke into Strauss' home and shot him."

Ward gestured at all of the bullet holes in the walls. "I'm guessing the top suspect is the A-Team?"

"And what about Magda?" Katrina asked. "What's the cover story for her swan dive off the balcony?"

Merlin looked toward the windows. "Suicide. Guilt over a lifetime of crimes and atrocities." Katrina involuntarily laughed.

Elaine Kopek cleared her throat. "Sir, I work for the FBI, not for you. You and the CIA can shape any response to these events you like, but my report to my superiors will be the truth, the whole truth, and nothing but the truth. I understand your work sometimes involves deception, but I took an oath."

Merlin nodded sympathetically. "I appreciate that principled stand, Agent Kopek." He removed his cell phone and dialed a number.

"Who are you calling?" Kopek asked.

"Robert Mueller, he's an old friend, I'm hoping he can communicate to you the importance of keeping this confidential in the name of national security."

Elaine gulped. The phone connected, Merlin cheerfully greeted his old friend, and chatted for a few minutes, updating the FBI director—now in his second year on the job—on "this thing up in New York" and mentioning "the place looks more shot up than Mutter's Ridge."

Then, with no words and only a satisfied look, Merlin handed the phone to Elaine. She held it to her ear, greeted the director, and listened quietly as Mueller explained that with both the bureau and the agency having so much on their plates, and with the terrorist threat requiring full cooperation between the two government agencies, this was not the time for the FBI to pick a fight with the CIA when the agency had asked nicely and had made a strong case that revealing the details of Strauss' plot would stir up additional fear.

Elaine agreed that her report on the incident would be full, detailed, and truthful, and then, if the director deemed it necessary, highly classified.

Once that was settled, the team was finally cleared to leave the scene by the FBI and NYPD.

"How much trouble are we in?" Raquel asked.

Hare had a faraway look in his eyes as he waited for the elevator.

"None, although I want all of you on desk duty for the next few months," he sighed. "If you hadn't done this, and Strauss had gone through with it—well, people would be in a panic. Jonestown meets Columbine meets Heaven's Gate, less than five miles from Ground Zero! If people started believing that millionaires were secretly running child abduction rings, the whole country would start drowning in paranoia."

Raquel smiled. "After tonight, boring old desk duty in the office looks pretty appealing!"

Katrina nodded. "Relax, Merlin, we're not going to make a habit of this."

2021

CHAPTER THIRTY-SEVEN

LIBERTY CROSSING INTELLIGENCE CAMPUS
TYSONS CORNER, VIRGINIA
JULY 2, 2021

"**W**hatever happened to the Pachen Lama?" Katrina asked, suddenly wondering whether that child's mother had been still alive, or whether Magda had killed her during the kidnapping. "I don't think China ever acknowledged he slipped out of their custody."

"They didn't," Alec nodded. "Sometime in April or May 2003, they grabbed another kid from Tibet around the same age and claimed that one was the Pachen Lama. Gedhun Choekyi Nyima went to India, but he ended up coming back to America a year or two later—I think the Dalai Lama was afraid the Chinese were closing in on him. So, he lived a normal life under a new name with adoptive parents, I think either Colorado or upstate New York or someplace, and got accepted to Cal Tech. Studying quantum physics, the interconnectedness of all living things. But shortly after graduation, he disappeared. If the Buddhists know where he is, they're not saying. It's probably safer that way."

Alec paused. "He would be in his early thirties now."

They looked around the small conference room, down the hall from their bullpen of offices in the Liberty Crossing complex. While most of the Clique had been dealing with the Iron Wolves at the brothel in Budapest, FBI special agent Elaine Kopek had continued to retrace the steps of the team's first mission. Elaine had listened to all of the team members tell their version of how that formative mission had proceeded—what had gone right, and the considerable amount that had gone wrong. While there were a few contradictions, it wasn't quite *Rashōmon*. Then, earlier that day, she had declared she had made a breakthrough, and a strong possible suspect for who had been trying to kill them.

And she had kept them waiting in suspense, arriving five minutes late, and removing a thick stack of files from her satchels.

Elaine began by noting a couple of different offshoot terrorist groups had used the name Brotherhood of Eblis over the years, and Raquel recalled Director William Peck mentioned them when he was having his meltdown during a television interview a few years earlier. But none of those other groups amounted to much—bands of jihadist burnouts, looking for work. She slid the short stack of the first files to the side and picked up the next one.

"Consuela Zambada Cardenas, founder of the Grand Bazaar, dead."

Elaine dropped a file on the table, for dramatic effect. She picked up the next set of files.

"Brotherhood of Eblis members Kadir, Abbad, Hamid, Jasem, and Raqif all killed in the apartment. Dead, dead, dead, dead."

She picked up the sixth file, a thin one.

"The lone survivor, Abbas, captured by Raquel in the parking garage, was sent to prison on a thirty-year sentence—but he was diagnosed with terminal cancer and died in 2011."

She dropped his thin file and picked up a thicker one.

"Vasco Gianni, Italian recruiter of mercenaries. Dead."

She picked up the thickest file of all and shot a look at Katrina.

"Notorious Chechen mercenary Magdalena Kurbikka Vagabova, a.k.a. Magda. Dead."

She picked up the last file and looked at Alec.

"Deranged zealot multimillionaire Linus Strauss. Dead."

She dropped his file and paused for dramatic effect.

"I see why you guys were so befuddled. Everyone who you fought on that first mission is indeed dead. I went and reviewed every last bit of information in every file that Raquel was cleared to obtain. I cross-checked everything in all of those files and records against everything Dee and the NSA could find. And then, thanks to investigative skills taught and honed by the bureau that you spies keep underestimating, I found one last possibility."

From her bag, Elaine removed another file.

"Emir al Eblis, or Abu al-Saqat, founder of the Brotherhood of Eblis. Presumed dead, but not confirmed."

Katrina nearly leaped out of her chair. "*What?*"

Elaine gleefully slid the folder across the table toward Katrina. "The Jordanians never got around to doing DNA testing on the bodies from the helicopter crash near Petra. Jordanian intelligence told the CIA's Amman Station he was dead, so you guys recorded him as dead. Raising the question…is Emir al Eblis actually dead?"

Ward's eyes grew wide. "Because if he isn't…we shot down his helicopter, nearly killed him, killed his client and all of his lieutenants and followers…"

Brimming with satisfaction, Elaine sat back in her chair and pressed her fingertips together. "This is a guy who would want revenge against you. And he's had, what, eighteen years to move his chess pieces into place?"

Raquel nodded. "Okay, *now* we go to Director Stern with all of this. We've got to find out if Emir al Eblis is still alive, and if so, where he is."

Everyone nodded, but before anyone could rise from their seats, Elaine took one last file out of her briefcase.

"Wait!" She ordered. "As Lieutenant Columbo used to say, 'just one more question.'"

She picked up a thick stack of legal records from the last folder.

"There was one other avenue of investigation that I found curious: Who got Linus Strauss' remaining fortune? He had spent a ton on Magda and the kidnapping plot, but between his investments, the Manhattan apartment, his places he owned in Tahoe, Aspen, and the Hamptons, he still had a lot left. He was divorced and had no children. Apparently, there were a ton of lawsuits, everything went into probate, until a few years ago someone claiming to be Strauss' legitimate heir won their case and founded a charitable foundation, the Linus Strauss Institute for Community Change."

"*What?*" this time Alec did leap out of his chair, waves of shock and outrage washing over him. His chair fell backward.

"I'm sorry, wait..." he blinked rapidly, and shook his head. "You're telling me this guy... *plotted... to... kill... children...*"— Alec paused after each word for emphasis—"and had a knife to the Pachen Lama's jugular, and now somehow he's got a charitable foundation named after him?"

Elaine nodded. "You do have to admit, Linus Strauss was indeed committed to changing the community."

Elaine watched Alec's reaction: incredulous horror and outrage with a mixture of sympathy and amusement. She held up a glossy brochure for the institute, flipping to the back. "Institute Director Madison Reed, who looks young enough to be one of those idiotic TikTok stars." She rolled her eyes. "It's a crazy theory, but I started thinking, what if someone was afraid you guys might someday reveal to the world that Linus Strauss wasn't killed during a burglary gone wrong? What if they were afraid you were going to reveal the truth, or the bureau was going to release that psycho video he recorded with the images of the kidnapped kids, and just ruin his reputation?"

The team around the table mulled over the possibility.

Katrina first shook her head. "It's intriguing, but I don't see that as sufficient motive to send a guy with a truck bomb to the gates to CIA headquarters. And remember, whoever's doing this has been digging into our past, talking to our old enemies."

Raquel nodded. "This is personal. This is a vendetta. You don't go on this kind of a warpath just because you're afraid of some really bad publicity."

Dee concurred. "Targeting us, sending the note that refers to 2003—all of that would make it more likely that the truth is exposed, not less likely." She glanced over to Ward, who had been stroking his beard and looking at the long-out-of-date surveillance photo of Emir al Eblis.

"I'm thinking Occam's Razor, simplest explanation is most likely," Ward declared. "Long-lost jihadist burnout looks like a much stronger possibility." He looked at Alec, who had been studying the brochure for the Linus Strauss Institute for Community Change. "What do you think, buddy?"

The institute had a small office in New York City, where a bust of Linus Strauss smiled to visitors in the posh lobby.

Alec held up the photo of Madison Reed, who looked barely old enough to be out of college, like the stereotypical cute girl next door who had put on her mother's work clothes and posed with her arms folded, pretending to be a nonprofit executive. He smirked. "Does this look like a terrorist mastermind to you?"

CHAPTER THIRTY-EIGHT

LIBERTY CROSSING INTELLIGENCE CAMPUS
TYSONS CORNER VIRGINIA
JULY 6, 2021

"You want to know why Emir al Eblis, or Abu al-Saqat, has never popped up on video surveillance at all, anywhere in the world, since 2003?" Dee asked the rest of the team.

She adjusted her screen from the last known photo of Abu al-Saqat. She added an eyepatch, a massive scar from his forehead, down through his eye, down his cheek to the side of his chin.

"Because after that helicopter crash, he didn't have the same face anymore. Once I plugged that new variable into the search algorithms in our databases ..." She paused and contemplated explaining that facial recognition never worked as quick as it did in the movies or television shows, even with the advances in artificial intelligence and algorithms, and realized it would take too long and the team never seemed to absorb her lessons anyway.

"In late 2003, a one-eyed man named Moussa al-Baal popped up on the agency's radar screen in Damascus, involved in the arms trade." The image of Moussa al-Baal was the same as that of Emir al Eblis or Abu al-Saqat, but with terrible scarring on one side of his face and an eyepatch.

"Two-Face," Alec declared.

"Close. His street name was One-Eyed Moussa," Dee declared. "Small world, Katrina. Apparently he worked with your old buddy Rafiq the Rat once or twice."

Katrina thought of her old source, Rafiq Tannous, a man who disgusted her, but who had met such a sudden and violent end she couldn't help but feel some sympathy. She hadn't realized it at the time, but their last conversation had been his desperate, if characteristically opportunistic, warning of the coming of the Atarsa terrorist group.

"One-Eyed Moussa bought and sold small arms—nothing too dangerous, nothing that would put him on anybody's priority lists," Dee continued. "Illegal, working around embargoes, but really small-time as far as underground arms dealers go. Honestly, there was not a ton about him in our files."

"Almost like a man who had tried for the big score once, and the experience nearly killed him in a helicopter crash," Katrina observed.

"Gradually, over the years, One-Eyed Moussa moved with his markets," Dee continued. "Syria. Yemen. Pakistan. Bangladesh and Myanmar. Two years ago, we lost all track of him. But you're not going to believe who was the last Agency case officer to check in on him, and who apparently tracked him as much as anyone else here."

She paused again for effect, before continuing. "Sanai Sato."

Katrina swore.

CHAPTER THIRTY-NINE

ULURU-KATA TJUTA NATIONAL PARK,
NORTHERN TERRITORY, AUSTRALIA
JULY 8, 2021

Many years ago, when Sanai Sato graduated from the CIA's case officer training program at the Farm, her superiors had lectured her about her personal apparel and grooming choices and how her taste for high fashion and style often made her stand out in a crowd. She answered that she was only interested in going undercover as a woman with good taste. She had argued to a few male instructors and handlers that a beautiful woman who tried to not look beautiful was incongruous and more likely to arouse suspicion than a woman who was beautiful and knew it and didn't mind showing it off. Some agreed, some didn't.

Sanai Sato left the agency about a year before the Atarsa attacks. She had a distinguished career as a case officer that involved several stints with the Dangerous Clique, and Raquel had written her a glowing recommendation. The paperwork didn't reveal that Katrina and Sanai had a relationship accurately characterized as "frenemies." Perhaps the two women were just too similar—both beautiful, smart, exceptionally skilled at their work, and working in a CIA that still had traces of the old boys' network and that didn't quite fully recognize all the potential of the women in its ranks. Katrina and Sanai were both used to being the alpha within their respective groups, and a sibling-like rivalry slowly poisoned their working relationship. Strangely, once Sanai left the team, her teammates felt simultaneously relieved and a bit betrayed that she had left them.

Sato's new residence was just down the road from Longitude 131, Australia's most celebrated luxury camp, with views direct to Uluru/Ayers Rock and across the desert to Kata Tjuta. Her home was easy to miss, and that was the point. The two small aboveground portions looked like a pair of natural hills—one an "upstairs" observation deck looking at Ayers Rock, the second a skylight for the cavernous living space below. At the press of a button, retractable covers designed to look like the terrain could cover the windows and door, making the home seem to just blend in with the landscape. Even with the windows uncovered and open, it was extremely difficult to spot on a satellite image or surveillance drone.

A road seemed to lead into the middle of nowhere; closer examination revealed the road ended with a declining, curved ramp, leading to the underground four-car garage. The garage entrance was similarly difficult to spot from the air.

Inside, the home's underground chambers were spacious, climate-controlled, a seemingly endless series of curved walls and hallways. Beneath the stairway leading to the observation deck, large video screens mimicked window views of the outdoors. Five bedrooms, four bathrooms, an independent power generator and backups, an underground swimming pool and jacuzzi with teak deck.

The Dangerous Clique was pleasantly surprised when Sato responded to their inquiries, saying that she would welcome them dropping by.

"Nice place," Alec said, wondering if the vast underground home had ever been used as the set of a villain's lair in a James Bond film.

"Yes, it is," Sanai declared proudly. "The previous owner ran a private investment firm whose clients included some unsavory figures whom he didn't want publicized, which made him much more cooperative during our negotiations. He had named it the White Lodge, and when I bought it, the whole place was done in stark white—which I couldn't stand."

The entire interior had been redone in black, polished to a fine shine.

"So now it's the Black Lodge," Alec remarked to himself.

"Must have cost a pretty penny," Katrina remarked, trying and failing to hide her contempt.

"I guess life is sweet working for ... *consulting firms.*" Katrina's tone for the words *consulting firms* was the one most people reserved for *human traffickers* or *North Korean border guards*.

Sanai met Katrina with a hard look of contempt that gradually evolved into a smug smile. "I did. The consulting firm led to private security contractors, who led to extremely wealthy clients who were willing to finance the lifestyle I always deserved."

Sanai could tell Katrina saw her as a sellout.

"Katrina, you and I are women with a very particular set of skills. The difference between you and me is that while you're still slaving away for Uncle Sam, I know my worth."

"I'm sure Mika Brzezinski will be proud," Katrina declared dryly.

Katrina had known going into the agency that she would make less money at the CIA than she could in the private sector. Working at the agency, and in particular the Dangerous Clique, offered alternate perks: knowing her actions could mean the difference between safety and disaster for an unknowable sum of innocent lives, de facto legal permission to hunt down sociopaths and radicals plotting terrorist attacks and terminate them with extreme prejudice, travel to exotic lands, and unlimited premium coffee.

Alec smirked. "Hey, Sanai, for a hundred bucks, will you switch back to our side?"

Sanai glared at Alec with anger. "What kind of a woman do you think I am?"

He smirked. "Oh, Sanai, we've established what kind of woman you are; now we're just haggling over the price."

Ward cleared his throat, feeling a little out of place as the team's focused voice of reason. "What's with the luxury bomb shelter?"

Sanai stared in a bit of surprise, and then chuckled. "You're telling me the great Dangerous Clique has no idea what's coming?" She shook her head, genuinely amused. "You guys really are overrated."

"What's coming, Sanai?" Katrina demanded.

"Storm clouds are gathering," Sanai said, raising her eyebrows. "See, the world can handle one crisis. There's always one crisis going on. Two or three, people start to feel it. But what's coming? It's not even two or three crises at once. It's at least four. Probably five. I'm guessing China, Russia, Iran, one non-state actor, and one we aren't even thinking about."

Sanai stared, intensely amused that her old colleagues seemed so clueless.

"Boy, you guys aren't hanging around arms dealers and mercenaries anymore," she mocked. "Gotten soft and comfortable in those Virginia suburbs, and out of touch. Otherwise, you would be moving into a luxury bunker like me. You guys really think when push comes to shove, Americans are going to defend Taiwan from China? Or the Baltics or Ukraine from Russia? Or anyplace in the Middle East from Iran? Think a lot of Americans will be willing to make any sacrifices to protect South Korea from North Korea? You guys couldn't even get your own people to take lifesaving vaccines. The Taliban's back to their old tricks, all over Afghanistan. The forces of chaos are on the march."

Katrina noticed Sanai now referred to Americans as *you guys*, and not *we*.

"I can't believe you guys are so blind to this. Americans can't unite against threats anymore. There's just too much temptation to turn everything into the same old red versus blue fight. You guys will never be unified on anything ever again. You guys are still afraid to blame China for the virus. The night watchman is gone, my friend. America's not riding to the rescue the next time some Hitler or Stalin rises to the top. Most people in the Western world are still walking around, acting like everything's normal. Those of us in the international underground? We can already see it. We see the stockpiling of weapons, the testing of new tools for asymmetric warfare, the probing of defenses, the testing of response times. You think China's testing hypersonic missiles just for fun? Think Russia's testing anti-satellite weapons for no particular reason? You think the Saudi royal family just woke up one morning and decided, 'Hey, wouldn't it be neat if we had some intercontinental ballistic missiles'? Iran's building up an arsenal of kamikaze drones—think of a swarm of flying IEDs. They can all see it. Everybody's on their own now. Those of us who can see it are just grabbing what we can and hunkering down before the storms hit."

"You're expecting a war?" Ward probed. "Some global disaster?"

"I'm expecting at least five global disasters, all interconnected. Five gathering storms. Take your pick from a long menu. Combat applications of artificial intelligence. A worldwide scramble for resources with climate change hitting hard. Mass migration. Cyberattacks knocking out power for months. Governments collapsing. Terrorist groups like ISIS and Atarsa. Your friends like the Shedim and their ideas of ethnic bioweapons. It'll be like a reverse singularity. Everything turns to chaos at once."

"We're bringing two children into this world," Alec announced.

"Man, you just have to tell everybody, don't you?" Ward grumbled.

Sanai laughed, until she saw the look on Katrina's face. "Oh, God, you're serious. Oh, no. What a terrible time to do something like that."

Having just dropped this atomic bomb of pessimism and gloom upon them, Sanai went to her decanter and poured herself a drink.

"So, I guess you won't be needing a drink, Katrina," Sanai teased. "What else can I do for you?"

"Where can we find One-Eyed Moussa?" Katrina demanded.

Sanai continued her infuriating chuckle. "Funny that you're looking for him! He was one of the people who told me the rumors about the Five Gathering Storms. And that was before the coronavirus—he knew global calamities were coming. He had the same idea—find a remote corner of the world, build your top-of-the-line bunker and stock up supplies, and get ready to spend a decade or two riding out the storm."

"I asked for his location, not a thesis on what kept him up at night!" Katrina snapped.

"You're on edge," Sanai observed, tilting her head and studying her frenemy closely. "If I didn't know better, I'd guess you thought he was connected to the Langley bomb, but you're much more tightly wound than normal. All of you are. Something's hit very close to home." Sanai smiled.

"Sanai, don't play games with a pregnant woman," Katrina seethed. "Tell us where he is, or else you're going to get that fight that you've been asking for, almost since the day we met."

Sanai clucked her tongue. "I find it refreshing that you're no longer trying to hide that you've always felt threatened by me."

Alec held up his hand. "Sanai, before you escalate this any further, I feel obligated to inform you that the last guy who gave my wife attitude the way you're doing right now was Sergei Markov. You know, the Boris Badinov of the Iron Wolves?"

Sanai's eyes widened.

"The hit that got him in Budapest?"

Katrina gave a little satisfied smile and shrugged—and made a mental note that Sanai, the semi-retired former case officer, was still plugged in to the international espionage and mercenary rumor mill.

Sanai put down her drink, as if this revelation changed her understanding of recent events considerably. "Everybody said it was the Chechens! That was you guys?"

"That was *Katrina*!" Alec clarified. "One of the world's most notorious mercenaries, the biggest, baddest Russian this side of Ivan Drago got a little too big for his britches, wouldn't cough up any answers, and got his ticket punched. And Sanai, that's not even the worst part: Katrina killed him just because she really needed to pee."

That cut the tension like a knife, and everyone laughed. Sanai nodded and raised her glass.

"Then this will be my baby shower gift," she chuckled. "There's this South Korean island, Ulleungdo, that's almost halfway between Korea and Japan," Sanai explained. "Supposed to be sacred, with positive energy or something like that. Moussa saved up a ton, made a bundle on his last few arms deals with Burmese militias killing off the Rohingya. He bought this seaside cliff resort, Kosmos, and turned it into his own private mountaintop hideaway. It looks like something out of the Jetsons or something—space age and futuristic."

Alec called Dee to start tracking it down.

"What's a guy like One-Eyed Moussa doing there?" Katrina asked.

"Same thing I am, stocking up and battening down the hatches," Sanai answered. "The last time we talked, we figured it would be the last time, and we said our goodbyes. He's convinced the world's ending—or at least the world we know. Time to settle all accounts and go to ground."

Katrina looked around Sanai's home, which probably ranked among the world's most luxurious fallout shelters.

"And you buy into that too, huh, Sanai?"

Sanai swallowed the remaining liquor in one gulp and winced.

"The world out there doesn't exactly seem to be calming down, now, does it, Katrina?" She put her glass down. "More like it's teetering, and one good shove will send it over the edge."

Katrina met Sanai's stare.

"All the more reason for some of us to keep shoving in the other direction," Katrina declared. She realized she wasn't mad at Sanai, she was disappointed. Her old teammate could have been so much more than she was. Sanai thought she was being sophisticated and realist, but she had ultimately settled—content to enjoy the decline, instead of trying to reverse it. And who could possibly enjoy a luxury underground bunker if the world outside was falling apart?

But Katrina studied Sanai's defiant stare, and realized Sanai probably thought she was naïve.

"Good luck to your twins, Katrina," Sanai said, coming as close to genuine warmth as she could.

"They're going to need it."

CHAPTER FORTY

"One-Eyed Moussa has motive. Did he have the means? Opportunity?" Elaine asked. "Is there anything actually tying him to Harvey Lawrence Godula?"

The team had returned from Australia on an extraordinarily long and twice-delayed flight, and dragged themselves, groggily and exhausted, into the office the next morning. Alec and Ward joked that they wanted their coffee administered intravenously. Katrina fumed that the doctors were limiting her to one cup of coffee per day.

"You're supposed to be avoiding caffeine," Alec reminded her.

Katrina glared. "I'm also supposed to be avoiding stress, and you see how well that's going!"

Raquel rubbed her eyes, overcome with frustration. "For God's sake, will someone please get Katrina a decaf latte so she can at least feel like she's getting coffee?" She sighed and tried to get the meeting back on track. "Dee, please tell me NSA found a smoking gun."

Dee winced and held up her hand in a shaky *maybe* gesture.

"Once we had his location, finding and reading through at least one of his e-mail accounts was like cracking an egg," Dee shrugged. "We didn't find a smoking gun, but One-Eyed Moussa is in contact with a half dozen semi-retired arms dealers, smugglers, terrorists. He's got a few suspicious messages around the time of the attempting bombing—inquiring about a package that was not delivered and getting the answer that it was lost in transit."

Alec let out a little scoffing laugh. "So, there's this little problem going on with the supply chain right now—"

Dee ignored him. "But there was one really big find. Ward, you're gonna want to sit down for this."

"I don't faint, you know." Ward, having poured himself a third cup of coffee, returned to his seat.

Dee took a deep breath. "We finally found One-Eyed Moussa's real name by going through old information the Egyptians shared back when their intelligence services were feeling more cooperative. Before he was One-Eyed Moussa, before he was the Devil's Prince, before he was Abu al-Saqat or 'Father of the Fallen,' before he was Emir al Eblis, he was born with the name Tarek Nuru. Nuru was born in the south end of the Manshiyat Naser ward in Cairo, the Garbage City where the city's waste gets dumped. The poorest neighborhood in a city where there's a lot of competition for that title. He and his mother and brothers were one of the Zabbaleen, or *Garbage People* who try to eke out a living by going through the trash and finding something useful or valuable in it. No sewers, little electricity, little fresh water."

She displayed a horrific picture that looked like someone had taken the entire contents of the Fresh Kills Landfill in Staten Island and dumped them atop an already crumbling, densely packed Middle Eastern urban slum, with smog so thick it looked dystopian.

"Everything we've heard about the guy's childhood makes it sound like hell. Easy pickings for a recruiter of the Muslim Brotherhood, then Egyptian Islamic Jihad."

She displayed a poor quality black-and-white mug shot or passport photo.

"Tarek Nuru did go to Afghanistan in the late 1980s, probably just in time to watch the Soviets withdraw. After about a year or two, he went back to Egypt, and apparently signed on with Hamas. After another year or so, Egyptian state security starts looking for him, so in the early 1990s he gets out of town and goes to the Philippines. This is the big discovery."

She paused and took a deep breath. "In December 1994 and January 1995, Tarek Nuru was in Cebu, Phillippines."

Ward's posture immediately changed. It took a moment, but Raquel realized why that place and time would be significant to Ward.

Katrina squinted and tried to remember the significance of Cebu—she knew she had read about it at some point.

After a moment, it came to her. "Ramzi Yousef, one of the bombers of the World Trade Center in 1993, was there!" she said, her tone shifting from excitement to soft anger over the course of the sentence. "He was planning Operation Bojinka, the plot to bomb all of those airliners."

"And while Yousef was in Cebu, so was Terry Nichols, the partner of Timothy McVeigh," Ward rumbled quietly, like embers of a fire on the verge of sparking back to life. "No one was ever able to prove a foreign connection to the Oklahoma City Bombing, but a lot of law enforcement and intelligence officials thought it was weird that two of the perpetrators of two of the worst bombing terrorist attacks of the 1990s were in the same city of about 600,000 people at the same time. They both used truck bombs, and they both used ammonium nitrate. Nichols went to the Philippines as a guy who couldn't get his bombs to work when he tried test runs. He came back capable of building a bomb powerful enough to be measured on the Richter scale."

"And we're looking for someone who sent instructions on how to build a truck bomb to a paranoid nut, with instructions on how to drive it up to the gate of CIA headquarters," Alec said. He held firmly to his coffee cup, thinking of the closing scene of *The Usual Suspects*.

"It's not a smoking gun, but there's a whiff of smoke in the air," Raquel declared. "And the gun is still warm."

She looked around the table.

"*Now* we go to Director Stern with all of this."

CHAPTER FORTY-ONE

Under normal circumstances, a man like One-Eyed Moussa—born one of Cairo's "Garbage People," once a hunted Islamist terrorist under another name, then a notorious mercenary commander under yet another name—would never have been able to afford purchasing a mountaintop seaside resort and convert it to his private residence. But recent years had been anything but normal.

Starting in 2017, the Myanmar military accelerated an ethnic cleansing campaign against Rohingya Muslims—mass arson, killing, rapes, torture, and looting, destroying hundreds of villages and forcing an estimated 700,000 Rohingya to flee across the border to Bangladesh. Once again, the United Nations issued sternly worded statements of disapproval that did nothing to change the conditions on the ground. A few countries enacted a few formal arms embargoes against Myanmar. But many of the world's major arms dealers were sufficiently fearful of being accused of profiteering from genocide; profiteering from war was sufficient. They postponed delivery on existing contracts with Myanmar, citing the need for "internal reviews."

One-Eyed Moussa, who had spent fifteen years as small-time but reliable small arms dealer developing contacts all over the

Indian Ocean, found himself perfectly positioned to take delivery of arms from third-party buyers and resell them, off the books, to the Myanmar military. A long-comfortable profession became wildly lucrative overnight, giving One-Eyed Moussa three spectacularly profitable years and leaving him ready to retire.

Then in early 2020, the COVID-19 pandemic brought global tourism to a halt, and the gorgeous, otherworldly Kosmos resort on the South Korean island of Ulleungdo was forced into bankruptcy. The Kosmos resort had only twelve rooms and was built for no more than double that many guests. The architectural marvel was full of high, swooping archways and smooth, white curved walls, creating a sense that the resort building was not constructed so much as born, and that guests were entering and staying in warm, soothing, womb-like chambers. The high windows were designed for stargazing, and rooms had astrological and elemental themes—Mars with fire, Mercury with water, Jupiter with the woods, and Venus with gold. The resort featured two long, narrow, curved saunas with high ceilings that felt like sliding into the belly of a whale like Jonah, or perhaps some other warm, wet part of a human body. Outside, an infinity Jacuzzi using water melted from snow stacked in Nari Basin was designed to make guests feel as if they had become part of the sea over the cliff.

Kosmos was one of the most unique spa resorts in the world … but it couldn't operate without guests. As the pandemic raged through Asia, with little prospect of reopening and returning to normal operations, the owners were desperate to get rid of it—and didn't care too much that the new purchaser, the eye-patch-wearing Moussa al-Baal, had made his fortune in "international shipping" with some shady characters.

"One-Eyed Moussa al-Baal"—formerly known as the Devil's Prince—stood on his balcony looking out at the sea.

The sky was overcast, but the sea before him was somewhat choppy. But every time he picked up his newspaper or checked the Internet, the five storms were gathering more quickly and growing stronger.

Afghanistan was careening toward an epic, generational humanitarian disaster, the likes of which the world had never seen. The virus that was supposed to be in the past continued to spread, mutate, and infect new victims. Killer floods had hit wealthy neighborhoods on two continents. Heat waves popped up in unexpected corners of the northern hemisphere, where almost no one had air conditioning because they had never needed it before. Hurricanes and typhoons would be coming soon. War still raged in the Ethiopia and Sudan border region, Yemen, Somalia, Congo—all spots that most Westerners would have difficulty finding on a map. The bloodshed there didn't affect their sheltered lives—but the growing prospects of war in Ukraine and Taiwan would. When Taiwanese electronics stopped shipping, atop a global supply chain crisis, everyone would sense that the good days had come to an end.

On paper, One-Eyed Moussa realized he should have been happy; for a child of the Zabbaleen to retire, living like a king in a mountaintop castle would be, on paper, a triumphant life. But he figured he would be one of the last ones. As a young man, he believed in a cause. After enough bitter defeats, driven by hypocritical and selfish leaders, the disillusioned warrior shifted to renting himself out to someone else's cause. Money was pure. Simple. It had no pretensions. Money was honest; it never pretended to be something it was not.

But even fighting for money carried its price, as the fires of a helicopter had taught him, and reminded him every time he looked in the mirror.

He looked out and spotted a small boat off in the distance. He wondered if whoever was on that boat had any inkling of the metaphorical storms that were coming.

***

"I'm going to be seasick," Katrina mumbled. She also needed to urinate—these days she always felt like she needed to pee, a change driven more by her hormones than the tiny weight of the two minuscule human beings growing within her. But she resolved that she would white-knuckle her way through this portion of the reconnaissance mission.

"It's choppy water, there's just nothing to be done," Alec said, putting his arm around her. Three U.S. Navy personnel in plainclothes were taking the pleasure boat out, freeing up the four CIA personnel, posing as tourists, to continue their monitoring of the shore and the giant white ovals of the former Kosmos resort.

For the first time since Fox Plaza in Los Angeles, Raquel made the executive decision to deploy with her team into the field, flying to Seoul and helping arrange the surveillance mission on Kosmos. The first step was reconnaissance by boat, followed by some sort of in-person confrontation with Moussa. Ward, Alec, and Katrina were still debating the best course of action on that.

"I see the little bugger standing out on his balcony," Ward declared, still holding up the binoculars. He watched Moussa for another moment, then lowered the binoculars and shook his head. "Dude seems awful cool for a guy who's masterminding a plot to kill us."

Raquel was about to say something but was interrupted by insistent chimes from her secure satellite phone. She answered and turned away.

"Just because the guy's chilling on his balcony doesn't mean he can't be a mastermind!" Alec argued. "Every James Bond villain is always sitting there in his space-age Barcalounger with his femme fatale and stroking a pussy! *'Ah, Mr. Bond, welcome to my humble abode. I hope you enjoy this death trap I had installed off my remodeled kitchen. It went forty percent over budget and two months behind schedule, because I used union contractors.'*

"The guy studied up on us!" Ward said, skeptically. "He knows the reason nobody's ever heard much about the Conspiracy of Fire Nuclei, the Afrikaner Resistance Movement, the ISIS Bengals, and Nigerian Ansaru is because we killed almost all of them before they could build a reputation. He knows we're the crew who took down Atarsa, Hell-Summoner, the Shedim network. Despite your best efforts, they don't call us the Gregarious Clique! I pride myself on having killed more terrorists than cancer. And after trying to kill me and failing, this guy doesn't even change his address? No guards? No visible security? He's just sitting, chilling on his balcony, having coffee like it's a friggin' Folgers commercial!"

He shook his head skeptically, then checked the binoculars again. "Now he's in the kitchen."

Alec shrugged. "Everybody we've ever gone up against has underestimated us!" he countered. "It's the only advantage we can ever count on!"

"What if Moussa isn't the guy?" Ward shouted back, generating concerned looks from the three Navy personnel on the boat. "If somebody's trying to kill me, I want to make 100 percent sure I get the right guy!"

Their argument was interrupted by Raquel suddenly shouting into the satellite phone.

"Madam Director, you are making a mistake!"

Alec and Ward turned in surprise, and Katrina gritted her teeth and ignored her seasickness.

Raquel cupped her hand over the phone. "Director Stern is ordering us to stand down."

"Stand down?" Alec exclaimed in disbelief. "What, they want us to stop watching him?"

An infuriated Raquel held up the phone and put the director on speaker.

"Raquel, I've taken everything you told me to the White House, and they resolved to address the threat of One-Eyed Moussa al-Baal through other means," Stern announced, with all of the passion of a recorded voice informing you that they had been trying to reach you about your car's extended warranty.

"What other means?" Raquel demanded, shaking the phone.

They could hear a sigh on the other end of the line.

"Raquel, I think you have to understand that the administration wants a really clean narrative on this one," Stern acknowledged, her voice betraying just a little bit of discomfort with how the decision had been reached. "They've got a lot on their plate right now. Afghanistan. China. Russian hackers. Fears of virus variants. They really need a win to restore everyone's confidence. The president wants to be able to say to Americans we've dealt with the terrorist who tried to blow up the CIA."

"Dealt with … how?" Raquel insisted.

Stern seemed to sigh again. "Look, you'll see soon enough, just don't get too close to shore."

Stern hung up, and the four members of the Dangerous Clique looked at each other in confusion. Then they heard a thunderous roar, at first distant but soon almost deafening. Ward and Katrina had heard that sound before, many years earlier in Afghanistan.

A Hellfire missile.

Everyone on the boat turned in time to see the missile slam into Kosmos, right into the kitchen. But what they witnessed was not a normal Hellfire missile. The recently deployed R9X, nicknamed the Flying Ginsu, struck the upstairs kitchen off the balcony of the remodeled resort tower.

Seconds before impact, the missile deployed six long blades that shredded anything and everything in their paths. Previous uses had demonstrated that the blades of the Flying Ginsu cut through building walls, car roofs, and human flesh in a manner that would have brought the late Ron Popeil to tears of joy.

The Flying Ginsu indeed sliced and diced and could cut through a tin can and then slice a tomato. It had been developed to counter terrorists who attempted to hide behind women and children, or other innocent civilians. The U.S. intelligence community and Pentagon characterized it as the "right seat, left seat problem"—when a particularly wanted or dangerous target was in one seat in a vehicle, but the other passenger or driver was considered an innocent civilian. The Flying Ginsu improved the odds of survival of the surrounding civilians—but couldn't guarantee it. While the blades were exceptionally dangerous, the site of a Flying Ginsu strike experienced no explosion, little or no fire, and little or no debris or scorch marks.

Kosmos was left largely intact, except for Moussa's kitchen. It was as if the whirring blades of a sawmill suddenly detached and flew directly at Moussa—slicing his midsection, neck, and three of his four limbs.

On the boat offshore, the Dangerous Clique team watched in stunned silence.

"Any chance he made it?" Raquel asked, knowing the answer but feeling obligated to ask anyway.

Alec grabbed the binoculars and surveyed the scene. "Moussa's kitchen is now, uh …" He looked for the right words. "Think of a giant marinara stain."

Katrina winced and suppressed the urge to heave what was left of her most recent meal over the side of the boat.

"Gee, I sure hope we got the right guy!" Ward announced sarcastically.

Raquel lowered her head in frustration and started muttering about how she had hoped Stern would be different.

Katrina slammed her hand against the seat.

"The whole point of our surveillance was to make sure Moussa was the right guy!" she fumed. "We didn't know it yet! We were supposed to capture and interrogate the bastard! The damn Seventh Floor was so eager to see what they wanted to see that they just blew him up, thinking the odds that he was the right target were pretty good! This is Curveball all over again!"

CHAPTER FORTY-TWO

REMARKS BY THE PRESIDENT ON THE AIR
STRIKE IN SOUTH KOREA
JULY 15, 2021

My fellow Americans. Today we tracked down the mastermind of the attempted bombing of CIA headquarters, and in an air strike, targeted and killed him, eliminating the threat forever.

Over the course of his long career in international terrorism and the illegal arms trade, this mastermind went by many names. Tarek Nuru. Emir al Eblis. Abu al-Saqat. One-Eyed Moussa. He's been a jihadist, a mercenary, and an illegal arms dealer. And now, he is dead, and will never menace anyone ever again.

This is as clear a signal as this government—as this country—can possibly send. To anyone who gets the wrong idea, let me say it clearly. To those who wish America harm, to those who engage in terrorism against us and our allies, know this: The United States will never rest. We will not forgive. We will not forget. We will hunt you down to the ends of the Earth, and we will make sure you will pay the ultimate price.

This is a new world. The terror threat has metastasized across the world. The fundamental obligation of a president, in my opinion, is to defend and protect

America—not against threats of 2001, but against the threats of 2021 and tomorrow.

I urge all Americans to join me in grateful prayer for our troops and diplomats and intelligence officers who carried out this mission.

***

CIA HEADQUARTERS
JULY 19, 2021

CIA Director Barbara Stern did not rearrange her schedule when a senior case officer demanded an in-person meeting, even for a senior case officer with the distinguished record of Katrina Leonidivna.

When Stern had presented the Dangerous Clique's information to the president, national security council, and the Director of National Intelligence, everyone had concurred—Tarek Nuru's past experience with bomb-building, along with his previous conflicts with the CIA in 2003, made him the person most likely to send instructions to Harvey Godula to blow up CIA headquarters. The president, secretary of defense, and chairman of the joint chiefs—all facing considerable public criticism over ominous developments in Afghanistan—were eager to "send a clear signal." With Tarek Nuru now dead, the administration was ready to declare that justice had been done and a threat had been eliminated.

But when it became clear that the entire Dangerous Clique team was in near-open revolt about the decision to strike Tarek Nuru, Stern relented and asked her scheduler to clear out a space.

The early morning meeting started badly and went downhill from there.

"I don't know how many more ways I can say it," the director shrugged. "The administration wanted a clean narrative on this.

They determined Moussa was a threat and took action to eliminate the threat. Case closed."

"Did you not hear anything we just said?" Katrina exclaimed. "We're not a hundred percent sure Tarek Nuru, or One-Eyed Moussa, is the right guy! For all we know, this government just blew up a retired arms smuggler for no good reason!"

Stern stared back blankly.

"Nothing the FBI turned up in the investigation of Harvey Lawrence Godula pointed in any other direction," the director responded, shaking her head. "Your lead on this guy was the best option we had, and between Afghanistan, China, and Russia, the White House wanted this issue dealt with and resolved."

"Sounds like a bunch of gathering storms," Alec muttered into his hand.

"Resolved?" Katrina was beside herself. "What if we killed the wrong man?"

"Tarek Nuru's crimes over the course of his life more than justified his termination," Stern insisted. "Unless you think we should just let him enjoy a quiet retirement in a luxury resort, spending the fortune he made in arms deals to genocidal regimes."

"You're dodging the issue! This may not have been the guy who sent the truck bomb to our doorstep!" Katrina fumed. Raquel gave her a look, trying to signal her to dial back her anger.

Katrina ignored Raquel's glare and pointed her finger at Stern. "You're worried that the inability to generate any other leads on the truck bomb attack makes you look weak, and that the president, who's already worried about his poll numbers, might replace you. So you went along with a White House that was desperate to find a quick and easy solution!"

"I followed the orders of the president!" Stern said, with about as much emotion as the team had ever seen in her.

Katrina was like a pot ready to bubble over. "We had options! There's this process called indictment, and extradition, and this group called Interpol, and—"

Stern nodded. "Mmm, and did you say any of that to Sergei Markov before you murdered him in cold blood?"

Katrina froze in shock, briefly contemplated lunging across the desk to strangle the CIA director in indignant rage, then composed herself. "Sergei Markov was trying to kill me and my unborn children."

"Katrina, I'm not mourning the man," Stern declared. "I'm just calling you a shameless hypocrite."

"That's not an improvement," Alec observed.

"I don't have to justify myself or my decisions to you or anyone else," Stern declared icily. "Judging from the insubordinate tone from both of you, I think the stress of impending parenthood has compromised your judgment."

Ward raised his hand. "Madam Director, I'm already a parent. And I'm pretty sure the impending parenthood of Alec and Katrina is not compromising my judgment." He paused. "And with all due respect, ma'am, I still think the decision to drone Moussa was crap."

"Noted," Stern declared through gritted teeth. "This conversation is going in circles. I think we're done here." She gestured toward the door.

Raquel rose to her feet. "Madam Director, telling us to get lost isn't going to change anything, and this is the sort of decision that looks bad in the history books." She paused. "Or in an inspector general report."

Stern glared back with indignation as she rose to her feet and leaned over her desk. "Do you know who you're talking to? Do you know how many women have run this agency?" She held up two fingers. "Gina Haspel and me! That's it! I didn't get here by telling presidents that I can't deliver on their priorities! I didn't get here by telling them that I can't solve a problem, or that their policy proposals are asinine and unrealistic, even when they are! When the president of the United States gives an order, and you have doubts, you have two options. You can quit and let somebody else replace you, who might be a fool or sycophant, and who will just make things worse. Or you can salute, carry out the order, and use what limited power you have to steer government policy in the right direction next time."

Katrina dismissed it with a hand wave.

"You're making excuses," Katrina concluded, her voice dripping with contempt. "Our whole purpose is to ensure the people running the American government have the right information—and when they make a decision *before* they have the right information, we're enabling bad policies that have life-and-death consequences! If we're not going to stand up for what's right, and oppose what's wrong, then what are we doing here? What's the point?"

Raquel stood frozen, unnerved at how heated the argument between Katrina and the CIA director had grown. This meeting that had originally aimed to clear the air had simply thrown gasoline on the fire—maybe it was because Stern felt more pressure to go along with administration decisions, or maybe Katrina's pregnancy-driven stress was becoming uncontrollable. But Raquel sensed the dispute had just leaped past the point of no return—there was no way they would leave this office without some sort of disciplinary action.

But strangely, both Stern and Katrina seemed to find raising their voices cathartic. Perhaps the two women had stumbled into an opportunity to drop their consummate professional facades and vent their spleens with wild abandon. If there was no chance this meeting could end in anything but disaster, there was no point in holding back any long-repressed opinions or truths.

"I don't have the luxury of sitting there and insisting we do the right thing, or to try to please everybody's conscience!" Stern snapped, with as much anger as anyone on the team could remember ever seeing in her. "I work in a messy world, with unclear answers and competing pressures, and no easy answers! I have to make the best call I can with the information I have! You can live with it, or you can resign!"

"The person who sent that truck bomb to our front door might still be out there!" Katrina barked. "And you're in denial! You're blind to it, because you're afraid if you tell the president he's wrong, he'll get rid of you! So you end up enabling the president's wrong decisions!"

"If the president makes the wrong choice, it is not my responsibility to fix it!" Stern insisted. "My job is to carry out his orders. If he screws up the orders, that's the responsibility of the American people!"

Alec found himself trying to nudge Katrina toward the door, but it was too late.

"Coward!" Katrina roared, pointing an accusatory finger. "This was the wrong call, and you knew it! You *know* you should have pushed back more! And you're so mad at yourself about it that you're taking it out on us!"

"One more word out of you, and you're both fired!" Stern roared back. Her nostrils flared.

The door to Stern's office opened, and Stern's assistant and a member of her protective service detail entered, with concern. They had heard a few heated arguments in Stern's office during her brief tenure so far—in fact, they seemed to be occurring with greater frequency and intensity—but today's rising crescendo of indignation was the angriest they had ever heard the director.

The arrival of two other people caused everyone in the room to freeze, as if Stern and the Dangerous Clique had been caught doing something embarrassing—and perhaps they had.

"Raquel, all of you are suspended from field work until further notice," Stern declared, quietly but firmly. "Take some time off and cool your heads. Think long and hard about how you want to approach your duties, and my instructions, from here on out. Because as illustrious as your team's record is, *I'm still the director here.*"

"Yes, ma'am," Raquel and Ward murmured. Katrina stared in fury. But Alec couldn't help roll his eyes so hard he almost pulled a facial muscle.

Stern noticed. "I knew that sooner or later I was going to have to decide whether Harold Hare's crazy idea for a lightly managed globe-trotting assassination team was compatible with where this agency was headed." She gave them all a contemptuous glare. "This meeting is helping clarify things a great deal."

Alec paused before the door. "Well, Madam Director, I'm glad you found the true villain in this story."

"Get out of my office!" she shot back.

***

Raquel, Katrina, Ward, and Alec walked back into their office, silent, glowering, simmering with frustration. Dee had warned the others that confronting Stern with the team's doubts was likely to end badly. Even if Stern had agreed with their fears that Tarek Nuru was just a scuzzy retired arms dealer with no clear connection to Harvey Godula and his truck bomb, she was likely to scapegoat the team, as they were the ones who had brought her the intelligence about Nuru in the first place.

Dee watched as her teammates walked through the doors and slumped into their chairs, their body language signaling that they had entered the meeting with faint hopes … and then Stern had stomped all their hopes out of them.

"So …" Dee said, interrupting the awkward silence. "How did it go?"

"We're not going back into the field until Stern gives us the green light," Raquel informed Dee. She shook her head. "Which may well be never."

Dee sat back in her chair, exhaling slowly in disappointment. She had expected the meeting to go badly. She hadn't expected the director, who had seemed to have handled the tensions of the Hell-Summoner crisis well enough, to grow infuriated enough to contemplate pulling the plug.

"Fools!" Alec fumed. "Bureaucratic fools! They don't know what they've got there!"

"I'm like Michelle Obama's old quote in reverse," Ward sighed. "For the first time in my adult life, I'm not proud of my country."

"Directors come and directors go," Katrina murmured. "Since I've been here, we've had, what, nine or ten? And they never learn. Half of them never even study their predecessors. They all come in, from Capitol Hill or the Pentagon or wherever, thinking we're just another top-down federal agency. They don't understand that because we've got unique duties, we've got unique responsibilities."

Katrina thought about continuing, but she felt emotionally spent. She had offered versions of her spiel many times over the years. Even with all its problems, even with China on the march and Vladimir Putin gleefully flexing his regime's muscles, the U.S. government was still the single most powerful institution on the planet.

Even aside from its nuclear arsenal, the U.S. military could strike any site on the planet within hours, if not minutes. The U.S. Navy could reach almost any corner or depth of the sea, the Air Force boasted that it controlled the skies, and the various branches of the U.S. armed forces operated out of 750 bases in eighty countries around the world. U.S. Cyber Command could take down computer networks and shut down the power just about anywhere in the world, and U.S. Space Command was perfecting the art of taking out the satellites of opposing nations and ensuring enemies couldn't do the same to America.

America's satellites watched from above and its surveillance stations listened throughout the world. The entire government spent roughly $6 trillion in a year, had embassies in just about every other country on the planet, and had still unrivaled, or barely rivaled, economic and cultural power. Even after the pandemic, riots, intense political divisions, al-Qaeda, ISIS, Atarsa, and the rest, the United States was still the closest thing planet Earth had to a global ruling power. If hostile aliens landed tomorrow, everyone would turn to the American president to lead the response; no one would be asking what the head of the European Union thought.

Katrina described the U.S. government as a lumbering colossus, heavy and slow-moving but still immensely powerful once it determined its objective and built up a full head of steam. (When she got to this point, Alec added, "we're like a big red-white-and-blue kaiju," but she surprised him by responding that the better metaphor was Voltron, because Americans are all a little different and come in lots of different colors, but they get stronger when they work together. Alec marveled that Katrina had come up with her own pop culture reference.) This colossus was steered by an executive and a Congress that relied on the intelligence community to know what was going on in the world—to be the eyes and ears of that Voltron.

Because the intelligence community uniquely sat in that pivotal role, Katrina believed, it had a special duty to make sure they get it right. They informed the brain, the source of all the key information. Or at least, that had been their role in the past. In recent years, she wondered if the brain of the American colossus had started making its decisions based upon what it saw on Twitter, or one of the cable news networks, or what someone on the *New York Times* editorial page or YouTube had said.

If the American Colossus stopped getting good information—or if it stopped caring what was true and what was false—it was destined to become power without responsibility. Just another scorpion.

She held her hands to her face, inhaled slowly, and willed herself to keep it together.

After a long silence, Raquel asked, "Katrina, how much vacation time do you have saved up?"

Katrina paused. "Uh … a lot."

"You and Alec should go," Raquel declared. "Your doctor told you to avoid stress—well, here's the opportunity. Go on vacation, paint a nursery, just do all the things in life you've been putting off because of what we do."

Katrina looked at Alec, and they reached out and held each other's hands.

"Great," Katrina said, with a little laugh. "Now all I have to worry about is this pregnancy and the possibility that someone is still out there, trying to kill us."

After a long sigh, Alec asked, "What are we going to be coming back to?"

Raquel shook her head, and tilted back her chair, staring at the ceiling.

"Honestly, I have no idea," she lamented. "I've wondered if this team was living on borrowed time. Half the times we survived the organization-chart reshuffling and the chopping block because people forgot we existed." She shifted forward and shrugged. "Maybe we're just not compatible with how this agency sees its mission anymore."

"It's a different world from when we started," Dee chirped. "After nine-eleven, as bad as it was, it was simple. Stop the next attack, catch the bad guys, whatever means necessary." She sighed, realizing that the seemingly simple directive had taken the CIA into murkier and murkier waters. Americans could argue whether black sites, enhanced interrogation, waterboarding, extraordinary rendition, and all the rest of the peak War on Terror tactics were morally justified. But even the most ardent defenders would recognize an organization that wholeheartedly adopted the practice of inflicting pain upon prisoners was not what any American intelligence organization would *want* to be.

"Now?" Dee gestured to the television in the corner. "A prerequisite of national defense is a widespread belief that the country is worth defending. Lots of Americans hate each other's guts. They're convinced the real 'bad guys' are their neighbors and politicians they didn't vote for, not Xi Jinping or Vladimir Putin or the Iranian mullahs."

Ward cleared his throat.

"The world's not that different. What's changed is our willingness to see the world as it is," he muttered. "Lotta people in this country want the problems of the world to go away. I can't blame 'em, I feel the same way myself sometimes. But the problems over there never seem to stay over there. We're too angry at each other to see what's happening—those five storms or whatever Sanai was rambling about."

CHAPTER FORTY-THREE

AUGUST 13, 2021

Alec could have gone to any Trader Joe's, but he picked the one at the intersection of Little River Turnpike and Pickett Road because it had a Total Wine next to it. Katrina couldn't drink, but that didn't mean Alec wasn't going to go to his happy place, staring at a wall of bottles of exotic microbrews and assembling his six-pack of oddities. He didn't know if working at a microbrewery was as happy as it seemed—working with beer was probably much less fun than consuming it—but the funny caricatures, pun-filled names, and colorful art certainly made those small independent breweries feel like an ongoing party of goofy personalities that just happened to produce and ship beverages on the side.

The past three weeks had ended or alleviated some forms of stress for Katrina and Alec but cracked open some two-liter bottles of new stresses.

They spent one weekend and change visiting Katrina's parents in the Bukharian Jewish community of Miami Beach, Florida. Both sets of parents were thrilled at the thought of becoming grandparents. Abraham and Ziva Leonidivna concluded they didn't like the prospect of living several states away from their grandchildren and announced their intention to move closer. Katrina suggested they move back to Queens and lamented that the Washington D.C. area didn't have much of a Bukharan Jewish community. After immigrating to the U.S., the

Leonidivnas had learned early on that while they shared religious beliefs and certain cultural traditions and felt welcomed by other Jewish communities—native-born, Israeli, Russian, Ukrainian, or Persian—none of those other those Jewish communities ever quite felt like a precise fit, the way they felt among neighbors who remembered the old country.

"There's a Bukaran Jewish community in Atlanta," Alec observed.

"But that's almost as far away as Miami Beach!" Abraham objected.

Alec gave his father-in-law an innocent look. "Is it, now?"

Then Alec and Katrina rented a car and drove up to spend another few days with Alec's parents in Nag's Head, North Carolina.

Alec particularly enjoyed the visit to his parents, in large part because his impending parenthood meant he had beaten his two older brothers in what had been an exceptionally slow-moving competition to give Joseph and Aneta grandchildren. If Katrina's pregnancy ran smoothly—Alec instinctively knocked on wood every time he mentioned it—he would be ahead of his brothers Martin and Michael, two to zero. This led to phone and Zoom calls that featured a blizzard of spectacularly unsubtle nudges to Martin and Michael, inquiring when they were going to meet nice girls, settle down, and get married. The cascade of excuses was spectacular.

After their trips, Katrina and Alec had begun parenthood preparation in earnest. They indeed painted the spare bedroom that would become a nursery, a neutral yellow as they hadn't wanted to know whether the twins inside Katrina were two boys, two girls, or one of each.

The couple assembled two cribs, a changing table, and the diaper caddy that promised to keep horrific smells away but that every parent they knew said wasn't quite as effective as advertised.

For the longest time, Alec had believed working with the Dangerous Clique was the only job that he—and likely Katrina—could truly be happy. With minimal supervision and input from Stern or most of her predecessors, the completion of each mission meant a new blank page, waiting to be filled with new assessments, analyses, and plans of action. Alec and the rest of the team could choose from any trouble in the world, look for someone who represented a threat to U.S. interests, and figure out a way to make that person's life miserable. The travel was frequent, the scenery was always changing, the adrenaline was regular, the camaraderie made work feel like hanging out with a close-knit group of friends, and when things went right, the sense of accomplishment was unparalleled. At their Christmas party a few years ago, when a long-lost friend had asked the couple what was new, Alec cheerfully answered, "Katrina killed the mastermind of Atarsa with a dead-center headshot from across the room. How have you been?"

Maybe age was catching up with Alec. Maybe it was the prospect of having children. But for some reason, he wasn't itching to get back to work, and dreaded travel. Maybe a desk job wouldn't be so bad. Raquel regularly joked that she was unimpressed with the "kids" coming out of the Farm these days, but sooner or later, somebody younger was going to have to do what Katrina, Alec, and the rest of the team did.

Alec decided it was time to ask Katrina if the two of them should ask for desk jobs in Langley when her maternity leave ended.

He had just put his assembled six-pack and groceries in the back when he turned and something heavy and metal collided with his face. Pain exploded outward from his nose and cheeks, reverberating around his skull, shooting down his neck and up to his scalp. He closed his eyes, winced, and tried to open his eyes but couldn't—passing into unconsciousness.

***

Despite the crowded parking lot, only a handful of shoppers saw what happened, and only much later did they relay what they witnessed to anyone in law enforcement. A trio of men—all big, burly, wearing sunglasses and Covid masks—had converged on the man's car. When he turned from putting his groceries in the back of his SUV, one of the men had hit him across the face with a wrench. The man was knocked out cold, and within seconds, a black GMC Vandura cargo van—one so old, it might have gone back to the 1980s—pulled up behind the man's prone body and the three assailants. The van's side door slid open and the three men tossed him inside and hopped in themselves. Within twenty seconds, the van had zipped past the Einstein Bagels and exited to Pickett Road, disappearing as it sped north.

About two minutes passed before someone told the Trader Joe's general manager about what they had seen, and then the general manager's call to 911 had been directed to a Fairfax City emergency operator instead of Fairfax County, as the shopping center was directly on the line between the two jurisdictions. The Fairfax City emergency operator told the general manager to call the county police, as the listed address was in their jurisdiction.

By the time the first patrol car arrived, the black van was long gone. But the officer diligently took a statement from the woman who spoke to the general manager.

"So, three guys come up to another guy, who's loading groceries, hit him and knock him out cold, grab him and throw him into a van, and speed off," the Fairfax County police officer summarized. "And nobody else seemed to think this altercation was unusual or worth calling 911 about?"

The woman shrugged. "You have to understand, parking is always a madhouse here."

CHAPTER FORTY-FOUR

When the knock came on the door, it awoke Katrina Lenonidivna from a restless sleep, filled with dreams that were not quite nightmares but had a persistent tone of anxiety and menace, the way spooky music in a horror movie trailer can make mundane images of suburban domestic bliss seem ominous and foreboding.

Katrina saw an African American woman in a plainclothes suit and two Fairfax County police officers through the peephole and braced for the worst.

The woman began, hesitantly, bracing herself for a wide range of potential reactions: "Does Alec Flanagan live at this address?"

"I'm Katrina Leonidivna. Alec is my husband. What happened to him?"

The detective nodded. "His vehicle has been abandoned and we have eyewitnesses saying he was abducted."

***

The woman at the door, Detective Lucia Robbins, had dealt with a handful of kidnapping cases in her law enforcement career, but they were nothing like this—custody disputes, one creep who had attempted to talk schoolkids into his car, and the abduction of a witness who testified against a particularly vicious local gang, the Reccless Tigers. The description of multiple kidnappers, operating quickly and efficiently, made Robbins suspect the parking lot abduction outside Trader Joe's was related to a gang.

But Katrina Leonidivna did not react like any other wife or family member whom Robbins had ever dealt with. Katrina nodded calmly, asked for details, and immediately called a number she had on speed-dial. Within a few moments, Robbins found herself on speakerphone with an FBI special agent Elaine Kopek who, upon getting the full account, declared that Flanagan's abduction was likely connected to matters of U.S. national security and that the investigation would be managed by the bureau.

Robbins wasn't pleased. "State and local law enforcement agencies are not subordinate to the FBI," she curtly declared into the phone.

"Oh, I want you to keep looking for him," Elaine replied. "You keep doing everything you would usually do. But at this point, Alec's abduction is likely connected to his work at the agency, and the threatening note that his team received. And if that's the case, whoever took Alec has probably already taken him out of your jurisdiction."

***

Within an hour, Kopek was at Liberty Campus, and Dee had established a teleconference with the FBI's Strategic Information and Operations Center. Katrina and Raquel were already there, and Katrina had rather brusquely brushed off expressions of sympathy.

"Let's just find Alec," she kept repeating. Clearly, One-Eyed Moussa hadn't been the mastermind who was targeting them. But everyone else from 2003 was dead. The questions kept running through her head. Who was left? Who was tormenting them, and now dared take her husband away from her? She and her team had been doing this a long time—a kidnapping in broad daylight on American soil was a spectacularly audacious move, even for the rogues' gallery of foes they had fought over the years.

Fairfax County and Virginia state police had distributed a BOLO and APB with Alec's driver's license photo. The witnesses from the Trader Joe's parking lot were being reinterviewed for any additional details they could recall, with a particular focus on the description of the van.

Shortly after Ward arrived, steaming and fuming, the bureau announced that they had set up systems to flag the use of Alec's credit cards.

"This wasn't thieves," Ward said firmly. "Thieves steal things, they don't kidnap people. This is whoever set up the Front Gate Bomber!"

Even Patrick Horne had arrived and surprised everyone by being vaguely reassuring.

"That may be the case, but if whoever this is wanted Alec dead, they would have just shot him right there in the parking lot," Patrick declared. "All other things being equal, Alec is alive. Whoever took him wanted him in one piece. Ordinarily I would suspect a ransom demand, but there are much easier ways to make money than kidnapping a CIA employee. A possibility I don't think we can rule out is some foreign intelligence service getting way too cocky and operating through cutouts."

Katrina stared at the table and wondered if the Russian FSB knew who had killed Sergei Markov. Perhaps Zoya had told Moscow, or Markov's friends, the truth.

Patrick gestured to Raquel. "Can I speak to you in your office?'

***

Raquel closed the door behind her.

"What's up?"

"I've discreetly notified all of our personnel to keep their eyes open for Alec and asked my team with the DNI to review anything that pointed to anyone plotting an abduction of agency personnel, going back years," Patrick declared. "It's a long shot, but I figured it was worth it."

"Thank you," Raquel exhaled.

"But there's something else I think we need to talk about," he said, looking at his shoes briefly. He raised his head. "How certain are we Alec didn't fake his disappearance?"

"What?" Raquel frowned. "We're a hundred percent certain! There are witnesses!"

Patrick shook his head. "What's Alec's mental state right now? He just had somebody pledge an intent to hunt him down and kill him, his career just derailed, and he's about to become the father of twins. He wouldn't be the first man to snap under the pressure of impending fatherhood."

"Patrick, stop wasting my time with this." She reached for the door.

"Wait!" Patrick insisted. He took a deep breath and rubbed his eyes.

"Look, you know Alec and I have a history, but I'd never do wrong by Katrina, and that's why I'm bringing this up where she can't hear us," he said. "I'll move heaven and earth to find the big idiot, but I'm just asking—could this be him panicking? He's got every reason to freak out. He's older than most new fathers. And it's one thing to live with life-and-death risks when it's you, or your wife, or your friends. But a child or children change everything. He's facing something unlike anything else he's ever dealt with. I'm just saying it wouldn't shock me if Alec felt overwhelmed and wanted to escape everything in his life that is stressing him."

Raquel paused. As Patrick laid it out, it didn't seem quite so unthinkable.

"People go through intense changes when they're about to become a parent! Katrina's always been the gorgeous, unflappable assassin—and now she's barfing on people! Alec always thought he was this wisecracking hero, and now he's about to transform into the sleep-deprived, bags-under-his-eyes, suburban dad in sweatpants with spit-up on his shirt, trudging through the aisles of Wal-Mart at two a.m. because they're out of formula."

Patrick painted a vivid image. But Raquel wondered if Alec could successfully completely hide a deep-rooted internal panic.

Finally, she shook her head. "Not buying it," she declared firmly. "Alec's problem isn't burying his emotions and hiding them from the rest of us, it's the opposite. When something's on his mind, he never shuts up about it."

***

Raquel returned to find that Elaine had taken over a cubicle and seemed to be getting somewhere in the investigation.

"Dee, open up the file that just arrived in your e-mail," she instructed. A moment later, she started narrating. "We went through traffic camera footage of all of the surrounding intersections. We identified a black van—within a few minutes, it was on the Beltway, heading north toward I-95."

"Did we get the plates?" Ward asked.

"Take a look," Elaine grumbled, gestured in frustration to the screen. On the video, the license plate of the van seemed to be glowing white light, with no discernable numbers or letters. "My guess, some sort of acrylic and resin reflective tape or gel. It looks normal to the naked eye but obscures the image on video. They're smart. Did their homework."

"Foreign intelligence?" Raquel guessed.

"Nah, you can learn how to do this on the Internet," Elaine sighed. "But this is different from Godula's truck bomb. He was an angry nut, sloppy, didn't check and test his detonator. Hiding your plates from traffic cameras like this? This is thinking two steps ahead. Careful, methodical, knowing how we operate and using countermeasures."

Ward paused, realizing that if Alec were here, he would have joked that he would get that reflective resin and never deal with a red-light camera again.

Raquel speculated that there could only be so many black vans on Interstate 95. Within a half hour, the agency and bureau's contacts at the Virginia Department of Transportation and state police had reviewed traffic camera footage to find the van again, now approaching Baltimore in the left-hand lane, above the speed limit but not quite fast enough to stand out from the rest of the traffic.

Katrina studied the screen.

"They're in a hurry."

***

The hunt for the black van appeared to end a half hour later, when Maryland State Police thought they had spotted it north of Baltimore. But the police found only two construction workers who spoke limited English inside, with no sign of the missing Alec Flanagan. Subsequent investigation determined that this van's license plates had no reflective resin; the police had lost the van.

The FBI expanded the BOLO—be on the lookout—to state police and highway patrols up the east coast. A few hours later, the New Jersey State Police thought they had found a black van matching the description that had no license plates just past Exit 16W on the New Jersey Turnpike. But instead, the state troopers found a small group of human traffickers.

After a few hours of mounting frustration at Liberty Campus in northern Virginia, Elaine Kopek asked law enforcement agencies to stop looking for black vans, and instead look for any van with license plates that did not appear on traffic cameras.

Ninety minutes later, the NYPD responded they had hit the jackpot. A red van that otherwise matched the make and model of the previous traffic camera footage with reflective plates had driven into a parking garage at 25 Albany Street in lower Manhattan.

Further examination of the video of the van entering the garage determined that the bottom of the red van had stray bits of black, as if the van had once been covered in black spray-on matte finish that was designed to be peeled off quickly.

CHAPTER FORTY-FIVE

Elaine put in a call. The FBI had a helicopter not in use that day, an American Eurocopter single-engine AS350 B2 that could carry one pilot and up to six passengers. With a top cruising speed of roughly 152 miles per hour, that helicopter could get her, Katrina, Ward, Dee, and Raquel from northern Virginia to the downtown Manhattan heliport at Pier 6 in about an hour and a half.

The FBI's Strategic Information and Operations Center communicated to the New York office that the kidnapping case involving the black-turned-red van involved national security issues and was a high priority to the Central Intelligence Agency—and that the director had personally requested the FBI leave no stone unturned. CIA Director Barbara Stern was infuriated with Alec after the angry meeting in her office, but she wouldn't—and couldn't—treat Alec's kidnapping as anything less than a major crisis. In addition to the Dangerous Clique's anger over her leadership, the agency's many veterans of Afghanistan were grumbling with how she had acquiesced to the president's deeply flawed vision for withdrawing from that country. The rank and file were growing restless; Stern needed to reassure them that she believed in pulling out all the stops to protect agency personnel—even if the endangered soul was a notorious wiseass like Alec Flanagan.

For better or worse, Kopek had a preexisting relationship with the new assistant director of the FBI and chief of the New York field office—her immediate superior from eighteen years ago, Raphael Davino. He and his team greeted her as she and the rest of the team emerged from the FBI helicopter.

"Kopek. Glad you're still around and kicking. So, this is the CIA's notorious gang?"

"They're the Dangerous Cli—you know, just bring us up to speed."

Davino shook his head dourly, in a way that unnerved Katrina, Ward, Raquel, and Dee. Elaine knew that deep existential depression was Davino's default facial expression.

"My guys have been scanning traffic camera footage," he said, leading them toward a row of black government SUVs. "Before going to the garage, a red GMC Vandura cargo van with reflective plates stopped by the freight and delivery entrance of One World Trade Center. They unloaded one large crate onto a wheeled cart, and three men brought it inside, while the fourth moved the van to the garage."

"Big enough to hold a grown man?" Elaine asked.

"Uncomfortably," Davino nodded. "Assuming that's your missing man, the good news is we can narrow down his location to one building." He pointed up. "The bad news is that it's one of the biggest buildings in the world."

Katrina paused, and her knees seemed to wobble. Elaine, Ward, and Dee immediately grabbed her sides, fearing she would faint.

"I'm okay," Katrina said, wincing.

"What is it?" Dee asked.

Katrina looked up at the Freedom Tower with trepidation and swallowed hard. "Agent—"

"It's assistant director, but my friends call me director," Davino responded. No one could tell if he was joking.

"I don't think my husband's abduction is simple kidnapping or even tied to espionage," Katrina declared. "Whoever took him could have taken him anywhere—some abandoned warehouse or safe house or out to the middle of nowhere. These bastards took him straight to the biggest skyscraper in New York City, right next to the site of the biggest terrorist attack in American history, a place crawling with cops."

Davino's expression somehow managed to shift from dour to even dourer. "What are you saying, Mrs. Flanagan?"

Katrina was sufficiently worried to ignore one of her biggest pet peeves, being called by her husband's surname. "I think whoever took my husband picked this location because they're planning something big and symbolic. This isn't just a kidnapping. I think this is terrorism."

***

Built for the astonishing sum of $3.9 billion, One World Trade Center, commonly called the Freedom Tower, was the tallest building in the United States. It was also the tallest building in the Western hemisphere and ranked as the sixth-tallest building in the world at 104 stories high. The building's total height, including the spire, is 1,776 feet—designed deliberately to reference the year of the signing of the Declaration of Independence.

One World Trade Center's top floor is officially designated as floor 104, even though the tower only contained ninety-four actual stories.

The building encompassed a gargantuan 2.6 million square feet, with eighty-six usable aboveground floors, with seventy-eight floors used for offices.

Somewhere in that colossal tower was one missing Alec Flanagan.

***

Katrina paused before getting into the black SUVs.

"These SUVs just scream government," Katrina said, throwing up her hands and shaking her head disapprovingly. "If we roll up to the tower in these, with you guys in suits and earpieces, looking like the Men in Black, we might as well announce to Alec's kidnappers who we are and that we're here!"

"Nobody's going to think we're the Men in Black," Davino objected. Slightly doubting his own denial, he quickly removed his dark sunglasses.

Elaine scoffed. "Raphael, you dress like an undertaker. Katrina's got a point. We'll take an Uber or something."

"Element of surprise is gonna be hard to keep," Ward said, looking up at the tower. "Whoever this is, we know they studied us, talked to our old enemies, and recognized Alec. Good chance they know our faces, too."

Katrina nodded. She suddenly reached out and took Davino's sunglasses.

"Grab hats, sunglasses, and Covid masks," Katrina instructed. "It'll help a little."

Davino started instructing Katrina to be careful with his sunglasses, because they were some designer brand. Elaine, sensing Katrina's growing impatience with her colleague, tried to steer the conversation in another direction.

"Has anyone tracked down video footage of where those guys took the crate once they were inside the tower?" Elaine asked.

"Nah, my guys already talked to building security, and they said—"

Davino paused, as if he had just realized something important.

"They said what, Davino?" Elaine sensed whatever it was, it was something bad.

"They said the building's video surveillance system had been glitchy since this morning," Davino said slowly. "Their tech guys were looking at it, thought it was the usual problems with a software update, but … now I don't think it's a coincidence."

"Ya think?" Katrina muttered softly.

CHAPTER FORTY-SIX

Where the hell was he? Wherever he was, it was under construction, maybe some sort of office suite. The doorways had plastic tarp zipper doors for dust protection, and the floors were covered with taped-together patches of cardboard from wall to wall. Exposed wiring hung from holes in the ceiling, and the room was lit by well-worn portable construction lamps. The room had a couple of office chairs like the one he was tied to, a pair of folding card tables, and a laptop upon one of them. A massive, seven-foot-tall and eight-foot-wide mirror leaned against a wall, waiting to be installed.

Through a doorway, Alec saw three men who might as well have been giant slabs of beef, dressed in dark gray work coveralls, elbow pads, and knee pads. He had a vague memory of being in a van with them. The malevolent trio noticed he was awakening, and then injected him with something. All the helpless Alec could do before passing out again was ask whether the injection had been fully approved by the FDA or was merely under an emergency use authorization.

Alec realized he was tied to an office chair, looking down and seeing a pair of plastic zip-tie flex cuffs on each wrist, binding him to the armrest. He pulled and felt similar pressure around his shins and ankles.

Alec realized that in addition to binding his hands and legs to the chair, someone had apparently had fun tying up his thighs, midsection, and shoulders with black electrical tape. He could breathe, but he didn't like the constricting feeling.

"Somebody really enjoyed themselves doing this," Alec mumbled.

The double girls chuckled.

He realized he wasn't seeing double; there were two women, who were identical to each other. Twins.

Alec knew he had seen their face before, but the throbbing in his head left him seeing double, with the same smiling face on either side of him. His mind felt disassembled, and Alec felt like he had to put all of his neurons back together, piece by piece, like they were Legos.

"Why am I running into so many pairs of twins all of a sudden?" he muttered. "What, is this kidnapping sponsored by Doublemint?"

The twins smirked at each other, and then smiled at him, but not in a way that made Alec feel reassured. He felt like dinner.

One of the twins took a step to the door.

"He's awake. Well done, we'll take it from here, boys," she cooed. "Stay close, we've still got a lot to do after this." The three men in the doorway turned and stepped away, as if they didn't want to see what was coming.

The other twin dropped her smile, stepped closer, and brought her face inches from his. "I've waited so many years to ask you this," she said, studying his face intensely. "When you killed Linus Strauss ... did you hesitate at all?"

"What?" Alec asked in confusion. He thought back to that fateful night.

"Answer the question," the twin demanded, seething. "Did ... you ... hesitate?"

"No, as a matter of fact, I didn't," Alec said.

His still-foggy mind remembered how Ward had nodded in approval that night, and how proud Alec felt. Always distant from his two older brothers, Alec had wanted a wizened, tested, well-worn male role model. While he was technically a year younger, Ward suited that role perfectly. Alec believed he had passed the former Army Ranger's test that night.

"You knew nothing about him, did you?" the girl asked.

Alec knew he had seen her face before—and finally a key Lego piece in his reassembling mind snapped into place.

"Madison Reed!" he exclaimed. "You're the baby-faced one running the Strauss Foundation."

"And I'm Tiffany Reed," the other twin declared. "Older by about seven minutes."

She paused.

"Linus Strauss was our father."

CHAPTER FORTY-SEVEN

Alec shook his head in confusion, then disbelief. "Wait, no. No. Can't be. Linus Strauss didn't have any children!"

Madison and Tiffany smirked at each other again, shaking their heads, if Alec was proving himself a hapless fool.

"Our father married a woman before he met our mother," Tiffany began. "It wasn't a happy marriage. She was apparently the kind of woman a man like our father was supposed to marry—some frigid high-society Connecticut WASP."

"Our father divorced her in 2002. He had already established a relationship with our mother, Victoria Reed. She was a professional escort." Madison announced it with no shame or hesitation. She noticed a small scoffing exhalation escape Alec's lips.

"Oh, you think there's something wrong with that? The world's oldest profession? Ever hear of Sydney Biddle Barrows? Descendant of the *Mayflower*, ran a multimillion-dollar high-class escort service in the 1980s. Thousands of powerful men as her clients. It's an industry. Marketing, health insurance, public relations. Our mother was a businesswoman. She knew how to use what she had to get what she wanted."

Alec looked down, then up at the twins. "So, she was your *good* parent."

"Some men said our mother was most desired woman in the city in her day," Tiffany said, with the kind of pride appropriate for a boast that her mother had won several Nobel Prizes. "But she did what a woman in her profession is never supposed to do. She fell in love with him, and he loved her."

Alec frowned. What the girls were telling him did not match the man he had killed in 2003. None of the intelligence they had hastily assembled for their dossier back then included anything about a paramour or children.

"He planned to marry her. He loved her, and us. Linus Strauss took care of our her, under the table," Madison explained.

Alec visibly recoiled, calculating this revelation. "Father of the year."

"He was going to take care of us and our mother!" Tiffany raged. "Until you killed him! See, he didn't leave any legal record of us, or his relationship with our mother. His will went into probate. Our mother had to hire some ambulance-chasing lawyer and file suit after suit to get any share of the fortune, even though we were his only children. But she was a strong woman, and things still might have turned out okay for us … if she hadn't gotten cancer."

Alec winced.

"Yes, Alec Flanagan, in this world, even the people who you think are *bad* get cancer," Madison hissed, her voice dripping with condescension. "We're flesh and blood human beings, just like you. Not so much fun to think about, when you're killing people like our father, now, is it?"

Tiffany continued, the pair walking around him in a circle, like sharks.

"It took years and years to sort it all out in the courts," Tiffany seethed. "DNA tests to prove paternity. Dad's ex-wife kept insisting she was entitled to his fortune, even though she signed a prenup. That bitch and her lawyers kept filing appeals to drag out the process, hoping mom would give up. During all of this, our mom was getting chemo, beating it, then the cancer would come back. Over and over again! Almost three years ago, the two fights ended, six weeks apart. First, mom died. Then the courts finally agreed, once and for all, that we were the legitimate heirs of Linus Strauss."

Tiffany stopped in front of him and grabbed his face by the cheeks.

"We would have had a happy life, if it wasn't for you! Dad's fortune might have helped her get into some clinical trials, finance research! But we didn't! Because *you*, Alec Flanagan, murdered our father in cold blood!" She released his cheeks from her grip, ready to savor her captive's sudden onslaught of guilt.

But Alec shook his head in disgust. "Yeah, well, I hate to be the one to break it to you when you're all ready to go Inigo Montoya on my ass, but your daddy was a psycho! He kidnapped kids and planned to kill them! He had a knife to a—"

And then, just before he finished the sentence, Alec had a terrible realization.

Linus Strauss had gone mad, and plotted to kill children, shortly *after* he had become a father. Strauss *knew* he had two daughters when he hired Magda and the Brotherhood of Eblis and plotted to murder five children on camera to prove a point about organized religion. He *knew* he had a woman who loved him. He knew he had all of this, and had thrown it all away, concocting a bloodthirsty sacrifice like something out of some ancient pagan ritual.

Fatherhood had not brought out all of Linus Strauss' paternal, nurturing, loving instincts. It must have terrified him, Alec realized. He strongly suspected that what Tiffany and Madison were telling him was their mother's edited and rewritten version of history. The one where Linus Strauss loved them and had planned to form a loving family but had been somehow unjustly struck down by an intruder—an intruder whom the girls had tracked to a black ops, off-the-books out-of-control CIA team.

As Alec thought through the ramifications, he wondered whether Strauss had pressured Victoria Reed to abort his children. Strauss may have fallen in love with Manhattan's most desired escort, but he didn't necessarily want to start a family with her. He was a multimillionaire in Manhattan, raking in money with his investments, enjoying Robin Leach's champagne dreams and caviar wishes. He had worked hard climbing to the top, and he wanted his life to be sex and money and a nonstop celebration of himself and prioritizing his own desires. He wanted parties and vacations and adventure and an endless avalanche of tributes to his ego. He hadn't signed on for the responsibilities of fatherhood, changing diapers, worrying about daycare, coaching soccer games, and helping with homework. Strauss had already grown bored with one marriage; Victoria wanted to drag him into another, this one for life, with a responsibility for new lives he would never escape. He had found his perfect sex goddess, and in his mind, she had betrayed him by wanting to be a mother.

If he had pressured her, Victoria had refused to abort their children, obviously, and maybe some dark, long-repressed, secret part of Linus Strauss was unlocked by his overwhelming fear of becoming a father. All of that disbelief and fear and resentment of how parenthood would change his life curdled into a murderous rage. Something had held back Strauss from killing Victoria or her baby girls, thank God. But Linus Strauss had been ready to kill *somebody*. Alec remembered reading disturbing statistics about the number of pregnant women killed by their boyfriends or husbands. The creation of new life marked a turning point, a sudden change away from the way things had been. Some psychotic people must see that sudden change as the end of a life, one that justified ending other lives.

And then Alec felt the metaphorical light bulb above his head. Organized religions told men they had to marry the women they loved. They told men like it was wrong to see a woman as a disposable object, and not commit to her. They instructed men to raise the children they sired.

Being caught in the cloud of 9/11 and extremism was just an excuse for Linus Strauss, Alec realized. In the end, he was enraged because organized religion told him that he couldn't keep living his life the way he wanted, and he had to prioritize the needs of others. And he lashed out at what had caused his world to change so suddenly and dramatically: children.

Linus Strauss had plotted an elaborate suicide-by-cop, and would kill some children along the way, because his new children promised to change his life against his will. And Alec had played the role Strauss had wanted all along.

"Hello!" Tiffany slapped Alec a few times. Alec realized he had spaced out, thinking through Linus Strauss' true motivations.

"Calm down, Tiffany," Madison said, with a strangely gleeful smile. "He's starting to realize he was the villain of this story all along."

She dragged a chair, and sat opposite him, uncomfortably close.

"So, there we were—eighteen, legal adults, with access to millions from the sale of dad's properties. Enough to finance a thorough search for the people who killed him. Police records indicated the FBI was there that night. FOIA requests with the FBI gave us just enough to confirm our suspicions that the official story about the robbery gone wrong was a lie. I mean, if this was just a routine break-in gone wrong, why did the FBI have files on it, anyway? We knew the redactions pointed to something classi-fied, something to do with national security. We swore we would do whatever it took to hunt our father's killer down. It took two years, Alec Flanagan. We even found some guy claiming to be a mole within the CIA, and it sounded like he could tell us every-thing. But when we asked about one of the names we had found associated with this secret team, the guy just disappeared."

Alec's eyes bulged.

"Wait, you found the mole?" Alec exclaimed. The twins' revelations were piling up in his head like one of Dagwood's sandwiches. "Who is it?"

"Just some pain in the ass who wouldn't help us!" Tiffany groused, with a dismissive wave of her hand. "Finally, we found this prosecutor over in Germany. This guy was investigating a claim that a few years ago, part of a CIA team—a man and a woman—had left some café in Berlin right before it blew up."

Alec realized that was when Katrina narrowly avoided being killed in an Atarsa bombing of Café Vernuft, after a meeting with her source nicknamed Rat.

Alec's expression betrayed his sense of getting caught with his hand in the cookie jar, and the twins laughed.

"Once we had your faces from closed-circuit television video…then we could start matching it to other databases," Madison crowed. "We got some of your aliases, your passport photos and records, and started putting together your past travels. We spent a lot of money in bribes. But the best part was learning all about you from your enemies—the Jaguar, the Iron Wolves, One-Eyed Moussa."

Alec bit his lip, contemplating how spectacularly compromised he, Katrina, and the rest of the team had been these past few weeks. He was fully clothed but might as well have been naked. He tried to shift gears.

"Say, did you notice any pattern in all of our enemies? Like the fact that they're all a bunch of psychotic murderers? And that maybe that makes my friends and me the good guys?"

"There's nothing good about you, Alec Flanagan," Madison declared. "There's nothing good about your wife, either, or your burly buddy with the big beard. You're murder for hire, just hiding behind an American flag. You kill people on behalf of the U.S. government. The same government that drone-strikes weddings, detains terrorists without a public trial, turns a blind eye to brutal regimes if they're 'pro-American,' and sells arms all around the world. You thought our dad's a monster, you think we're monsters … this whole time, you never saw that you're just another monster."

Alec remembered, years ago, Katrina expressing a fear late at night that she was becoming "just another scorpion."

"We know everything, Alec Flanagan," Tiffany boasted. "We know you and your monster wife are going to have some little monster kid."

That last word gave Alec a little hope. Clearly, the psychotic, vengeance-obsessed pair didn't know everything.

"Kids," Alec corrected. "Twins. Just like you two. And I can't help but notice that if you kill me, and leave my unborn children fatherless … that would mean you've done to my kids exactly what I did to you." He gave them a glare of satisfaction at their surprise. "Careful, you can get sick from consuming that much irony."

Madison and Tiffany exchanged a look.

"Who said anything about killing you?" Madison said in mock confusion. "Or your wife? Or your child or children?"

Alec exhaled. Then he looked at his captors in confusion. "So, wait, what are you going to do? Whine me into submission?"

Tiffany smiled a grin that made Alec more nervous—"crazy eyes," was the common term. "No, silly! We're going to destroy your children's future."

Alec suppressed a flinch at the threat. "What, you're going to keep them out of an Ivy League school?"

CHAPTER FORTY-EIGHT

After stopping in what may well have been the cheesiest and most overpriced tourist souvenir store in all of New York City, three-fifths of the remaining Dangerous Clique emerged in their best approximation of lower Manhattan camouflage. Katrina wore a purple NYU jacket, Yankees cap, and Davino's sunglasses. Ward opted for a black leather Brooklyn Nets jacket and black newsboy cap. Dee had refused to wear the Jets jacket that Katrina had recommended and opted for a deep blue and orange Knicks jacket. They all put on black Covid masks to further obscure their identities.

Raquel and Elaine had refused to change from their business attire. "The tower is an office building," Raquel said. "Most of the people inside have jobs."

"Lots of tourists going to the observation deck," Katrina retorted. "Even if this just buys us a few extra seconds, it might be worth it."

When they entered the building's massive lobby, they were nonplussed to find Davino and his men were already chatting with building security—and he and the dozen members of his team, with their earpieces and G-man postures, still looked like the Men in Black.

Now Raquel's patience was wearing thin. She gently pulled Davino aside.

"Davino, your team isn't exactly blending in," she whispered. "I thought we didn't want the kidnappers and/or terrorists to know the FBI was here looking for them!"

Davino took a moment to appreciate the Clique's hasty disguise efforts and one muscle in his face moved slightly in amusement.

"I'm sorry, are you under the impression this is a Langley operation? Because this is bureau, through and through," he declared—not quite obnoxiously, but treading right up to the line. In Davino's mind, he was the alpha wolf, asserting his dominance over the pack. But every woman on the team in front of him had dealt with these sorts of jurisdiction fights before.

"It's our man up there, Davino," Raquel stated coolly. "You cannot sideline us."

"The mobile operations center is not the sideline—"

Katrina reached up and put a seemingly reassuring hand on Davino's shoulder. Raquel braced for a volcanic eruption from Katrina, the exhausted, pregnant senior case officer who had dodged a truck bomb, been marked for death, and didn't know if her husband was alive or dead.

But instead, Katrina offered a sweet smile.

"Assistant Director Davino, there is no one I would rather have managing this operation than you," Katrina purred, zigging when everyone expected her to zag. "Elaine told me all the old stories of you guys in New York. If it hits the fan, I have absolute confidence that you and your team are the ones who can bring back my husband safe and sound."

Davino, who had been prepped for a turf fight, was confused. He looked at Elaine—he didn't think she had been particularly fond of him as a supervisor—but felt flattered. "Er ... thank you."

"I just need one thing from you," Katrina pivoted. "I've got a theory about where my husband is being held in this building. It's a long shot, a vague tenuous connection to a past operation of ours, and it could be nothing. All I want from you is the opportunity for Ward and me to go upstairs and check it out. It'll take … fifteen minutes, tops."

Davino studied Katrina.

"We've got a lot of ground to cover, and I figure this is a way for my team to be useful to you."

Davino swayed his head, not quite an affirmative nod, not quite a negative shaking of *no*.

"Okay, but take one of my men," Davino offered.

"I'll take Elaine," Katrina countered. "This isn't our first rodeo."

Davino weighed her counteroffer for a moment, then shook his head *negative*, and was about to speak, but Katrina spoke first.

"You're a pro, and I'm a pro," Katrina cooed. "I trust you, and you trust me. I would take one of your agents, I'm sure they're among the best, but I've never worked with them before, and we don't have time to get in sync. Elaine and Ward and I have done this before."

"Hell, this isn't even the first time we've raided a skyscraper this year," Ward quipped, thinking back to Fox Plaza.

Davino seemed reluctant, but finally nodded. "Fifteen minutes," Davino answered. He tossed Elaine an FBI walkie-talkie and pointed a finger at Katrina. "You see anything suspicious, you get out of there and my guys come in and take over!"

"With you guys watching our backs, I feel unstoppable," Katrina lied.

A moment later, they headed toward the elevators, with Ward and Elaine having no idea where Katrina was leading them.

"Since when have you had a long shot theory about where Alec is being held?"

Katrina let out a little grim chuckle. "Since the moment I scanned the list of building tenants and saw the Linus Strauss

Institute for Community Change on the twenty-second floor."
The eyebrows of Ward and Elaine leaped skyward.

"Hell of a coincidence, don't you think?" Katrina asked dryly.

Ward murmured to himself as the elevator doors opened.
"The Dangerous Clique will pay for its crimes from 2003."

CHAPTER FORTY-NINE

"See, killing you would barely be any punishment at all—you'd be dead," Tiffany said with glee. "Who wants that, when we can do something terrible, something that will have consequences you will have to live with, forever?"

Alec's mood darkened as Madison departed the room. She returned a few moments later, holding a heavy sack a bit bigger than a loaf of bread. She tossed it, and the sack landed roughly in Alec's crotch. He winced and caught a whiff of something that reminded him of cleaning solution.

"One floor above us, we've got a huge office just stuffed, floor to ceiling, with sacks of ammonium nitrate like that one. Picture a bunch of the Ryder trucks from Oklahoma City, all lined up next to each other," Madison described, with the cheerfulness of envisioning a dream exotic vacation.

"If it goes well, we'll send the top three quarters of the Freedom Tower crashing into lower Manhattan," Tiffany added, her eyes widening with excitement. "If it doesn't go well, it will be like the first World Trade Center bombing. Either way, it's going to freak people the hell out."

***

Knowing the fate of the towers that had previously stood near this spot, the architects and builders of One World Trade Center tried to foresee every conceivable terrorist threat.

The tower's cubic base was covered in luminous materials—a mixture of stainless steel and titanium—that was simultaneously shimmering, light-reflective, and blast-resistant.

The tower boasted three-foot-thick reinforced concrete walls in all stairwells, elevator shafts, risers, and sprinkler systems. There were also extra-wide stairwells with pressurized ductwork designed to ensure a supply of fresh air in case of fire, as well a dedicated set of stairwells exclusively for the use of firefighters, and biological and chemical filters throughout the ventilation system. The stairwells featured low-level emergency lighting and concrete protection for all sprinklers, as well as interconnected redundant exits, additional stair exit locations at all adjacent streets, and direct exits to the street from tower stairs.

What the architects, security builders, and small army of security consultants had not imagined is that a potential threat would plunk down the $31,250 per month for a five-thousand-square-foot office on the twenty-second floor, and then another $62,500 per month for an even larger suite of offices on the twenty-third floor. Yet by selling off just one of Linus Strauss' vacation homes, Madison and Tiffany Reed had nearly two million in cash and secured yearlong leases for those spots.

As tenants, the Linus Straus Institute on the twenty-second floor and RS Holdings LLC on the twenty-third floor could come and go, and bring in large crates, with minimal suspicion.

Once Madison and Tiffany sold off the Hamptons estate, they had more than enough to hire "employees" for their elaborate venture of revenge. The pair found Cody Washington, who was overqualified to lead their personal army.

Washington's once-promising Army career with the 75th Ranger Regiment had derailed after drunken nights and brawls during his deployment to Kosovo as part of Operation Joint Guardian. Facing a court martial, Washington laid out the horrors he had seen during his tour in the aftermath of the Balkan wars—everything from babies abandoned by their mothers because they had been conceived during rape, to booby-trapped grave sites, to bodies left hanging in the town square overnight. The formal wars and ethnic cleansing had stopped, but the campaigns of revenge continued. Washington described one former paramilitary member who casually remarked he had killed children during the war. When Washington asked him how he could kill a child, the man answered simply, "you aim a little lower." Washington said he had stopped respecting the lives of the civilians around him because they had so vehemently and passionately refused to respect or coexist with each other.

Washington narrowly avoided a dishonorable discharge, as military judges determined that Washington's actions were the result of post-traumatic stress and placed him on the Permanent Disability Retirement List. But his reputation was ruined, both within the ranks and in the lucrative world of military contractors. Cody Washington was an undisciplined hothead whose aggression and lack of impulse control made him a liability when it mattered most.

Back in the United States, Washington gravitated toward extremist movements, and when

Madison and Tiffany said they needed muscle, Washington knew the right men to contact. He used their cash to recruit and employ two dozen men, almost all with military or police experience, and almost all of whom had lost their jobs in those institutions with cause.

These men were easy to find, all eager to send a message to a government they had deemed irredeemably corrupt and a threat to the American people. These men had all variously believed that the federal government had created the coronavirus or used it as an excuse to seize control and suspend the Constitution—a seemingly paranoid argument that particularly cloddish lawmakers strengthened with idiotic, far-reaching, arbitrary quarantine and restriction edicts—or that the previous presidential election had been stolen, or various other conspiracy theories indicating that modern American life was a hideous series of sinister lies. And one or two of the men said they hadn't yet ruled out the theory about lizard people.

With a newfound army, it was relatively easy to accumulate sack after sack of ammonium nitrate, diesel fuel, and other explosive materials, as well as long stretches of wire and improvised detonators.

The twin sisters with the deep pockets had instructed Washington and his team: "Make it like that big shock wave that everybody saw in Beirut!"

Washington warned the sisters he couldn't guarantee that the blast would topple the tower at the twenty-third floor, bringing seventy-one stories of skyscraper down upon the streets of lower Manhattan, an unthinkable mass murder committed in the same spot for a second time in twenty years. But he was certain that, at minimum, their massive, room-filling bomb would create a blast at least as strong as the 1993 World Trade Center bombing, and many times more powerful than the Oklahoma City bombing. And if enough of the blast tore through the support of the rest of the tower's twenty-third floor ... perhaps the entire structure would topple.

Alec contemplated the monstrous scale of the sisters' plot.

"Either you're lying, and you are going to kill me, or you're not worried about me telling the world that you two were behind all of this."

***

Tiffany casually unwrapped a candy bar.

"Look, he's trying to think!" Tiffany giggled. "No, we're not worried. See, that's not even the big part. We're not just blowing up the Freedom Tower." She slowly and dramatically ate a piece of chocolate.

Madison gestured for and received one of the Kit Kat pieces.

"Part of our delayed inheritance was what our father kept from some tech company that spun off of GlobeScape before it went under—it was small search engine company trying to become a rival to Google," Madison explained between bites. "The company went under, but not before it had created some very useful tools for finding information from obscure corners of the Internet. They just never figured out how to monetize it."

She paused, noticing Alec had stopped taunting her. Mentioning the bomb upstairs had really rattled him, and this pleased her.

"We took what they had built—think of it as like an early Google, with really good ways of finding out how to reach people by e-mail or text," Madison continued. "We named it Gjallarhorn. It's the horn from Norse mythology that announces Ragnarok, the great battles that will end the world."

She paused again. No snark from Alec, no jokes about Thor or Loki, no cracks about dot-coms. He was sweating and, as far as she could tell, genuinely scared. He was beginning to realize how much they had thought through their plans, dotted the *i*s, crossed the *t*s, and methodically contemplated every detail.

"Moments after the bomb goes off, we've programmed Gjallarhorn to send out manifestos," Tiffany boasted with glee. "See, our GlobeScape AI scans people's social media histories to determine which groups they hate the most: Antifa, white nationalists, the militias, Proud Boys, the Deep State, Boogaloos, Incels, ISIS or other jihadists, anarchists, the Klan, QAnon, the cartels, Black Lives Matter, La Raza, Atarsa … the CIA."

"Right as the bomb goes off, millions of Americans will receive manifestos declaring that the bombing was the work of whichever group our AI determined they hate the most,"

Madison declared with an unnerving excitement. "Those manifestos will establish people's initial impression and understanding of what happened. When law enforcement says it wasn't these groups, the conspiracy theories will spread like wildfire. You know people will start saying the government is covering up the perpetrators because that group has infiltrated the highest levels of government, FBI, DOJ, the works."

Alec had a sinking feeling that the twin sisters' elaborate disinformation campaign would work. In fact, it might work exceptionally well. A disturbing number of Americans were eager to believe the absolute worst about those who disagreed with them politically.

"Atarsa had a good idea, they just didn't have the vision that we do," Tiffany boasted. "Once we do this, paranoia's going to blow up far and wide. Every faction in America will be convinced they're being scapegoated and that others are getting away with literal murder. The Second Civil War won't be two sides hammering it out. It's going to be the American Balkans, a million little factions leaving pipe bombs on each other's doorsteps."

"Every day's going to be Charlottesville or Ferguson or the Capitol Hill riot!" Madison squealed. "We're going to be long gone, off on an island resort in the South Pacific somewhere, sipping mai tais. We shorted the insurance industry, which will go under once every American city's crippled with riots. The next few months are going to make the summer of 2020 look like the best of times. And once we've got this country choking itself to death on its own hate and divisions? I'm no expert, but I'll bet China and Russia and Iran and the rest will get frisky. They've been looking for a chance to kick this country when it's down. Hacking, sabotage, disinformation, maybe even terrorism. By this time next year, you'll be lucky if the United States is still one country."

Alec tried to hide his dread and failed. The twins' plan sounded unnervingly like the forecast of five gathering storms from Sanai Sato. The last few years had been hellacious for America's social fabric; he couldn't say, with confidence, that the psychotic twins' plan wouldn't work.

"Now, I'll admit, there's a chance that the blast from the bomb upstairs is going to maim you," Tiffany warned in mock concern. "Hell, if it kills you, we're not gonna complain! But right now, the plan is to leave you...to live...in the squalor of this collapsing empire, knowing your children will have just enough memories of the fading glory to feel disappointed with the rest of their lives."

Madison smiled. "That's our revenge, sweetie. We're not ending your life. We're tearing the whole system down and ruining your children's lives. That's how you will pay for killing our father."

Tiffany and Madison saw genuine fear in Alec's eyes and turned to each other and shared a look of satisfaction.

Alec looked down and took some deep breaths.

"Oooh, he knows he's screwed, Tiffany!" Madison cackled. "No wisecracks or insults."

CHAPTER FIFTY

The first tenant of the twentieth through thirty-ninth floors of One World Trade Center was Condé Nast, the massive media company that published *Vogue, Vanity Fair, GQ, The New Yorker*, and other prestigious magazines. But the pandemic's disruption to work life and advertising revenue prompted the company to consolidate, opening space on the lower floors.

Now the twenty-third floor was entirely leased by RS Holdings LLC. Anyone who researched the firm would find scant business records and paperwork; the company described its business as "art and antiquity imports and exports" and appeared to be founded one month before the lease offer. The pandemic's lingering effect on Manhattan business life meant that One World Trade Center management was not about to turn down a client willing to pay a year's rent in advance—and that came with a letter of recommendation from a tenant that had moved in a year earlier, the Linus Strauss Institute for Community Change.

The only thing the managers of the building knew about RS Holdings LLC was that almost all their employees were large men and they always seemed to be moving massive crates into and out of the office space.

Beneath RS Holdings, the twenty-second floor housed offices for a real estate firm, a financial management company, and the Linus Strauss Institute.

Ward, Elaine, and Katrina exited the elevator on the twenty-second floor, walked down the hall, and found the seemingly nondescript door to the institute. Unlike the other offices on the floor, the institute had wooden doors instead of glass ones, and the blinds adjacent to the floor-to-ceiling window were closed. The double doors were locked.

Ward tried to peek between the blinds.

"Closed up the office early today?" he asked skeptically.

"That's what they want people to think," Elaine said, pointing to scuff marks on the floor. "Looks like the sort of tracks from a large cart, the kind you would use to bring a big, heavy, man-sized crate."

Katrina removed a set of lockpicking tools from her messenger bag.

"If we've still got the element of surprise, I want to keep it," she murmured.

Ward and Elaine positioned themselves on either side of Katrina, scanning the hallway. After a moment, Ward removed his Glock 20 and offered one of his smaller-frame spares to Elaine. "We're going to want all the stopping power we can get in there," he warned. "Fifteen ten-millimeter rounds can go hypersonic and go deeper into soft tissue."

She shook her head. "Glock 17 gives me two extra rounds before reloading," she explained, holding up her bureau-issued sidearm. "Seventeen shots of nine millimeters still gives me better odds than fifteen shots of ten millimeters."

Ward pantomimed adding numbers, and chuckled. "It was my understanding that there would be no math!"

Below them, Katrina grumbled. "I am trying to concentrate down here!"

***

Just three doorways away, Alec composed himself.

"Okay, I've got a counteroffer. Don't blow up the tower, and in exchange I'll give you everything you need to disgrace me."

The twins stared at him, curious enough to let him continue.

"Listen. In my wallet, in the change pocket, there's a small, flat thumb drive, one that plugs into a USB port. I figured there was a chance someday I might find myself in a situation where I would need leverage. On that thumb drive is every secret about the CIA I've ever learned. All the dirty laundry, everything in Harold Hare's secret diary, you name it. You can let the world know that I let you have it. I'll be considered a traitor—a pariah—and I'll face charges."

He paused. "Let me make the sacrifice for my children that…" He paused, knowing he had to choose his words carefully. "The sacrifice your father would have made for you." It was a lie, but it was what the twins wanted to hear.

Tiffany walked over to the table with his wallet, fished through it, and plucked out the thumb drive like a ripe berry from a bush.

"Mmm, a tempting offer," she said, examining the thumb drive carefully. "Here's what I'm going to do. How about we take what you're offering us, ensure you get disgraced and branded a traitor, and *then* we blow up the tower anyway?" she laughed.

Alec raged, strained against his bonds, and swore furiously as Tiffany walked over to her laptop, plugged the drive in. With one or two clicks, she decided to see what Alec had been hiding, right under their noses. With a wicked smile and a wink, she made a big, slow, showy demonstration of pressing the mouse button to open the video file.

The computer's speakers suddenly burst forth with a heavy, quick drumbeat, and the screen filled with the image of a tall, lanky redhead—who looked a little like Alec—dressed in a hideous late 1980s fashion—a striped shirt, black blazer, and white pants, dancing awkwardly behind an old-fashioned silver microphone on a stand.

We're no strangers to love…
You know the rules and so do I…

Had Tiffany and Madison been looking at Alec's face, instead of the screen, they would have seen his look of horror and rage quickly drop like a sandcastle hit by a wave, replaced by his own wickedly gleeful smile. Alec started laughing.

A full commitment's what I'm thinking of
You wouldn't get this from any other guy

"Did …" she gasped. "Did you just Rickroll us?"

Alec was laughing so hard, Tiffany wondered if he might choke to death.

"*Hahahaha!* That's not just a Rick Astley video!" Alec struggled to speak between bursts of hysterical laughter. "You've just activated—*hahahaha*—a tracing program that Dee designed! This location—*hahahaha*—just got sent to every law enforcement agency, the FBI, Langley—*hahahaha*—and my teammates! You're so screwed!"

Tiffany leaped across the room and started hitting Alec across the face. He wouldn't stop laughing, though.

"You're so—*haha!*"—little drops of blood splattered from his crimson-smeared lips. "Oh, my God! You're so stupid! *Haha!* You just walked right into it!"

Tiffany, swearing and enraged, hit Alec harder and harder until the chair he was handcuffed to flipped and he landed on his back with a painful thud. The three slabs of beef in jumpsuits rushed into the room, concerned about the commotion.

"Hey, is this trouble—"

"Yes! Yes, it is trouble!" Alec laughed from the floor. "You are in so much trouble!"

Madison looked up at the three towering men. "He says he's triggered an alarm! Get upstairs and make sure everything is ready to go!"

Behind her, Tiffany continued to whale blows down upon Alec, kicking and then punching. Alec kept enraging her further with his laughter. He was in terrible pain, but he wasn't going to let her know.

"Hey, uh … is your sister okay?" the first slab of beef asked.

Madison looked back and sighed. "She's fine. She doesn't handle adversity well."

The three beef slabs nodded and headed out of the room. Enraged at Rick Astley's promises and how they started to sound like a political campaign commercial—*never gonna tell a lie and hurt you, never gonna give you up, never gonna let you down*—Madison picked up her laptop and threw it to the floor, smashing it to pieces. Rick Astley finally said goodbye.

From the floor, Alec kept laughing.

"Hey, did you know the word *gullible* isn't in the dictionary? Look it up!"

This sent off another frenzy of slaps from Tiffany.

"Tiffany!" Madison shouted. But her sister was overcome by uncontrollable rage.

***

Katrina had found picking the lock tricker than she remembered—or perhaps being pregnant, coupled with the anxiety of her husband missing, meant her hands weren't as steady as she was used to them being. Thankfully, no one had come near this end of the hallway—even with the pandemic's effects fading, many of New York's professionals were still working from home, giving the office tower a strangely empty, almost abandoned feel.

"I've almost got it," Katrina whispered while wincing.

They stood, tensely, in the hallway, desperately hoping no oblivious office worker would stumble into the hallway, right before they raided the Strauss Institute.

Ward tilted his head. "Do you hear that?"

Elaine leaned her head against the door. "Music?"

Ward's eyes narrowed, as face was overcome by an expression of confusion. "Is that ...'Never Gonna—'"

Before he could finish the sentence, the FBI walkie-talkie on Elaine's belt squawked to life.

Dee's voice reverberated through it. "Alec's distress signal just activated, location is on the south side of this floor."

Katrina dropped the lockpicking tools in exasperation. "After all that ..." She rose to her feet, accepted Ward's offer of a Glock 20, checked that it was loaded and the magazine was full and prepared to breach the door.

"Copy that, Dee, the Linus Strauss Institute, we're right outside!" Elaine confirmed. "Davino, we're going in hard, right now! You're invited to the party, but we're not waiting!"

Davino answered with curses and the huffing and puffing sound of him running. "That's not what we agreed to—"

"The father of my children is in there!" Katrina hissed into the walkie-talkie. "Davino, once I'm done with whoever took him, you're welcome to whatever's left. You might need a mop," she warned.

Elaine and Ward exchanged a look, a little unnerved at the aggressive gleam in Katrina's eye.

CHAPTER FIFTY-ONE

"Tiffany!" Madison shouted. "That's enough! We've got to get out of here!"

Tiffany stood above Alec, having beaten him bloody but failing to stop him from laughing.

"I don't care about your trauma!" Alec laughed through bloody teeth. "I'm sorry you went through all that crap with your parents, but it's not my problem! I've got my own problems! Everybody's got their own problems! You could have done anything you wanted with your lives, and you've chosen to waste them—"

He was interrupted by the sound of gunfire from elsewhere in the office suite.

***

The three slabs of beef had gathered their satchels of weapons and rounds in a large room with twin rows of cubicles that stood between the institute's reception lobby and the under-construction inner break room that the twins were using as an interrogation chamber.

A moment earlier, they heard a loud *bang* and realized the office's front door had just been kicked in. The biggest beef slab grabbed his walkie-talkie.

"They're coming for us, front door!" he shouted, and within a second, his buddies started firing at the intruders. They were answered by gunfire and a woman screaming furiously.

"Where is Alec Flanagan?" Katrina demanded between gunshots. "Where is he?"

The trio of beef slabs ducked down behind a cubicle wall.

"Sounds like she's really pissed at him," the second beef slab observed.

Katrina had wanted to jump and roll toward cover, but her body wasn't feeling as nimble and mobile as she was used to, and she didn't know how much jostling and jumping and impacts were okay for her babies, particularly during her so-called geriatric pregnancy. She ducked down in a crouch and sort of scuttle-dashed to her right, scrunching in a spot behind the platform featuring the bust of Linus Strauss. The three beef slabs popped up and fired again; Katrina took a grim sense of satisfaction when their gunshots tore into the marble bust, and broke off pieces of Strauss' scalp and nose.

"Send out Alec, and we'll let you live!" Katrina shouted. "Otherwise, I'm going to make an example out of you!"

"Whatever, bitch!" One beef slab called out. His closest buddy laughed, and in their crouching positions, they high fived each other. "She's over in the corner," the beef slab whispered, and he raised his head a few inches above the cubicle wall, ready to fire.

Katrina popped up, used what was left of Strauss' marble head as cover, and fired five shots, with one going through the top of the head of the particularly obnoxious beef slab. The beef slab's body slumped backward, face frozen, staring upward and bloodied, as if someone had carved a divot right through the center of his scalp. The beef slab's shocked partners stared down in horror.

"Was I not *clear* enough?" Katrina shouted, incandescent with rage. "*Donde esta Alec Flanagan?! Где Алек Фланаган?! Arekkufuranagan wa dokodesu ka?! Alec Flanagan nerede?*"

CHAPTER FIFTY-TWO

Within the plastic-sheeted room, Alec, Tiffany, and Madison heard lots of gunfire and Katrina's livid voice screaming the same demand in multiple languages.

From the floor, Alec's laugh changed pitch, getting a little higher. "Oh, my God, you're so screwed! You're about to see why I never win any arguments with my wife!"

The twins realized how quickly the tables had turned and shared a panicked look.

Tiffany grabbed the sides of her head. "They weren't supposed to find us until—"

"I know!" Madison barked. She grabbed a walkie-talkie from the table. "We are under attack down here! Washington! I want you and every last one of your guys down here!"

***

Katrina, Ward, and Elaine drove the remaining two beef slabs farther back, behind the last row of cubicles in the room. All of them were crouched down, behind or underneath desks, tables, or cubicles, popping their heads out, peering to see where their enemy was, squeezing off a shot or two, advancing to the next spot, and then ducking back down. Ward felt like he was in a giant game of Whack-a-Mole and realized how much squatting he ended up doing on these missions.

Elaine was assigned to watch their six, and she was the first to spot the pair of rough-hewn men in similar dark gray overalls peering through the door they had just kicked down, cradling machine pistols with so many attachments they could easily be mistaken for submachine guns. When she saw they were armed, she fired a short burst of shots to halt them by the doorway, sending them diving to the floor. They scrambled over, pushed the waiting room couch over, and used it for cover.

Elaine sent a lot of shots through the couch and heard at least one howl of pain. *They've got far too much faith in that upholstery*, she thought.

"They've got backup coming behind us!" Elaine shouted, realizing that maybe the three of them should have waited for the FBI team after all. She grabbed the walkie-talkie. "Any day now, Davino!"

The walkie-talkie buzzed. "Oh, *now* you want me and my guys up there!" After a moment, he added, "Almost there! We're taking fire in the stairways!"

Elaine realized that two more men had appeared in the doorway where the first two had just been a moment earlier, before another half dozen shots sent them to the floor.

"Where are they coming from, a clown car?" She turned to where Ward had been a moment ago, but Ward had moved ahead a few more cubicles.

"I'm going to need you to cover me while I reload!" Elaine shouted. She looked around, keeping her head on a swivel, trying to keep an eye on multiple doorways at once.

Ward popped up above a cubicle wall and nailed one of the armed goons by the office entrance.

"Right in the pie hole!" Ward exclaimed, ducking back down. "Reload, I've got ya!"

Elaine peered out from underneath the desk. "Where's Katrina?"

Ward popped up and peeled off a few more shots, winging one of the other guys scrambling behind the overturned couch. Ducking back down, he leaned over. "Katrina tore off! She saw two figures going down a hallway!"

Elaine responded with an incredulous *what is she thinking?* frown, and slammed a fresh seventeen-round magazine into place. Ward shrugged.

"I know, right?" he said, scanning the doorway. "I'm used to being the wild man around here! Between Alec, the pregnancy, and all the guys shooting at us, I think she might be losing her cool! It's like watching Gal Gadot on a coke binge having road rage!"

Now Elaine popped up, and spotted one of the remaining beef slabs, plugging him right below his Adam's apple.

"That's funny!" she shouted. "You weren't this much of a kidder back when I first met you!"

"It's Alec's fault," Ward said, taking his turn to reload. "All these years, he's rubbed off on us."

Ward noticed some movement behind a doorway that had floor-to-ceiling semi-opaque plastic sheeting, sealed by a zipper. It was hard to see what exactly was moving back there, but someone was in that room under construction.

"We're at your floor!" they heard Davino announce over the walkie-talkie, and from the hallway beyond the institute office entrance, a combination of shouts of "FBI!" and "Put the gun down!" and gunfire. Apparently the third pair of reinforcements thought they could win a shootout with the FBI.

"Cover me!" Ward requested, and he rose to a running stance, and tore off toward the doorway with the plastic sheeting.

***

Instead of taking time to unzip or cut the plastic sheeting covering the doorway, Ward figured he could run right through it. He did, but then a chunk obscured his vision and he was tangled in it at the precise moment he needed to be ready to confront whoever was in the room.

He thrashed his arms, getting the plastic sheeting away, and saw the under-construction room was empty—except for a bloody Alec Flanagan, still tied and taped into a chair, lying on his back.

"Alec!" Ward gasped.

Alec turned his head and smiled with a bloody mouth.

"This is not how I expected today to go," Alec groaned. "I figure someone's stolen my groceries and beer by now. Really glad to see you, buddy!"

"Elaine!" Ward shouted, scrambling over, putting down his gun, and whipping out his tactical knife to start cutting away the tape and plastic restraints around his wrists and ankles.

"What did these bastards do to you?" Ward moaned, in deep concern. "Jeez, you look like they used you as a piñata! You're supposed to keep all that red stuff on the inside, buddy!"

Alec gingerly rose to his feet. "I'll explain later, but let's just say my Ransom of Red Chief strategy didn't work out the way I hoped," he said, punctuating his sentence with a long groan. "They heard you guys coming in and ducked out and are headed upstairs. We've got two big problems."

Then the giant mirror on the wall behind Alec shattered, pierced by a bullet. Alec fell to the floor again. Ward picked up his gun, but before he could pull the trigger, Elaine appeared in the now plastic-free doorway, and sent four rounds toward the doorway on the other side of the room, and there was a sound of a body falling back against the door.

"Okay, new rule, from now on, we wait for the FBI backup!" Elaine announced. She looked down at Alec and saw how bloodied he was. "Alec! Are you okay?"

Alec realized he had hit the floor and been pelted with mirror shards, leaving little cuts on his arms and knees.

"You're lucky that bastard was aiming at your reflection!" Ward muttered.

"Gets you seven years bad luck!" Alec shouted from the floor. He wiped the mirror shards off him.

"Okay, we've three big problems. Maybe more." He shook his head, as if trying to clear cobwebs, and blinked with effort, as if trying to clear his vision. "Wait, where's Katrina?'

"She came here with us!" Elaine said, putting a hand on Alec's shoulder. "She's hunting down the folks who took you. Apparently, your kidnapping unleashed all her brewing momma bear instincts."

Now Alec looked concerned, and his eyes bulged. "She's taking our children into a gunfight?"

"Well, they're kind of attached to her."

Ward grabbed Alec by the shoulders. "Alec, what are these problems?"

Alec winced. "First, you're grabbing two of the many, many places she punched me! *Urg-agh!* Second, one floor above us, there's a room full of ammonium nitrate! They gonna try to bring the whole tower down!"

Ward's face erupted in horror. "Who is 'they'?"

Alec waved his arms. "Oh, that's the best part! Linus Strauss had twin daughters we never knew about! Madison and Tiffany Reed!"

Elaine's jaw dropped.

"Eh, don't beat yourself up over it, your theory came closest!" Alec quipped. "I'd beat myself up over it, but the twins already did that." He grimaced. "Too long, didn't read version: they're psychos. Bin Laden agendas in Bella Twin bodies. Oh, and last big problem, somewhere on the floor above us, there's a computer that's gonna send out false claims of responsibility for the blast, pointing the finger at every nutjob extremist group in the country, from Antifa to the Klan."

Elaine groaned, contemplating the frenzy of paranoia, fear, accusations, and counteraccusations that would surely overtake the country. Then she paused. "Wait, won't the blast blow up the computer?"

Alec thought for a moment.

"They're going to send out the claim of responsibility before the blast," he realized. "Then when the bomb goes off, it's going to destroy the evidence!"

They heard the gunfight getting louder from the adjacent office.

"Please tell me the FBI is winning," Alec muttered.

Elaine nodded. "I trust Davino for this part of the job, but we can't wait for his team to get here!" She held up the walkie-talkie. "Raquel, you getting all this? We've recovered Alec, he's banged up, but alive! There's a massive bomb on the floor above us, and some computer that's going to send out a message designed to stir up paranoia and panic! We've got hostiles everywhere, and the FBI is still trying to fight their way to us!"

"Got it," Raquel echoed. "Where's Katrina?"

"She took off after some hostiles, we've lost track of her," Ward barked. "There are three of us and a lot of problems! The bomb takes priority, right?"

"Hell yeah, it does!" Raquel's voice squawked. "Dee's got the floor plan on her tablet here—four main office complexes above you, north, south, east, west! Usually, I'd want to keep you all together, but there's a lot of ground to cover and we don't know how much time we have! Can Alec move with you guys?"

Simultaneously, Alec answered "Yes," Elaine answered, "No," and Ward answered, "With difficulty."

CHAPTER FIFTY-THREE

Madison and Tiffany were livid with Cody Washington, as he and three of his men hustled them toward a stairwell. One of Washington's men entered the stairwell and descended a floor, checking to see if the path was clear. The two others knelt and held their Anderson Manufacturing AM-15 M-Lok pistols, which to the casual viewer would look like an MP5 submachine gun, with the shoulder brace, longer barrel, scope, and curved magazine. Washington's men knew the guns didn't have nearly as much power as a real submachine gun but figured the sight of them would terrify any New York City civilians who got in their way.

"You were supposed to handle this!" Madison shouted.

"Little girl, you are in a world you do not understand!" Washington barked back. "You two cuties chose to mess with the deep state, and now they're here to hunt you down! This isn't NYPD like we expected, those guys coming up are FBI! It's probably Peter Strzok's personal hit squad!"

His men elsewhere on the floor were only giving sporadic updates through the walkie-talkie, but it seemed at least three threats were converging on the twenty-second floor. A main FBI team had just arrived in one stairwell and was engaging a half dozen of his men. His men inside the Strauss Institute offices had been nearly wiped out by a bearded man and a woman in a suit, likely the Army ranger and FBI agent the twins had warned them to watch for. But the other one who entered with them—the

Eurasian woman—had seemed to disappear into thin air during the gun battle.

A few of Washington's men had taken up defensive positions between the Institute offices and the stairways, and one by one, they had reported all clear, not seeing any sign of anyone approaching and then they mysteriously stopped responding. Washington felt like his men, some of the roughest, most ruthless, and unscrupulous militiamen he knew, many of whom had done time in prison or military brigs, were being picked off like naïve teenage swimmers in a *Jaws* movie.

"That's why we paid you and all these guys!" Tiffany shrieked. "We're supposed to be long gone out of the city before the bomb goes off!"

They heard a lot of gunfire, and the sound of someone—judging from the tone of the voice, one of Washington's men—moaning in pain. The moaning stopped after another gunshot. Whoever was hunting them was relentless, methodically picking off the mercenaries, shooting to kill, and, if hit, leaving them no chance to play possum.

Madison noticed a twitch beneath Washington's left eye. Her big, muscular roughneck who boasted about how he was too much of badass for the U.S. Army to allow him in the Balkans was scared.

"Hanson, go take position at that corner!"

Hanson gave Washington a skeptical look. His eyes indicated he felt like he had been chosen as a sacrificial lamb.

"Get out there!" Washington snarled.

Hanson crept slowly, keeping his AM-15 raised, finger on the trigger, and crouched at the corner. He reached into a pocket, removed a small mirror, and thoroughly studied the hallway around the corner.

"There's nobody here, man," Hanson declared.

"If there's nobody here, why do our guys keep getting shot?" Washington demanded.

"Dammit, we're moving to Plan B," Madison announced, whipping out her cell phone and dialing. "Roger? This is Tiffany Reed. This is your chance at that big score we talked about. I'm going to need rapid extraction and a quick trip to Buffalo."

Washington turned back from his prone position.

"Who's Roger?" Washington demanded. "Trip to Buffalo? Is that some code?"

"Private executive helicopter service," Madison gloated as she covered the phone. "I figured getting out of the city might be complicated—traffic is a mess even when the city isn't dealing with an ongoing terrorist threat!" She turned back to the phone. "Roger, we need pickup ASAP at the helipad on the top of the Freedom Tower! Don't file any flight plans, don't worry about the FAA! Just get there, and get us out, and we will make you an exceptionally wealthy man!" She hung up before he could haggle.

"Let's go, Tiffany, up the stairs, not down," she declared. "Good luck, Washington!"

Washington exchanged surprised and incredulous looks with his remaining man by his side, Conrad, and Hanson, crouched down the halls.

"I told you those chicks were crazy, man," Conrad muttered.

"Which ones aren't?" Washington sighed.

***

Katrina tried to control her breathing and listened carefully.

After Katrina saw two young women and four burly men in coveralls flee out of the institute offices, she tore away from Elaine and Ward—only to find that the retreat of the sextet from the institute was bring covered by four other men, all taking positions in the hallways of the twenty-third floor.

Katrina shot the glass door of the closed offices of the financial management company across the hall, and dove inside. *Land on your limbs, protect your womb*, she thought. She heard shouting from the goons in the hallway, but they didn't seem eager to pursue. If, as she had suspected, the base of operations in the biggest skyscraper in the country was not a coincidence and terrorism was some part of their plan, her team's assault had disrupted something—but what, and for how long?

Once Katrina felt secure that no one was trying to pursue her into the financial services firm office, she reached into her messenger bag. She removed the item she thought might have been useful if circumstances permitted a slower, more thorough search of a location where Alec was being held: The RANGE-R radar system, a small handheld device that claimed to allow the user to see through walls. A few years ago, Ward used one while monitoring an Atarsa sleeper, but contended the readings were defective—"I could tell where he was in the house, but the images made him look like a giant bug or something" was how Ward had put it. The device used radio waves, like the stud finders that people used for construction projects, and that every dad in America joked he kept accidentally setting off.

Katrina knew there were four men, armed with small submachine gun–like short rifles that might have been MP-5s, taking defensive positions in the hallway on the other side of the wall. She walked along the wall, maneuvering around desks and filing cabinets and bookshelves, periodically pressing the RANGE-R against the wall. Finally, she saw exactly where the first man was.

She raised her gun to the level and position of his head and pressed it against the wall.

***

Robinson knew this was it, the grand battle, the day that would be remembered like the Boston Tea Party. They had struck hard at the deep state, kidnapping some CIA goofball, but that apparently had more to do with some vendetta those rich twins had. No, he and his patriotic brothers would really strike a blow once they blew up the Freedom Tower. Real freedom had been blown up a long time ago, he knew. Everybody rejected what Timothy McVeigh had been saying just because he blew up a daycare center. The government was full of power-mad and petty bureaucrats, each eager to control the lives of the citizens. Mask them, force vaccines into them, take away their guns, arrest them if they leave their homes, take their money, take them off social media for dissenting. The pandemic had made the government's true agenda clear: force the citizenry into obedience and submission.

Bringing yet another skyscraper crashing to the ground will get their attention, Robinson thought, smiling.

***

That was the last thought Robinson had before a round tore through the wall, through one side of his head above his ear, piercing his skull, penetrating through his brain, and exiting the other side, piercing the other wall. His body tumbled to the floor, shocking and frightening his partners. It took them about five seconds to realize Robinson had been shot through the wall, and they fired a few shots at the spot where the kill shot emerged—but Katrina had already moved to another location, low to the floor.

This process repeated itself three more times. Washington's men in the hallway moved, retreated, got lower—and each time, within a few minutes, Katrina figured out a clear shot from behind the wall next to them. One time she chose to remove a framed motivational poster asking, WHAT DOES YOUR FUTURE HOLD?

After the third militiaman succumbed to another single headshot, the fourth just emptied all of his rounds into the wall—but Katrina had already ducked low and behind a metal filing cabinet.

The fourth and last man reloaded and fired more shots—creating a noisy racket that obscured the sound of the office suite's back door opening.

"Where are you?" the enraged militiaman screamed in frustration and rage at the bullet hole–riddled wall.

"Right here." He snapped his neck to his left, just in time to see Katrina's gun in his face. His eyes huge, he gasped in shock, and she pulled the trigger.

"I told you I was going to make examples of you," she declared icily. She kicked the corpse. She knelt next to his body and started methodically taking his gun, looking for extra ammunition, grabbing his walkie-talkie, and any other gear she figured would be useful.

"You wanted this!" she snapped down at him. "I tried to warn people! I didn't want to be a scorpion! I didn't want to take my 4.0 GPA and Georgetown scholarship and spend my life becoming the Serena Williams of murder! All I wanted was to make a better, safer world, and you assholes just keep coming up and picking fights that you should have known you were going to lose!"

She methodically moved on to the next body, farther down the hall.

"And even then, almost twenty years, I've tried to keep it professional!" she fumed. "After the virus, I was trying really hard to avoid killing people! I kept trying to give everybody a chance of redemption if they would just take it! It would have been just as easy to kill Hell-Summoner and Shakira Eribat as it was Sarvar Rashin!"

She slapped a fresh magazine into her newly purloined AM-15 and decided to use that until she ran out of ammunition for the small rifle—and decided she should check the other four bodies for more magazines. "But you idiots really wanted to taste it, didn't you?" she continued to seethe at her fallen foes, imitating a big dumb guy's voice: "*What's Katrina Leonidivna like when we really piss her off?*' You wanted to see what happens when I can't keep it professional anymore, and I'm losing my mind with fear and grief and rage, because you've gone after my family? Well, welcome to the show! Ignorant bastards! What did you think was going to happen? I will tear your world apart, thank you very much! This is what I've been trying to keep in check all my life! Now you know!"

She thought of Alec and let out a little chuckle at what he would say if he were here. "And knowing is half the battle … that you just lost!"

She looked down the hall and realized which stairway these men had been protecting.

***

Outside the entrance to the stairwell, Washington sweated and swore, contemplating his next move.

"Boss, sounds like we just got fired," Conrad said, rising to his feet. "I say let the twin bitches shoot it out with the FBI if they want. We need to get our asses outta here! I don't trust those bitches not to set off the bomb as soon as they're clear!"

Washington nodded. He had thought his men were ready for a challenge like this, but apparently, he had completely miscalculated. He called down the hall. "Hanson, what do you think?"

Hanson turned back and shook his head. "We've got a mission, boss! We can't just—"

***

He never finished the sentence, because a round erupted from the wall, right next to his head, entering behind his left ear and emerging above his right eye. His body jolted, then tumbled to the ground.

***

Washington and Conrad screamed, turned their rifles in their direction of where the wall had been pierced, and fired everything they had. When they were out of ammunition, they heard only silence.

"Some jobs aren't worth it, Washington," Conrad muttered.

***

The building's security alarm system started going off. What Washington and Conrad didn't realize was that Davino, Raquel, and the NYPD Emergency Services Unit had been arguing for the past five minutes about whether to activate the alarm system. Attempting to evacuate the building might save lives, or the decision could move more of the building's roughly eight thousand workers and the tourists on the observation deck into the line of fire. The decision was made to disable the elevators' ability to stop on floors nineteen through twenty-four; in theory, workers and tourists on the floors above would just descend past the ongoing gun battle on their way down.

CHAPTER FIFTY-FOUR

In a stairwell diagonally opposite the one that Washington guarded, and one floor above on the twenty-third floor, Ward, Elaine, and the gingerly walking and wincing Alec emerged and debated which of the four wings to begin searching.

"If they're trying to bring the tower down into the heart of lower Manhattan, they're gonna try to knock out the support on the north side, so it falls in that direction," Alec groaned. "Ward, you take that one. Elaine, you and I will try the, eh, I guess the east side is second most likely."

Ward left Alec leaning against a wall and kept checking the hallway intersections, fearing some of the terrorists remained. "Seventy-some stories of crashing skyscraper is going to kill thousands, no matter which way it falls!"

The walkie-talkie squawked, with Dee sounding panicked. "Guys, the message went out," she said. "Have you checked your texts?"

Alec rolled his eyes and grabbed the walkie-talkie. "Well, we've been a little busy up here, Dee, what with all the being kidnapped and shooting and maiming and all," he replied. "I was hoping this whole threatening electronic message thing could be handled by somebody else, because I have this distinct memory of going out and hiring the world's greatest hacker for this team, *so I wouldn't have to worry about stuff like this!*"

"Love you, too, Alec! Glad you're well enough to be snarky!" she answered. "I just figured you should know because I figure this means they must be intending to detonate it soon!"

"Great, thanks, love you, too, bye," Alec sang, sarcastically.

"Sending that message out is going to get every pair of eyes and camera in lower Manhattan looking right here," Elaine checked her phone, and realized she had received a text from an unknown number:

AMERICA YOUR PUNISHMENT FOR YOUR CRIMES IS HERE
WE ARE EVERYWHERE
WE HAVE INFILTRATED ALL YOUR INSTITUTIONS
YOUR GOVERNMENT WAS EASILY CORRUPTED AND BRIBED AND TURNED AGAINST YOU
THE DESTRUCTION OF THE FREEDOM TOWER IS JUST THE FIRST STEP
TODAY'S DEATHS ARE JUST THE BEGINNING
JOIN, SUBMIT, OR DIE
FEAR THE ARYAN NATIONS

Ward checked his phone, and realized he had a message, too:

AMERICA YOUR PUNISHMENT FOR YOUR CRIMES IS HERE
WE ARE EVERYWHERE
WE HAVE INFILTRATED ALL YOUR INSTITUTIONS
YOUR GOVERNMENT WAS EASILY CORRUPTED AND BRIBED AND TURNED AGAINST YOU
THE DESTRUCTION OF THE FREEDOM TOWER IS JUST THE FIRST STEP
TODAY'S DEATHS ARE JUST THE BEGINNING
JOIN, SUBMIT, OR DIE

FEAR ANTIFA

Across the country, hundreds of thousands of Americans simultaneously received the same terrifying message, all similarly worded except for the last line, which told various recipients to fear a wide variety of extremist groups and movements. Most recipients were concerned, but quickly determined, through social media or other media reports, that "the destruction of the Freedom Tower" had not occurred; the building was still standing.

But the relief was short lived, because moments later, more reliable news sources offered an update:

REPORTS OF SHOTS FIRED IN FREEDOM TOWER IN NEW YORK

"Hey, that's us!" Alec exclaimed.

***

Cody Washington told Conrad that if he wanted to, he was free to leave. Conrad didn't look back, tearing off down the hallway.

Cody entered the stairwell and thought about descending . . . but then he heard the voice.

The voice wasn't on the walkie-talkie, and Washington was certain he was alone, now that Conrad had run off. The voice kept giving him the same order.

Set off the bomb. Set off the bomb. Set off the bomb.

***

Down the hall, Conrad stashed his gun, ammunition, stripped off knee and elbow pads, and peeled off his jumpsuit to reveal relatively normal white-collar-worker casual Friday wear. Slightly heavyset but beefy, white-haired, Conrad figured he might blend in as an older, gruff finance guy who kept the boy-genius geeks in line at one of the building's many tech firms.

Conrad went to the nearest bank of elevators, and pressed the buttons, but realized none of them would stay lit—he suspected that the building had bypassed these floors. He decided to try the other stairwell at the end of the hall—but as he was reaching for the door, he realized a woman was standing in the office doorway with shattered glass that he just passed.

He turned. She had ditched the NYU jacket, Covid mask, and Yankees cap. She was down to a tight black T-shirt and black yoga pants, and the smallest and most stylish Under Armour tactical boots he'd ever seen. Conrad shuddered, knowing that the dossier the twins had assembled made this woman sound like some modern CIA samurai. He had initially figured this operative's reputation was hype—but his doubts had recently rapidly dispersed, much like the contents of Hanson's head.

And right now, she had a gun pointed right at Conrad's face.

"Did you kidnap Alec Flanagan?"

"Yes, but—"

***

Katrina pulled the trigger and watched Conrad's body fall back against the door.

"There's nothing you can say after the *yes* that makes it okay," she told him. "Consequences, jackass!"

Breathing heavily, she realized she was nearly echoing her husband; Alec liked to tell his foes that he was the consequence of their bad actions. She sighed and wondered if, after sixteen years of marriage, some of his identity was destined to bleed into her personality, and vice versa. She hoped whatever Alec had absorbed from her would help him endure his kidnapping.

She wished she had grabbed an extra FBI-issued walkie-talkie and had meant to take one of the walkie-talkies she had taken from her foes and adjust them to the bureau's frequency. But the one she had grabbed was starting to squawk with frantic messages; apparently the remaining men were debating surrendering to the FBI.

"The twins who took the CIA guy are running to the roof!"

Katrina smiled. She stepped over Conrad's bleeding body and peered up the stairwell.

***

Working together, Elaine and Alec had enough weight to knock the door to the eastern suite of offices open—unfortunately, they tripped and tumbled into the room.

The suite was covered corner to corner with small burlap sacks, each slightly larger than a loaf of bread, sometimes in piles five feet high, with long wires running everywhere, and connecting all of them, burrowing deep into the giant piles of the burlap. The room was thick with a stench reminiscent of cleaning fluid.

"Great news, Raquel! Found the bomb!" Alec reported, into the walkie-talkie. "This day just keeps getting better."

Elaine gasped at the sheer scope of how many sacks of ammonium nitrate had been stuffed into the room. She yanked back the walkie-talkie. "Davino, evacuate the building! Raquel, this thing is huge! There must be enough here to level the building—it's like, it's like—" Words failed her.

Alec grabbed the walkie-talkie back. "Pretend little bags of ammonium nitrate are reproducing like Tribbles, and you've got the gist!" He handed her the walkie-talkie back. "Okay, Elaine, you've always had much better judgment than me," he said. "How are we going to get out of this one?"

"Ideally, keep everything under control until the bomb squad gets here, but God only knows how many hostiles are still between them and us!" Elaine groaned. She squinted and tried to remember courses about bombs at the academy. "Okay, what do we know about ammonium nitrate? White crystalline power, more likely to explode when compressed or heated … Not likely to detonate just because it's moved or jostled, or else it would have blown up in the process of getting moved in here …"

Davino's voice came through Elaine's walkie-talkie. "NYPD bomb squad and FDNY are on their way up, but we've still got get them a clear path—taking heavy fire in the stairwells! They said rulebook for an ammonium nitrate fire is to evacuate beyond the perimeter—"

Elaine interrupted. "The perimeter is going to be lower Manhattan, Davino!" A series of incomprehensible sounds indicating stress, fear, and anger erupted from somewhere in her diaphragm, finally turning into a series of four-letter-words that climbed like a series of musical notes.

"You sound like Dave Chappelle's version of Maria von Trapp," Alec quipped. He pointed to a cell phone embedded in one pile in the corner, with all kinds of wires coming out of the power charging port. "Does that look important?"

"That's our detonator," she declared, calming down again. "Okay, in a detonator, an electrical charge from a capacitor heats a bridgewire, the bridgewire heats up so quickly that it vaporizes and creates a shock wave that detonates the explosive," Elaine muttered, trying to remember the last time she had attended one of the mandatory briefings updating special agents on terrorist bomb-making. It had been too long, she concluded. "No sign of a timer. They're going to call the phone, and the incoming call should provide the electrical charge."

"I don't want to move this," she reported into the walkie-talkie. "Dee, can you jam cell phone signals on the twenty-third floor?"

"I can try," Dee responded, not sounding confident at all.

Elaine realized Alec wasn't paying attention and had pulled an office chair and climbed atop it.

"Can you give me a light?" he said, standing well above her.

"I don't smoke, and I don't think an open flame is a good idea around—" Elaine stopped, realizing that Alec was reaching up to the sprinkler system.

"Let's give the firefighters a head start!" Alec exclaimed. "Sprinklers are temperature based, I heat up the sprinkler, it sprays water, soaks everything and maybe all this stuff doesn't ignite when the call comes through!"

Elaine nodded. "Dee, set off all the sprinklers on the twenty-third floor—hell, set them all off on all the surrounding floors!"

A moment later, they—and everything around them—were doused in water.

"Is that going to stop it?" Elaine asked, wiping wet hair out of her face.

"Should give us a fighting chance of minimizing any explosion," Alec guessed. "Tough to burn anything's that wet, right?"

"Sure, other than oil, gasoline, turpentine, paint thinner, hand sanitizer, rubbing alcohol, nail polish," Elaine recited. "I'd still feel better if I could put that phone into a lead-lined case that would block all incoming signals."

Alec shook his head and wondered if being showered with the cold water from the sprinklers would give him pneumonia on top of all of his bruises from Tiffany's punches and the throbbing pain in the back of his head.

"I've got to find Katrina! And once you've stopped the tower from blowing up, figure out where Ward wandered off to! I'm the one who gets kidnapped, but everybody keeps disappearing on me!"

As if struck by inspiration, Elaine suddenly ran into the hallway.

"It's happening again!" Alec exclaimed. He groaned, wiped water out of his eyes, attempted to stretch his back, and concluded that movement was painful in any direction. "Elaine? Elaine! You're not supposed to abandon me in the middle of—"

Elaine reappeared in the office suite doorway, holding a long, narrow cardboard box, about an inch and a half by an inch and a half, and about sixteen inches long. Aluminum foil.

"We passed a small pantry a minute ago," she explained—opening the box and taking out the roll of foil. Elaine tore off long stretches of it, and started methodically covering the cell phone, making sure to not apply any pressure on it.

"An aluminum foil blanket or something?"

"Faraday cage, it's why you usually lose your cell signal in elevators, it's a big metal box," Elaine concluded.

Alec nodded, impressed. "Put enough layers of aluminum, and the signal can't get to the cell phone—"

"—and if the cell phone can't get a signal, they can't detonate the bomb! I think! I hope!"

She concluded. "Okay, now, you go find Katrina, I'll find out where the hell Ward wandered off to—"

Alec departed up the nearest stairwell—and then Elaine heard sudden loud shouting from Ward, and gunshots on the other side of the floor.

CHAPTER FIFTY-FIVE

An objective observer would likely conclude that despite their all-consuming fixation for revenge, Madison and Tiffany Reed were surprisingly resourceful, and had demonstrated an intelligence, determination, inventiveness, and creative thinking far beyond their years. Despite being just barely adults, they had leveraged their mother's lessons and their considerable inheritance into the tools to change the world.

Victoria Reed hadn't believed the official story on Linus Strauss' death, and when discussing her lover's murder, Victoria displayed a level of obsession that Madame DeFarge would have found troubling.

Determined to learn the true identity of their father's killer, the Reed twins had methodically uncovered clues about a CIA team that large swaths of the rest of the U.S. government didn't know existed. Once they knew about the team, their exhaustive research over flight manifests, passport records, the dark web, and a series of bribes revealed the real names of the team members, once the man known only as "the mole" cut off contact. The twins had met with Mexican-assassins-turned-pirates and Russian mercenaries, learning more about the team, its history, and its habits on missions. Finally, the autopsy report on Strauss had indicated he was shot from the side, and the angle of the bullet's trajectory strongly suggested the shooter was likely at least six feet, two inches. Alec Flanagan was the only team member that met their criteria.

Godula and his truck bomb were a test run that they doubted would kill the Dangerous Clique team members, but they figured would get their attention. The twins assumed the anonymous note would terrify them. They had debated sending similar, more-certain-to-detonate truck bombs to the Leonidivna–Flanagan house, the Holtz residence, and Rutledge's farm outside Williamsburg, but they decided it wasn't satisfying enough. Madison said she needed to look in Alec's eyes and confront him with the consequences of him pulling the trigger.

They had found the home addresses of the core and reserve members of the Dangerous Clique, but initially feared that the team's unpredictable and far-flung travels would make an ambush difficult. They debated sending Cody Washington and his recruited roughnecks to ambush them, but Cody's team might sit around waiting for days, because the Dangerous Clique was off in Hungary, or Australia, or South Korea for the devil knows how long. Sooner or later, one of the neighbors would get suspicious. And the Reed twins wondered if the CIA did its own security surveillance on employees' houses.

But about a month ago, the team's behavior seemed to change—trips into the Liberty Crossing Intelligence Campus stopped, and Alec and Katrina left for the airport and were away for more than a week. But after that, the couple seemed to settle into a routine—it was as if their tradecraft habits had been interrupted by something that had completely disrupted their usual thinking patterns. Tiffany had followed Katrina on certain days and noted her shopping trips included purchasing prenatal vitamins.

By the time the twins' "detonation day" was ready, Cody and his team were in place to follow Alec and abduct him when the opportunity arose.

Madison, the more cerebral of the pair, had thought through everything, with one glaring exception.

The roof of One World Trade Center didn't have a helipad.

***

"Where's the helipad?" she shrieked, in between gasps for air. She repeated her cry, over and over, walking around in circles by the door. The view was spectacular, with the lattice-steel 411-foot spire past towering above them, even at this height. The roof had catwalks, cooling towers, HVAC equipment, and a permanent crane for moving additional equipment to the roof in the future if needed. But Tiffany was certain that somewhere at that jaw-dropping height was a big, flat, empty, reinforced and secure octagon, or square, or circle with an *H* painted on it. There just had to be one.

Tiffany grabbed her by the hand and pulled her back inside, and they descended the metal staircase down to the one hundred and fifth floor, which contained only roof access points and mechanical equipment—the building's heating and ventilation systems, air conditioning units, water tanks and pumps, electrical generators, chiller plants, and so on. Tiffany had been surprised that the top floor of the tallest building in North America was so … ugly and industrial, nothing like One World Observatory two floors below them—with its luxurious and ludicrously overpriced observation deck, restaurant, and bar.

Instead, they were in a dark, noisy, intermittently lit labyrinth of steel and iron mechanical equipment, all with myriad dials, panels, electronic monitors, and small keypads that might as well have been alien technology.

Madison realized she that because she had once read that police helicopters had rescued people during the 1993 bombing of the north tower of the World Trade Center, she had just assumed the new replacement tower must have a helipad. What Madison didn't know was that helipads on the tops of New

York City buildings had been almost entirely phased out since the 1977 disaster on the top of the old Pan Am Building, where rotor blades from a tipped helicopter came crashing down to the street. Hospitals and emergency service units still had helipads for medevac, and the constant buzz of tourist flights and wealthy businessman, taking off and arriving from the city's three commercial heliports made it easy to believe that helicopters could land atop flat-roofed skyscrapers.

Madison frantically tried calling Roger again and again, but he didn't seem to be answering. She could barely hear anything next to the vents and fans of the mechanical equipment anyway.

They emerged from the noisiest and darkest mechanical room into a lighter and quieter one, and were headed back toward the elevator bank when they heard a stairwell door open.

"Madison, we better—"

Tiffany froze.

A feminine silhouette stepped into the doorway they were approaching. As she came closer, the twins recognized the woman in the black shirt and yoga pants, holding a Glock 20 in one hand and one of the short rifles of Washington's men in the other: Katrina Leonidivna.

She was breathing heavily, but after a few moments, she seemed to resume her icy demeanor.

"Somebody said, 'the twins who took the CIA guy are going to the roof,'" Katrina said evenly. "You must be the twins."

Tiffany gulped and looked at her sister. Madison was just as terrified.

"You know, not too far from here, I killed someone a bunch of years back," Katrina whispered. "I had killed before—Afghanistan, some sniper shots in Mexico, a gunfight in Jordan. Heat of the moment, kill-or-be-killed from a distance. But this one was different—I could feel it as I watched her fall. As I watched Magda plummet down to the street below, I realized something: Killing another human being can get really easy, if you let it. And ever since then, it's been a struggle."

For a brief second, Tiffany contemplated trying to run, but realized there was almost no way she could move faster than Katrina's trigger fingers.

"Turns out, the CIA keeps finding people who are so threatening, that the world is safer with them dead, and it also turns out I'm really good at killing people when I stop holding back," Katrina continued, speaking softly—neither boasting nor regretting, just offering a statement of fact. "Men are usually too busy checking me out to see me coming, and all the size and strength in the world doesn't mean much to a bullet in the right place. They say God made man and woman, but Samuel Colt made us equal. But every day, I've had to hold it back, hold it in check. Because I don't want to be a really good killer. Or at least I didn't, right up until the moment someone told me my husband had been abducted."

Katrina stepped closer and was the most terrifying vision Madison and Tiffany could ever imagine. Tiffany thought back to Alec's insufferable laughter during his interrogation, and his confident boast that she and her sister were screwed. Katrina Leonidivna was not a cruel woman, but that did not mean she wasn't capable of a certain ruthlessness, an obsessive determination that could be as all-consuming as their hunt for their father's killer. Katrina could have walked away from counterterrorism missions or the CIA entirely at any time, Madison realized. Katrina's refusal to walk away meant that, on some level, she had not just begrudgingly accepted the use of murder as a tool of her work. Katrina had grown *just fine* with killing someone to make the world a safer place.

And Katrina had the twins literally square in her sights.

"Do you realize that in all the years I've been doing this, the Russians never went after my family?" Katrina inquired, her voice dripping with contempt. "The Chinese, al-Qaeda, ISIS, Atarsa, the Shedim—none of them dared go after my family. None of them *dared*! Some of the worst, most evil, most ruthless *ublyudki* on the planet, and even *they* realized that if they crossed that line, all bets were off! Might as well open up Pandora's box and start an all-out war. I like to think they knew what I was capable of. So, before I shoot both of you—a *lot*—tell me, just who the hell do you think you are—"

"You went after our family first, when your husband killed our father, Linus Strauss."

***

Katrina felt a wave of emotions crashing over her—shock, revelation, anger, dread, and maybe a few molecules of sympathy.

CHAPTER FIFTY-SIX

When Elaine finally found Ward, he was on the floor and bleeding.

She had just kicked in a door to the north wing, gun drawn, ready to pull the trigger on the center mass of anyone she deemed a threat. But no one had been standing in the room occupying the north side of the tower's twenty-third floor, which looked like a data center, with a dozen man-sized trays of servers all connected to each other. But no lights had flashed, and no fans hummed; the entire array of servers had been shot up like a target on the range at the Quantico training academy at the end of the day.

Another man in gray overalls lay dead, with four bullet wounds forming a line stretching from his sternocleidomastoid muscle in his neck, down to his deltoid, further down to his oblique, and clipping the side of his hip.

"Ward! What happened?" She spoke quickly into her walkie-talkie. "Twenty-third floor, north side! I have a man down! FBI ... er, *consultant* shot and in need of immediate attention!"

Ward grimaced and groaned and rolled over, showing a disturbingly large pool of blood beneath him and a large bloodstain toward the rear of his right side, just above his hip.

"Winged me, in and out like a burger!" He gestured to his satchel and the gauze and tape in front of his bloody fingers.

"Lie still!" Elaine ordered. She peeled back his shirt and winced at the sight of the wound. "It's not an in-and-out, at that caliber, it would have punched a huge hole in you! It's technically a graze, but it's so big it's like … poking a ball-point pen through your love handle."

"I don't have love handles!" Ward objected—before Elaine doused the wound in disinfectant, making him nearly curl into a ball from stinging. Once the pain subsided, he insisted through gritted teeth, "My dad bod has very masculine, manly 'brotherhood handles'!"

Elaine patched the gauze on as best she could and decided to keep Ward's focus away from his wound.

"So, how'd this guy get the drop on you?" she asked. "You getting old?"

Ward's eyes flashed with indignation.

"I walk in, and saw that guy in a ball, muttering to himself, something like, 'don't make me do it,'" the former Army ranger croaked. "Turns out I know him—or, I guess now it's I *knew* him. Cody Washington. Guy was screwed up ever before we got to Kosovo."

Ward grunted, adding a groan and then a chuckle. "He was one of those guys running around, yelling, screaming, looking for a fight—terrified anybody might think he was weak. He didn't realize the strongest ones are strong enough to be gentle." Ward looked across the room.

Elaine wondered how many men in the world would be better off if they had adopted Ward's expansive definition of strength.

"Twenty years later, here we are. I walk in, he's muttering, 'don't make me do it,' like he's arguing with someone not there. And I'm like, 'Washington, it's me, Rutledge. Who's making you do what?' And he looks at me with this desperate look in his eyes, Elaine, and he says something crazy like, 'the Voices from Cyprus' or something like that. And then he pulls his gun and it's the shootout at the OK Server Corral. He got me, but I got him worse."

"I can't believe it," Elaine muttered, applying pressure to the wound.

"Believe it," Ward grumbled. "The world is that small."

"No, I mean I can't believe that we've been fighting an anti-government militia extremist trying to tear down the federal government, and his name is *Washington*."

Ward chuckled, coughed, and let out a long, loud groan in pain. "Where's Alec? And Katrina? Why am I always looking for one of them?"

CHAPTER FIFTY-SEVEN

A lec's chest heaved. He had to climb another five flights of stairs, and then, exhausted, he tried to see if the elevators were working. Finally, he found an elevator that would take him directly to the one hundred and fifth floor. Dee reported that Davino's men had captured several armed men, but that the twenty-second floor was full of similarly dressed and armed men, who had all been shot through the head, some seemingly through a wall.

"Jesus Christ in Heaven, it's like a bloodbath in those hallways," Davino muttered. "I count at least six. I'd say these looked like professional hits, but whoever it was didn't even bother with the hearts once they had hit the heads!"

That sounds like somebody I know, Alec thought, growing increasingly worried.

Alec emerged at the one hundred and fifth floor—after a moment, he turned in the right direction and saw exactly what he feared—Katrina, a gun in each hand, standing over the bodies of Madison and Tiffany.

Alec screamed, *"No!"*

It took him a moment to realize that Madison and Tiffany were on the ground, handcuffed, but alive.

"Katrina!" he shouted.

Katrina tucked her Glock 20 in her belt and realized that wasn't as easy as it used to be, because her pants had gotten smaller, or her gun had gotten larger, or her pregnancy wasn't quite as invisible as she thought it was a few days ago.

"Oh, thank God you're alive, Alec!" They embraced.

"I never want to lose you again," she whispered.

He kissed her on top of her head. "I never want to shop for groceries again."

After their long, long embrace ended, Alec pulled away and marveled.

"I can't believe these two are alive," he mumbled.

Katrina took a deep breath. "It was … *extremely tempting*," she said, loud enough so that the twins could hear her. "But I just finished explaining to them, quite clearly, that when you killed Linus Strauss, he was an immediate threat to Gedhun Choekyi Nyima, holding a knife to his throat. You had, as the law puts it, a reasonable apprehension of death or great bodily harm to an innocent human life. A textbook case. No prosecutor ever would have brought charges, no jury ever would have convicted you."

She crouched down.

"These two are unarmed," Katrina declared. "And it might have been the only smart decision they've ever made."

"I would have thought somebody like you would have shot us in the back," Tiffany fumed from the floor.

Katrina looked down. "Suka, the day I shoot you it will be from the front, you'll be armed, it will be to kill you, and I will be looking right into your eyes when the life leaves your body." She could see in her eyes that her ferocity made Tiffany's blood run cold.

Alec looked down at his former captors and shrugged.

"Hey, don't look surprised, girls, I tried to warn you."

CHAPTER FIFTY-EIGHT

The one hundred fifth floor soon was filled with FBI, NYPD, forensics teams, Department of Homeland Security. Elaine reported that Ward was transported to New York-Presbyterian Hospital for stitches and possibly a blood transfusion.

"He'll be in pain for a while, but he'll pull through," she updated. "He'll have a hell of a story to tell. Chilling, even. There's something he told me that ..." She paused. "I've just got to check something out when I get a chance."

Davino's men were about to transport Madison and Tiffany Reed downstairs, but Alec tugged at Katrina and jostled his way closer to them.

"Excuse me, excuse me, gentlemen, I've got something I need to say to them," Alec insisted. The FBI men glared and scowled but nodded. They had already been telling their arriving colleagues, with wide eyes, about some sort of super-assassin from Langley who had cut through the hostiles like a hot knife through butter, shooting through walls.

"You wanna give 'em a piece of your mind, go ahead," one agent muttered.

Madison and Tiffany Reed stared at Alec—hardly overcome with guilt but defeated.

But Alec shocked everyone within earshot. "Listen, before your father died, he looked up at us and said, 'take care of my girls.'"

The girls' eyes bulged in surprise, and they started to cry. Katrina did a double take. Her memory was crystal clear: Linus Strauss never said any such thing.

And yet Alec was selling this alternate version of events with emphatic sincerity.

"His last thoughts were of you," Alec emphasized. "He was an extremely flawed man, driven to do terrible things. I don't regret shooting him to save another life. But if you've been spending your whole life wondering if he loved you, and whether he would have loved you if he had lived, rest assured … Madison, Tiffany … he loved you. As you get ready to spend …" he swallowed down his sense of satisfaction from the words that would follow, "… the rest of your lives in prison, console yourself with this knowledge: Your father loved you."

Madison raised handcuffed hands and wiped her tears.

"Thank you," she nodded.

Tiffany reached out to hug Alec.

"Nope, no!" Alec said, pulling back. "Less than an hour ago, you beat the hell out of me, or tried to beat the hell out of me!" He gestured to the FBI agents. "Book 'em, Dano!"

"I don't work for you," the FBI agent gruffly replied.

After the FBI team had taken the twins to the elevator, Katrina finally dropped her poker face.

"*Your father loved you*'? What … was … that?"

"Well, they're psychos, and I look forward to them rotting in Supermax for the rest of their lives," Alec chirped. "But they're probably psychos because of their dad and what they were told about him by their mom. And maybe they're psychos because they feared their father never loved them. And Katrina …" He looked both ways, as if he was about reveal a terrible secret, and needed to ensure no one was within earshot. "He *didn't*. Strauss never put them in the will, never left any legal tie, his name isn't on their birth certificates—there's a reason they never showed up in our original investigation way back when! Those girls weren't stupid. They've spent their lives suspecting that their dad didn't love them—and that maybe he got himself killed just to avoid being their father."

Katrina gasped at the thought and wondered what a revelation like that would do to a young girl's psyche.

"Jesus!"

"Yes, I think even He would be shocked by this, too," Alec quipped.

"They did all this, even though they thought he didn't love them," she marveled.

"They did all this *because* they thought he didn't love them," Alec corrected. "What better way to prove themselves to him, or his ghost, or his soul…" Alec paused and looked down. "his soul *rotting down there in Hell!*—than to hunt down his killer? Anyway, I just felt… in this particular circumstance, maybe it was worth telling these girls what they wanted to hear, if it would bring them some peace. I don't want them staying psychos and giving birth to new psycho children who will come after our kids in a few decades. Two generations of Strauss family terrorism is enough."

She reached up and pulled him in for a passionate kiss.

"That was uncharacteristically mature of you," she observed.

"There are two little people living inside of you, who get evicted in a few months," Alec quipped. "I guess I'm starting to think about what kind of a father they're going to have."

CHAPTER FIFTY-NINE

While Alec and Katrina were piecing together the motivation of the Reed twins, Elaine, Raquel, Dee, and Davino contemplated how much to reveal to the public. Davino was on the phone, on a conference call with the FBI director, the Department of Homeland Security, and the White House.

Raquel's cell phone buzzed as well. It was Director Stern.

"Don't let them say anything about your team!" Stern ordered.

"It's lovely to hear your voice, Director Stern, I'm so glad we're on speaking terms again." Raquel's voice walked the tightrope between sincerity and sarcasm. "I don't want that to happen, either, but the whole reason the Reed twins were trying to level lower Manhattan ties back to us and Linus Strauss!"

"At least a couple hundred thousand Americans got those claims of responsibility," Davino repeated from his call. "We've got to tell them something, and sooner rather than later."

"The online rumors are already getting crazy," Dee reported, pointing to her combination laptop-tablet, pacing behind Raquel. "People are saying it's ISIS, Atarsa's back, rogue Canadians, UFOs, lizard people." She shook her head in frustration. "The lizard people get credit for *everything*!"

"This whole mess all goes back to our bosses in government choosing to tell a convenient lie instead of revealing a painful truth," Elaine declared. "Harold Hare and the CIA thought they were so much smarter than the rest of us, and that their noble lie would serve the public better. When has that not ended up blowing up in our face eventually? How well did all those 'noble lies' work out during the pandemic? If the Reed twins knew their dad was a homicidal nutjob, maybe they wouldn't have been so motivated to avenge his death with all of this."

The White House chief of staff, the CIA director, the secretary of Homeland Security, and the FBI director all started speaking at once.

"This is going to go disastrously," Raquel sighed. "We won, and now we watch our bosses screw it up."

She was surprised to feel Davino's hand on her shoulder, a lumbering and awkward attempt at being reassuring. "Have a little faith," he urged.

***

Roughly ninety minutes later, the assistant director of the FBI and chief of the New York field office, Raphael Davino, stepped to a lectern piled high with microphones. Behind him stood the mayor, the NYPD commissioner, the superintendent of the Port Authority Police Department, and Elaine Kopek, although only a handful of the assembled reporters could have picked her out of a lineup.

"Today was a challenging day, but it could have turned out so much worse," Davino began. "Early in the day, the FBI was notified of a potential terrorist threat from group that had rented space within the Freedom Tower. Working with other agencies, FBI agents raided the office and found explosives. Our team, along with the support of the excellent men and women of the NYPD bomb squad—nerves of steel, those folks—neutralized the threat. An extended gun battle on the twenty-second and twenty-third floors resulted in I believe ten terrorists killed, eight wounded, and another six arrested—those numbers are preliminary and may change. Several FBI agents and agents of other U.S. government agencies suffered non-life-threatening injuries and have been taken to NewYork-Presbyterian Hospital for treatment. At this point, the tower is secure, the threat is eliminated, and the tower will be open for business and operating normally within a few days, probably this coming Monday morning."

"What was the terrorist threat—"

"Yes, I'm getting to that," Davino said, more amused than irritated. Elaine could remember when her boss would have snapped at the impatient reporter. "The group behind the attempted bombing was a collection of domestic extremists—working as mercenaries, really, operating on what I think can best be described as a neo-anarchist ideology—they just wanted to turn Americans against Americans. These mercenaries were employed by the Linus Strauss Institute and a related company, both owned and run by Madison and Tiffany Reed, the daughters of Linus Strauss."

Most of the reporters didn't recognize any of those names, but the graybeards among the scrum inhaled some air upon hearing that name. The shooting death of Linus Strauss had become something of a local legend, spurring one or two true crime podcasts to speculate about who had killed him—a burglary gone wrong, the mob, some sort of religious extremists, or, in the wildest theory, the CIA.

"A lot of you will be too young to remember this, but I worked the Linus Strauss killing back in 2003," Davino said. "There were certain details of the case that were never revealed to the public, at the direction of my superiors at the time. They've long since passed on or retired, and I feel in light of today's events, it is worth revealing the whole truth. Back in 2003, in the weeks before he was killed, the multimillionaire Linus Strauss was involved with a network of foreign criminals in a child abduction plot."

***

All across the country, every QAnon believer jumped off their couches and shouted, "I *knew* it!"

***

Davino waited until the spontaneous cacophony of shouted questions died down.

"The night of his death, some independent group, not U.S. law enforcement, raided his apartment and killed him and his associates—disrupting the effort to harm those children. The NYPD responded to shots fired, and a team from the FBI—including me—returned the abducted children to their families. Because the FBI did not want to encourage vigilantism or to stir public panic, previous occupants of this office made the decision to create a cover story of a botched robbery. I understand why my predecessors took that action, and I believe they did so with the best of intentions. But I think time has proven that approach was wrong. Noble lies are still lies. The citizens of this country deserve the truth, even when it is difficult."

The crowd of reporters in front of Davino erupted with an even louder clamor of hollering questions, in a tone and with a volume made Sam Donaldson seem demure and soft-spoken. He shook his head, waved his hand like a frustrated teacher, and pointed to one reporter, a crusty old veteran who he knew was reasonably professional. "Yes?"

"Today's messages and the bombing—could you clarify how they connect to this killing of Linus Strauss?"

Davino nodded. "From what we have gathered, Madison and Tiffany Reed believed the U.S. government killed their father and were eager to strike back at the United States in revenge. Next, yes?"

Another reporter: "The FBI has no leads on who killed Linus Strauss in 2003?"

Davino shrugged. "Linus Strauss was working with dangerous people—men connected to al-Qaeda, a Chechen mercenary—the kinds of people who ping the radar of all kinds of intelligence agencies around the world. I don't have any solid answers—but I would say the circumstances of Strauss' death indicate someone figured out what he was up to and decided to put a stop to it themselves—and there are a bunch of kids who got to grow up because they did."

A local television reporter who had aspired to be the next Geraldo Rivera, but who was not as reserved and taciturn as the fearless explorer of Al Capone's vault, ignored Davino's finger and shouted over the print reporter in front of him.

"How did the FBI stop the media from investigating Strauss' mysterious killing?"

Davino let out a little chuckle. "We didn't. If I remember correctly, a four-paragraph story ran on page B6 in the *New York Times* two days later, and that was about it. We had just gone to war with Iraq, remember. Nobody was paying much attention to anything else."

***

In the end, the revelations of Davino's confession barely made a ripple in the news cycle, much like the killing of Linus Strauss back in 2003. In fact, the reports of the attempted terrorist attack were overtaken in the news and the national conversation within a day, because on the day the Reed twins had tried to blow up the Freedom Tower, the Taliban captured another six provincial capitals, as the Afghan army's collapse became undeniable. Within two days, the Taliban subjugated Kabul and completed their reconquest of the country, and an American foreign policy crisis stepped front and center into the spotlight. Within a week, "that thing at the Freedom Tower with the strange messages" had faded from the public consciousness.

2022

CHAPTER SIXTY

JANUARY 18, 2022

O utside the hospital room window, life went on. Some nut had taken hostages at a Texas synagogue. Everybody and their brother seemed to have winter colds and wondered if their sniffles and cough were symptoms of the Omicron variant. China had announced there would be no spectators for the upcoming Olympics and offered up another serving of its habitual aggressive rhetoric toward Taiwan. Meanwhile, over in Eastern Europe, Russia was deploying more and more troops to its border with Ukraine. If an anxious person was looking for the signs and had confirmation bias, they could easily conclude that up to five storms were on the horizon, gathering strength.

But none of that mattered to Alec and Katrina; Katrina had just given birth to two healthy boys. Alec already realized that Ward's assessment was right: nothing would ever be the same again.

Two sets of new grandparents and two new uncles were already on their way from other spots along the east coast. Every friend had texted immediately that they would stop by at the first opportunity.

Ward was already driving up from Williamsburg. His wound had long since healed, although he didn't mind mentioning it whenever he wanted to get his way. He and Alec had talked incessantly about fatherhood, with Ward laughing as he was reminded of all of the challenges surrounding the arrival of a new baby. He assured his friend that strategically applied amnesia was a necessity for most parents. A few weeks earlier, Dee had casually mentioned that she and her husband were discussing adoption more seriously.

Katrina's maternity leave had forced Raquel to start evaluating potential recruits, and the team's relationship with director Barbara Stern was steadily thawing.

Alec had said he wanted to name one of the boys William after his grandfather. Katrina decreed that they would name the other Harold after the late Harold Hare, who had helped set them on their courses in life. Alec had offered Abraham and Leonard as middle names, honoring Katrina's father, but Katrina said Jews weren't supposed to use the names of living relatives. She reached back a generation and chose Caleb and Asher, rough English equivalents of her grandfathers' names.

"You realize that by naming our sons Will and Harry, people are going to think we're really big fans of the British royal family," Alec observed.

Katrina looked out the window.

"I don't care what anyone else thinks," she smiled. "These are our children. We'll raise them as we see fit."

She wasn't thinking about terrorists, rogue states, loose nukes, assassins, ransomware, or any variety of the malevolent and maniacal men plotting in the far-off corners of the world, hell-bent on unleashing chaos upon the globe. As far as Katrina could tell, they all seemed to disappear at once. For her, for once—perhaps just one shining moment—all was right with the world.

CHAPTER SIXTY-ONE

U.S. Department of Justice

Federal Bureau of Investigation

Washington, D.C. 20535-0001

TO: RAQUEL HOLTZ
FROM: ELAINE KOPEK

Wrapping up my report to Wray on all of this, I went back and reviewed the videotape seized by the FBI from Strauss' apartment that night. The tape is in good condition and the audio is generally clear—it has been sitting in an evidence storeroom in the headquarters building basement—next to that creepy guy's office. (Don't even ask what I had to do to find a machine and television that could play VHS tapes.) But once I did, I recognized a pattern and now I have absolutely no idea what to do.

March 19, 2003: Linus Strauss, upper West Side of Manhattan, shortly before he died: "Meaning has no meaning! Man has triumphed! The Voices were right! The throne is empty, which means I can sit upon it!"

April 2, 2019: Atarsa terror cell sleeper Norman Fein, while being interrogated by Ward Rutledge at the

Chicahominy Wildlife Refuge in Virginia: "The Voices need it this way."

April 3, 2019: Atarsa terrorist mastermind Sarvar Rashin, shortly before she was killed by Katrina while inside the abandoned Nicosia International Airport in Cyprus: "Let me give you a final lesson from the Voices: There are no consequences, no cosmic justice. Only chaos."

August 13, 2021: I checked the Freedom Tower security tape, and Ward's memory was correct. Shortly before he started firing at Ward, Cody Washington said he was being told to do something by "the Voices from Cyprus."

Could you please help me find a rational explanation for why four individuals that we have run up against over an eighteen-year span have made references to "The Voices," three of which shortly before they were killed?

***

●●●○○ Sprint LTE   2:38 PM   75% ▬▶

< Messages   **ELAINE**   Details

**DESTROY THAT MEMO
YOU SENT ME**

MERLIN WAS RIGHT

CHAPTER SIXTY-TWO

The mole reviewed the latest round of requests and offers.

None of them interested him. The offers were lucrative, but he had stashed away more than he would ever need. He hadn't really done this for the money, anyway. He had become the Central Intelligence Agency's most dangerous mole in decades as a giant middle finger to a world that deserved it.

The mole realized that no offer had really intrigued him since the inquiry from Madison and Tiffany Reed a few months ago. This was one of the rare times he cut off contact with a potential client abruptly and with no explanation. If they had inquired about the CIA's almost-off-the-books counterterrorism efforts in general, he might have been willing to negotiate.

But in the course of their inquiries, Madison and Tiffany Reed had asked specifically about a senior case officer named Katrina Leonidivna.

The Reeds had asked about Katrina based upon their suspicions that she had been part of the team that had killed their father, but he didn't care about their motives. Katrina represented the mole's red line. He could not cross that line. His entire endeavor was because of her.

Had the mole been a crueler and vindictive man, he would have endangered Katrina Leonidivna's life, a consequence for her unconscionable betrayal. In many ways, she deserved it. She walked through life, beautiful and driven, smart and charming, the woman men wanted, and that other women wanted to be. It was bad enough that she was such a merciless, relentless agent of chaos, but what really galled the mole was how oblivious Katrina was to the consequences of her actions. The mole watched her strutting around the CIA, and gallivanting around the world, unknowingly exacerbating the fundamental unfairness of life.

The stories of her killing Magda or Sarvar Rashin or Sergei Markov gave a hint at the well-hidden cruelty in her heart and soul. Her husband boasted she was hot, her friends saw her as warm, and the young recruits thought she was cool. But the mole knew the truth. Katrina Leonidivna was cold.

She had once expressed fears she was turning into a scorpion, a creature that killed out of pure instinct, with no thought of right or wrong—and the mole understood why. She had spent her life pretending she was more than a scorpion, better than a scorpion, but the mole knew the truth. Take away the smile, the beauty, the sex appeal, the skills, the reputation, the friends, the oath, the pledges and the principles … and underneath it all was a cruel creature morally indistinguishable from a scorpion.

Katrina crushed dreams without a second thought. She was offered everything, all a great man could offer, and Katrina turned him down with the casualness of ordering off the menu. And as far as the mole could tell, she never looked back, never regretted it, never doubted her instant judgment.

Katrina Leonidiva was the beautiful, curvaceous, charming, smart, near-perfect endless lesson that the world was not fair, and never would be.

If the world was fair, she would never have chosen Alec.

Patrick Horne stared at the screen and wondered whether the time had finally come to betray the long-lost love of his life, Katrina Leonidivna.

ABOUT THE AUTHOR

Jim Geraghty is an award-winning senior political correspondent at *National Review*. His work has also appeared in *The Philadelphia Inquirer* and the *Washington Examiner*. He is also the author of the first two books in the Dangerous Clique series *Between Two Scorpions* and *Hunting Four Horsemen*, the novel *The Weed Agency*, which was a *Washington Post* bestseller, and the nonfiction books *Voting to Kill* and *Heavy Lifting* with Cam Edwards.